THE WAR REPORTER

The

WAR
REPORTER

A Novel

Martin Fletcher

THOMAS DUNNE BOOKS
ST. MARTIN'S PRESS ❧ NEW YORK

This is a work of fiction. All of the characters, organizations, and events portrayed in this novel are either products of the author's imagination or are used fictitiously.

THOMAS DUNNE BOOKS.
An imprint of St. Martin's Press.

THE WAR REPORTER. Copyright © 2015 by Martin Fletcher. All rights reserved. Printed in the United States of America. For information, address St. Martin's Press, 175 Fifth Avenue, New York, N.Y. 10010.

www.thomasdunnebooks.com
www.stmartins.com

Library of Congress Cataloging-in-Publication Data

Fletcher, Martin, 1947–
    The war reporter: a novel / Martin Fletcher.—First edition.
        pages; cm
    ISBN 978-1-250-07002-9 (hardcover)
    ISBN 978-1-4668-7992-8 (e-book)
    I. Title.
    PS3606.L486W37 2015
    813'.6—dc23   2015025545

Our books may be purchased in bulk for promotional, educational, or business use. Please contact your local bookseller or the Macmillan Corporate and Premium Sales Department at (800) 221-7945, extension 5442, or by e-mail at MacmillanSpecialMarkets@macmillan.com.

First Edition: October 2015

10   9   8   7   6   5   4   3   2   1

For Marc Kusnetz

ACKNOWLEDGMENTS

If anyone inspired Tom Layne, it would be Neil Davis, a true war-reporting legend, who, after nearly two decades covering Vietnam and Cambodia, was killed by a tank shell in Thailand. He was a handsome rogue and the nicest man I ever met.

In addition to Neil, I would like to thank some of the many people who helped flesh out my meager understanding of post-traumatic stress disorder, love life in the Balkans, Balkan politics and modern history, and in particular, the pathetic progress of the hunt for Ratko Mladic, and his ultimate capture and trial.

They are: Mark Brayne, former BBC correspondent and now psychotherapist specializing in trauma; Bruce Shapiro of the Dart Center for Journalism and Trauma; Rachel Irwin of the Institute for War and Peace Reporting in The Hague.

In Belgrade and Sarajevo: Vladimir Vukcevic, the Serbian war crimes prosecutor; Dr. Zoran Dragisic of the International Security Institute; Jovan Stojic, chief of staff of the Security Information Agency; Ljiliana Smaslovic of the National Journalist Federation;

Aleksandar Vasovic of Reuters; and Danika Draskovic, Lidija Popovic and Suzana Vasiljevic, all of whom guided me in my quest for the truth about Ratko Mladic's evasion of justice. And thanks also to the half dozen other Serbs and Muslims who were beyond helpful but did not want me to mention their names.

Thanks also to my NBC colleagues Subrata De and Miguel Almaguer for their hilarious accounts of the HEFAT training course which inspired the prologue. And to my colleagues during my own time reporting from the Balkans in the '90s, in particular Masha Macpherson, Hanani Rapoport, Yossi Greenberg, and Dubi Duvshani, whose characters inhabit this story, if only in spirit. Those were life-changing years.

And deep appreciation also for those first-draft readers whose comments helped make this, I hope, a better book: Dina Shiloh, Robbie Anna Hare, Merle Nygate, Eliza Dreier, Marc Kusnetz and Jerry Lamprecht. And as ever for Marcia Markland, my trusty editor at St. Martin's Press, who always makes the whole book process a pleasure.

As for the villain of the story, Ratko Mladic, he was finally captured after sixteen years on the run. At the time of this writing he is on trial at the International Criminal Court in The Hague charged with crimes against humanity and genocide. A verdict is expected soon.

So many years and war zones later
I sense the dangers so much greater,
And I have met the enemy
Who is no longer him but me,
The anger, hate and animus,
That lurk in every one of us,
And, baleful as the years that pass,
I see him in the looking glass.

—MARTIN BELL, 2010

PROLOGUE

The sack clung like a death mask; Tom's eyes bulged. A fiber caught in his throat, he hacked and fought for every breath. By his side Nick struggled to his feet but a body slammed into him. His nose hit the earth and he felt the clinging ooze of blood. He was panicking, fighting against the pressing weight. The man yelled into his ear: "Keep down or I'll kill you."

The two friends sprawled on the ground, hoods blinding them, choking, hands tied, shocked by the speed of the assault.

Hauled to their feet, pulled along by their thumbs bent backwards. Such a little thing: helpless, relieving the pain only by stumbling forward.

Nick Barnes tripped on a tree root and lurched against the man pulling him. He pushed Nick back and wrenched his thumb, almost snapping it; Nick retched in pain. A branch whipped his face.

The ground leveled into a clearing where they were knocked to the ground. Nick breathed long and deep, trying to control the adrenaline, the pumping of his heart. At least they could sit. He tilted his head down, his chin touched his chest. His hood loosened. Through a slit at the bottom he could see the legs of the men. Black combat boots, olive fatigues, the stocks of AK-47s, at least half a dozen kidnappers. They were stamping on the grass, pushing other journalists into a line. Where were they? Jihaditype music was blaring. A man shouted to someone else, "Get the fuck down or I'll kill you."

Now Tom Layne could breathe again. His voice came out muffled through his hood: "We're just journalists, we didn't see anything; take our money, take what you want."

"Pipe down," someone said, and jabbed him in the stomach with his gun. Tom gasped and doubled up.

They heard a woman scream and the sounds of dragging and scuffling. She bumped into Nick. He grabbed her foot with his bound hands and wouldn't let go. A man prised his fingers open. Somebody else was dragged across his legs. Nick's heart pounded again. A moment later there was a gunshot and then quiet.

So this is how it is.

The shocked silence was broken by Tom, struggling to sound calm: "Let . . . us . . . go. We didn't see anything. We'll just leave, we won't come back. Let us go."

Nick whispered to Tom. "We have to make a run for it."

"No, no way. Just keep quiet. Keep calm." He called out, "Take off my hood, let me talk to you."

Nick raised his head and peered down through his narrow field of vision. He couldn't see any of the black boots or guns. He thought, No one's close, it's now or never. Do it! "Tom, now!"

Nick rolled to his side.

"No, wait," Tom hissed.

"I'm off," Nick said. "Good luck, mate. See you in the bar." In the same motion he jumped up, pulled off his hood, and raced to the trees.

Nick was fifteen years younger than Tom, a college runner, middle-distance. As he sprinted, his bound hands swung from side to side for balance. He leapt over a fallen tree trunk. He raised his elbows against the whipping branches. He heard yelling. His lungs slammed against his ribs. Sweat streamed into his eyes. He heard more yelling and a gunshot. He glanced back as he dodged round trees. A bulky man with a headband was chasing him, shouting, trying to point a weapon. Fear hurtled Nick on.

He slithered on damp leaves, nearly fell; blood dripped from his eyebrow where a branch had whacked him, the plastic zip tie dug into his flesh. But a slow smile spread across his face. That fat ass will never catch me. I'm getting away.

Half an hour later the seated journalists were still slouched forward, heads covered. Nick, on his stomach, watched them from the shadow at the edge of the trees.

He had escaped, rested, and made his way back to Tom, his buddy, his mentor, his tennis coach. He had freed his hands by rubbing the plastic zip tie against a rock until it tore. He picked at dried blood on his eyebrow and rolled behind a bush.

The guards, in combat gear, were talking in a semicircle by the gate of a house.

Nick inched along a ridge in the ground, followed the dark line of earth and grass as he'd been taught, focused on the guards, who didn't see him. At the last moment he stood and raced forward. He reached Tom, whose hands were now tied behind his back, tapped him on the head, and pulled his hood off. He ruffled his hair. "I made it," he said with a laugh. "And you're as good as dead."

"Sure, sure," Tom said, blinking in the light, straining to scratch his neck with his shoulder. "Untie me, I've got an itch, it's driving me nuts."

"I got away," Nick said again.

"Yeah, right," Tom said, as two off-duty New York cops walked toward them, AK-47s slung across their chests. "What a hero. You're going to get yourself killed one day."

"You're just a sore loser, grandpa," Nick said as he untied Tom's hands. "Too old to run for it."

"Just don't try that in real life, not with me around anyway," Tom said, scratching his shoulder. "My life's too valuable. And dinner's on you tonight."

But it wasn't. The last night of the HEFAT course—Hostile Environment and First Aid Training for war reporters—was always on the ex–Special Forces who taught survival to journalists in the Girl Scout camp at Cliff Manor, upstate New York.

PART ONE

The nurse told Tom Layne to stay out, so of course he went in.

As soon as she left the corridor, he opened the forbidden door and slipped into the small dark room off the children's ward. In the gloom he made out the outline of four empty cots along the walls, until he sensed, rather than heard, movement in a fifth crib beneath the shuttered window. He inched forward, running his hand along the cold metal rails of the infant beds, freed the window latch, and pushed it open. A rush of air blew out the staleness, and light glinted on the rails and brightened the faded sheets and blank walls.

A bare, severe room.

A little boy, too big to be a baby, yet drooling like an infant, brought a chubby hand up to protect his eyes from the sudden light, and rolled onto his side, trying to push himself up from his elbow. He gasped from the effort.

The boy wobbled upright, like a bowling pin finding its balance. He supported himself on one hand. His head seemed too big for his body, and a harelip bared his front teeth, yet his eyes were smiling.

Tom stretched his arm toward the boy, to stroke his head. His skin felt warm and in his widening eyes Tom now saw despair.

He heard the clacking of determined footsteps.

"Let's go," the nurse said, "I told you not to come in here."

"Who is he?"

"We don't know. Nobody knows his name."

"What do you mean? Why not?"

"Nobody visits this one."

She took Tom's elbow and pushed him toward the door.

He resisted, pulling out his notebook. "Wait a minute. You must know something. How did he get here?"

"Outside now, please." She was a stout woman and used considerable force. As she closed the door he walked to the nearest bench, gesturing for her to join him.

"No time. Very busy," she said, glancing over Tom's shoulder. There was a bandaged child in every bed, surrounded by anxious family, while groups of visitors searched for friends.

She clenched her lips in disapproval as she watched the man with the big camera move closer to a bandaged girl's head. The other loud, clumsy one held a big microphone pointing at her mouth. The girl's parents sat on the edge of the bed and tried to smile. The nurse snorted. She knew what the parents were thinking: Foreign television. Maybe they can help.

Tom kept asking questions until the nurse called out in Serbo-Croat to a colleague, her exasperation clear in her tone. As she walked away the younger, pretty one sat next to him and said in English, "Yes. What you wish?"

"We're from American television. Please, would you mind telling me what you can about the little boy in there?" he said, looking at the closed door. "The boy with the harelip?" He pointed at his lip to help her understand.

She looked away, as if for help, and then back at Tom.

"But first, what is your name, please?"

"Fata. Fata Gorani."

She nodded as he spelled it out.

"That's a Muslim name, isn't it?"

"Yes. From Fatima." She shifted on the bench, unsure what Tom wanted.

Tom tried a reassuring smile. "The daughter of the prophet."

That seemed news to her. Tom's eyes wandered. She had deep brown eyes and red lips, and a full body that strained against her white uniform. With her olive skin and dark hair, framed by a white cap and blouse against a white wall, she'd be beautiful in close-up. Better than that other old bag.

He waved over Fata's shoulder until he caught the cameraman's eye. Nick took one last wide shot of the family by the bed. As he left he dug into his camera bag and held out a Snickers bar to the girl.

With an encouraging smile and gentle pressure on her shoulders, Nick guided Nurse Fata so that daylight from the window backlit her, giving a white frame to her pinned-up hair, and then he nudged Tom a few inches forward to get the right composition for a two-shot over Tom's shoulder. Nick didn't bother with the tripod but kneeled, resting the camera on his knee and thigh. He liked to move around while shooting. He squinted through the viewfinder, found focus, and gave the thumbs-up to Tom. Zoltan held the extended boom mic out of shot, pointing up to her mouth.

Tom hated the boom mic, it was too big, too intrusive. He liked to work quietly with a small hand mic, just slide in and do it; that's how he usually worked with Nick, who was so discreet you hardly realized he was there. But with Zoltan's bulk and wild gray hair, panting and sweating lemon vodka from each exertion, every head was turned toward them.

Fata had been in the ward for only four months, she said on camera, and she checked on the boy whenever she could, which wasn't often because the ward was just too busy with dozens of children arriving every day, many crying and bleeding from shrapnel and bullet wounds; it's all very hard, very sad.

She told Tom what she could, which wasn't much, and back in the Holiday Inn that night he filled in the background for his report.

The day before the siege of Sarajevo began, a woman from a distant village brought her two-year-old son to the hospital for an operation on his harelip. In the evening she returned home, meaning to come back in the morning, but that same night, April 5, 1992, the Bosnian Serbs blocked the roads, shelled the town, and the mother was never seen again. Probably she phoned the hospital, but after a few weeks all phone lines in and out of town were cut.

Now, two years later, the town was still surrounded, bombed daily, with all supply routes closed. After a mortar shell set fire to the records office, the hospital had no knowledge of the child's name, home, or next of kin.

All they knew was that he had come in for a routine proce-dure on his harelip, but the doctors never had time to do it. And no wonder, Tom said in his standup in front of the hospital as an ambulance disgorged more wounded behind him. The Serbs fired an average of 330 shells a day from the hills and forests overlook-ing the town, with the heaviest bombardment on Bloody Thurs-day, July 22, 1993, when 3,800 shells slammed into the homes and

streets of Sarajevo, a town of half a million. In the two years of
the siege so far, thousands had been killed and tens of thousands
wounded. So who had time for a little boy with a harelip who had
never learned to talk?

How could he, if nobody spoke to him?

"But why is he all alone in that room?" Tom said to the nurse
in the interview that aired. "Why isn't he out here with everyone
else?"

The nurse shrugged. "I don't know."

Tom rose, shook Fata's hand, thanked her for the interview,
and asked for her telephone number. In case he had any more
questions, he said. Nick winked.

She laughed. Telephone? Sarajevo? Come here if you need me
again. I'm always here.

Tom walked with Nick and Zoltan to the other end of the ward,
explaining what he wanted. Slowly, making a show of filming
more children and families, he and Nick edged their way back to
the corridor with the forbidden door. He had told Zoltan, who
stayed at the other end, "Make some noise. That shouldn't be hard
for you. And we'll slip in when nobody's looking."

At the door Tom said, "Nick, you ready with the hand mic?"

"What do you think I'm holding? My dick?"

At the entrance to the ward a tin bowl clanged to the floor, and
as all heads whipped toward the clatter, which seemed to take on a
life of its own, Tom and Nick slipped through the door and
closed it after them.

The boy was sitting against the side of the cot, his head leaning against the metal strut, playing with his hands, threading and
unthreading his fingers. The shirt of his white hospital pajamas
was too small and his trousers were too big. A soiled white sheet
was crumpled in the corner of the cot.

"Sometimes I pick him up or take him for a walk. Give him a hug," Fata had told Tom on camera.

"When was the last time?" he had asked.

"I don't remember."

That was one of the sound bites Tom used in his story, over pictures of the boy abandoned in the corner of his cot, in the corner of the little room. Light from the window behind gave him a hazy, transparent look, pale and wan against the white paint. He looked as if he would fade into the wall, or fade away altogether.

Tom had sighed.

"Quiet," Nick hissed. Tom was holding the hand mic against his face, and the sudden expulsion of air exploded through Nick's headphones like a wave crashing onto rocks.

For an instant Tom's thoughts had gone to the elder brother he'd never known, who had died in infancy. And he saw himself too, for one sad thought always succeeded the other, alone with his parents on every birthday, with no other family, just the three of them. It was lonely. And as he looked at the lonely boy in the cot, he remembered his guiding creed: I can't stop this from being a world that tortures children, but I can stop some children from being tortured.

It isn't fair. Maybe you have to pay money to get attention? It's true they really are busy out there; it's a zoo. Who are the kid's parents? Two years he's been here without a visitor? How sad is that?

When Nick finished filming, Tom took the boy's dimpled hand, soft like a baby's, held it and stroked it, while the boy's head hung.

Tom Layne's report, featuring Nurse Fata Gorani and an interview with the hospital director, library pictures of earlier shellings, and the drama of the children's ward, all framed around the story of the abandoned child, led the news that night, even though it was more of a news feature than a hard news report.

For Tom knew how to spin a TV yarn: beginning with the feel of the lonely boy's soft skin, a close-up of the yearning in his eyes, the silence in his bare room emphasized by the noisy children's ward outside. Tom paused in his narration so the viewer could hear the boy's panting in the silent room, broken by the sudden boom of a mortar landing. More wounded children rushed into the emergency ward, followed by crying parents, and then back to the little boy . . . all alone . . . without a name . . . and the nurse who couldn't remember when anyone last held him in their arms. The story ended on a close-up of the boy's brown eyes, a blank appeal for love.

"The network switchboard's gonna light up," Nick said. "Adoption city."

Tom had made his reputation from just such tales in every war and disaster zone for close to two decades. Nobody married pathos and drama so well, nobody brought dry facts to life like Tom. When Tom arrived on a story, the opposition groaned.

Yet only Tom knew that each time he came home from a war zone, a little bit less of him returned with him. All that time looking out of the window meant he spent less time looking in the mirror. By embracing the reality of others, he was fleeing his own.

But what was his reality? A Coke in a bar after work? People were always surprised that he didn't drink. Another herogram from the show? Another girl swept off her feet by the dashing foreign correspondent with the curly locks, which by the way were graying at the temples?

Was he an eyewitness to history to avoid looking at himself?

Anyway, what was there to see?

He thought, Not a hell of a lot.

That night the foreign editor messaged: *Another winner for the reel. Keep your head down. Don't do anything dangerous.*

Oh right, so why send me to Sarajevo.

Around midnight, after they had fed the cut story on the satellite and the New York producer had goodnighted them, Zoltan took Tom, Nick, and a few others to a bar in the Old Town, in a cave-like basement, walls of exposed rock two levels below ground. The music was pounding, the cigarette fumes choking, the girls sexy and clinging, the message: Anything goes, what's to lose, we're young and we're all going to die anyway. Nick, smoking at the bar, fit right in, living every day as if it was his last, trusting Daddy Tom to keep him safe. They were more than just mates on the road. He was learning from Tom every day and Tom loved the role of teacher. Tom was the TV vet from a humble home in Queens who'd carved his way to the top, while Nick was the exact opposite, a privileged child from the stockbroker belt of Surrey, outside London. Before taking over his father's road haulage empire, he had chosen to taste the glamorous life of a television news cameraman. The experienced Yank and the dilettante Brit. Both single. Their eyes met and Nick smiled. But not at Tom.

Nick had felt pressure on his thigh. Leaning hard into him was that girl from a few nights ago, in tight jeans, with frizzy black hair and big round earrings that hung to her bare shoulder; after a swallow of beer she gently bit his earlobe.

"So what did you say your name was?" he said, pulling the hair from her eyes.

Tom turned away with a wry smile as Zoltan banged his glass with his own. *"Zivjeli, Zivjeli!"* he shouted above the din, for the sixth or seventh time, and knocked his drink down in one.

One of the mysteries of Sarajevo under siege was where the alcohol came from. The good stuff was smuggled in through the secret tunnel under the airport runway and was hard to find and cost a bundle. But someone was making a fortune churning out slivovitz by the vat. The brandy tasted of ripe pear, or so it seemed. In fact, said Zoltan, whose every pore oozed musty alcohol sweat, it's fermented grass.

Zoltan threw his arm around another man who had pushed his way to the bar. Tom looked down at his drink and sipped it carefully, frowning, wondering what it really was. They called it Coke.

Nodding his head to the music, Tom thought, I wonder what his name is. After Nick had enough pictures, and had turned his camera off, Tom had picked up the boy, held him, hugged him, murmured to him, and stroked his head like a puppy's. At first the boy had shrunk from him, with wide eyes, and had grunted.

He must be about four years old, Tom thought. Yet his hands were as smooth as a newborn's. He probably hasn't even had a chance to get them dirty. For two years in that cot he must have done nothing with them. When Tom had set him on the floor to take him for a walk, it was lucky he held his hand, because the boy had sunk to the ground. He didn't even have the muscles to hold himself up.

His arms and legs felt like sponges.

But after a few minutes, in which Tom had kissed him on the cheeks and waved him around in the air, despite his weight, he had brought a kind of smile to the boy's face, and the memory made Tom smile too, now, as he sipped his so-called Coke. It had been a feral smile, a slanting of the lips that revealed more teeth and gum. He only realized it was a smile because the boy's eyes had widened and for an instant gleamed with life. And when Tom tickled him and gently pinched his bare tummy he had twisted and gurgled with pleasure.

At two in the morning Zoltan drove Tom back to the hotel, without lights, in case the snipers hidden in the tall buildings across the Miljacka river were also having a late night. Zoltan dropped Tom off at the back entrance, the most protected spot. Inside the hotel the only dim dots of light, moving and glowing like a cat's eyes, came from head lamps worn by reporters on late deadlines to write in the relatively safe dark corridors. The generators didn't operate at night because light in the rooms lit up targets for the snipers, even through the curtains.

"Thanks, Zoltan, enjoyed that. Late start tomorrow," Tom said. "Ten o'clock?"

"That's late? And Nick?"

"Don't worry about Nick." He had disappeared with the girl half an hour earlier. "It doesn't matter when that guy goes to bed, or who with. Always on time in the morning."

Tom's mind was tired and blank as he undressed in the dark room, trying to avoid the air-conditioning—the funnel of icy air that blasted through the mortar hole and shattered window. He turned on the tap, which gargled and expelled a trickle of brown drops before tapering off. With a glass he scooped water from the bath, which he had filled when he arrived a week earlier in case the taps went dry, brushed his teeth, and fell into bed.

With his eyes heavy, drooping in mid-read, Tom went through his telex messages by flashlight, screwed up the last one and aimed for the hole in the wall and missed. They really didn't let you rest. It had read, *Another great story tonight. What are you thinking of for tomorrow?*

He shivered and pulled up his coat that half covered the blanket. What am I thinking for tomorrow? Fool question. What else is there to do? Chase the bombs, find a family.

Tom felt the weight of his eyelids, and his thoughts drifted to his mother, bless her. What a worrier, always had been. He smiled to himself: Remember when I told her not to be afraid, that when I go to work I wear a flak jacket and a helmet. She said, "Tom, if you need to wear a flak jacket and a helmet to work, you should get a new job."

He chuckled in the dark. That made sense; she always did. She was a tough old bird, so was Dad. You didn't survive the war in Europe by being Mr. Nice Guy. All he knew was that they had met in the woods in Lithuania and fought with the partisans against the Nazis. They never talked about it, but the more he reported on wars and met killers and their victims, the beaten and defeated, the more the curtain was drawn on what his own parents must have gone through to survive. And it wasn't always nice. In fact, it never was.

Tom shook his head, and the movement, with eyes closed, left him nauseous for an instant. When his giddiness settled, he arranged his pillow, brought his hands together on his chest, and opened his eyes.

It was a perfect frame, the stars through the hole in the wall, carved by a mortar a week before. His room faced west, above the hotel's main entrance, the side that caught most sniper fire. The east side got the learner snipers, for some reason. Must be a training camp there. The south faced the Serbs directly and got the mortars, so no one wanted a room there. The north got far fewer hits, but when it did, they were big caliber. The best was a low floor facing east, and whenever somebody there moved out journalists besieged the front desk, offering envelopes of cash, cartons of cigarettes, their female colleagues, anything to get the room.

He felt himself beginning to drift, at last, tuning out his tinnitus, that merciless tone that pierced his thoughts. As darkness and peace embraced him, Tom had a final distant thought, a smile in a mist of clouds behind his eyelids: Tonight, that kid, that was one hell of a story.

Sleep well, little boy. I'll see you again. Good night.

The next morning when Zoltan looked around the crowded breakfast room in the hotel basement he saw Nick at a refectory table full of press, but no sign of Tom. Nick was staring at his plate and the goo on it. He heard Nick's voice over the crowd. "What the fuck is it?" The British journalist next to him shrugged. He was savoring a fried egg, tantalizing everyone with the aroma. He'd brought in a dozen and nobody could understand how they hadn't broken on the journey. He even had a sachet of salt. Zoltan pulled up a chair, called for a black coffee, and lit a cigarette. Although there was no real food, the waiter served him in a pressed white jacket and bow tie.

"How did it go yesterday?" Zoltan asked Amber, Tom's producer from the London bureau.

She had been out all day with Nina, their alluringly moody Bosnian translator, looking for matching tires for their bulletproof Audi. Two days earlier, when they were racing down Sniper Alley, Sarajevo's main boulevard, a bullet had struck the inch-thick side window with a thud, sending spiderlike cracks to the corner. With everyone yelling and cursing, Nick, at sixty miles an hour, had swerved, hit the ragged edge of a mortar hole, punctured the two right-hand tires, and barely managed to keep the car on the road. They had skidded and the steel rims screamed and smoked until Nick clattered into an alley, hidden from the Serb snipers. There he had scattered half a dozen boys playing soccer.

"We got them," Amber said with a smile. "Cost a fortune though."

"I bet they did. How much?" Zoltan asked.

"For me or for New York?" They didn't get danger money, so evened things up by fiddling their expenses. It was only fair, they claimed. If the bean counters spent one day in Sarajevo they'd shit themselves. Everyone knew of NBC's New York unit manager who thought the crews were spending too much money during the Iranian revolution. He sent an exasperated message over the open telex saying he would come the next day with forty thousand dollars cash and would handle all the bills himself. Ten minutes after he checked into his room in the Intercon, before he'd even unpacked, there was a knock on the door. He opened it to find a masked man pointing a Kalashnikov at his chest. He pushed the bean counter back into the room and said, "Give me the money."

Amber loved to tell that story and it was always met with peals of laughter and knowing looks.

Zoltan felt a tap on his shoulder. "Come here a minute, will you?" Tom said. Zoltan pushed back his chair and walked with Tom to the door. "Sure, what's down?"

"What's up. We say 'What's up.'"

"What's up?"

"Can you spare some batteries? About thirty. A box. Double A."

"Uh, yes, if you want, sure. When? Now?"

"Yeah."

"What for?" Zoltan asked as they walked to the storeroom.

"Something, no big deal. Tell Amber I'll be back in a couple of hours. If anything big happens go shoot it and I'll take a cab there, but otherwise just wait for me."

· · ·

On the way out Tom picked up a package from reception, and called a hotel taxi. "Bolnica," he said, trying to get the accent, which sounded to him like the hiccups. "Bolnica Kosevo."

Ten minutes later he reached the hospital, where he told the driver to wait for him in case he had to rush off to a shelling or a sniping. The mornings were the worst.

Men had to find the day's food, women looked for water from a working well, and children needed to play outside.

While the snipers were freshest after a good night's sleep.

It was quiet today, so far. No ambulances or sirens or gunfire or falling mortars. Just lines of hunched people at water pumps or hurrying about their errands, looking for bread and vegetables, one eye on the enemy in the hills.

What Tom wouldn't give for a steak. The Holiday Inn had always been surrounded by dogs looking for meat, but there wasn't any. Then for a few days there was plenty of meat, but no dogs.

At the children's ward Tom walked straight toward the closed door at the end, nodding curtly to the nurses, his parcel under his arm. He wasn't going to let them stop him.

When the chill air had woken him that morning and he had curled up in bed, trying to stay warm, all he could think of was the little boy, who he thought of as the harelip kid. Is he cold in bed too? When was the last time someone hugged him? What about his mom and dad? Are they dead? Or desperate? Maybe they were glad to be free of him. Who knows? But no, if they didn't care they wouldn't have brought him in for surgery. He must be so lonely. He probably hasn't had a toy in two years. Imagine never having a toy. Tom felt heat in his eyes, and remembered the way the boy's eyes briefly lit up as he held him.

In bed Tom decided: I'll buy him a toy.

But what?

He went out at nine o'clock, when the shops opened, looking for something the kid would like, but he couldn't find anything. Toys were hardly a priority in a town under siege where the only gift was life. Shops had run out long ago. Who had money for such frivolous items? The driver took him from one area to another. He had almost given up when he walked into a hardware store and saw, on a shelf, covered in dust, a box with a toy electric guitar.

It looked cheap and tinny, probably made in Belarus or Bangladesh, Tom thought, but it was perfect. He can use his hands and fingers, he can hear the sounds, he'll love it.

The storekeeper couldn't believe his luck at finally unloading the waste of space and even thanked Tom for buying it. But you need eight batteries, he pointed out, a fair man, and he didn't have any to sell. Nobody did.

"That's all right," Tom said. "I know where to get some."

He had decided something else. He wasn't going to ask anyone's permission. He was going to go straight to the kid's room, open the door, and give him the guitar.

And that's what he did, and for the next three days the boy had a visitor at last. Someone who held him and stroked him and even sang to him. When Tom left on the fourth day the little boy looked after him and kept looking at the door, and hours later when Nurse Fata brought his food, there he was, leaning against the side of his cot, gripping the slats and staring at the door.

The nurses kept the shutters open now and there was light in the room.

Tom had tried to show the boy what to do with the guitar—he twanged away, tinny notes clunked out—but maybe the deep notes reminded him of the booms of the bombs, or the high notes the screams he heard through the door, because he had shrunk from the sounds. The guitar scared him.

On the third day his hands had inched toward the guitar, which Tom proffered from the corner of the cot. Tom had watched, smiling, nodding, and saying, "Yes, yes," until the boy's fingers met the shiny red toy, and the next day he drew his fingers across the strings. And then again. And again.

The kid must have been practicing, because on the fifth day he was strumming like a champ. Tom laughed out loud. "Go for it, little feller!"

Attracted by the noise, Fata leaned in through the door.

Seeing her, the boy stopped, and as he held the guitar tight against his chest a beatific, wondering smile lit his face, a smile so wide it hid his harelip. He twanged the strings again and as the tinny tones mixed and merged and he tapped the guitar like a drum and made more sounds come from the big red thing, his happy burbling and the guitar sounds filled the room. All the while he looked deeply into Tom's eyes like a puppy looks into the eyes of its master.

Fata beckoned to other nurses to see the miracle.

Tom was sitting on a stool by the bed, playing with the boy's bare foot, and as their eyes held he felt the tickle of a tear on his cheek and he wiped it away, hoping nobody saw. A chink in his armor: the cool reporter whose tears flowed freely, but only in private.

He felt a warm hand cup his head. It was lovely Fata at his side.

As he had driven to the hospital each morning, telling his team he'd be back soon, they had joked that he must have a girlfriend in town. And as he had sat back in the cab, staring at the drizzle sliding along the window, he had wondered why he really did care so much. Was it truly concern for the boy, who somehow reminded him of his lost brother? Or because of the admiring looks from the pretty nurses? Could his good deed really stem from such a base motive? Uh, hello, yes.

And now, as the boy smiled happily at him and he felt Fata's warm touch, he thought, Jeez, I'm gonna get laid tonight.

Instead he worked past midnight on another short "news of the day" piece, which he managed to turn into a little movie. A mortar had fallen on a building in the town center, which happened many times a day, but what made this one special, Zoltan had told them, was that Serb families shared the building peacefully with Muslims and Croats, even though their Serb cousins were shelling the town. It had been an oasis of reason in a mad world, and now it was in flames. Tom milked the metaphor, even showing a Jew who also lived in the building playing his fiddle while the residents wailed and cursed as their home burned behind him. "You can't make it up," Nick muttered as he filmed the flames licking the collapsing walls, pulling focus from the devouring orange tendrils to the violinist's dancing fingers on the strings, his mournful notes merging with the crackle of burning beams.

And again, as Tom fell into his freezing bed, he tore up that dopey nightly message: *So what are you thinking of for tomorrow?*

He wasn't thinking of a story, he was feeling Fata's hand on his head. It was warm and gentle. As he curled up he tried to remember. Had she stroked his ear too? He thought so. It had made him shiver. Was it an invitation? He felt himself stir, and a smile came to his lips as he thought of her lush hair pinned up into a bun and the stray strands around her eyes and mouth and the length of her neck. The full flow of her breasts filling her blouse and those eyes, oh those beckoning eyes. He closed his eyes and turned on his back and imagined it was her hand: a nurse in Kosevo hospital, why not, she must need relief from all that pain and fear. All I need is to invite her out for a drink, in that bar with Zoltan and Nick, and then, and then . . . and she's the only nurse who seems to care for the kid. He had even found her playing the guitar with him. Just like a mother.

The idea came so suddenly Tom jolted up. His eyes strained in the dark room, the air-conditioning chilled his nose, and he knew he was concentrating hard, because he felt his tongue between his lips, its tip exposed, which happened when he was truly focused. Nick laughed at him for that. It made him look simple-minded.

Like a mother. And just like that, for once he had an idea for the next day. It's brilliant, he thought. Risky, but brilliant. Well, risky may not quite cover it. Fucking dangerous. He played the idea out in his head, calculated the upside, the downside, and knew he could do it. Only one thing. Don't tell New York.

They'd never buy it.

At first light he called Zoltan on the satellite phone and told him to come in early, wheels up at eight. The rest of the team gathered for breakfast at seven as usual, bleary-eyed, unwashed, cursing the lack of water, blaming the Serbs for their lack of sleep. The Serbs had woken them at four in the morning with a mortar into the top floor.

"Fucking bastards," Amber said, leaning back and tucking her shirt deep into her trousers. "Don't they ever sleep?"

"Will you stop putting your hands inside your pants?" Nick said.

"God, you must be hard up. That's sexy?" Amber said, pulling at her zipper. "And stop looking at me. Drink your coffee. Anyway, what about the hot chick with the earrings?"

"She's upstairs."

"Really?" Zoltan said, sitting down.

Nick smirked and raised his eyebrows.

Tom smiled at Nina, their Croatian fixer, shaking his head at Nick in mock disapproval. She half winked back, the dreamy Slav, and as she raised her coffee cup in an ironic toast, their eyes lingered. What is she thinking, Tom thought, and not for the first time. So young and so knowing. His look flitted from her to Nick and back, and he thought, They're made for each other. Except for one thing; he fancied her himself, like crazy. Who wouldn't?

Each time Tom and Nick came to cover the wars in Slovenia, Croatia, or Bosnia, Tom called Nina. She was young, twenty-four, but hardened, as were all the local fixers and translators. Two of her close friends, one a fixer with CNN and the other with the BBC, had been killed in Croatia, and the week before they arrived in Sarajevo another had lost an eye and half an ear to shrapnel from a mortar.

But as she told Tom over dinner one night, as she finished the wine, their fingers grazing, she was not really hardened, she had only developed a defense against the hardness around her.

"So what are you then?" Tom asked, his hand resting on the middle of the table, hoping she would lay her hand on his.

"Naïve, I'd say. And genuine. Genuinely naïve." And that throaty laugh again, those mischievous eyes.

Nina pleased him in the languid, knowing way of the Balkans, with her long auburn hair, wide cheekbones, and full sensuous lips that transformed with the instant wide smile of youth. When she held a glass of slivovitz poised in one hand and a cigarette between the fingers of her other, explaining in her throaty purr the violent intricacies of her homeland, Tom would admire her and desire her in equal measure, although she was almost half his age. He loved her faultless logic and fearsome temper when anyone disagreed about the war. Her family name was Ibrahimovic. Half Serb, half Muslim, she came from a small farming village not far to the east, where her family still lived. She spoke Serbo-Croat, which she insisted on calling Bosnian, as well as excellent English, French, and German. When Bosnia claimed independence from Yugoslavia, and the Yugoslav Serbs attacked to maintain their dominion, she had dropped out of law school to serve her fledgling country as best she could, by assisting the foreign media in Sarajevo.

She liked Tom but she liked Nick too, who was almost her age, older by a couple of years. And if Tom was swashbuckling and exciting, Nick was the same but youthful too. And handsome. A rogue. While there was something smug about Tom . . . look at him, he really thinks I'm going to hold his hand on the table.

She loved their stories from East Timor or Somalia or wherever they had just been, driving in a jeep and hoping for the best. In Operation Desert Storm in '91 they didn't sleep for three days as they swept into Iraq with the 82nd Airborne and later won just about every television news award with their series on one Texan father of three, the division's youngest paratroop captain, whose exploits Tom spun daily into golden yarn. It was Tom's mantra: Find the little story that tells the big one.

"Lean in, guys," Tom said now. In a few words Tom laid it on the table, his nighttime inspiration. He spoke quietly so none of the other journalists would hear him. He summed it up: This is what the siege is all about, he said, families torn apart.

"I don't know," Zoltan said.

"I do," Amber said. "Forget it."

Tom scrutinized her. "Let me guess why."

"Because New York will never go for it. It took them ages to get you in here. Now you want to leave Sarajevo? What happens if you can't get back in? New York will go nuts."

Zoltan broke in. "Those hills are very dangerous. It's not a one-day thing. Where would we sleep?"

"Nick, what about you?" Tom said.

"Me? If it's okay with you it's okay with me. I'd rather not over-night though. Personally."

"Don't worry, she'll wait," Tom said.

"You think? Okay then, whatever. Fine by me."

"Nina?"

She shrugged, took a drag on her cigarette. Breathing smoke out through pursed lips, she said finally, "I think it's a wonderful idea."

"Good, so that's it, we're agreed then," Tom said.

"No, no, no," Amber yelled. But added, quietly, "Great story though."

Tom looked at her, nodding slowly. "Amber, it is, it really is, and we can do it, too. I've got a good feeling about this. But you'll have to stay behind. Zoltan too."

"Oh, good," Zoltan said. "That's the smartest thing you've said so far."

Amber stood up. "No way. I'm coming too—"

Tom interrupted. "Sit down. Listen, if something does go wrong, which it won't, but if it does, you'll need to manage things from here. Also, you'll need to take calls from New York and London while we're out of town. Don't tell them we're gone, just say—"

"Oh no," she broke in. "No way I'm lying. What if something big happens here, the hospital gets hit or something, and you're not even in town? They'll have me for breakfast . . . especially Bill fucking Perkins." Her running battle with the cranky London bureau chief, aka the Screaming Skull because of his shaven head, was the stuff of legend.

"Okay, you're right. But don't tell them till we've left, all right?"

"Sure. I'll tell them you're off the reservation, you just left, nothing to do with me."

"You'll go far," Nick said. "Management material."

"Oh, drink your fucking milk."

"It should work," Tom said, mostly to himself. "It's a damn good story."

It was a simple idea, but then they were the best. "Don't know why I didn't think of it earlier," Tom said to Nick as they climbed the stairs to get their overnight stuff.

"Doesn't matter," Nick said, pausing to catch his breath on the seventh floor. "We've been on the air almost every night anyway. How we going to find her, though?"

"No problem. We just drive around asking. How many mothers left their harelip kid for an operation two years ago and didn't come back because of the siege? We'll find the kid's mother in no time, trust me."

They didn't leave till the next morning though. It took half the day for Amber and Zoltan to find a spare tire and enough black market gas to fill the tank. They attached the roof rack for spare gear but after loading it they took it off again. They didn't want to draw attention. Cowboys in the hills had a habit of stealing whatever they could, at gunpoint, so there was no point advertising their wares.

Tom and Nina went to the UN in the old post office to consult with Captain Sam Morissey, a wiry man with a thin mustache, an American who'd been seconded, nobody seemed to know why,

to the Canadian 3rd Battalion. He should know the latest loca-
tions of all the militias and the best path through their lines.

He did, and his summary was curt: Forget it.

"She could come from anywhere," he said, tapping the aerial
photos and maps pinned to the wall, dragging his pointer across
a radius of three hundred kilometers. "And the villages are all
mixed up in the hills—they don't call the country a leopard skin
for nothing. Serbs, Muslims, even some Croats, and there are out-
of-control gangs like the Scorpions, Red Hand, Black Hand, Hand
Jobs; if you go up there alone anything can happen. And you,
Nina, you're the translator?"

"I am."

"Well, I strongly recommend against it. It's the Wild West out
there. Who's going to look after you, pretty boy here? But look, if
you're going anyway, you have my numbers, why not check in
every couple of hours, tell us where you are, at least that way
we'll have a general idea where you got kidnapped."

"That's kind, Sam."

"You're not married, are you, Tom? No children? That's all right
then."

"Get lost."

"You're a free agent. Care to tell me why you're going?"

"No," Tom said. "You wouldn't understand."

Tom barely did himself. He wasn't going just for a good story;
there were plenty of good stories here in Sarajevo. He always
measured the downside and the upside. Upside, on a scale of one
to ten, a story was a nine or even ten. Downside, in terms of
danger, for him and Nick, four to five. But worse for Nina, with her
Muslim name, cruising around those hills full of Serb militias.
Verdict: too close to call. But it wasn't just about the story anymore. He wanted to find the harelip kid's mother. She hadn't seen

her little boy in two years—two years of war, shelling, shooting, hunger, disease—she must be terrified for her child. And he could help. Do something good for a change. Maybe. Bring her news that her child was well fed and in good hands. He had even brought a tape to show her of the grinning boy playing with his guitar.

A great story too, yes, but he had done plenty of great stories. On the risk/reward scale, it didn't measure up. He was trying to persuade himself: the reward this time was of a different measure. The reward would be a mother's joy.

Really? That's why he would risk all their lives?

Why did he care? He couldn't say.

He turned, shook the captain's hand. "Sam, we'll check in. If not with you, with Amber. A couple of hours go by without a call, send in the cavalry."

"Tom, don't you get it? There is no cavalry. Secure the airport, humanitarian aid, that's us. You're on your own and it's pretty daft, if you ask me. But then, you are a journalist."

Tom laughed. "Guess so. Thanks, Sam, see you in a few days."

"Tom, I'm serious, how many journalists have been killed so far?"

"In Yugoslavia? Croatia, Bosnia? In the last couple of years? Oh, a few dozen."

"Exactly."

"Cheer up, Sam, it may never happen. Drinks at the officers' club when we get back."

"There isn't one."

Tom laughed and walked out, holding the door open for Nina.

They left at sunup, hitting Sniper Alley before the gunmen rose and while the insomniacs among them were too tired to shoot straight, and floored it. This was always a white-knuckle ride.

People died here; charred car wrecks lined the tram tracks. Ropes were tied to lampposts for people who had been shot to drag themselves to safety. From the back Nina said, in a tense voice, as if to distract herself, "Did you know that the real name for Sniper Alley is Dragan of Bosnia Street? Ulica Zmaja od Bosne?"

"Well, whaddya know?" Nick said, eyes fixed on the road a hundred yards ahead. Tom was eyeballing the buildings across the way, as if trying to stare down Serb snipers. "Thanks. I'll try to include that in my story tonight," he said.

Amber had made them an appointment with a Serb spokesman in their headquarters in Pale, a ski resort about ten miles away, on the slopes of the Jahorina mountain, and with their blue-and-black UNPROFOR press passes they had no problem passing through the UN roadblocks at either end of the airport runways. The front line was quiet that morning. Even inside the bulletproof car their helmets were strapped on tight, their flak jackets snug, as they snaked past the white tanks and armored cars at the UN barriers. The one-mile drive through no-man's-land was eerie, made odder by a cart delivering groceries to the one store in the wasteland of damaged homes.

Their plan was simple: before the final climb to Pale, hang a left and head for the nearest village. If anyone stopped them they would show their telex with the Serb rendezvous at HQ and claim they were lost. Meanwhile they'd drive from village to village asking about the family of the harelip kid lost in Sarajevo.

"Simple," Tom said.

"Unless we get kidnapped, shot, bombed, or beaten," Nina said.

At the wheel of the Audi, Nick half smiled. Another day at the office. He liked nothing more than heading into anarchy, camera ready, Tom at his side, a pretty girl in back. This was his seventh war, all with Tom, and he was only twenty-six.

As he thought of it he looked sideways at Tom, who was staring ahead. You couldn't find a better buddy. One problem: Tom started out as a cameraman too, and kept giving advice, mostly bad. He was a great correspondent but everyone knew he'd been a lousy shooter. And as for women, he's like a kid. Nick grinned as his eyes met Tom's. They both nodded over their shoulders toward Nina with the same unspoken message: Lay off, she's mine.

"I saw that, boys," she said, and they laughed. But Nina didn't. What am I, she thought, a piece of meat? They're all the same, they all want the same thing. But then, why not? She gazed out the window as trees flashed by and through them the sky came and went. She thought of her brothers and hoped they would stay out of the war. And she hoped they were having fun while they could. She should do the same. So who was she to object? And they're both so cute . . .

The camera was big and heavy, propped up on the backseat with Nina's hand holding it steady by the mic attached on top. Nick had set everything on automatic. Tom had a radio mic already pinned to his lapel; to turn it on he just had to flip the little switch on the transmitter clipped to his belt. When they got to the badlands, he'd tell Tom to switch it on and leave it on, sod the battery, they had plenty more; when the shit hit the fan it was hard for Tom to remember. And between Tom's legs was a small Sony amateur camera that acted as backup video, ready in case something happened as they drove. Tom could just turn it on and point it. Even Tom should manage that. Nick sighed and looked into the mirror, where his eyes met Nina's.

"You all right? You look tired," he said.

She raised an eyebrow and smiled. Look at his lovely brown eyes, the hint of a rogue. More than a hint. As their eyes briefly held, Nick winked, which made Nina laugh. "What is it?" Tom said. She leaned forward and messed his hair, soft and full. He liked that.

Like father and son, she thought. Hmmm. Autumn and spring. Which one?

"Nothing," she said.

She looked out of the window again. The red-roofed homes of Sarajevo lined the valley along the river like embers and climbed the ravines until they petered out in the mountain woods, the war's front lines. Through flashing gaps in the trees she saw the early sun glittering on rooftops, birds wheeling overhead. It seemed so close you could throw a stone onto her house. It was beautiful, once. Now it was just a sitting duck for Serb gunners.

The road narrowed into a winding mountain path, a canopy of pines almost concealing the sky. Rocks jutted out and little gleaming waterfalls wet the pebbly road, which crunched as they drove. "Slow down," Tom said on a sharp decline, gripping his seat.

Three minutes on, around a long bend, half a dozen gunmen in olive green fatigues and green cloth caps lounged in chairs beneath a tarpaulin hung between tree trunks. They waved their arms. Two stood and took positions on either side of the road, their weapons pointing at the car. Nick slowed and halted a dozen yards away. Leaning out the window he shouted, *"Novinar."* Press.

One of the gunmen beckoned the journalists forward with his left hand, his right hand leveling the semiautomatic at their vehicle. The other soldier stood straight, legs apart, rifle aimed from his shoulder at Nick's head. "Show them your hands," Tom said, placing his own on the dashboard. He didn't worry though. There was no tension here, the guards were just going through the motions. Four of them continued to play cards on a table of sandbags. Five yards away the guard showed them his palm, like a traffic cop. Nick stopped the car. "Out." The man gestured, jerking his gun. The other gunmen looked up from their game. A transistor radio was playing what sounded like a love song. A chicken tied by string to a chair leg jumped and squawked in place. Rescue? He hopped on one leg and strained against his shackle.

Nina opened her back door and got out. "Good morning," she called brightly in Serbian, nodding at the chicken. "Lunch?"

"Who are you?" the soldier said.

"Journalists," she said, pulling her Serb press pass from her pocket.

"Them?" he said, walking along the car and peering in. Nick smiled and handed over his ID card. Tom shook a Marlboro loose and offered the soldier one. The soldier snatched the pack and wriggled his fingers. Tom gave him his press card.

"Stay. Wait."

Reading their cards, he walked to the tent and called on his walkie-talkie, mangling their names. They heard the crackle.

Tom tuned the radio to Serb music and turned it up. The other guards lost all interest and returned to their card game.

Ten minutes later the soldier waved them away.

"Okay, you can go. Be careful," he said in Serbian. "Terrorists ahead."

They drove on in silence, broken after a minute by Nina's snort. "Terrorists! They are the Chetnik scum."

Ten minutes later the road led them into a cobbled village square with a chapel on a raised brick island in the middle. Low wooden houses with sloping red-tile roofs overgrown with climbers merged into the woods like fairy-tale homes. Old women at the water pump followed them with their eyes and men smoking on a bench turned their heads.

"I bet they know about the kid," Tom said as Nick halted by the chapel. They got out, yawning and stretching. They had been on the road for three hours, and it was approaching noon. The clouds were darkening as a chill wind rustled the trees. Tom pulled on his heavy jacket and turned up the collar. While Nick consulted his map in the driver's seat, Nina and Tom approached the men.

In room 921 of the Holiday Inn, Zoltan was doing his Slavic best to reassure Amber after she finished pummeling a pillow. "Come, my dear, let's go for a slivovitz, it'll do you good."

"I can't go downstairs. I'd have to climb up again. Can't you get me a lower floor, ferchrissake?" She was slumped back on the lumpy bed, one side of her face showing through long curly locks, jeans-covered legs wide apart, a study in dejection. "You've been promising for a week. Where's your pull? What do we pay you for?"

"To make slivovitz."

Zoltan's was foul but mind-numbing. "Let's go for a slivovitz" was his euphemism for "Come to my place," which meant what it meant. The crew could be away overnight; this was his chance. He'd been trying to pull Amber ever since he'd met her, which was the reaction of most men. She had an air that was both distant and inviting, a wall of reticence that didn't say keep out so much as climb over, if you dare. She was a most attractive mystery, her olive skin and fine-boned face a beautiful ethnic mix. In short: to die for. There didn't seem to be anybody in her life and Nick kept telling her she was wasting a national treasure. Whenever it got a bit hairy he would offer to tighten her flak jacket, while Tom stood in front of her, his lips inches from hers, pulling the cords of her steel combat helmet. She appeared exasperated at the attention: "I'm not a fucking action doll!"

She pushed herself up and swung her feet to the floor, shaking her head in disbelief. "They've really fucked me now, they really have." It was the third time she'd said that since she got off the phone with the London news desk. "Oh, shit!" she shouted.

She threw her pen to the floor, watched it bounce and clatter behind the lamp in the corner, and went onto her knees to feel behind and retrieve it. "It's my last goddamn pen!"

Zoltan watched her rear with a grin, it rose as she thrust forward. Dissolute didn't begin to describe his looks. His face was lined, his gray hair was disheveled, his eyes bloodshot, and he tended to pudginess and perspiration. "Have a drink," he said, "it'll do you good."

"Oh, get washed!"

"Can I use your shower?"

"There's no water. And anyway, no you can't."

Amber was at the end of her rope. The news desk had called, looking for Tom. She had said he was out on a shoot. Brinley, the London desk manager, had left a message: Tom should call the morning show directly, they may want a piece, sorry about the short notice, but it shouldn't be a problem, they could cut it in London, he just needed to file a track. There were good agency pictures of part of a convoy of humanitarian aid vehicles that had slid off a mountain road, killing a driver. Boxes of food were scattered all over the place and militiamen were stealing it, all on camera. Good stuff. We're telexing you the wire stories. The show may need a minute twenty, not sure yet, but could Tom do it if needed? With a standup. And the show says he must wear a flak jacket this time, orders from on high. We're booking time on the bird, protectively.

That was the message. Amber said she'd tell him, sure, no

problem, which she'd regretted as soon as the words were out of her mouth. And now, when she had called Tom and told him of the request, he had flatly refused. "Can't," he had said, "we're in a village, we'll never get back in time, I think we're on to something," and he'd hung up.

Hung up! He'd hung her out to dry. Selfish bastard. Doesn't give a shit about anyone else. Now what? What if they want a piece? She'd have to explain that he was out of touch. But if they asked where he was, then what? She couldn't lie. But the asshole was outside Sarajevo. She shook her head again, curls flopping from side to side. If he didn't get back in, she was toast. She had let him leave town. And part of a producer's job was to manage the talent, aka correspondent. Tom was a star, too big to fail, too respected, too big a deal. But she wasn't. If he was out of pocket when the main news wanted him, well, heads would roll—or rather, a head. Hers. She could hear Screaming Skull ranting from a thousand miles.

Fuck!

Why did she let him go? He better find the mom and get his ass back to town quick.

Looking up from his map, Nick saw a man emerge from the shade of two houses, holding something long. His neck hairs stood. A weapon? Tom and Nina were thirty yards away, stooped over the old people, their backs to the approaching man. He was walking slowly, resolutely. The women at the fountain had seen him too. Two of them got up and walked away, two more rose and walked toward Tom and Nina. Nick's heart began to pound. Think! He grabbed the small camera, turned it on—may as well get whatever was going to happen. He put it on the seat, at least he'd get the sound. He switched the ignition and rolled the car forward slowly. Not too fast, no sudden move, but he had to get the armored car to Tom and Nina, between them and the man.

He imagined shooting, muzzle flashes, everyone running. He closed his eyes. Get a grip, he told himself, just drive the car, stay calm, what would Tom do? Smile and talk. Talk, talk, talk.

The man was closer now and Nick chuckled with relief. The man had reached the people on the steps and offered them glasses of tea from his tray. Tom raised his in salutation, clinked glasses with Nina and the men. Nick sighed heavily, turned off the car, and walked over to take a glass too.

Tom shook his head at him. "What?" Nick said.

"They don't know anything. But this guy," Tom looked at the least wizened man, with a dirty blue beret, "this man says we should go to the next village, it's much bigger, and ask the priest. He should know, the church knows everything."

"Good idea," Nick said. "Where is it?"

"Don't ask me. Nina's finding out."

"Maybe I can do it by phone," Nina said. "This woman is inviting me to use her phone at home."

"It works? She's got a line?"

"So she says."

"Great," Tom said, "that'll save us time. And time on the road." The less time spent driving, the better. Most bad things happened on the road.

"Or we can use ours," he said. At that moment their satellite phone in the car rang again. It had a shrill beeping sound like a fire alarm. They had already ignored it once. Nick and Tom's eyes met. Tom shook his head.

Amber gripped the phone with hatred. Don't tell me they can't hear it.

. . .

In the narrow entrance hall of a low-ceilinged house, Nina was pleading on the phone. Tom could hear it in her tone; she was talking with her hands. *"Hvala. Hvala lijepo. Da. Da."*

The old lady brought more tea in little glasses, offering a bowl with cubes of sugar.

"We can go see him," Tom prompted in a whisper. "He'll tell us if we're face-to-face."

Nina shook her head, made a rubbing-out gesture with her forefinger. She held the phone to her side. "He wants to know why we want to know."

"What?"

"He doesn't know who we are. We could be anybody. Police, enemy, who knows?"

"Does he speak English?"

"No."

"Tell him this is a terrible war and we just want to do a little good, it's the truth. Tell him we need his help so that we can help this poor family."

Nick said, "Just say we'll give him a hundred bucks."

Fifteen minutes later they were back in the car, each lost in their thoughts. The priest had advised them to avoid the main road; farther along, Bosnian Serb artillery was moving positions and they wouldn't take kindly to journalists giving away their new co-ordinates. So now they were rattling along a rutted track that skirted sloping fields and should lead them through the woods toward the village of Bukomir, an hour to the north.

It was getting late, past one thirty; they'd have to push to make it back to Sarajevo that night. But Tom was smiling quietly to himself.

It would be a moment to cherish.

The priest had described Aleksandar and Ema Cordas as simple farm laborers who prayed in church every morning for their lost son, Petar. For six months they had walked to the road-block, begging to be allowed through. They had brought presents, fresh vegetables, for the soldiers, who commiserated and said they too had children, but it was too dangerous, their orders were that nobody could pass for any reason. One day an officer from head-quarters had ordered, "That's final, stop bothering us," and at last they had given up.

Everybody knew their story, it was a tragedy, but it was not for man to understand the ways of the Lord, but to accept. And when the priest had accepted that Nina and her friends were genuine journalists and that their intentions were good, he had blessed them over the phone.

Tom closed his eyes: for once he would be the bearer of good news.

They would show the parents the tape of their boy in his cot playing with the guitar, with his smile and glinting eyes. Two years with no news! Half the boy's life. There would be weeping, tears of joy.

Tom looked at Nick, who was driving with one arm resting on the window frame, relaxed. You'd never think he was driv-ing through a war zone—he could be driving to pick up his girl back home in England. Although she had just dumped him be-cause he was hardly ever at home. She'd met someone else. Nick was upset but Tom had told him, "It goes with the territory. You want a stable life, work in a bank."

He looked out of the window and tried not to dwell on the dan-ger, from militias, shelling, bandits, worst of all, the unexpected.

Stay focused, that's all. He cleared his mind of all bad juju, and felt a smile.

Reporting on every war eventually came down to one question: How far is it safe to go down the road? Nick always said, "If it's okay with you, it's okay with me." Tom, at forty the grizzled veteran, hadn't put a foot wrong yet. He was a lucky bastard, everyone told Nick, stay close to him and you'll be all right.

And that was a two-way street. Nick would go anywhere, do anything, they shared a certain recklessness, yet there was a soft side to Nick too. He always carried candy bars to hand out to children. Tom couldn't imagine anything ever happening to Nick, he was too kind, he deserved a long and healthy life. Stay close to Nick, Tom's instincts said, he's the lucky type, and as Napoleon said, he'd rather be lucky than good.

Nick was also almost young enough to be the son he'd never had. Tom had been married once, to a television producer, briefly and disastrously. "Son," he would warn Nick over a soft drink at the end of the day, with as much deep-voiced pomposity as he could muster, as if he were delivering the evening news: "Man is incomplete until he's married. Then he's finished." That always cracked him up.

Nick had been even more excited than Tom when the priest gave the names. When they met the parents he'd have to keep filming throughout—anything could happen. The mother could faint with joy. On camera. What a story.

There was a jolt, and another. The car bounced as Nick hit a series of hard ridges in the track and bumped through them. Nina called out in alarm, one hand gripping the camera on the backseat so it wouldn't fly into the air.

And then she couldn't help herself, she yelled in surprise, and even Tom's heart leapt. Nick hit the brake and they all shot forward.

The explosion seemed on top of them. Birds screeched and lifted from the trees, long thin legs following beating wings. Nina hit her head on the roof, Tom stopped himself with his arms on the dashboard, Nick was already opening his door and yelling, "Give me the camera." There was another explosion, and another, they didn't seem as loud, and Tom yelled, "It's okay, it's okay."

He understood what those ridges in the road were, just where the trees thinned and the track widened. The ground had been churned up by heavy vehicles. Another bang, and another. Nick was rolling his camera for sound, looking for the source of the explosions. Nina was shaking on the backseat, peering up like a tortoise. Tom said: "Outgoing. Relax."

But there was no time for that.

A jeep hurtled out of the trees and halted next to them. Two soldiers jumped out with weapons raised. Tom lifted a hand to show everything was cool and said, "Nina, we got company. Tell them we're journalists. We want to film the artillery."

But it quickly turned bad. The soldiers, both with bandannas, could not care less. One barked an order. Nina called, "Nick, put the camera down. Right now."

Nick turned it off and pointed the lens at the ground. "Get in," the same soldier shouted at Nina, gesturing to their jeep. She looked in alarm at Tom, and shook her head. "Why?"

"What is it?" Tom asked.

The soldier grabbed Nina by the arm and pushed her into the front seat of his jeep, yelling at her. The other soldier, the one with a topknot, with sharp features smudged with earth, jerked the camera from Nick's hand.

"Hey, don't touch the camera," Nick said, more out of habit than conviction. This was no moment to argue—the Committee for the Protection of Journalists was on three hundred something Seventh Avenue, New York, not on this isolated track in the woods in the middle of fuck knows where.

Tom went round the car to Nina, who sat trembling in the jeep. He smiled at the two soldiers, making eye contact, talking all the time. "Nina, tell them not to be concerned, we're just journalists, we have press passes, we'd like to speak to their officer."

Nina began to talk, when without warning Topknot shoved Tom against the side of the jeep. "You, shut up," he shouted in English as Tom stumbled and had to catch himself.

The other one, with hair pulled back tight in a ponytail, climbed into the jeep, said something to Nina, and roared away with her. Over her shoulder she saw Topknot pointing his weapon at Tom and Nick, who could only call out after her, "It'll be okay, call the officer."

"Where are you taking her?" Tom said as the jeep disappeared into the trees.

As quickly as he had exploded, Topknot relaxed. He stood his weapon against the car's wheel, leaned back against the door with one leg drawn up behind him, and lit a cigarette. He offered it to Tom, who took it, and looked at Nick. Nick shook his head.

"Do you speak English?" Tom said.

The soldier nodded, lighting his own and blowing out smoke with a loud sigh. "Where from?" he asked.

"New York, but I live in London," Tom said. "Where's your friend taking her?" He had already stopped worrying. He realized they had lucked into one of the new artillery positions. They must be very close, judging by the force of the booms, and the two guys must be field security. They'd check their passes with headquarters and let them go. Tom looked at Nick, who nodded back. Nina was fine, she just didn't know it yet. The only real questions were: Where was the battery and could they film it?

A crackling voice came through the soldier's walkie-talkie. A moment later they were driving across a potato field, Nick guiding the heavy car along the tops of the ridges, hoping they wouldn't bog down. The soldier tapped the windshield. It had a dull sound. "Stop bullets?"

Nick nodded. "Bulletproof. Yes."

"Good," Topknot said, tapping his side window, feeling the leather seat, his mouth curling in appreciation. "Nice. Lot money. I keep."

"I don't think so." Nick smiled.

"I do," he said, and smiled back, the automatic rifle between his legs moving from side to side with the motion of the car.

It was a roundabout drive to an open field on the other side of the trees where they had thought they were being shelled. A cluster of military vehicles, jeeps, half-tracks, and tow trucks surrounded a dugout and a bunker of sandbags. In the center, seated at a white folding table, was Nina, surrounded by Bosnian Serb militiamen with their shoulder flashes of the Serb cross and four Cs, symbols of their fight for independence.

Spread around the field were artillery pieces, each with a knot of men smoking. The guns were silent now.

They must have been shelling Sarajevo.

Nina was leaning forward and talking intensely to an older man. He had black hair that fell over his eyes and a natural scowl that made Tom—who knew how vulnerable she was; they all were, but especially her—uncomfortable. Nina, don't fight with him, Tom thought. Agree with everything the Serb says. For once.

Nina introduced him. "Tom Layne. Our chief correspondent. A star in America," she said to the man, who looked un-impressed.

Tom shook the officer's hand. "Through me you talk to America," he said, his usual spiel, which he delivered with a smile and a shrug, supposed to be in modest affirmation. "We have the biggest news audience in the country." All the networks claimed the title; it depended how you measured it. When pressed, the CNN correspondent explained that his viewers were the fattest.

It was supposed to make the other guy understand that Tom was worth talking to, that his presence wasn't just a nuisance but an opportunity that could be exploited. That was the idea anyway. The downside was that it also sent another message: kidnap him and you could get a lot of money.

Tea and coffee were served around the field radio, which stood upright in the center of the table. They were waiting to hear if headquarters would give them permission to film, but either way, Tom felt, nothing bad was going to happen. He looked at Nina, talking animatedly to the officer. Although she was half Muslim, and had a Muslim name, it was the half-Serb side that counted here. Most of the country was the progeny of mixed marriages, which made a mockery of their internecine slaughter. Who knew what it was really all about? One writer, when talking about the war in Bosnia-Herzegovina, a war fought in places like Srpska Kostajnica and Donja Tramošnica, said he would call it the Unspellables versus the Unpronouncables.

Tom looked at his watch. It was almost three and all that mattered to him was getting to the village to find the family. But slowly, slowly. He smiled as he accepted sugar. Take it easy, he told himself. No hurry. Get out safely.

The field radio crackled to life and the officer answered, looking at Nina. *"Hvala lijepo, hvala lijepo,"* she said. By now Tom understood a few words and looked at her. Good news?

"We can film."

"Really?" Tom was surprised. "We have permission?" He looked over at Nick, who was already fiddling with the camera, raising it to his shoulder.

At that moment the radio crackled again, more talking, more walking away by the officer with the receiver to his ear, and then, shouted orders. He pointed at Nick and gestured toward the big guns. He put one hand over his ear: they're going to shoot, get ready.

Tom ran to the car to get the tripod and set it up for Nick. Nick kicked the legs out further till it was stable, slid back the clasp, and clamped the camera onto the tripod head and found the horizontal. He focused on the nearest gun but before he could turn on the camera it fired. A jet of flame shot out with the shell. "Shit, missed it," he shouted. "Nina, ask which one is next!"

He picked up the tripod and camera and walked quickly back till he could see three guns lined up in one shot. "Just run the camera, leave it on," Tom shouted.

"You don't say," Nick said, switching on the camera and letting it run. Everyone else bent over or turned away, hands pressed against their ears. One gun fired, then almost simultaneously the booms of the second and third. Nick got it all on a wide shot, and zoomed in to the smoke curling out of the middle barrel. Minutes later he got a close-up of the barrel as it fired again, orange flame and black-gray smoke pouring out with the shell, then he did a fast pull-back to the first gun just as it fired too. A casing was ejected, the gunners reloaded efficiently. A moment later, silence.

Nick stood up straight with his arms wide, triumphant. "Got it all," he said.

Tom laughed at their good luck. Till he saw Nina. She looked as if she could cry. She was crouching, her long auburn hair hiding her face.

They were shelling her city.

And now she had to make conversation with the gunners. The killers.

"What's wrong?" the officer said to her, pushing his hair from his eyes.

Nina looked up at him and shook her head. Her heart was pounding, she told Tom later, she wished a sinkhole would swallow them all, she was sure they could see her trembling. Maybe you felt that, Tom told her, but you didn't look it. He had intervened, asked her to translate a question, to distract her from what he knew she was thinking.

Tom's question, as Nick rolled the camera, didn't help, but it was the obvious one: What was your target?

"The criminals," the officer said, and abruptly turned away. "We will drive them mad until they surrender." He told Nick to stop filming. "We may have a surprise for you," he said. "Save your film."

Tom, Nick, and Nina went to their car, where Nick told Tom what pictures he had shot. "I'm amazed they let us," Tom said. "And they didn't say anything about giving away their location."

"You can't tell anyway," Nick said. "It's just ground, trees, and sky. Great stuff though. Good sound."

The firing had been deafening. Tom's ears were still ringing even though he had covered them with his hands. They were so close they could smell the cordite, had felt the displaced air.

Now it was silent around them as they discussed what to do. "Too late to go on," Tom said, "right, Nina?"

She had recovered. It was always like this. Either the Muslims insulted the Serbs or the other way around. Half of her was always wounded and upset. What a horrible war. "Yes, I think so. I don't really know where the village is and it's getting dark. It's too dangerous to drive around at night."

"Sleeping bags in the car," Nick said. "Just for a change."

"Well, we have all we need," Tom said. "In the morning we—"

He broke off and tilted his head, cocked an ear and an eye. "What's that?"

A distant throbbing, a vibration among the trees, a beating of the air. The officer and his men around the table also looked up. The throbbing became a roar and Nick filmed the helicopter as it appeared from the north, low over the trees, its nose dipping as it hovered fifty yards away over open ground, blowing up a storm of earth and dust, before settling with a final bump.

The door swung open and two men with guns jumped out with lowered heads. A moment later a bulky man in camouflage fatigues emerged, holding an attaché case with one hand while keeping his cap in place with the other. He strode forward as the rotors beat above him, flattening the grass and throwing out pebbles like grapeshot, while the officer and his men rushed toward him, arms outstretched.

"Holy cow!" Tom said, looking sharply at Nick. No worries, Nick was always a step ahead. He was focused on the tall, sturdy man with swept-back gray hair under his cap. Binoculars hung from his neck. Wind blew out his open flak jacket, making him look even stockier.

Nina was staring. "Oh. Oh. I've never seen him before."

"Sssshh," Nick said. "I'm recording."

The man embraced the officer, shook the hands of the others, and as the chopper rose in another roar of wind and dust they all walked to the little table, where the crowd quickly grew as soldiers left their field guns and gathered around. Voices were raised as one, a sudden shout of greeting and defiance. It sounded like a toast to war. The TV crew filmed from a distance.

Until, half an hour later, a young soldier ran toward them, waving and shouting. Nina cupped her ear with her hand. "Is this good or bad?"

"What's he saying?" Tom said.

"He wants to meet you."

"All right!" Nick said with a grin. "The Big Cheese. The ten-ton gorilla. The mountain comes to Mohammed."

"I think this is called a scoop," Tom said. "He never speaks to the press. Let's go."

The crowd of soldiers around the table parted as they approached, and there he was, sitting at the head, legs outstretched, hands folded on stomach, watching them as they walked—the tormentor of Sarajevo, whose orders to his gunners were: "Beat them senseless!" and "Torch them!"

Nina hung back but Tom strode forward with Nick behind him, camera rolling to get the two men meeting. "Good afternoon, General," Tom said, as they shook hands.

"Hello, welcome," said General Ratko Mladić, feared commander of the Bosnian Serb army, most powerful man in Bosnia, most hated too. Patron of rape, murder, torture. That was all the English he knew, and he waved Tom to a seat before going back to Serbian with his men. The soldiers melted away, leaving the officer, a couple of aides, and Mladić around the table with Tom and his team.

His next words, translated by Nina, surprised Tom. "Do you play chess?"

"Why, yes. I'm not much good but I love the game, yes. Why, do you?"

"The game of kings. And bored soldiers," he said in Serbian, and Nina translated.

It was agreed. The crew would sleep in the car, be given food and drink, and Tom would play chess with Mladić. "I often visit the soldiers in the field, sleep over," he said, through Nina. "Evenings can be long. And cold. Chess warms me, I find."

Tom only smiled. What do you say to that?

The sky had turned leaden gray, clouds and the onset of dusk flattening the light, turning the trees into shadows. Nick murmured to Tom, "We're losing light. Fast." They had to film now or it would be too dark. And they might not be allowed to use lights.

"Sir. General, would you mind if I ask you a few questions, on camera, first?" Tom asked. "I mean, now, while we still have daylight? This is an opportunity to talk to America."

"You think I want to talk to America? You think I need an opportunity?"

"No, yes, well, I just meant . . ."

"I am joking."

"Oh."

Maybe it was because they had driven through potato fields but, as he looked into Mladić's face, while Nick prepared the camera and microphones and Mladić spoke to the officer, it was hard for Tom not to think of a potato. His head was square, like a block, yet puffy, his complexion ruddy and bland. His eyes, a penetrating blue, seemed dark holes too small for the whole. Truly, he thought, like the eyes of a potato—and are they really poisonous? His receding hair, iron gray, was swept back at the sides but fell forward in the front, an old-fashioned quiff. His mouth was set firm with down-turned edges, as if he was frowning even while he talked. His jowls were heavy. He looked like a broad-shouldered street fighter. The one thing everyone said about his military career was that all he knew was to attack, with great force. And that, Tom thought, is what he looks like: an armored bulldozer.

"Ready," Nick said, as Nina smoothed down Tom's collar, and he added quietly, "We have about ten minutes of light, Tom."

"So we'll start, General," Tom said.

He nodded.

"Forgive me, but as we don't have much light, I will get straight to the point."

Mladić's eyes bored into Tom. He nodded again. To hear better, the officer and soldiers closed in from the sides, like a pincer movement.

"Why are you shelling the town of Sarajevo and killing and wounding thousands of innocent civilians?"

Nick's face, cheek pressed against the camera, didn't change, but he smiled inside. Doesn't mince words, he thought. Does Tom realize, to all intents and purposes, we are prisoners here? 'Course he does.

"Innocent?" Mladić said, and paused, considering Tom, before answering.

Tom didn't want a discussion, he wanted a short, strong sound bite, and now. So he added:

"You know. Massacre."

Mladić's lips tightened even more. "Massacre? Massacre? They do massacre, not the Serbs." He listed names: "Kupres, Doboj, Samac, you know these places? Modrica, Derventa, they burned down a hundred Serb villages along the Drina river. They did it to us. Did you ask them why? Did you? Did you? Did you ask them?"

Tom shook his head. Before he could rephrase the question,

narrow it so that Mladić would give an answer he could use, Mladić went on, "Do you know what my name means? Do you?"

Tom shook his head again.

"Ratko. From Ratimir. My name means 'War or Peace.' You see? We want peace, not war, but they attacked us so we must fight back. And you? Are you better? You are worse. You can say I have horns on my head if I had invaded Vietnam, Cambodia, or the Falkland Islands. If I sent my armies to other countries like Somalia or the Gulf. Oh, but wait. That wasn't me, that was you. That is what you do. Who is the devil here? We are fighting for our own homes. I am defending my people. That is my patriotic duty. America, England, NATO, you are the devil."

Tom shifted in his seat. All good stuff, but he saw a story forming in his mind. In Sarajevo they had filmed the shells falling, here they had filmed the shells being fired; here they had the snipers getting into position and there they had sniper victims dying and others running in the streets for their lives. They had both sides of the story, they could cut back and forth. Now here was the Serb army chief, and he needed him to talk about why he was shelling Sarajevo, not all this self-justification stuff.

"But why take it out on civilians? Fighting the army, fine, but killing old men, women, children. You should see the hospital wards. They are full of children. Why?"

"Look, we don't want this war, nobody does. It is a war among Serbs. You know that Bosnian Muslims are really Serbs? Under Turkish rule they became Muslims four hundred years ago. These are my people, but misled. Did you know I lived in Sarajevo, in Pofalici, with my brother? The house we lived in burned down too. You think I like that? This war must end. It must end. That is my message to America."

Tom was getting nervous. Mladić was giving him nothing.

"General, forgive me, not my word, but the world is calling you a murderer."

Nina, translating, felt her heart grow cold. She would have found another word, softened it, but didn't think fast enough.

Mladić pulled back in his seat and considered the interviewer. His mouth formed a kind of grim smile and his eyes were deadly. Words emerged like a snarl, but he caught himself.

"Sir," he started again. He turned to look into the camera. Nick had him in big close-up, face puffy and reddening. "I have an unfortunate role in an unfortunate war in an unfortunate country—people in Bosnia wish for peace. There is a habit amongst people in our country of saying the words 'peaceful Bosnia' at the end of a sentence. This tells you how rarely it is peaceful in Bosnia."

They went back and forth a bit more but Tom could not pull out of him any emotion or threats against Sarajevo, no sense of the bullying killer he was known to be. In short, Mladić had won—he would come across as a man of reason and integrity.

"Almost out of light," Nick murmured. "I need time for cutaways, wide shots. Or the light won't match."

Tom sighed. He'd blown it. "Well, thank you, General, if you could just sit there a moment while we get—"

"If you could talk to the people of Sarajevo now, what would you say to them?" Nina threw in the question. Nick quickly reframed for a close-up.

"What would I say, young lady?" Mladić said. "You ask me what I would say?" he repeated, his voice louder and harder, his eyes boring into her. "To those terrorists? This is what I would say. Enough. Enough fighting. People of Sarajevo, surrender, surrender now. Or we will burn you all, we have all the power, all the guns, enough shells to bomb you for years and to turn Sarajevo into a graveyard. We will drive you to the edge of madness. And we will, to save our country, we will destroy you. Women, children, we are sorry but," and now he was jabbing with his finger, "tell your men to stop attacking Serbs, to stop killing Serbs, for hundreds of years the Muslims tortured and raped and killed us, now is the time, our time, we will do anything for our people to live in peace. Anything at all." His voice had risen to a shout. "You are warned, you are warned, that is what I tell the people of Sarajevo, we will turn you into toast! Tell America too. NATO? I spit on NATO. These are our hills, our mountains, our homes, these green fields have run red with our blood for centuries but today we are strong and united and any foreign invaders will rue the day, rue the day." He was red with anger, leaning forward, in Tom's face, and poked him in the chest with his finger. "We will never give in, if I have a million men, a million men will die, because we will never be defeated!"

As Nick pulled wide to show the Serb soldiers listening they began to laugh and applaud their leader, clapping and stamping their feet.

General Mladić sat back with folded arms and looked along his nose to Nina, to Tom. "Does that answer your question? Does it? Does it?"

Nina had been whispering the translation into Tom's ear, racing to keep up as Mladić ranted. Tom said, "Oh, yes. Oh, yes it does, thank you."

Next morning it bucketed down. The windshield wipers flew, pushing water to the sides, giving a straining Nick brief moments to glimpse ahead. The track had turned into a pebble-strewn lane, so at least they shouldn't get stuck in mud. They were following the soldiers' directions to Bukomir. "There should be a right turn soon," Nina said, "opposite white crosses, where there's a steep drop down the mountain."

Moments later: "Here's the turn. Slowly." It was a sharp bend that had surprised many, hence the cluster of crosses.

Now the thick trees gave some protection from the driving rain, enough to see, and Nick accelerated a little, displaced pebbles flying to the sides.

The phone rang, shrill in the enclosed space. It was wedged behind the driver's seat. Tom looked at it. He was lying on the backseat, knees up, his back against the door, with his sleeping bag as a cushion. At last he was comfortable after a cold night where all three had strained and groaned, seeking relief for their arms and legs, with Nick and Nina cramped in the front seats, and Tom, exercising droit du seigneur, spread out in the back. That had annoyed Nick, who said at least the lady should have the back. "What lady?" Tom had replied.

With a sigh Tom leaned forward and picked up the phone and said, "Ratko Mladić."

"Tom? Is that you? Tom?"

"No, it's Ratko Mladić."

"Who? Tom, don't mess around, New York has been trying to get you since last night."

"Good morning, Amber. How are you? Did you sleep well? We had to switch the phone off, the battery is going down already."

"What about the spare?"

"Oh, right. Anyway, what is it?"

"You won't believe it."

"Try me. And you won't believe what we lucked into." Tom outlined the story so far. "I don't think anyone's ever interviewed Mladić like this before. We played chess, three games, he murdered me. But Nick was filming, with lights, we did an interview and continued the talk over the game. And that's just for starters." Amber was trying to interrupt but with the delay on the phone line he spoke over her. "So that's one story, a separate story. And guess where we're heading now?"

Nick grinned at Tom in the mirror; he was sitting up with excitement. "The mom. And dad. We're heading there now. We're going to have two fantastic stories."

When he had told her everything, Amber was at last able to make herself heard. "Great, great stuff, Tom. But listen. Prepare yourself. Big Bucks is going to London." She hesitated.

"So?" Tom said, but his heart was already sinking. Whenever the network anchor, Buck Johnson—Ten-Million-Dollar Man, Big Bucks for short—traveled to London, or almost anywhere, he wanted the veteran foreign correspondent, his anchor buddy, by his side.

"Why? What's the story?"

"Okay, remember, I'm just passing this on. Don't shoot the messenger. He's got a one-on-one with Prince Charles." She began to speak quickly, racing through it, trying to finish before Tom erupted. "Charles fell off his horse. Twice. There were complaints that the heir to the throne could kill himself playing polo or something. So that's the story and it's huge. The big question: Not war in Bosnia or peace in the Middle East but, and as I say, I'm just the messenger: Will Prince Charles give up polo? All the papers are leading with it. So you know Buck and the palace, he thinks it's named after him, I think he wants a knighthood, so he's doing a one-hour special on the Royal Family set around his exclusive interview and he wants you there. They want you to do a piece on the princes, William and Harry. They need you to break off whatever you're doing and get to London. ASAP. Jim Miller is on his way to replace you."

Silence.

"It's not my fault, Tom. Tom? Hello? Hello? Tom?"

Tom had to smile. He slowly replaced the receiver in the cradle and leaned back against his sleeping bag, shaking his head at the wonder of it all. You couldn't make this shit up.

Nick was gaining speed now; the track had turned into a real tar road. Seeing Tom lie back with a grin on his face, he smiled too. "What is it, Tom, what did they say?" Nina turned her head too.

"What did they say?" Tom repeated. "Nick, are you holding the wheel tight? Don't hit a tree, but get this. Are you listening, Nina? Have I told you often enough how beautiful you are?" He put his hand in her hair and mussed it up playfully, although after a night in the car it was already a bird's nest. "Listen and learn. Do we have the greatest job in the world? Yes, we do. Do we get to see the world in all its misery and make it a better place, in our own tiny way? Yes, we do. Do we love to spend shitty nights in the car in pursuit of important stories that can help people understand their lives a little better? Yes, strangely, we do. Lastly, do we have the biggest jerk-offs for bosses? All together now: yes we do."

"Let me guess," Nick said, slowing down, looking at Tom's reflection in the mirror. "They want you back in London for another story on the Royal Family."

"Yes."

"Yes? You're kidding me! I was joking."

"You got it in one. A story on William and Harry."

"Who?" Nina said.

"Big Bucks is doing a one-hour special on the palace, it must be his fifth, and they want me on the set."

"Huh?" Nick could only grunt.

"Exactly."

"Fuck that."

"Exactly."

"The phone just went down."

"You're learning fast."

"William and who?" Nina said.

Tom lapsed into silence, Nick drove on, and Nina said, "About another twenty minutes, we should arrive."

Tom opened his wallet and took out the visiting card Ratko Mladić had given him, shifted it between his fingers. When they had woken that morning, early as it was, Mladić had already left by car. A soldier had handed him the general's visiting card, on the back of which Mladić had written a few words. Nina said, "This could be very useful. He's written, 'This man can be trusted. Call me if necessary.'"

"Useful here, maybe," Tom said. "Kiss of death in Sarajevo."

He slid the card back into his wallet, looking at the back of Nina's head. She was lolling in her seat, her hair falling to the side, loose tresses spilling over the back, auburn and wavy. He took them in his hand, stroked her hair. "Tired, Nina?"

"No," she murmured. "Well, a little."

"You saved the interview."

"I know."

"In return, if you like, I'll brush your hair. Do you have a brush?"

"No. It's in my bag. In the back."

"Must make a good impression on . . . on . . . what are their names again?"

"Aleksandar and Ema Cordas." Nina's vowels came from deep in her throat. Tom tried to say their names but only made her laugh. He leaned forward and whispered them again, and she laughed harder. "No, no," she said, as Tom stroked her hair, "that's terrible pronunciation."

Tom wanted to kiss her ear, and Nina wished he would.

Nick glanced sideways. *The old guy, he never gives up.*

. . .

The rain had stopped and the gleaming earth and the slick red pines smelt of fresh herbs and wood smoke that rose through the trees. The valley below was alive in shades of green and strips of glittering water, and dotted with homes and fields in clearings in the woods. Bukomir.

Their journey had taken them almost back to where they had started. On the other side of the wooded slopes lay Sarajevo. If they had turned right before Pale the day before instead of left they would have come upon the place within an hour. They could see it was a mixed Serb-Muslim village by the church steeple and the mosque's minaret, and relations must have been good, once, because the prayer houses stood in a lane almost side by side.

Everyone knew the Cordas home, and their story.

Outside, Tom pinned his tiny radio mic onto his collar, turned on the transmitter, Nick checked the receiver, made sure his batteries were full, turned on the gun mic, the directional microphone attached to the top of the camera, and they were ready. Nina went first, followed by Tom and last of all Nick, filming point of view as they walked. He wanted to shoot the meeting as it evolved from Tom's point of view, which should make it more immediate, intimate, dramatic. Close-ups of his feet walking, his hand outstretched, his tense profile.

It was a low brick house with a wooden extension on top and a thatched roof. The small windows were closed and shuttered. At close to midday, not a good sign. Tom pushed open the gate and let Nina lead the way.

She knocked on the door, once, twice. They waited with pursed lips. Light footsteps inside, the rattling of a key in the lock, and the door was slightly ajar to reveal frightened eyes in a thin face.

A small, pale woman clasping a faded dressing gown to her throat recoiled at the sight of strangers.

"Hello, sorry to bother you. We are journalists, are you Ema Cordas?" Nina asked.

The woman was clearly deciding.

She nodded.

Nina told her why they had come.

It was good that Ema Cordas was so short, because she didn't have so far to fall. Tom lunged forward, too late, then fell to his knees and took Ema's trembling hand. She was calling "Petar, Petar," and gripped his hand so tight it hurt.

"Quick, get some water," Tom said.

Nina called out but nobody else appeared to be home. She pushed past and returned with a basin of cold water. She dabbed Ema's forehead and slowly helped the weeping woman to her feet.

"Petar is well looked after, he is healthy and growing, you can be proud," Nina told her, translating for Tom. Why make it worse? "The nurses love him and care for him."

They told her as much as they could, as she nodded open-mouthed and crossed herself repeatedly and kissed the crucifix around her neck. She didn't say a word; the news had struck her dumb.

"Ask her if she'd like to see pictures of Petar," Tom said. Nina translated and as she spoke the mother's eyes widened until they seemed to take over her whole face. She nodded furiously as her eyes welled with tears. She trembled so much Nina had to take her arm.

Nick, quiet, discreet, had filmed it all. He set up a small video player and monitor and slid the tape inside, then took up the camera again and began to roll. All Tom had to do was push the Play button.

"What about her husband, Aleksandar, is he around?" Tom asked. "Maybe he wants to see too. Any more kids?"

Ema Cordas spoke rapidly, at last able to talk.

"She says she knew Petar was in the hospital but hadn't heard anything for months. Her husband was wounded, he isn't here," Nina said. "She didn't say what happened. I don't want to ask. And they don't have any other children."

Tom nodded. No need to press her about her husband. The priest would know.

Ema was now perched on the edge of the sofa, looking at the TV, muttering to herself as if in prayer. A black kerchief around her head, she had dressed hurriedly. She was wearing a gray woolen jacket on a dark leather sofa, in a room with musty walls and one dim light, windows shut—everything about the small room was dark and heavy. The house smelled stale and sad. A baby photo had been enlarged until it was almost blurred, and was pinned over the cold fireplace without a frame. On the mantelpiece there was a shrine of little stuffed animals and two pacifiers.

Nick gave Nina a small battery-driven sun gun and guided her hand until the edge of the light cast a glow across the mother and gave some depth to the room.

As Nick prepared, Tom sat next to Ema with a reassuring smile, trying not to look smug. They'd done it, found her. What a story. Yet what a poor woman, so little, so vulnerable. When would she see Petar again?

"Ready," Nick murmured, rolling the camera, and Tom smiled at Ema, indicating the TV monitor on the low table. As she looked from him to the screen he leaned forward and pressed Play.

The countdown began at 10 and reached 3, 2, 1, each numeral

accompanied by a beep. Nick focused on Ema's face, allowing it to fill the screen, knowing he could film the monitor later. The story was Ema's emotion when she saw her baby for the first time in two years.

Tom had been doing this for two decades but didn't predict what happened next. Neither did Nick. As the black-and-white numbers on the TV monitor morphed into Petar, wide face smiling at the camera, holding the guitar between his legs and playing with the strings, nodding with each note; as Ema's eyes flooded while she stared, transfixed, and her jaw dropped open; as Petar leaned over with his pudgy arm and his hand went out of the screen and came back with a slice of apple which he put into his mouth and his mouth worked and he stretched out his hand for another piece; and as Nick gently, sensitively, zoomed in to a tight close-up of Ema's wondering wet eyes, Ema suddenly disappeared from Nick's little screen in the eyepiece. Gone.

Ema shot forward and fell onto the TV monitor and embraced it, sobbing, and kissed her baby on the screen, kissing and hugging and crying and calling out, "Oh, Petar, Petar, I'm sorry, I'm sorry I left you, I'm so sorry, oh Lord, forgive me, please forgive me."

She slid to the floor and lay at the foot of the monitor, prostrate with grief and relief, her shoulders heaving, her body wracked with sobs, calling to God and to Petar for forgiveness.

Nina, next to Tom, burst into tears and Tom struggled to hold his back. He took Nina's hand, and she squeezed so hard he had to pull free. Petar smiled down at his sobbing mother. His hands on the cot's rail, he pulled himself to his feet and banged and shook the guitar at the camera, smiling, rolling his head from side to side, his harelip stretched by his radiant smile. Reflection from the screen cast a blue glow onto Ema's lowered head, and Petar's gurgles merged with his mother's sobs.

Only Nick worked calmly on, wide shot, medium, close-up, from the side, pan down from the TV to Ema's tears, back up again. The distance created by the lens distanced him from what was real, happening before him, only feet away. Ema's sobbing seemed in a different dimension.

Now Nina was sitting helplessly on the floor with her hand resting on the head of Ema, who appeared to be sleeping by the TV. Ema was exhausted. Drained. Of tears, of emotions, of . . . of what?

Tom, on the sofa, making notes, searching for words, could find no more. He wondered how much of the crying pictures they could use. Not too many, just a few seconds. It was too intrusive, too heartbreaking, too raw. The mother deserved her privacy. And yet, again, his conundrum. When does reporting become exploitation? When does the bad outweigh the good?

They stayed like this, as the room grew darker, until Ema finally rose, like the phoenix, to make tea.

Outside in the car the phone rang, but they were deep in conversation. Tom had had another idea, he'd thought of it while wondering when Ema would ever see her son again: Why not smuggle Ema into Sarajevo? To reunite her with Petar? They could pay someone to take her through the secret tunnel under the airport, which was used to smuggle in food, weapons, people, medicines, not to mention booze and cigarettes. They could meet her at the other end, inside Sarajevo, and take her to the hospital. Can you imagine what that would look like? When she actually picks him up and holds him?

They could even get them both out the same way, they could go back home through the tunnel. It would be an extraordinary story, maybe they could film her all the way, Nick said, he could even go through the tunnel with her, filming every step. "Doubt it," Tom said. "It's too secret. We probably couldn't even mention the tunnel. Just that we helped her. We'd have to say that."

Ema was sitting on the sofa, her thoughts with her son, and it was so easy for Tom to imagine her holding Petar. A mother, a lost child, reunited; he wanted that more than anything, an echo from his own home. But he imagined also the cut story, the heart-rending report. He shook his head, a smile playing on his lips, as he questioned himself, and not for the first time or in the first place. What came first, the story and the glory, or helping someone? He didn't know the answer. Does it even matter why you do a good thing, as long as you do it?

Nina asked, "What are you thinking about?" He shrugged, and she said, "I think I know."

"Maybe you do," he said. "I doubt it."

"I may be naïve," she said, "but I'm genuine. And so are you."

It was not to be. When Tom finally answered the phone, on the caller's third attempt, and the New York desk assistant told him, "One moment please, Boone wants you," his stomach had clenched. Boone was the senior vice president for news, aka the Terminator, because that was what he spent most of his time doing. Everybody was afraid of the next round of cuts.

Boone's response, after Tom had outlined his proposed scoop, was this: "Ratko . . . Ratface who? Nobody can tell Ratface Mladić from a hole in a doughnut, nobody in the front office gives a rat's ass about some kid in a hospital, or his mom; what the front office does care about is getting your ass back to London for the Royals, and in the future if you don't answer the phone when you're in the field you won't be sent into the field again, I don't give a crap who you are. And why the hell aren't you in Sarajevo?"

. . .

"Well, to be honest, we couldn't really have smuggled her in," Tom said, recovering quickly after hanging up. "Great idea, but I don't think we want to play God too much. What happens if she got caught or shot or something? We would have made that happen. Why? For a story?"

"To help her," Nick said.

"Good point. Still, really, that's a step too far, we can't get that involved. It isn't right."

"The poor woman," Nina said. "Isn't there anything we can do for her?"

They left Ema Cordas money, the rest of their food, the tape of course, even though she didn't have a way to watch it, but best of all was a gift from Nick, who always traveled with a Polaroid camera—he took six photos of Petar on the screen and gave them to her. She kissed the pictures, careful that her tears would not wet them, held them to her breast, kissed them again, and placed them on the mantelpiece by the pacifiers, then packed all her fresh-baked cookies in a paper bag.

"For Petar, and for the nurses caring for him, so they will love him even more.

"And please, take this photo," she cried, pressing one into Tom's hand. "Give it to Petar, tell him it is his mommy and daddy. Tell him we love him. Tell him one day we will be a family again."

In the driver's mirror Nick saw her becoming smaller and smaller, walking after them and waving, until finally he turned a bend and she was gone.

They didn't say a word until they reached the roadblock outside Sarajevo.

. . .

Petar and Ema's tale stunned the New York control room. When Ema fell forward and hugged the television, there were gasps. When Ema gave the cookies to Tom and asked him to give them to Petar, and then there was Petar in Sarajevo sitting in his cot, smiling and eating his mother's cookie, with Tom's closing words, "Baked with love," there were sobs.

The *New York Times* media correspondent wrote that for all the years of shelling and explosions and sirens and shooting, and wounded and dying, no image had ever conveyed so authentically what a siege really means to the people. And what hammered the message home, he wrote, was the perfect simple line that was reporter Tom Layne's particular genius: "This is Tom Layne on day eight hundred and four of the siege of Sarajevo."

Even Boone sent a message: *Your mom and kid report—I told you it was a great story. Viewers calling in all day asking how they can help.*

The next morning Tom woke early, sweating. The heating, set at maximum, had come on for the first time in months, and there was no air-conditioning. The hotel had nailed a sheet of hardboard over the mortar hole and broken window, stopping the stream of cold night air. He had made his way in the dark to the door and left it ajar to get a breeze, returned to the bed, thrown off the cover, and fallen asleep in his underpants.

Until he felt a shifting on the mattress. His heavy eyes came open and there, through a daylight blur, was lovely Nina, smiling down at him, sitting on his bed, her leg touching his bare thigh. As he sleepily smiled back, she took his warm hand in hers. Their fingers curled and it was tender and sweet and loving. It was natural to bring her hand to his mouth and kiss it, hold it there, and for her to lean down and kiss his forehead and then his nose, and next their lips met for an instant, just an instant.

A brief, sleepy kiss, the princess awoke the frog, with the fragrance of soap and youth, and yearning.

Nina, slowly, knowingly, pulled up the cover, letting the brush of her hands tease his skin, as she said, "So are you leaving today?"

"Now I'm staying."

"No you're not. Do you know when you will come back?"

"Yes. As soon as possible."

"Please do."

Now she lifted his hand to her lips, and kissed his fingers, and walked slowly from the room.

Flying out of Sarajevo on the UN C-130 nicknamed "Maybe Airlines" (maybe it will land, maybe it won't), his mind lurched between Nina's teasing lips and the sneer of Ratko Mladić. One moment his heart melted with memory of her—what had happened between them?—the next it hardened. How to describe Mladić? When Tom landed in London, a limo brought him straight to the bureau to cut the piece for that night's show.

He wanted to give a sense of the contradictions of the man, the chess-playing charmer, the adored leader, the thug, the calculating killer who included mass rape in his arsenal of intimidation. After much searching for the exact phrases and pacing around and sighing and moving around sections of text and sound bites, he decided to juxtapose something Mladić had said while playing chess: "Stay calm, move wisely, and the pawns will fall one by one, and then the path to the king will open by itself. There is no need for force," with Nina's question followed by the rant: ". . . we will burn you all . . . we will drive you to the edge of madness . . . a million men will die . . ."

Mladić had tried to pass himself off as a philosopher and a gentleman, but the facts and the lurid juxtaposition of the quotes told a different story. Tom's version included a roll call of mass rapes, massacres, ethnic cleansing, and of course the merciless battering of Sarajevo, the greatest civilian siege since Stalingrad. The most sinister part was that there was nothing schizophrenic about Mladić. He didn't have the excuse of insanity, a military analyst told Tom on camera. He was cold, calculating, and brutal. True, he has two sides to his personality, he said, but both are evil.

Next up for Tom was the inescapable, his nemesis, the Royals report. Could there be a greater contrast with the plight of Petar Cordas than the heir to the British throne, twelve-year-old Prince William, and his younger brother, Harry? Or Ema Cordas's scrawny yard and the grounds of Kensington Palace? Or the battered bulletproof Audi with splintered window, and the stretch limo with cocktail cabinet that transported Big Bucks, Screaming Skull, and Tom Layne to their rendezvous with royalty?

In the neck-snapping life of a foreign correspondent, it was business as usual for Tom, who scrubbed up well in his dark gray pinstriped suit and Valentino cream cotton shirt with gold cuff links. He wasn't allowed to interview the boys on camera but did spend a few moments chatting with them as they watched their father being interviewed by the American network anchor.

When Buck Johnson asked Tom, a few days later, live on the set at Canada Gate, what the young princes were like, expecting a long, gushing response, Tom had to banish a sudden association of Petar and his guitar from his mind, and this threw him, so that all that came out was, "Delightful." His brevity caught Johnson on the wrong foot because he hadn't prepared a follow-up question.

"Informative," said Boone later, along for the ride on the royal junket. "I think you nailed the character of the two princes in one word. A bit short on context though. Big Bucks was pissed."

"So, back to Sarajevo then?" Tom replied.

He was in a hurry to return. To cover the war. To see the harelip kid. And, especially, to get back to Nina.

Four weeks later Tom got his wish, and it ruined his life.

Sarajevo had a hold on everyone it touched. The siege, that alien medieval concept, united townspeople, foreign journalists, and NATO soldiers in a pressure cooker of heightened emotions. The city's hair was always standing; everyone's eyes darted, they edged into doorways, flinched at booms. The whining bullet, the crashing shell. Who'd get it next? It was claustrophobic; at least journalists could leave when they wanted, even if the riskiest part was crossing militia lines on the mountain roads.

The correspondent Tom was replacing had not yet left town, so the day after Tom returned, even before he could visit the harelip kid, when news came of the torching of some small villages over the hills halfway to Kladanj, about twenty miles up the main road to Tuzla, Tom, Nick, and Nina set off in the bulletproof Audi. Road M-18 took them into the hills where they made good time, skirting the woods. There were very few cars on the road. *None* would be a warning. *Few* just meant there was little reason to use the road. It led to Sarajevo and you couldn't get in. The only traffic would be to the villages scattered along the road or in the woods.

Tom and Nick were in high spirits, relieved at getting out of town for a bit, even if Tom had only just returned. They didn't know their exact destination but, as usual, planned to get to the general area and then Nina would ask around.

All three had eaten in a tavern the night before, and toasted the work they would do, but Nick didn't miss the knowing glances between his companions. He grinned to himself: Tom got in first, he's gonna seal the deal. Good for him. He'd go back to the bar and find Suzana.

Back at the Holiday Inn, Nina and Tom had lingered on the unlit stairs, giving Nick time to make his excuses. Tom, wound up, didn't want to appear overeager. Slowly, slowly. Beneath the stairwell, out of sight, they took each other's hands and resumed that gentle month-old kiss, and Tom trembled in Nina's arms. Hand in hand Tom walked Nina up the stairs to her room, where she wanted to pull him in, but he did not ask, and she didn't want to appear too forward. And as they bought time with another kiss, the moment was lost when two Brits from CBS, a camera crew, suddenly appeared out of the staircase. "Well, well," the cameraman said, grinning, walking towards them. "Hope your condom doesn't tear again, Tom." And the other added, "Hey Tom, can we watch?"

"Assholes," Tom answered as they walked by, and the soundman had the last word. "Keep it down, I'm next door, I can hear everything."

Nina, red-faced, quickly said good night as she turned the key and closed the door behind her, leaving Tom cursing the jeering Brits.

They parted for the night, though how Nina and Tom longed for each other.

Now it was the usual gray cloudy day. Nick had the music up loud, next to him Tom was moving his head and tapping in rhythm, with his window open, elbow out, enjoying the wind in his face, feeling Nina behind him and close.

But the closer they came to the villages, the more subdued

Nina became. The foreign journalists she worked with, in their excitement, never seemed to realize that their great story was her shattered life, and the tragedy of her homeland. Tom was different; that was one reason she felt so drawn to him. He understood. And he was so sweet. She had looked forward so much to his return. Yet although it was plain what she wanted—and what he wanted too—Tom couldn't seem to get over the fact she was almost young enough to be his daughter.

They had held hands at the stairs, their good night kiss was lingering and loving, they had stroked each other's hair, but it had ended at her door. For how long? She should have invited him in. Just said it. Now she looked at his neck, the packed waves of his chestnut hair brushed back over his ears, his head moving with the music.

But her thoughts were turning elsewhere and she felt her stomach knotting.

Tom turned. "Should be around here, no? One of these villages? Let's ask the next person."

She nodded slowly, her lips tight. They were getting close. Too close.

"Are you all right?"

"Yes."

They stopped at a stall among the trees for a cold drink.

"He says we're his first customers in two days," Nina said. It was quiet; the only sounds were from birds in the trees and the rustling of the wind through the branches, and the occasional distant boom. Sarajevo getting blasted.

They sat on white plastic chairs and drank as Nina spoke with the stall owner.

She turned pale.

"What does he say about the villages?" Tom asked.

"One village. He just told me which one. I know exactly where to go."

"Are you all right?" Tom asked again. Her voice seemed weak and muted. Tom didn't like to touch her in front of Nick but he took both her hands. "You look pale. Really. You want to go back? We don't have to do this. Are you sick?"

"No. No. We must go there."

Nina knew where to leave the road and take a track, which they followed for a couple of miles, through small clusters of homes, one of them adorned with Serb flags, until the track opened onto a clearing, where at the far side a row of homes began, with fields out back. On the other side of the fields was another row of houses, with more homes in the distance. Flowers, fields of yellow and blue, were in full bloom. The only sound was the distant mooing of a cow. There were no people, just the bitter smell of embers.

"Spooky," Nick said, approaching one house with his camera on his shoulder. Plaster was crumbling in the front, cratered by bullet holes. Wisps of smoke curled round the charred front door. Words were daubed on the walls of the next house, along with the Serbian cross. The windows were smashed, the front door hung from a hinge. They went inside. Furniture was upside down, clothes were strewn everywhere, water was pouring from the tap into the sink. Nick filmed it, then turned the water off. A photograph album lay torn on the sofa. There were burn marks in the bedroom. Someone had tried to set the room alight but the fire didn't catch. He filmed four thin parallel red lines that reached from waist height to the floor where there was a pool of dried brown blood. The wall was pocked with bullet holes. Nina looked in horror. Someone must have been shot there and tried to grasp the wall, smeared it with his bloody fingers as he slid down. The body was gone but the house smelled of gore.

Nina gagged and stumbled out. The lane was deserted, a silent trail with silent houses in the woods.

"What do you think? Anyone around? Is it safe?" Nick said to Tom, who was carrying the tripod.

"I don't like it, to be honest," he said, looking around. "It's very fresh. Let's get what we need and get out."

"Look." Nick nodded at a body in a garden, another one lying across its chest. As Nick filmed, a dog appeared by the corpses, whimpering, trembling, its tail between its legs. When they moved, it fled.

They walked along the lane, past the burnt and looted homes, passing more corpses, one mutilated, and a burned-out tractor.

"Okay, let's leave," Tom said. "I don't like this. We've got enough."

But they saw Nina, walking into the field.

They walked round one house to join her. Tom called out, "Nina, let's go."

At the sound, an old man appeared in the doorway of an untouched house. He was bent, gaunt, and unshaven, with a black cap and baggy trousers. He watched them approach. Tom and Nick stopped in front of his house, miming, Can we come in?

The man turned back into his house.

"Nina?" Tom called. Where was she? He needed her to translate. This could be the only eyewitness. He called again, louder, "Nina?"

Nina appeared from inside the neighboring house, walking with wooden steps.

The old man came out, peering. "Nina?" he said. "Nina?"

"Nina?" Tom said again.

Nina was crying. Her shoulders shook as she walked through

the gate and hugged the old man. She said to him, "Adjin, have you seen my parents?"

"No," he said. "Have you seen my children?"

She shook her head and buried it in his chest and he stroked her hair.

Nina turned and pointed at the house she had just left, her hand trembling and her voice too. "That is my home," she said. "Everyone's gone. Where are they?"

"I don't know," Tom said, looking away.

Adjin made sweet tea as they sat together in his kitchen. After a while Nina switched to English. "Everyone has been taken away. He doesn't know where to. All this was done by the Serbs. They live in the next village. He says they've always wanted our fields and now they will take them. All this," and she started crying again, struggling to talk, "it's got nothing to do with the war or the country. It's one family, they've always been jealous and they want everything and now they have an excuse. My parents are helpless, they are just farmers, they are old, they wouldn't hurt a soul." She paused for a moment and said, in a small voice, "Thank God my brothers weren't here. They would have tried to fight back.

"I must find my parents," she went on.

"How is your house?" Tom asked. He wanted to take her hand, to caress it, to comfort her, but he knew it would be no comfort.

"It's hardly touched. We're lucky."

In the neighbors' house on the other side they found the body of a little boy, about six, folded over a wooden bench. He had wild blond hair, sturdy legs in shorts, and a small hole in his back. Nina fell to her knees, weeping. "Dragan. My nephew."

Tom took her arm. "Nina? I'm sorry, but we should go. We have to report this, get people to come and look after the bodies." He looked anxiously toward the woods, toward the houses, along the lane. "They may still be here. Let's go. Quickly."

He pulled her from the boy and they walked back to the car. They passed more bodies. A bucolic farming village, now a killing ground.

Before leaving, Tom took the wheel and drove slowly through the village and out the other end so that Nick could get one last traveling shot from the moving car, showing the devastation of the row of shattered homes.

And that was their mistake.

Just as Nick took the wheel back from Tom, and was turning the car to leave the way they had come, Nina suddenly screamed, "Stop!"

She was staring at the very last house, where a middle-aged man had emerged, walking down the path to the gate, waving at their car. He wore blue overalls and a military cap with an insignia. "Drive," Tom said to Nick, but at that moment Nina moved so fast they couldn't react and nor could the man. She threw open her door, grabbed a rock, ran at him screaming, and smashed it on his head.

Tom and Nick stared open-mouthed. "What the fuck . . ." Nick said.

The man was on his knees, shouting, holding his head, blood streaming through his fingers.

Another man came running out of the house. "Oh, no," Tom yelled. "Get in, Nina, get in quick."

She fell back into her seat as Nick finished the turn and roared away. Nick and Tom were shouting, "Are you nuts?" "What did you do?" "Ferchrissake."

Tom twisted round, saw the second man running back into the

house. "Faster, Nick," he shouted, "let's get out of here. Oh, Nina, what the fuck did you do . . ."

"He did it," she screamed, "he did it. That's the family, Popovic. He's Darko." She was trembling so hard her teeth chattered.

"But you can't do that, we're journalists," Tom shouted at her. "Oh, for God's sake, we're screwed."

Nick gripped the wheel, his face taut, the car throwing up a cloud of dust as he almost lost it on a bend, and he pulled the car straight and put his foot down all the way. The engine roared as the car leapt over bumps and ridges in the track; trees and fields flashed by. "About a mile to the road," Tom said, trying to slow his breathing.

"You're American television, they can't touch you," Nina said, shrinking into the seat.

"Oh right, right," Tom said. *You goddamn idiot.*

"Well, that's a first," Nick said, eyes fixed on the road.

"It is. It is," Tom said. *Where is that damn main road?*

He knew what would happen. They'd have walkie-talkies. That house with all the Serb flags. "Get off this road, Nick. Take a track. Anywhere."

But there was no track. The only way was straight.

He stared ahead, trying to see through the trees, and a minute later saw three small dark figures in the middle of the road. The men held guns, pointed straight at them. Nick slowed, his heart exploding, and Tom shouted, "Don't stop! Go! Go! Drive through, we're bulletproof, go!"

But Nick couldn't, he just couldn't. He couldn't mow down people. He slowed more. "Go!" Tom shouted again, but Nick was frozen. He came to a halt.

"Shit," Tom said.

Two men stood, legs apart, aiming automatic rifles at the car, while the third stepped slowly toward them, aiming his weapon at the driver's head.

In the back, Nina was trembling. "Black Hoods," she said. The men wore gray fatigues and black hoods.

"Lock the doors," Tom said, pushing down his lock. "Nick, listen, accelerate, this is bad, Nick, look at me, lock your fucking door and drive. It's bulletproof, we'll be okay if you just put your fucking foot down."

But the man had pulled Nick's door open. He had Nick by the arm and jerked so hard Nick fell out of the car and onto the ground where the man kicked him in the head. He shouted something in Serbian. One man moved forward until he touched the hood, his rifle pointing straight at Tom, whose mind fixed on the question: How bulletproof is the window, will it stop a rifle shot at six feet?

Doesn't matter, he thought, too late now.

The first man pulled open the back door and pulled at Nina's arm. She yelped and struggled but he forced her out. She fell to the ground next to Nick, who was holding his head and bleeding from the nose. The third man moved from the hood to Tom's door and pulled, and then started jerking the handle. *"Otvori vrata!"* he shouted. *"Otvori vrata!"*

Tom struggled to appear calm. He nodded and pulled up the lock and got out of the car, talking slowly. "It's all right, we're just journalists, we're driving to Sarajevo, you can let us go. We didn't see anything, we'll just leave, we won't come back, we—" He doubled up when the man jabbed him in the stomach with his gun— it was straight to the gut, like a hammer. He couldn't breathe, and waved his arms. "No, no . . ."

As the man pushed him around the car to Nina, Tom managed to say, "Nina. Nina, tell them we have money, they can have it, all of it, we didn't see anything."

Her lips moved but nothing came out.

Tom staggered, nearly falling over Nick, who pulled himself to his feet. The three gunmen spoke quietly to each other, looking at Nina.

Now Tom could hear music blaring from the houses. Female singer, rock. The one with a bandanna spoke into his walkie-talkie, then hitched it onto his belt next to his pistol. He took Nina by the arm and began to pull her away. Tom said, "No, no," and Nick grabbed Nina's other arm and tried to pull her back. It's what they had learned on their HEFAT course—don't let them separate the women from the men. Hold on—keep talking. Nick held Nina by one arm while the gunman, weapon in one hand, backed up, pulling her with the other. Nick hung on. Nina, looking as if she was being crucified, was in shock, whimpering. Tom was talking, he hardly knew what he was saying, anything, just keep talking, they couldn't understand anyway, he was begging, when the gunman, moving backwards, hauling Nina, stumbled. As he fell, Nina tripped over him and Nick, still holding her arm, fell onto her. The gunman released Nina to break his fall, and the butt of his weapon hit the ground, his finger still on the trigger.

It all went quiet for Tom, even his tinnitus was silenced, he didn't hear a thing, not even the shot. He didn't see anything outside a narrow tunnel of vision, like looking through a telescope. Through which he saw the rifle butt hit the ground, a spurt of flame, and Nick jerk back like a puppet.

The bullet shot through Nick's skull and killed him instantly, so quickly he didn't have time to close his eyes, and Tom looked into them and saw Nick's soul escape.

Time stopped. Tom's heart stopped, and lurched forward, making him gasp. His mouth went dry, his eyes widened in shock, he saw Nick's blood on his shoes.

The gunman stood up, looking at Nick's lifeless body, and cursed. The other two gunmen had jumped back at the gunshot but quickly recovered. They pulled their hoods off and forced them over Tom and Nina, backwards, so that they couldn't see through the holes.

They pushed them, stumbling, choking, blind, into the house. Nina tried to shout but gagged on a strand of wool; she hacked and hacked as the clammy, smelly hood stuck to her face.

They hit a wall hard and heard the thunk of a heavy door slamming and the click of a key turning. They sank to the floor, leaning against each other, and tore off the masks, gasping and sucking in air, their hearts pounding.

"They're . . . Black . . . Hoods," Nina said again, through gasps.

The words fell on Tom like a guillotine. Of course! He hadn't realized, it had all happened too fast. Black Hoods—the deniable shock troops of the Bosnian Serb army. A paramilitary gang of crooks, rapists, and killers.

They were fucked.

They leaned on each other, slumped against the wall. Tom saw Nick, in flashes of images, behind his closed eyes. The gunshot, the blood, the bleeding head. His dead, empty eyes. If only he could have closed them.

Oh, Nick, no, young Nick.

Tom's body was heaving. He leaned against Nina, who was whimpering. She took his hand.

"I'm sorry," Nina said, "I'm so sorry," and she sobbed.

The music stopped and started again, louder. More rock music.

After a few minutes Tom sighed, dried his face. "Listen," he said, taking out his wallet and finding Mladić's card. "When they come—"

They came.

The door flew open and men crowded into the room. "American

journalist?" a man said. He wore jeans and a black leather jacket and had a pistol in his belt. He seemed the youngest, black hair and mustache. "Yes, yes," Tom said, pulling himself to his feet. "You speak English? We didn't see anything, we didn't do anything—"

"Be quiet. Who are you?" Looking at Nina.

"Nina Ibrihimovic."

"You hit Darko Popovic with a rock?"

Nina looked away and shuffled her feet.

"Did you?"

"Yes, I did," she said.

"Well done. I have often wanted to do the same," he said, and repeated it in Serbian. His men laughed.

But then, in English, "Popovic is on his way here."

"Sir, please, listen," Tom said. "We are just journalists, all we want is to leave and do our work telling the world what it is that you want. Through us you can speak to America, to the world. We are not involved, we don't have weapons, we—"

"If you are not involved, why did she hit Popovic with a rock?"

Tom went on, his voice cracking. "Look, your commander, General Ratko Mladić, he knows us, please read this. You can call him, he will vouch for us, tell you that we are okay, he'll tell you to let us go." He held out Mladić's visiting card. The man read it, slapped it against the palm of his other hand, looking from Tom to Nina and back again.

"We play chess together," Tom added with an attempt at a smile.

"We shall see."

"Well, once," Tom said. "He won. Easily." *Make it personal, look into their eyes.*

The gunmen left, leaving Tom and Nina alone again in the bare room. Minutes later a man brought them tea and sugar.

"I can't," Nina said. She started to cry. "Oh, Nick . . ."

Tom held the cup to her lips. "Please, drink, it'll help."

After a moment Nina asked in a tiny voice, "Is this a good sign? The tea?" Her hands had stopped shaking.

"I suppose so. But better start praying right now. Pray that Mladić never saw our story on him."

They waited an hour, sitting side by side, against the wall, and hardly spoke. Tom stared at the blood drying brown on the white sole of his sneaker.

It's my fault. I'll have to break the news to the network. From the phone in the car as soon as we get away. He didn't know anything about Nick's family, he'd have to meet them, tell them what happened. Nick's stuff in his room, he'd have to pack it all up. The camera gear. How will we get his body back? He should call Morissey at the UN, he'd know what to do.

Morissey was right, after all. He screwed his eyes shut. Oh, Nick. I'm so sorry.

I'm in some kind of shock, he thought, I can't be this calm. I must, I must be feeling more than this. It'll hit me later. A part of him apologized, the part that was above this, separate, watching, seeing himself slumped against the wall, the girl at his side, but the other part, the real part, him, feeling the hard floor beneath him, was trembling again. What's going on? He felt his mind racing. None of this makes sense.

Oh yes, it does. The thought penetrated his shock. You fucked up, big time.

Stop it. First, get me through this.

The door opened, his head jerked toward it. There were three men with the English-speaker. "I spoke with the general."

Tom saw his grim face, and his hands tearing up the visiting card. Bile shot up, and he thought he'd vomit.

The man pulled his pistol from his belt, put it at Tom's head, and leaned into him. "The general says you are a bad loser." Two men kicked Tom behind the knees, then punched him as he fell.

One dragged Nina into another room where two more men waited. They wore jeans and black leather jackets.

The door slammed.

"I'm sorry," the man said to Tom, pulling him to his feet. "Orders." He slid a hood over Tom's head. "Can you breathe all right?" Tom nodded, straining to get his nose through the hole. "Good," he said, hissing into Tom's ear. "Because these are your last breaths."

He pushed Tom by the elbow, through the door, and into a field where Tom stumbled and bumped against a tree.

"Turn around," the man said. Tom shuffled his feet. His heart was pounding, sweat ran into his eyes. Is this it? He heard himself grunting, in anger, at himself. He cursed himself. I waited too long. No wife. No children. Nick, I'm sorry, so sorry, what a waste of it all. No more tennis. Oh, Nina, I want you so much. I'm so sorry.

He heard Nina's screams, a man shouting; the drumming music turned louder.

Nina. Oh, Nina. I love you, Nina. And I never told you. He called out, as loud as he could, he bellowed, "Nina!"

"Good-bye, American journalist," the man said. "Why did you come here, this is not your war."

Through the hood, steel dug into his temple. He felt the gun barrel dragged across his cheek, teasing him, and now it pushed into his throat, pointing up to his brain. He was panting, like a racehorse at the end. But his mind began to clear. Okay. So. It's over. All over. It can't be. But it is. And he knew then that the only moment of complete clarity in life is the instant of death. Nina . . .

"General Mladić says good-bye," he heard, and it was over.

PART TWO

Belgrade, twelve years later,
March 22, 2006

They were just agreeing that Indira Mladić, no relation, was the best Serb folk singer, even if her first name was Indian; and that her red tresses were fake but her glorious breasts were real, and that's what counted, when the direct line rang, the encrypted phone. The three men went silent and stared at it. It stopped after two rings, and only when it rang again, a few seconds later, did the man in the gray suit grab it. He listened to the brief report, and said to the room, "The Host is moving."

The burly man behind the desk, the oldest, nodded and took a deep drag on his cigarette. He blew out slowly from the corner of his mouth as the first man gave instructions into the phone: "Drive normally, under no circumstances let yourself be noticed, and if someone does see him, solve the problem. You understand? On the spot." He hung up.

Two hundred and twenty miles away in Serbia's wooded northeast, two black Mercedes swept round a bend into a long straight avenue bordered by plane trees, dim shadows cast by a sliver of moon, their leaves glistening in the drizzle. Windshield wipers working, headlights piercing the misty darkness. Wheels whined on the tar as the drivers accelerated, thirty meters separating them, walkie-talkies linking them.

"M1, from Control. Accident ahead. Go round, do not stop."

"This is M1, got it," the man in the passenger seat of the lead car said, twisting round. "Cover your face, Chief," he said to the man behind him, "just in case."

But he didn't. One hand caressed the other, balled into a fist.

From the opposite direction two cars flashed by, sending up sheets of water, and ahead, where the long road narrowed before the next bend, moving pinheads of orange light grew in size until they became an arc, formed by a traffic cop waving them to stop.

"Drive through," the man in the passenger seat said. His voice was tight and determined. Concealed between his knee and the car door, he gripped a pistol. The driver nodded, eyes fixed on the road. *"Nema problema."* No problem.

But as they approached the obstruction their beams lit up long black skid marks leading to an upside-down car half on the road, scattered parts, and another buckled car crushed against a tree. They were going too fast and had to jam on the brakes, lurching them all forward. The cop jumped out of the way, they saw his mouth move, heard his muffled curses through the shut window. Behind, the second Mercedes pulled out to avoid them, both cars slowing to a crawl. The accident must have happened a while ago because the only people at the scene were two angry traffic cops, one of whom now walked toward the first car, shouting, holding his flashlight in his fist at head height and pointing down into the car.

From behind the two cars a single beam of light bore down upon them.

As the cop loomed in the window, his flashlight lighting one face and the next, spinning his free hand to indicate they should lower the window, the man in the backseat jerked his head away. But it was too late. The policeman's eyes widened. Ten thousand cops in Serbia carried his photo and each day they had to report whether they had seen anybody who looked like him, the man at the top of Europe's "most wanted" list.

The traffic cop jumped back and shouted to his colleague.

"Shit," the driver muttered as the man next to him already barked into his walkie-talkie. He jerked the wheel to the side and put his foot down, brushing the policeman who fell, and with wheels screaming, he slalomed between the two wrecks and roared away, closely followed by the second car, whose spinning wheels kicked dust into the air. A wheel ran over a broken fender, which catapulted into the air and fell with a clang, narrowly missing the policeman.

The traffic cop scrambled to his feet as his partner ran to help him. "Did you see who that was? That's him . . ." he sputtered, his words falling over each other. Looking wildly after the disappearing cars he grabbed at his walkie-talkie. "Base, Base, this is 2040, 2040 . . . Base . . ."

He didn't finish the sentence. The motorbike that was trailing the two Mercedes had jerked to a halt, there was a tut from a silencer, and he collapsed like a puppet on a broken string, a spot of red between his eyes. The second cop stared in terror at the muzzle of the gun and the black helmet that concealed the face of the shooter who swiveled his arm and shot him between the eyes. The rider confirmed the kills with two more shots to the heads, pushed the gun back inside his leather jacket, checked there were no witnesses, and accelerated after the convoy.

He regained his watching post two hundred yards behind the Mercedes, ready to prevent any vehicle from overtaking, and spoke into the microphone clipped to his mouthguard.

Problem solved.

When they arrived, on schedule, just before dawn when the streets were still, the drivers stayed with the cars and the motorbike while the others walked the Host to the lobby of a scruffy apartment building. They took the elevator to the third floor, where one of the men produced a key for the wall-to-ceiling metal grille that separated the elevator shaft from the residential areas. An elderly woman waiting at an open door smiled and all but bowed as she followed the men inside. The flat was small, sparsely furnished, but the fridge was full.

The Host looked around and acknowledged the woman with a half smile. The men sank onto the sofa and chairs and opened the beers the woman had brought and banged them together with shouts of *"Zivjeli!"* and emptied the bottles and called for more.

The overheated room had a greasy smell of leftover kebabs and onion and flatbread. The direct phone rang again, twice, broke off, and then another call. This time the man behind the desk took it. Leaning forward, the phone at his ear, his shoulders bunched up, his biceps appeared about to burst his jacket. His narrow lips were pursed in concentration, his eyes staring at the other two through a haze of smoke. He tapped the ash from his cigarette, took a drag, listened silently until he had heard the full report, then spoke in a velvety voice, so at odds with what he said. "It's already taken care of," he told the caller, rubbing a large black mole on his left temple. "There will be a police press release in the morning. Two traffic policemen had an argument and killed each other. Their families have already been informed. Sad story. Poor discipline. Heads will roll."

He put the phone down and pushed himself to his feet with a loud yawn. "That's it, then. Bedtime." The man in the gray suit took a raincoat from the door peg and held it as his boss slid his arms through the sleeves. As they shuffled and dressed and put on their hats, one of them said to the older man, "So what about the reporter? What do we do with him?"

"Nothing. Don't touch him. He's American."

"And if he becomes a problem?"

"He already is. All reporters are a problem."

"So what do we do?"

"We'll see. There are many ways to skin a cat."

Belgrade, Topćider Cemetery, the next day

A gray-haired man crouched with a brush at a pale marble headstone and lovingly filled in the carved Cyrillic letters with white paint. He wore a sleeveless down jacket over a hooded sweater, and his glasses hung from his neck on a cord. His face was smooth, his brow unfurrowed, his touch gentle but sure, and Tom thought, as he filmed from the side, from his seat on the bench under the fir tree, that he must have loved her very much.

Tom scanned the hillside of densely packed graves overlooking Belgrade, a gust of cold wind tearing his eye. Several rows away a man with a blue-peaked cap paused at a tomb, his hands clasped behind his back, gazing at the marble busts of a husband and wife who shared the family plot. A couple pushing a baby stroller over the pebbly path crunched by. But still, at the tomb of Ana Mladić, no sign of a man with a wreath.

And there's Nina. The nearest café must have been a distance away; she had taken twenty minutes to find coffee. Her head bobbed up and down between the headstones as she walked up the hill toward him. The sky was overcast and a wind blew up from the valley, rustling the trees. He shivered, even bundled up in his down jacket. It was noon and they'd been waiting since eight o'clock. He took out his hip flask of brandy and as he brought it to his mouth he surveyed his hand. Strange. When he filmed, it was rock steady. Otherwise, the shakes. He watched it tremble. Not as bad as it used to be though. He took a long swig and let the brandy warm and turn mellow in his mouth, settle around his taste buds, and savored the gentle burn as he swallowed, and sighed, then took another long sip, again holding the rich amber liquid, teasing it, savoring its mellow oakiness.

Nina's long auburn hair, glinting reddish in the light and bouncing as she walked, and her growing smile as she approached, made him smile too. He was glad he had called her. He wasn't going to, it had been too long, it had felt too strange, maybe he was even scared, but he had done it. When he told her who he was, on the phone from New York, he could hear, in her long pause, her happiness.

Or was it? Was that long pause something else? Doubt? As in, Why reopen that can of worms? He had plowed on and the longer he spoke, as he related his plan, the more intently she had seemed to listen. Anyway, she didn't interrupt, there was just silence from her end of the line.

But when he finished, saying, "So that's it, that's the documentary—I hope," all she said was: "Well, well. Tom Layne, it's about bloody time."

And his answer surprised even himself. "Nina, I've missed you so much."

Was that why she'd agreed? Because she felt the same? But she didn't. She had the opening to say she had missed him too, and she didn't say it.

Did she just want to work with him to make some money?

For that matter, why did he really want to work with Nina? After all this time? There were plenty of other fixers. As Tom had fought for sleep on the seven-hour flight to Frankfurt, and had tried to study his notes on the connecting flight to Belgrade, Nina was on his mind as much as the doc. And so was the bad stuff too, the weirdness he had spent so long trying to forget.

It was his first time back.

That made him need a drink, but at four in the morning, in the dark cabin, hurtling eastward, with everyone around him snoring, he realized he'd forgotten to fill his hip flask. Lucky they charge for alcohol in coach, he thought; I can't afford to drink, in more ways than one.

So Nina had married. Of course, why wouldn't she? Like any mom, proud of her son, Sasha: "He's seven years old, you'd love him, the sweetest child, not always easy; with my mother in the village, where he stays when I'm on assignment. He's happiest there, trying to care for the animals, running free with the other children in the forest, swimming in the pond, the kids there accept him despite everything."

When they had met again, in the tiny hotel lobby bar, barely large enough for the sofa they occupied, she filled the silence with the photo she always carried. Sasha, aged six then, grinning hugely, flexing his thin arms in a skinny muscleman pose with water dripping off him, glistening in the sunlight, a bush of yellow blossoms behind him.

"He's adorable," Tom said, and without thinking kissed the photo.

After a brief marriage she had divorced Sasha's father. It was mostly her fault. She got angry quickly and at nothing, drank too much, and had nightmares that she never explained. He had always felt excluded, that he didn't really share her life, but there were things she could not say, so many, that in the end the silence destroyed them. "Goran, he was a good husband," she had said, "but I was a bad wife. I had affairs with other men and I didn't hide them. It was as if I wanted to hurt him, I don't know why." Nina shrugged and poured herself another drink. "It seems so long ago. What? Five years?" She lit another cigarette and stood at the half-open window, her arms crossed, blowing smoke outside. "I was afraid, too. But I could never tell him why, and I didn't really know myself. I do now, of course."

"Did you ever get any help?" Tom had asked. The first two nights they had gone for dinner at nine and talked until two in the morning, the second night in his room. At first they had both been reticent, but it soon became clear they didn't have much else to talk about.

She shook her head, taking another long drag and blowing more smoke out of the window.

"Never?"

"No." She turned toward him, as if assessing him. "I should have. But, no. We are not like you Americans." She threw her head back and laughed, throaty, mischievous. "We don't have insurance for that."

He tried to laugh—it came out as a snort, heavy with memories. "Insurance didn't cover what I went through, trust me."

It took Tom two months to go back to the London newsroom, another two months to realize he just didn't care anymore, and three more months before he got the call from New York. In all fairness, he had to hand it to Yvonne, his close friend and the senior vice president of the news division; it must have been a tough call for her to make, which she could easily have delegated, but as she said when she got him on the phone, at the fifth attempt:

"This is tough love, Tom, I'm going to say this more gently than anyone else would. There's been a lot of discussion here, but the word is, you're burned out, you've been saying it yourself."

He knew what was coming.

"Well, your contract's up at the end of this year, and the thinking is, as of this moment in time, that the news division will only give you a one-year contract this time, instead of the usual four, and—"

"The news division? You mean you."

"The news division, Tom. This isn't personal. You know if it was personal, we'd never be having this conversation, if it was just—"

"What conversation? You're doing all the talking."

"Come on, Tom, don't blow me off, listen to me. If it was just up to me I wouldn't be saying this—"

"You mean giving me an ultimatum."

"Okay, if that's how you want it, in so many words, then yes. An ultimatum. You've got one year to shape up, get over it. It happened. Everyone was devastated about Nick Barnes, not just you. If you're burned out, we can't use you. You've got one year to show us you can still perform. Otherwise, no more contract. That's the thinking."

"The thinking? Someone out there is thinking?"

"Yes, and don't be cute. I'm sorry, but I've been asked for an early answer about you accepting a one-year contract, on probation, although nobody uses the word. I'm just telling you the way it is, as a friend. Take a few days, think it over. Then, one word. Yes, or no."

"Make that two words?"

"Whatever."

"Okay, I've got two words for all of you. My early thinking is,

as of this moment in time, fuck off." Tom slammed the phone
down, looked at it, picked it up again and threw the phone at a
TV monitor, watched it bounce off the screen, and laughed so
hard he had tears in his eyes, the first good laugh he'd had since
before he thought he was dead.

The word that got around, from his startled colleagues at the
news desk who saw it all through his glass wall, was that Layne
had finally flipped. It was agreed. Everyone saw it coming.

"But nobody tried to help?" Nina said.

"No. Well, maybe that's not fair; I wasn't exactly welcoming.
You know, way too much drink, drugs, nothing too radical. I don't
think I had a real night's sleep in three years. I had girlfriends,
quite a few, nothing that lasted, I was difficult. Made a decent living. Freelancing, documentaries, I shot them myself. Mostly
porn, that kind of thing." He gave a goofy smile at Nina from
across the coffee table in his room. "That was a joke, right? But I
want to be totally honest, we agreed, right? What happened, with
one girl, I hit her. I didn't mean to, I exploded, it happened. I
lashed out, caught her on the ear. She called the police. It'll never
happen again. Another time, on the escalator in the subway, a guy
pushed in front of me, I grabbed him from behind and almost
tore his arm off. I yelled at him that I'd fucking kill him. He was
a lot bigger too, but I must have looked like a lunatic. He didn't
say anything, just stared at me, everyone did. So I walked down
first but I was shaking all the way."

His hand was trembling as he poured himself another drink.
Nina took the bottle from the table. "Thank you for telling me. You
know, I had some bad moments too. Not so different, either."

She hadn't left her room for three months, couldn't get out of
bed, and when she did she smoked so much she could hardly
breathe. She'd also had nightmares for years, and even during the

day the faces of her rapists appeared out of cupboards, through doors, in crowds, she could feel their touch. She had spat at a man in the street and didn't know why.

"There's always reason to spit at a man," Tom said. "If you don't know why, he does."

That made her burst out with laughter and Tom agreed: "We were pretty fucked up. Maybe we still are."

At last Tom had said, "I'm tired out, early start tomorrow," and he had walked her to the door, where they pecked each other on the cheek and both said, "Sleep well."

That was last night. And Tom, sitting on the bench, taking the coffee from Nina, satisfied that there was no activity at Ana's grave, smiled back at her smile and couldn't help thinking, I'm damaged goods and the good news is, so is she.

He could thank his new friends at the DART Center in New York for getting him to call Nina. He'd thought of her for years but he couldn't handle anything that reminded him of that hor-rific day, and nothing reminded him of it more than the mem-ory of Nina. He had never called her, not even once. He had left Nina in the hospital and returned to London with Nick's body, and they had never spoken again.

It gnawed at him, especially in the beginning, but what was there to say? How are you?

How do you fucking think I am?

Yvonne had put him in touch with Bruce Shapiro at the DART Center, over at Columbia, where they specialized in journalists and post-traumatic stress, and he'd been the one who had ex-plained: It's common for anyone suffering from PTSD not to want to be in contact with people who remind them of it. It's natu-ral to let sleeping dogs lie. But it's harmful too. However hard it is, connect, connect, connect, that's the way forward, relive the horror in a safe place. Still, it took a few more years for Tom to pluck up courage, to even try to talk about Nick's murder, Nina's rape, his own mock execution.

Details, long suppressed, came back, one by one. He remembered that after the gunshot he had closed his eyes tight, trying not to see Nick on the ground, with those empty eyes. He remembered the tight gripping of his own eyes. After he heard Nina scream he had tried not to hear, he had tried to blot it all out, even as it was happening.

It was all so fast, and as he had tried to relive it, in a quiet, warm room with some anonymous therapist, and he had tried to keep his mind focused, something came back—hard metal pushing into his throat, the sensation of choking, of wanting to vomit, and then—utter clarity. An opening, light, a whiteness. Not a glimpse of heaven. Just a void. That sense—it's over, my life, it's all over. He had cried in that therapy room.

But Tom's conclusion wasn't quite what the therapists had had in mind. All the seminars and sessions said: Confront your fear, relive the trauma, and only then can you escape from it, by converting trauma, which you can't cope with, into tragedy, which you can.

They didn't know Tom Layne. When they said confront your trauma, he wasn't only thinking of screaming in a small room with a sympathetic listener. He was thinking of the man.

Ratko Mladić. Europe's biggest killer since Adolf Hitler. And Tom didn't want to talk about him.

He wanted to find him.

He'd explained to Nina in that first phone call. "I'm going to make a documentary on Ratko Mladić. Why he hasn't been caught, even though he's been on the run for eleven years. There's no way the Serb secret service doesn't know where he is. Why don't they pick him up, put him on trial? Because they don't want to, that's why. He's a local hero. And I want to tell the story. What do you say? I need a fixer, I can pay; not close to what the network pays, but I'll give you a cut of the profit."

She burst out laughing, her first laugh. "Profit? From a documentary? Who are you kidding?"

"Well, you know . . ."

Nina knew. She was a freelance producer, still assisting foreign media. She worked on day rate. Money in the bank. She needed to pay the bills.

But work with Tom Layne? Is that what she wanted? After so many years of trying to forget, move on, all that drink, some drugs, too much sex with the wrong people; always trying not to think about it, not to go there. And, let's face it, failing miserably, for at least five years. Depression had ruined her marriage, and come close to ruining her life. She was through with it all now though; Sasha was her life. Tom Layne? I don't think so.

Yet . . . Tom Layne. When he called she could see his face clearly; well, it wasn't so hard, she'd seen him on TV here and there, his freelance work, mostly longer pieces, and she always thought how good he looked. He must have got over it quickly. Well, he didn't go through what she did. And Nick. Nick, she couldn't see at all. His face had gone. Maybe her mind was blanking him out, helping her in some way, for what happened to Nick, that was such a waste, such a waste. Oh, Nick. Nick, those eyes, those dead eyes.

And now, Tom is back.

Why didn't he ever call? Just once, in the beginning. To see how she was. Maybe to help? But what had she ever been to him? Dinners, a kiss or two, hardly that. Just a naïve girl whose head was turned by the handsome older man, the TV star. What a cliché. How many like her had he known? And if he had called, what was there to say? Maybe it was better that way.

So why now? Have things changed?

She wanted it, and she did not want it. But in the end, it was simple. She needed the money.

So after two days thinking it over, she had called Tom. "I'll help you, who would you like to interview? But forget about finding Mladić, everyone has tried."

"I know that. It isn't really about finding him. I want to do a documentary on the failure of the hunt."

"And if they suddenly find him?"

"Good point. They won't. But you know what? I hope they do, the bastard."

As she sipped the coffee, which had cooled as she walked through the Topčider Cemetery, Nina snuck sideways glances at Tom on the bench. Are we really going to wait here all day? She looked at him more boldly, his features flattened in the direct light. He had looked good on TV and now she knew why: makeup. In the flesh, there was something worn about him, used, his skin had become mottled. He looks his age, even older, she thought, which he didn't before. Still full of energy, but more nervous now, he seems fragile, too. He seems shrunken, his shoulders rounded, or was she just imagining that, projecting onto him the changes in herself? There's sadness in those eyes, even when he smiles, and dark, swollen eyebags, deeper lines, he drinks too much. But then, she thought, so do I. His nose even seems redder, or is that the wind? He does have the same thick wavy chestnut hair though, and the graying at the temples is nice.

She looked away, over the graves, and sighed.

"So?" Tom said.

"So? What?"

"So, what's the verdict? You were measuring me up, looking at me like a painter. Am I worth painting?"

She laughed. "Frankly? Yes." She hesitated, seeking the right word. "You have an interesting face. Lived in. I remember someone using that phrase, I didn't realize what they meant, until now."

"Hmmm," he said with a smile, and a quick check of Ana's grave. "I'm not sure that's exactly what I was hoping to hear. And as for you . . ."

"Don't you dare!"

Twelve years it had been. Of course she looked older. She thought of herself as he must see her. No longer a girl, a woman, approaching middle age. Thirty-six. Round glasses, shiny auburn hair, lucky she had prepared for Tom's arrival by going to the hairdresser; she had colored out the first gray strands. Plumper in places. The wrong places. She straightened. A woman in her prime, and proud of it, she thought. She wished she hadn't worn such tight jeans though.

"So, would you?" she said.

"Would I what?"

"Paint me."

But she had lost him. Tom half stood, holding the camera at chest height, staring hard over the headstones, to a man who had slowed at Ana's grave, and was looking around. Tom brought the camera to his eye and turned it on, then lowered it, turning it off. "False alarm," he said. "I thought he was stopping there."

The man, still walking slowly, passed by and turned left, up the hill, toward them, examining graves while scanning the area. "I wonder, though," Tom said.

"What?"

"Maybe he's checking the place out. Sit here." Tom placed Nina on the bench so that it looked as if he was filming her, but he had zoomed over her shoulder to a medium shot of the man looking suspiciously around and slowly circling the hillside.

And sure enough, moments later, two more men appeared through the trees to place bouquets of red flowers that stood out like blood flecks on the shiny black marble tomb of Ana Mladić. From this angle Tom had an unobstructed line of sight, with headstones in the foreground and a frame of foliage. The two men stood, heads bowed, by a wooden bench next to the grave. The layered clouds, pierced by sunlight that danced on the shimmering leaves, drenched the graveside in color and shadows. On the end of the zoom, Tom filmed them from their waists up, their faces sparkling as the sun came and went. Not wanting to draw attention to himself by using a tripod, he hand-held the camera and hardly breathed, to hold the picture steady.

Hard men, in regulation jeans and black leather jackets. About forty years old. Black hair, mustaches, grim, menacing. They looked vaguely familiar, in a threatening way, but then half the men in Belgrade had mustaches and looked as if they'd like to slit your throat. As soon as he had enough video, sixty seconds, he turned away and sat down. He'd rather make do with the minimum than be noticed by those thugs. He could use every frame. With the first guy looking around, he had two minutes' worth of material. He didn't need more. He'd go over later to film the flowers on the gravestone. He looked at Nina with a tight grin and a nod of triumph.

He'd been right. Half right anyway. On that day, twelve years earlier, on March 23, 1994, the attractive, dark-haired daughter of Ratko Mladić, who one day should have provided him with the joy of his first grandchild, had taken her father's ceremonial pistol and, at the age of twenty-three, killed herself with one bullet to the head. In a news film of the funeral, which Tom had bought for his documentary, the Bosnian Serb army leader moves as if on automatic, face frozen, accepting condolences for his daughter's suicide, until, standing, he lays his head on her coffin and weeps. Two women stroke him.

Shortly afterward, Mladić suffered a stroke. Some say he emerged convinced that his daughter's death was caused by a conspiracy against him, and that this unbearable blow caused Mladić to embark on Europe's biggest killing spree since the Nazis. Revenge for his daughter. Especially as he was a war orphan, his parents killed by the Ustache, the Croatian fascists. Now he was a hunted war criminal, charged with genocide and crimes against humanity.

Sometimes, on the anniversary of Ana's suicide, Mladić broke cover to mourn at her grave. That was Tom's hunch. He would wait all day and maybe Mladić himself would bring flowers. Instead, he had sent his henchmen, which wasn't too shabby either. But now Tom had another brainstorm.

"Quick," he said to Nina, "let's get ahead of them." He slung his gear over his shoulder, drained his coffee and, walking away from the men, they made their way to the nearest cemetery exit. It was a gamble, there were several, but it was a good bet the men had entered from the closest.

While Tom waited in the street at a discreet distance from the metal gate, Nina hurried away to fetch the car.

He was thinking, Great stuff. He had already filmed the grave with its headstone inscribed: ANA MLADIĆ 1971–1994, topped by a small white cross. Mladić hadn't come himself, but he had filmed the next best thing: his men, delivering a tribute from the grieving father.

His new idea was to follow the messengers—maybe they would lead him to Mladić.

Nina sat at the wheel of their car, facing away from the cemetery, eyes fixed on the sideview mirror, and within moments the three men appeared through the wrought-iron gate. Two waited while one went to bring the car. As soon as he reappeared, in a white BMW, and before the two men had climbed in, Tom told Nina to drive away slowly, down the hill, and to let the BMW overtake them. They followed the car through Belgrade's usual heavy traffic, Tom filming its progress through his windshield until it led them west across the Gazela Bridge over the river Sava, a tributary of the Danube, which it joined a mile to the east.

"No surprise, then," Tom said, half to himself, as they followed the BMW into Novi Beograd, New Belgrade, the gigantic city in a city, hundreds of grim, communist-era apartment buildings and shabby shopping complexes, all daubed in graffiti. If the best place to hide a book is in a library, then where else would Mladić be but in some anonymous apartment, among hundreds of thousands of others. In this drab gray place, home to a million Serb worker bees, General Ratko Mladić was a folk hero, a military icon the people would never betray.

They were fine following the BMW along a wide main road into the heart of New Belgrade, but when it did a U-turn and took the first right, and Nina without thinking turned with them, and even though she was three cars back, Tom's antennae began to quiver. "I don't know," he muttered. When the BMW found a parking space by a shopping center, and Nina slowed at the end of the line of cars, Tom hissed at her to continue. He had taken his small shoulder bag with the concealed camera and had filmed, through his open window, as they slowly drove by the BMW.

"Let me out," he said. "Meet me in the center here, in the café, there has to be one. Or if there isn't, on a bench."

He walked past the cracked concrete slides of a playground, his small bag over his shoulder, camera inside, screwed onto a built-in mount, the glass of the lens flush with a hole in the leather casing. From outside it looked like a large decorative button. The on-off switch was the zipper handle. He turned the camera on, pointing it at his feet walking, the streets he was passing, and it recorded the sound, his footsteps, traffic noise, although muffled. He couldn't see through the viewfinder but was experienced enough to know more or less what pictures the wide angle was capturing.

Good raw point-of-view material for a doc. Secret camera stuff always looked good. It made a glass of milk in the kitchen with Mom look like a Soviet espionage movie.

He quickly found the parked BMW but saw no sign of the three men.

The forest of apartment buildings was packed so densely it blocked out the afternoon sun. Everything was concrete—the crumbling benches, the playground walls, the buildings and the streets, even the few trees had low concrete walls around them. A cold and hard place. Tom mentally filed a phrase for his script: "Belgrade, bleak and bored." Men sat alone on the benches, gazing at nothing or reading. Morose, he thought: another good word for the script. Grim. Dark. As Tom pointed the hidden camera at him, a wrinkled man took out his dentures and wiped them with a piece of newspaper. Women in faded tracksuits walked by with half-empty shopping bags. As Tom walked to each corner of the little shopping complex, failing to see the men, he understood: they must have gone inside one of these buildings. Could Mladić really be here?

He approached one, hidden camera rolling, and entered the small, gloomy lobby where an elevator door closed with a snap, followed by the whine of the ascending motor. One wall looked as if someone had thrown a bucket of brown paint over a cartoon of a giant penis. An elegantly dressed young woman in a fawn wool coat and scarf and high heels tapped down the stairs and passed him into the street.

How the mighty have fallen, Tom thought, retracing his steps to the shopping center. Even the pigeons seemed to limp instead of strut. He had already filmed the fancy villa Mladić and his wife shared openly until 2001, in a quiet cul-de-sac in west Belgrade, surrounded by his private army of fifty-two armed bodyguards. The neighbors had called him "the General" but when Tom tried to interview them they turned away. From there Mladić's army buddies had protected him in their barracks, despite the so-called UN manhunt. Mladić had attended soccer matches, his son's ostentatious wedding, vacationed freely in the mountains and pristine bays of Montenegro, but the party ended when the new Serb government finally arrested his patron, the wartime Serb president, Slobodan Milosevic, and the writing was on the wall for Mladić and Radovan Karadzic, and all the other wanted Bosnian Serb war criminals. They quickly went underground.

Tom caught the bitter tang of urine as he passed the trees at the corner of the shopping center, behind a grocery store. And yes, sure enough, there was a café on the other side of the concrete square.

He went inside and found Nina, with two cups of coffee. "Black, no sugar, right?" she said, her soft voice mingling with a mournful Balkan melody from a wall speaker hanging from its wires.

"Thanks," he said, pulling up a chair. He placed the bag with the concealed camera on the table. "Got some good shots, point-of-view stuff, walking around. I lost them, though. They must have gone into one of these buildings. I went into the lobby of one and took some shots. God, it stank."

"So what now?"

"Well, wait here a bit, I suppose."

"Not too long, though, Tom, there aren't many outsiders here. Nobody comes here without a reason."

"Let's just finish the coffee then. Want a sandwich? I'm starving."

While Nina called the waiter and they ordered, he looked around. He laughed, "Look."

A motorbike was suspended from a gallery rail above them with an axe strapped to the front wheel. On the walls were paintings of mountains and lakes, and every inch of space behind the bar was taken with bottles of beer and spirits. It was a small café with six tables. They were the only customers.

"Nice place," Tom said with a grimace. "Coffee sucks."

"Too strong," Nina said, lighting a cigarette. "So tell me, has anything changed? How do you see the overall story?"

"Simple," Tom said. "We find Ratko Mladić. That's the general idea."

"Oh, sure, no problem. Then what?"

"Run for our lives?"

"No, Tom, really, what do you hope to get?" But as Tom talked about Ratko Mladić and his men and what they had done, and how the world didn't care, she felt her stomach tighten and regretted her question. As long as she didn't think back to that day, and night, and the next, she could continue as if nothing had happened. If her nights were bad, well, that didn't interfere with her days. So why, she had asked herself many times since that first phone call, had she agreed to work with Tom on a documentary about that monster? The money? Really?

She took another long drag on her cigarette and stubbed it out, and lit another.

With a sigh Tom pushed away the coffee cup. "Can you order me a tea? Mint tea, if they have it?"

Nina waved at the waiter behind the bar and he took Tom's coffee and soon returned with a glass full of hot water and generous sprigs of mint with a tea bag.

"Look," Tom said. "I don't want to get too bogged down with the background, everyone knows who he is by now, the real story is the failed hunt for Ratko Mladić. Why, with the whole world looking, has nobody found him?"

"But does anybody care though? Outside Serbia, I mean?"

"I care. You care. And they should. Think about it. He's like the poster child of everything that is wrong with the world, all the intrigue and blackmail and special interests. If it has a face, it's him. Look, here's a man, wanted for crimes against humanity in Sarajevo, genocide in Srebrenica where he let his men massacre nine thousand Muslims, he's the biggest killer in Europe since Adolf Hitler, as I keep saying, and he's walking around free, and nobody gives a shit."

He took a cigarette from Nina's pack. "Here, try this," he said, taking out his silver flask from his coat pocket. "Brandy."

Nina tried it, tried it again, and again. Tom took a long swig, sighed, smacked his lips, and put it away. He pulled on his cigarette.

"This is what I have to say in the film, early on, to set it all up, right? To tell the viewer, this is why it's important, this is why you're watching. I've got about five minutes to say that in 1995, there's the Srebrenica massacre, which Mladić does. Shortly after that the United Nations declares Mladić top of their "most wanted" list, along with his boss, Radovan Karadzic. All the forces of NATO in Europe are looking for him. Ha ha. Did you know that US officers actually met with him in the late nineties at an army base near Mount Zep? They didn't even want to capture him. The Americans thought catching him would put too much heat on their own troops and didn't want to lose more men for no good reason. Then they became too busy with Iraq and Afghanistan to care about a Balkan killer, even though he killed a lot more people than bin Laden. The Serb government? Too riddled with corruption and crooks, too divided between nationalist xenophobes and pro-Europeans."

Nina pressed his arm and looked around. "Speak quietly."

"There's nobody else here."

"Anyway."

Tom nodded and leaned toward Nina and went on, just above a whisper. "I need to get all this into the top of the doc, about five minutes' worth of context, that's enough. So, where was I? The International Court of Justice orders the Serb government to arrest him, but there's fat chance of that because he's a Serb hero and even if they wanted to, which they don't, the people wouldn't let them. The government's afraid of a revolution to defend him. And the rest of Europe? Politics. They're afraid too much pressure on strategic Serbia could push Serbia away from the West, back into the arms of Russia. The only people genuine in their hunt for Mladić are the Dutch, and that's only because they stood by and let the Srebrenica massacre happen in the first place—they're humiliated and they want revenge." In his excitement his voice had risen again.

A couple had entered and sat at the next table. Even though he was talking in English, Tom tried to speak more quietly.

"So this is all what I have to say in the beginning of the doc. After the Serbs finally had to do something, they picked up Milosevic, and then it became a bit more serious for Mladić. His protector was gone. Since then, what, five years ago? Mladić disappeared. All kinds of rumors. He's living on army bases, in Greek Orthodox monasteries, in caves in eastern Bosnia, in loyal mountain villages, in Russia, in Montenegro, here in some lousy apartment in New Belgrade. The real point, though, is that each time there was a real snatch operation, somebody tipped Mladić off."

He leaned back with a sigh. "That's where we come in. That's where the doc really starts. Who's tipping him off? Why? Who's protecting Mladić? It's a great story. We don't have to find him. Anyway, we never could. But that's the point of the doc. Nobody can find him. Why? I'll tell you why. It isn't hard to hide if nobody wants to find you."

As Tom had warmed to his tale, and had felt the anger rising, his voice had risen again too. Of course he was passionate. He hadn't been killed, but young Nick had. The couple in the corner had stopped talking and were looking at him, and so was the barman as he dried glasses. Nina noticed and whispered nervously, "Tom, enough. Anyway, I think we should go. You never know in this place who's listening, and why." She waved to the barman for the check. The music had turned to some kind of annoying Serbian rap.

Tom had just whispered that even if Mladić wasn't in a nearby apartment building, his messengers were, and they must be communicating with him somehow, they were getting warmer, and Nina was just answering that if it was so easy, then why hadn't other people done the same thing, and anyway, let's go quickly, when shadows appeared across the floor, and the two men entered.

The two men from the cemetery. Tom recognized them immediately and looked away and his heart began to pound. They stood at the bar, leaning against it, and ordered two coffees, staring openly at Tom and Nina. The waiter came with the change but Nina didn't take it. She was frozen, looking down at the table. Her hand was trembling. The couple at the next table shifted and went silent. As Tom turned, unsure what to do, what would happen, his eyes met the unwavering gaze of the taller, broader man. He had graying dark hair, his eyes were small in a pale hard face, and his trimmed mustache made him look, to Tom, comic, but there was nothing funny about his gesture. Looking into Tom's eyes, without stirring from the bar or worrying about the other customers, he held up his thumb and pulled it across his throat.

Tom felt his heart lurch and his eyes darted to Nina. Her back was to the man, luckily she hadn't seen, but she was so frightened she still hadn't raised her eyes from the table, as if she was looking away from a ghost. Her whole body was trembling, she was white. She tried to catch Tom's eye. They must leave. Now.

Tom tried to control his racing heart, he felt a chill through his pores, and even as his nervous system screamed Leave, one part of him said, This is too good to miss. He calculated quickly, the upside, the downside. Be careful, these are thugs, they're on home turf, don't upset them. But then, what could they do here, in a public bar? And this is great: Mladić's men threatening him.

Tom carefully took his bag from the table and slung it over his shoulder, as if he was about to leave. He held it in his arm and pushed the hidden Record button in the side zip, keeping the lens facing the two men at the bar. It was a wide angle, it would capture everything along the bar; whatever happened next would be on tape. Win win. He looked back and turned his palm, signing, I don't understand.

Again the bigger man looked straight at Tom, straight into the hidden camera, and with a sneer again pulled his thumb across his throat.

Tom shook his head, as if he still didn't get it, but inside he was jubilant. He had it. The man threatening him, on camera. The editor could zoom in digitally, make it a tighter shot. What a moment! What else could say so graphically that they were entering dangerous territory?

The universal sign: I'll slit your throat. *Yes! End of part one. Cut to commercial.*

This is gonna be one great doc!

Tom looked away, as if he was scared, which part of him was, but the larger part was smug and thought, Well, mate, you haven't lost your touch. He took Nina's limp hand, and only then, feeling her tremble, did he realize how terrified she was.

Forgetting the change on the saucer, and without glancing back, he led her out the door.

When the waiter knocked on the door with room service that evening, Nina had jumped and Tom had tried to laugh off her fear, but the more he thought about the men at the bar, the more he understood it hadn't been by chance. Either they knew they had been followed and were smart enough to trace him to the café, or someone in the café, probably the barman, had overheard his conversation and tipped them off. Whatever the explanation, Mladić's network of protectors was on the ball. No surprise there. And they were warning him.

"We're journalists," he said to Nina as he poured a glass of red wine. He didn't understand why she was so frightened. "We're making a doc on Mladić. So what's new? Everyone does docs on Mladić. What's there to worry about?"

"A lot," Nina said, and she meant it. "You don't understand." If things went wrong, Tom could just leave. She had to stay, her life was here. That simple idea of staking out Ana's grave and then following the messengers meant that in one week Tom had gotten closer to Mladić's men than all the other journalists she had worked with in a decade. But that wasn't what had scared her. She hadn't told Tom how terrified she was by the two men in the café.

And after their growing intimacy she didn't know how to tell him that she couldn't carry on with this project, that she shouldn't even have started.

She'd have to tell Tom she would not work with him anymore.

But she didn't want to. Tom had meant so much to her, even though he didn't know it. And she knew now how much he still meant to her, even if she hadn't known it either. Their few days together had brought it back, some of the good. For in all these years, a little part of Tom had been with her, watching from behind the bedroom curtains, talking to her as she walked in the woods. They had known each other so briefly, yet shared so much. Only he knew what she knew; but she had never dared to call or even e-mail him, that piece of her life he shared was the missing piece, the evil part, the place she would not go, although he was possibly even more hurt than she. She saw that now.

When he had phoned her, a window had opened. For both of them. She didn't want to close it now. But she must.

As their work drew them closer this week, sharing the car in the day, sharing meals at night, and circling around the forbidden subject, yet approaching it with an aside, an allusion, calling it "Then," and swiftly withdrawing, they both realized what was happening. This was it: talk therapy. What they had needed and never found, they were beginning to find in each other: a safe place to revisit that terrible day.

Word by word, in the dim light of the bedside lamp, before room service, they had circled and tiptoed and finally had broached, in the tenderest way, the overwhelming guilt Tom bore for the murder of his friend.

Not yet her rape.

"I know, Tom," Nina said, caressing his head, which rested against her shoulder, holding his two cupped hands. "I know."

Tom's eyes were shut, he was drifting, close to sleep. When he was brought home to London, and then went to live in New York after, instead of helping him recover, the network wouldn't re-new his contract ("You're phoning it in, these days, phoning it in"), he had lost himself in every avenue of escape, punished his body, cut off his friends, avoided any help, because nobody could know. Only Nina, Nina who he had loved, even if ever so briefly, so impossibly, so innocently, Nina, who had been there, who had suffered with him, only she could understand. But he couldn't bring himself to call her.

And now, here she is. Holding him. Beneath the bravado, weak and scared like him, they shared that, at least. He burrowed tighter, enjoying her softness and her warmth, and the safe place she provided. And so he could talk, and he did talk, as he never had before. What Nick had meant to him, the son he never had, cliché, I know. Nina knew that, she had seen it. How Nick had trusted him, and he had failed him. Nina knew that too, but it wasn't his fault.

"It was, it was," Tom said.

"Sssshh," Nina said at last, stroking him. "You did what you could, and nobody could have done more. It just happened. It was an accident. I know. I saw it." More of Nina's friends had been killed, the war had been long and terrible and claimed the lives of many young journalists, mostly students, like her, who had worked with the foreign media. She knew death. And she knew that nobody is to blame except the one who pulls the trigger. "We were doing important work," she said. "And we paid a heavy price."

Tom said, "Nick did."

"Yes."

"I went to see his family, you know. Told them what happened in those final moments. That he died a hero, trying to save you. It made it easier, you know. For them."

"I wrote to them."

"You did," Tom said, sitting up, and then settling into her body again. "I didn't know that."

"I had to. I wanted to phone them but I couldn't. I started dialing a few times. But I couldn't go through with it. So I wrote a letter. Saying thank you for such a noble son. How lovely he was. How he tried to help me. I told them what happened to me too."

"Everything?"

"No. Not everything. What for?"

"Did you stay in touch with them?"

"No. They never wrote back." There was a heavy silence until her body rose and fell with a loud sigh, and his head moved with it. "I suppose nobody really knows how to react. I didn't mind. I said what I needed to say. They don't owe me anything. I imagine it was just too hard to answer my letter. It takes so long to recover."

"Yes. Yes, it does."

"If you ever recover."

"You don't. Not really."

"You just have to move on."

"Yes. That's right."

They snuggled against each other, sipping from the wine, until the second bottle was empty, and the hip flask too, and the heavy gongs of the grandfather clock on the landing outside struck eleven.

Nina rose unsteadily. "I better go to my room," she said, "before I do something I may regret."

"And what could that be?" Tom said, holding her hand, pulling her gently down toward him, as she exaggerated her swaying and pulled away.

She put her finger to her lips. "Ssshh."

"Don't go," Tom said, "stay. Please."

Now Nina was by the door, framed by it. Later he told her, he had no idea why, but he switched on the hidden camera. Instinct?

Nina smiled, drowsily, and slowly shook her head.

There was a knock on the door. Nina, already standing, opened it. Two gloved hands shot in and grabbed her by the head and muffled her mouth while the second man pushed past and pointed a pistol with a long metal silencer at Tom's chest. The first man, gripping Nina's head like a heavy rock, leaned back against the door, closing it, and sat her in a chair, still holding her tight. She gasped through his fingers, her eyes wide with terror. Would they recognize her?

"Where's the camera?" the bigger man with the comic mustache said and it wasn't so comic now.

Tom, shocked and helpless, nodded at the pile of equipment in the corner, silently thanking God for his habit of putting all the used tapes in the hotel safe. "The tapes?" the man said. "In the case, the blue one," Tom said, trying to stay calm, giving up the unused tapes. "Please don't hurt her, take whatever you want, just don't hurt her." The man slung the case over his shoulder and took the camera. Tom began to protest but the man quickly shut him up.

"Don't bother. Keep quiet and you won't get hurt, this is a warning, a very serious warning. Stay away from us. Leave Belgrade. You don't know who you're messing with."

The first man released Nina with a push while the second one raised the camera above his head and smashed it into the marble fireplace with the crash of a gunshot. Nina hid her face with her hands, flinched, and almost fell off her chair. The lens shattered and hung from the body like a broken wing.

Mustache drew his finger across his throat again, snarled, "Last warning," and quietly closed the door after him.

Trying to stop his own trembling, Tom went to Nina and held her as she shook uncontrollably.

"Nina, they've gone. It's all right." He shook the brandy flask. Empty. He went to the shelf, took a new bottle, and handed it to her. She gulped and coughed. "Water."

He brought her some in a plastic cup.

"Are you all right now?" he said. "It's over."

She trembled so much she spilt the water. Tom helped her hold the cup to her mouth. "Don't be a fool," she said between sips. "Of course it isn't over. You'll have to stop making this film. They mean what they say."

"Has this happened to anyone else?" he asked.

"Not that I know of."

He stood behind her, holding her shoulders, trying to reassure her. "It's okay," he said, "it's okay now, they've gone."

Silently he picked up the camera and examined the drooping lens. The mount was dented and the glass was smashed. Lucky it was just the filter. The camera body seemed all right, just scratched and a dent in the bottom. The tripod screw might be damaged.

So, he must be closer. Closer to Mladić. Otherwise, why would they bother? He brought Nina to the sofa, sat her down. He sat next to her, took her hand. "We'll have to think differently. Be more clever. More discreet. Stay away from them for a bit while we do some more interviews, shoot other stuff. We need to—"

"Not with me."

Tom gasped as he realized.

It must have all been caught on the hidden camera. He'd just switched it on. To film Nina. He stood, grabbed the bag, opened it, checked the red recording light was on: Yes. In a daze, Tom switched it off, thinking, Oh my God, what incredible footage, even if they're out of frame half the time, great sound. What made me switch it on?

But then: "Wait a minute, back up," he said. "Did you say 'Not with me'? What do you mean?"

"What I said. Not with me. Listen, Tom." She had stopped shaking and lit up a cigarette and was pacing nervously. "Look, it's all right for you, you can leave any time you like. I don't have anywhere else to go. I have a little son to think about." Her voice changed, became more tentative, uncertain. "And there's something I didn't tell you." She paused, thought better of it, changed track. "I have a job. They must know who I am. Life means nothing to them. Other people's lives."

Tom felt his stomach sinking. Go on without Nina? "But everyone does these stories."

"Yes, but no one has upset them like you. You followed the wrong people. Or rather, the right people, apparently. You're too good a journalist." She tried to smile, and failed and glanced away. "It's too dangerous for me. I'm sorry, Tom, really, I am."

Her head was bowed, her hair fell across her face like a veil, he ran his fingers through the loose tendrils and pulled them back, and lightly brushed her forehead with his lips, and knew: half the reason he was doing the film was to see Nina again. When he'd first considered making the doc he had immediately thought of calling Nina to help—it would be the best excuse to call.

She had helped him so much already, and he had helped her too, he didn't want it to end. They had come so close together in the last few days, closer than he had been with anyone since, well, since he had last seen Nina. The women in the meantime, they meant nothing. Cold comfort, no more. Nina . . . Nina . . . He felt a welling of emotion and took her face in his hands to kiss her, on the lips, her velvety lips, that he had kissed once before, and dreamed of ever since, and as their eyes met, so close, and as his eyes turned misty and he lowered his face to hers, she turned away.

"I'm afraid, Tom. I have Sasha to think about."

You mean: And I don't have anyone.

His fingers trailed through the strands of her hair as she shifted away from him, and he pulled back too, a divide opened between them. "I'm sorry," she said, in a more determined tone. There was another long silence, as the gulf grew wider and a lonely vista opened up before him. He willed himself to believe it wasn't final; it couldn't be. He'd only just found her again. Nina was looking at him, and blowing smoke from the side of her mouth. "I'm sorry," she said again.

When Nina had gone to her apartment and double-locked it from the inside, Tom paced his room, anxious and disturbed, his mind racing. The thugs. Nina. He'd carry on with the film, he couldn't stop now. But what about Nina? Would she want to see him again, even if she wasn't working on the film, or would he be tainted, too dangerous to be around? He felt sick, and poured a brandy.

Woodenly he examined his broken lens; six thousand dollars. Maybe they can change the mount bit. Luckily the camera seemed to be undamaged, so the spare lens should fit, even if it was slower and not such a wide angle. No need to spend on rental, he still had a full kit. After all, he was financing the whole project from his own money.

I wonder what I got with the hidden camera, he thought. He unscrewed the camera from inside the shoulder bag, slipped on the headphones, peered at the tiny viewfinder screen, and, with a spreading grin of satisfaction, saw Nina open the door, being grabbed by the head and pushed out of shot, heard muffled screams and voices, the crash of something being smashed onto the floor, his own voice and then Mustache appeared in shot at the door, doing his familiar throat-cutting act, contorting his face into what he thought was an intimidating scowl, and the two men went out of the door.

Yes! Tom pumped his fist when it ended. Extraordinary, he'd never seen anything like it. It's the real thing. Even more spooky because you couldn't see half the action but just hear it, with the camera steady, showing an empty space. Yes! I can sell this right now, he thought.

Pity about Nina. That shot of the guy grabbing her by the head. Man! Of course she's terrified. Who wouldn't be? She just needs time to get over it, they have to be more careful, maybe she shouldn't come out with him on any more shoots, she could just do the telephoning and maybe log the tapes, transcribe interviews. But oh, these pictures, good stuff!

He looked at the time on his cell phone. Eleven forty. Six hours' time difference: it must be five forty in the afternoon in New York.

He lay on the bed, plotting Nina's return, stoked by the pictures. These guys were from central casting, with their cut-throat stuff. This is going to be a great documentary.

Time to call New York, get some buzz going, talk up the price. Lying flat, head resting against a cushion, a smile on his face, he caught Boone, the great survivor, between meetings. As carefully as possible, knowing the phone was probably bugged, he sketched out what he was doing, the brushes with violence, trying to hint that it was all on tape, without actually saying so in case any bad guys really were listening. The circle was closing on Ratko Mladić, he told Boone, stressing the historical significance of the man: the Greatest Killer in Europe since Hitler. But as he tried to explain the kinds of people he wanted to interview, people close to the farcical government hunt, he knew he was being too careful, too vague, and he felt the distance growing on the phone, sensed absence in the silence on the other end, that he was losing the Terminator, who suddenly broke in. "Tom, sounds great, really great, why don't you put it down in an e-mail, I'll take it to Productions, I gotta run, the show's on in forty-five minutes."

"*The Hunt for Ratko Mladić*—that's the title," Tom said, "and—"

Boone interrupted again. "Got it. But, okay, you know what, straight up? You want us to commit to buying *The Hunt for Ratko Mladić*? Let's face it, who the fuck is Ratko Mladić? Who cares? Call us when you find Osama bin Laden. Gotta run."

And Tom was staring at a dial tone.

"You damn dimwit." He crossed the room to his bag and swigged from his bottle, conjuring a dozen violent ways to make Boone regret the day he was born. Nothing changes, all they care about is ratings. I should do a doc on the Royal Family.

Sam Morissey wasn't much help either.

One of the first things Tom did on any assignment was to check out the names of the local US embassy staff to see if he had any contacts. And in a stroke of great fortune it turned out his old UN buddy from Bosnia and Croatia was attached in some obscure way to the military attaché in the Belgrade embassy. Since Sarajevo, Morissey had bounced around the Balkans and Central Europe in a variety of posts, all related to security. The more vague the public job definition, Tom had learned, the more specific the secret role; a more obvious spook there couldn't be, even down to the graying buzz cut, which Tom had admired when they met for dinner the day after he had arrived in town.

When he phoned Morissey the next midday saying he couldn't talk on the phone but something big had happened, the spook wanted to meet Tom immediately, if not sooner, and named a bar on a small side street in the Old City near the Hotel Balkan.

Tom found the place, small and dark, at the end of a cobbled lane on a hill.

They arrived together, shaking the rain off their coats into the street. Tom looked around. "There's a great bar in the hotel next door, why are we in this dump?"

"Because you're paying. I'm being considerate."

Tom nodded in approval. "Nice place."

They took their beers and brandies to a corner table, where Morissey extracted every last detail from Tom, from the moment the men had placed flowers on the grave of Ana Mladić until his midday phone call. Everything, except Nina. Tom wanted to keep her out of it.

Morissey said, "But you didn't mention lovely Nina."

"Is there anything you don't know?" Tom said.

"Yes. Why do you care so much about Mladić?"

"Do you know who's protecting him?"

"I already told you the other night, everyone has a general idea. But exactly who? Where? Nope. They don't want to hand him over, for a dozen good reasons."

"Good reasons?"

"Yes, very good reasons. From their point of view, that is."

"And from your point of view?"

"Good question." Morissey embarked on a convoluted explanation of American national interests and security concerns in the Balkans, as well as stretching into Europe and the Atlantic to the west and Russia and the Sea of Okhotsk to the east.

"Sea of what?" Tom said.

"Bottom line," Sam ignored him, "Serbia, as always, where East meets West, where Christianity meets Islam, where Harry meets Sally, is a powder keg. We do not want to rock the boat in the Balkans. Stability is the name of the game. Mladić may be a killer, evil, but in the final analysis he's a small fish in the big picture."

"That's a mixed metaphor."

"Whatever. You're the writer, not me. I can only say it the way it is. And the way it is, is: stay out of it. Drop it. They're a dangerous bunch, Mladić is still protected by the security services, and they don't miss a trick. That was a message they sent you, and you'd better get it. It's just a documentary, and you said yourself nobody wants it yet. There's plenty of other stories."

"You think I should drop it?"

"Yes. Absolutely."

"No fucking way."

But the spook had spooked him, no doubt about that. When Morissey left, Tom downed two brandies, toasting himself for not taking a third, and exactly when he shouldn't have, when the room began to turn and he hardly knew what he wanted, he phoned Nina. She was out of breath. She had just come in with the shopping, she had to leave to collect Sasha from school, she was late.

No, she hadn't found another fixer for him. No, she didn't

know where Mladić was. No, she didn't want to come over for a drink. No, she didn't want to sleep with him. And when he told her about Morissey, she said the same: drop the doc.

He considered the matter at leisure over that third brandy.

Tom was smiling to himself and humming as he unfolded himself from the cab and, moments later, coolly observed the hotel receptionist, who seemed to be swaying a fair distance away. *"Laku noc,"* he tried, gripping the marble counter. "And good evening to you too," the clerk answered, holding out an official-looking letter along with his key. *"Laku noc,"* Tom said again, and, extending his hand, at his second attempt connected with the letter. He opened it in the elevator, leaning against the wall, and did a double take at the embossed gold, gray, and blue badge with the stamp: Безбедносно-информативна агенција. That sobered him up. Serbia's Security Information Agency—the BIA.

At ten o'clock the next morning a stern-faced middle-aged woman in a calf-length brown skirt and blue blouse led Tom along a series of corridors till they reached the one open door. She waved him in. It was a small waiting room, where the typist did not look up from her work. The woman told Tom to wait, and said she would collect him when he was finished. Tom thought, In five years? Ten? He looked around: no chair.

They had walked through the grand entrance lobby of the BIA headquarters, with its heavy oil portraits, dark parquet flooring, and thick burgundy carpets, and with each turn and new corridor the surroundings had become less plush, until they had reached this part of the Tito-era edifice, where the walls were bare and the floors covered with linoleum: *easier to wash off the blood.*

There was a call and the typist looked up and nodded at the

direction of the shout. Tom pointed at the door. Go in? Her head was already bent over her work so Tom turned the knob and entered.

Another small room, another person working, ignoring his presence. Tom observed him: slight of frame, blue sweater over a white shirt. Short, dark hair; frameless spectacles; around thirty-five. One chair for a guest. Tom said, "May I?" and sat down.

The man looked up. "Tom Layne?"

"Yes, that's right." A polite smile.

"You used to be Tom Layne?"

That did make Tom laugh. "Yes, that's true. I am the man that used to be Tom Layne."

"I used to watch you when I was a student at NYU. You were very good at reporting from the Balkans. You were one of the few who understood the region and the people. I even remember some of your reports. Especially the one about Ratko Mladić."

"Well, thank you."

"I read that it got you into some trouble."

"You could say that."

"I am sorry. That is not how our people behave. Not usually."

"Not usually? You mean, sometimes they do?"

"You understand quickly. I knew you were a good reporter. But . . ." He flicked through some papers and looked up. "But, let's get down to business, I have another meeting. You do not have a work permit for Serbia?"

"No, no, I don't. As a visiting journalist here for just a couple of weeks I don't need one."

"Quite so. But . . ." Now he looked through a file and appeared mystified. "Are you registered as a visiting journalist with the Ministry of Information?"

"No."

"So you do need a work permit then?"

Tom didn't answer. No point. Whatever he said would make no difference to anything. What did the little man want? Journalists and bureaucrats are instinctively hostile, like cats and dogs. But he caught himself. This is the BIA HQ. This guy may look like a bureaucrat, but he's a secret service agent. Don't mess with him. Why had he been summoned?

He noticed the man's hands were trembling. Tom looked at his own. Steady as a rock. The man had taken a used teabag that was drying on a saucer and was playing with it, shredding it.

"Mr. Layne," he said at last.

"Yes?" Tom stared at him.

"Mr. Layne, what story are you working on?"

Tom understood it was easier to get into the BIA headquarters than to get out, and, as he had hundreds of times on hundreds of stories, he launched into a modified pitch that hopefully would satisfy officialdom long enough for him to finish his work. "Well, everybody is looking at Serbia as it applies to join the European Union," he said, "and one of the stumbling blocks is the question of the remaining war criminals, as defined by the UN and indeed your own government, that is, who are still at large. So I want to show how you are looking for them, at your successes and, of course sometimes, failures, and how you are trying so hard to—"

"And Ratko Mladić is a failure of ours?"

"I didn't say that. It's very hard to find him. You've even offered a reward, five million euros. That shows how sincere you are. But of course, no luck so far. So, yes, of course Mladić will be part of the story, but not all of it, by any means."

"Fascinating," the official said, nodding intently, "fascinating." He launched into a long explanation of Serbia's difficulties in tracking down war criminals and the eminent place the task occupied in government policy. He moved on to animated reminiscences of his student life in the Big Apple. After a few minutes he looked at his watch. Tom could see he was building up to something. The point of inviting him here? But his question surprised him.

"Do you have insurance?" the official asked.

Tom did a double take. "What do you mean?"

"Exactly that, do you have medical insurance? I know you are a freelancer now, and if something happens, if, God forbid, there is an accident, do you have medical coverage? This is a requirement for every foreign visitor who works in our country—we do not want people to become a charge to our state. Do you?"

"Yes, of course. Aetna."

"Me too! As a student in New York, I had Aetna. They're good. New spectacles every year. Do you carry their card everywhere, at all times?"

"Yes, actually."

"Good. Good. Hospitals demand it from foreigners. But I hope you don't need it here." With the palm of his hand he swept up the scattered tea leaves and the destroyed tea bag and, pushing the debris into his wastepaper basket, smiled at Tom with eyes entirely devoid of mirth. "This is a free country, Mr. Layne, a democracy. We have a free press, as you know. Still, some people are very jealous of their privacy, rightly so, I might add. I do hope you will be very careful, Mr. Layne. Very careful. Thank you."

In his hotel room, leaning back on two chair legs, feet up on the little desk, Tom said into the phone, "You know, I'm getting a little fed up with people telling me to be careful," after Morissey had just told him again to be careful.

He let his chair fall with a bang onto four legs and placed his elbows on the desk, holding the phone with both hands as if he was confiding with the instrument. "Look, Sam, here's the question. Three guys place a wreath on the grave of the daughter of Ratko Mladić, the most wanted man in Europe. We follow them and the next thing is we get threatened in a café, attacked in my own hotel room, and then the state security service warns me I may get hurt. Now you, my own embassy, say the same thing. What am I missing here? Aren't they supposed to be looking for Mladić? Aren't you supposed to be protecting me, with all those tax dollars I'm paying you?"

"You don't pay tax."

"I will if I earn some damn money from this doc."

"Tom, Tom, you're so naïve."

"Maybe. But my hands aren't shaking anymore. I was told to confront my fears to get rid of PTSD. It's working."

"You'll have more than a bit of stress, my friend. You'll have a blunt stake up your hairy ass. Remember Vlad the Impaler? He's from these parts. These guys mean business. You're not even with the network anymore, no one's got your back. You're out there, all alone, on a wing and a prayer, and you're pissing off the bad guys. What do you think I can do for you? All I can do is warn you to listen to their warnings."

"Sure, sure. Tell me, does Aetna have an air ambulance evacuation clause?"

"What?"

"Aetna. Do they do emergency medevacs? Just in case?"

"What are you talking about?"

As Tom logged his tapes, taking time codes and noting what pictures he had shot and still needed, and replayed on tape and in his head the growing tensions of the last few days, his stomach began to clench, it dug into his gut, what he called his nervous stomach. Now even his body was warning him. Hints of trouble had become open threats of real violence, and his insides weren't quite as sanguine as his outside. He'd lost Nina, the secret service was on his case, the bad guys could get worse, he had no real way to cover the story, which Boone, his most likely client, didn't want anyway.

Objectively, dude, Tom thought, popping the top from his pocket flask, you're screwed. He took a swig, washed it round his mouth and felt the brandy burn his throat, and took another big one. I really should check, he thought, whether Aetna does medevacs. What number do I call? It's probably on the card. He must remember to look.

On the other hand, it was all beginning to fall into place. The BIA's involvement in the bigger story couldn't be clearer. The guy in the office had known everything about Tom, yet had showed zero interest in Mladić's thugs. When Tom had tested him by describing the two men who had attacked him in his room, he hadn't jotted down a single note.

So now what?

First of all he should change hotels, even though they'd soon find him through the police visitor registration data bank. At least he could find a hotel that was harder for them to barge in on him.

Or what about not staying in a hotel? Stay in someone's flat? That would buy some time.

At least it's an excuse to call Nina.

Four hours later Tom followed her into the apartment, pulling his suitcase and three cases of camera gear on a folding trolley. "Nice," he said, surprised by the grandeur of the high-ceilinged living room, the shoulder-height marble fireplace, and the vaulted bay windows with floor-length lace curtains. "Big."

"Lovely, isn't it, lots of room and light," Nina said, pulling the curtains to reveal tall plane trees in a leafy garden. The marble in the fireplace was white-veined purple and on either side were recessed walls filled with shelves of books. Colorful African rugs were scattered over the sofa and across the hardwood floor. "Here's your bedroom," Nina said. "You're good for three or four days. When my friend comes back we'll find you somewhere else."

"He lives here alone?" Tom said, looking out the window. Third floor and sheer wall with no outside staircase. The only way in or out was the front door.

She smiled. "Not exactly. He's divorced. Who isn't?"

"You live nearby?"

"Yes, two streets parallel, toward the university. It's very lively here, very central, you can wander around."

From the doorway Nina watched Tom try out the bed, stack his cases in the corner of the room, hang his trousers and shirts. He only needed three hangers. She remembered he had always traveled light. She told him Sasha was back with her mother, school was out now for a short break, and anyway Sasha didn't always go to school. There was a story in the press about Mladić. A new report said that the army had sheltered him until 2003 but had then turned him over to secret services, old military comrades, family. More speculation that he was in New Belgrade. She was chattering nervously. Tom recognized the signs: she was building up to something. It was only after he had checked his camera gear and she had prepared two espressos and brought them to the cushions on the sunny alcove overlooking the garden that she plucked up courage.

Draining her espresso, she lit a cigarette and blew out of the open window. "So," she said, and when she finally got to it, it was with a firm voice. "Do you want to know why I changed my mind?"

It was late afternoon. A cold draft blew in, rustling the lace curtains. "I wasn't going to ask. I'm just happy you did."

"I must tell you. I haven't been able to sleep." She paused and continued only after a sharp intake of breath. "So it's like this. When Nick died, and they took me away. Well . . . you know what happened to me?" She glanced at him, then lowered her eyes, and continued with a harder voice, speaking to the window. "They forced me, you know, they raped me, you know that, of course." Tom's breathing changed. He shifted in his seat, turned toward her. He took her hand, and nodded.

This was where he never went; long ago a mist of dope, drink, cigarettes, women had wrapped him in a cocoon of, let's face it, denial. There were rare flashes—falling into the car. The slam of the door kicked shut. Nina crying. Him, silent, shocked. Stopping to vomit out the door. Nick's corpse under a blanket on the backseat. His smashed head bouncing with the car. Reaching back, covering it. A girlfriend prodding him awake, sweaty, nauseous.

"I had nightmares, for years," Nina said, and Tom thought, I still do. "I saw their faces at night, in my sleep, and in the days I saw them in crowds. I was always afraid. I thought they were following me. I drank a lot. I didn't trust men. I hated men. I couldn't bear to be touched. But then when I did it, when I had sex, it was as if I wanted to be punished. As if it was all my fault." Nina's face was hard, she sucked deeply on her cigarette. "I'll tell you something funny." Her short laugh was raw and unconvincing. "Often I thought of you. The love that never was." She looked at Tom and nodded sadly. "Yes. We loved each other. Am I right?"

The smallest smile played on Tom's lips, his eyes were heating, he held it in. She went on. "Everything was mixed up in me. I think what happened to us, to you and Nick and me, I don't think anything worse can happen to anyone. Right? What do you think? The worst things that man can do to man, or woman, they did to us. Am I right?"

Without thinking, Tom replied, "They killed nine thousand men and boys in Srebrenica, raped thousands of women."

"True. But is it worse? To do it to thousands or to do it to one? Especially if you are the one. And after they have done it to you, what is worse, to die like them or to live like us?"

Tom squeezed her hand and saw the dying light darken the shadow on her face, her taut brow and staring eyes, her lips clenched until she continued, and at the same time he wished that she would stop, and that she would carry on. Get it over with. He needed to hear it, from her lips, even while he shrank from the words.

"You know, when that happens to you, and they hurt you, you're just a piece of meat. They steal your being, your uniqueness, your worth. Nothing matters anymore. They leave you with nothing, you're a skeleton, a shadow. And I had no one to talk to. I kept it all inside. For a long time, too long, I thought it was better to die with Nick and I wished I had. I saw Nick's face, the faces of those two devils, and I saw your face, Tom, your lovely face. Because you know what? I loved you then, I did. And they destroyed that too. They destroyed everything good in me."

From the glow of her dying cigarette she lit another. Tom was breathing heavily. Me too, he thought. I loved you too. Why did I never tell you? There was a weight on him. He went to his bag and came back with his hip flask and offered it to Nina. She sipped at it. He threw his head back and took two long swallows.

She watched him, they were holding hands again. She fell silent.

He wanted to say it, he had wanted to for so long, and at last he did. "I loved you too, Nina."

"I know." Their fingers curled around each other. She sighed. "I heard you shout, you know."

"When? What do you mean?"

"When they attacked me, I tried to fight, at first. But it was useless. I didn't have a chance. I screamed. I remember the music. But somehow, I don't know how, through all the noise and everything, I heard you, you shouted my name. Niiiinaaaa. I heard you."

"I don't remember. Or rather, I don't remember anymore what is real, what isn't."

"I do. You don't know what it meant to me, to hear you. It helped me. In my nightmares, sometimes, I see their faces, but I also hear you call my name and it makes me feel better."

Tom wiped away her tears.

How he had tried not to remember.

"Did you ever tell anyone this?" Tom asked.

"No, of course not. Who?"

"Your husband?"

Nina snorted, blew her nose. "All he cared about was the football score."

"A psychologist?"

"No. I told you, no insurance. Anyway, rape. Who cares? Who wasn't raped? Wherever the armies went, the Serbs, the Muslims, the Croats, the women got raped. Men, they're all the same." She tried a little smile, it was bitter. "It's the men who need the psychologists."

"True. It haunted me that I wasn't able to help. I felt so bad."

"You felt bad? I've got news for you, Tom, this isn't about you. Excuse me, but I can't feel bad about you feeling bad."

Tom pulled back. That wasn't what he meant. "I'm not asking you to feel bad for me. I'm just saying . . . Oh, forget it." He stood, paced in the room. Nina stared out of the window. She still hadn't said what she wanted to say. It was too hard.

Tom was thinking of Nina, groggy at breakfast, Nina, sleeping and snoring in the car, Nina, looming above him on his bed, and, of course, as he always did, of their kiss. He had felt Nina's lips for a decade. He wished he had called her earlier, but how could he have, he who had failed her? As Nina stared out of the window, smoking, and the light became dim, he finally broke the silence. "So why did you come back then?"

It was now or never. Nina turned and looked at him. "Because the two men, in the café? The ones who broke into your hotel room? They're the ones who raped me."

A shiver ran through Tom. His neck hairs stood.

"Are you sure?"

"You can close your mouth. You think I could forget those ugly mugs? I see them every night."

"Still?"

"No. Not so often. I don't have nightmares as much as I used to. But it's them, all right. The big one, he started it, he was the worst, and the other one, he was just along for the ride. He actually helped me when it was over. The big son of a bitch, he just left the room. I recognized them as soon as they came into the café. I couldn't look up again from the table in case they recognized me too." She sucked long from her cigarette and held the smoke.

A chill settled over Tom. His voice was distant. "I wouldn't worry about that. All the women they raped."

"In the café I had my back to them." She breathed out through her nose, two columns of smoke. "But then when they barged into the room, they could have recognized me, but they didn't. You're right. What did I mean to them? Nothing. Anyway, that's why I came back. Let's make this film. At least it's a way of doing something. Maybe some good will come out of it. Get them arrested. Finally get over this whole damn thing."

"*Inshallah.*" Tom raised his flask in a toast, but his mind was racing. Rapists, killers, secret service. What was he getting into? What was he getting Nina into? Again. And why? Why was it so important? Morissey was right, there were plenty of other films to make that people would actually want to buy.

He downed a tot and handed the flask to Nina and as she threw her head back and swallowed, Tom gazed at her bare throat and felt a surge of warmth. Until he imagined fat fingers gripping that throat and his stomach wrenched at the thought of the brutes and he felt the gun at his head and he suddenly heard, at last, his own voice, his bellow that day as he understood what they were doing to her, and would do to him, his own voice echoing through time and pain. Suddenly he heard himself, for the first time. He shivered. Another piece of the puzzle—he had blotted out so much.

And its echo. When he was little his mother had told him of her first son, his brother. She had only mentioned him once, in tears, maybe because it had been his brother's birthday or something, and she had held him so tight he could still feel her, and he had said, "Mummy, stop, you're choking me," and she had told him to forget what she had just said, never to talk of it again. But he had not forgotten. At night he spun all manner of tortures for the Nazis who had murdered his brother and her first husband.

She never told him their names, and after all these years he had never dared ask; he had not wanted to hurt her more. But how can it be, he told himself in the long nights, as he fought for sleep: You don't even know the name of your own brother.

Friday evening was the big night out, so after they had calmed down and toasted their renewed partnership, Nina had suggested they go out for a drink, to cheer up for God's sake. Tom had wanted to film some nighttime scenes, crowds of Serbs, and ask them questions about Mladić. So here they were, in the block-forty-five area of New Belgrade, at the entrance to the Crazy House bar where Nina knew Misko, the owner.

The room was so packed at eleven o'clock they had to wriggle their way to the bar. A man with a wild mane of white hair and a white beard was singing loudly and badly, playing the gusle, a sort of one-string lute with a body of animal skin. He held it between his knees and sawed at it with a bow and every thirty seconds stopped to swig his beer. The large woman next to him tried to pull the gusle from him but he wouldn't yield the floor. He wiped dripping ale from his whiskers and belted out his song.

Tom laughed at the merry scene and focused his camera, the small Sony, whose automatic iris performed miracles in low light, but even before he could press the Record button a rough hand appeared in front of the lens and jerked it down. "No pictures" was a command Tom had heard in dozens of languages and it was usually followed by explanation, agreement, laughter, and the most vociferous objector usually turned out to be the most garrulous interviewee. But not this time. The man didn't say anything more, just held Tom's arm down by force.

In the crowd of shouting, singing, laughing Serbs, only Nina noticed. She said something to the man and pulled Tom toward her. "Misko isn't here," she said. "The manager said we can't film."

"But this is perfect," Tom shouted to make himself heard, then put his mouth to Nina's ear. "Look at the walls." Portraits of Mladić, Karadic, Milosevic, other Serb leaders, were framed in a neat row along two walls, a gallery of local heroes or, to them, mug shots of war criminals. Tom could hear himself recording the line, over the picture of Milosevic, who was already in a Dutch jail, while the camera panned to the two fugitives: "One down, two to go."

Never one to give up, Tom asked Nina, "Can you ask him if we can film from outside?" As they had entered, Tom had noticed a pool of yellow light that shone through the large window onto the path, lighting anyone who stood there, and he had seen that if he placed the interviewee at the right angle, part profile, close to the window, the light would balance well with the action inside the room. He'd film the interviewee with the dancers in the background through the window. The digital camera was a wonder, it would easily handle the light contrast. It would look somber and moody. "We can ask people outside about Mladić."

Two minutes later Nina was back with a smile. "He says we can do what we like outside, but don't expect anyone to talk about Mladić."

Tom knew right away how he would write it. Only being allowed to shoot from outside would just add to the drama, to the image of Fortress Mladić, where everyone rallied to his side, where even a reward of five million euros could not entice a single informer.

As it turned out, the manager was right—not one person agreed to talk on camera, even outside. Off camera they swore that if Mladić came in right now, everyone would buy him a drink, nobody would tell the police, and if the police did find out he was here, they would come and buy him a drink too. He could live in an apartment here for fifty years and nobody would rat him out. This is Mladić-land, the whole country is, he is a true Serb warrior. It was wonderful material for Tom, but if he didn't have it on camera, it was worthless. Increasingly frustrated, he became more reckless. Each person that entered or left he accosted, or rather Nina did in Serbian, with the request to answer a few questions about General Ratko Mladić, and especially, Where is he? until the manager came out, with two beers. He gave them to Tom and Nina and apologized that he had received complaints. "Come inside," he said, "enjoy the party. But no more questions, please."

With no choice, Tom shrugged. They had tried; time to relax. "Fair enough. We're not getting anything anyway. Let's go inside."

The room was alive with laughter and song. There were now two men and a woman, sitting on the bar, each playing the gusle, different songs at the same time, each drinking and singing, and occasionally, when they recognized something, the whole room sang along, swaying and raising their glasses, some banging them on tabletops, as the bartenders passed, holding trays of drinks above their heads, and the floor became sticky with beer.

If only, Tom was thinking, if only I could film this. It could even be the beginning of the doc—what a great scene of Serb unity and tradition, passion and defiance, camaraderie and soul. He'd find a line from a Serb poem or song to play over it. Something about timeless defiance. They all seemed to have the same beery square heads of Mladić himself.

Nina, who'd had a few beers herself, had given up shouting translations of the songs into his ear. But he had got the message: they were the usual epic poems of Serb heroes defying the evil Ottomans, of hopeless revolts and violent rebellions, of Tsar Lazar and Jug Bogdan, the maiden of Kosovo, and of the greatest glory, to fall courageously on the field of battle. Tom was writing in his head again: It's all for one and one for all, and here, in the Crazy House bar, the one is Ratko Mladić. They love him here.

Oh, sod 'em, he thought. This is too good to miss. I'm going to film anyway. He went to the bathroom and took the tape out of the camera with the few seconds he had shot before being stopped, and hid it in his back pocket. At least if they stopped him again and even confiscated the camera cassette, he wouldn't lose anything. With a fresh cassette loaded, he went back to work.

He positioned himself between two groups of people at the bar, from where he had the best view of the three wild gusle players, and held the camera surreptitiously at chest height, without looking through the viewfinder. Struggling to hold the camera steady as people pushed him from all sides, he filmed their manic performance, panned to the drunken audience clapping and singing, shot estimated close-ups of their sweating faces, beer-dripping beards and mustaches. When he had enough he moved to the back of the room and filmed over the shoulders of the crowd. He could make do with five minutes of film, and when he had it, rather than risk getting stopped or, worse, having the tape taken, he switched off the camera and lowered it.

Even Nina hadn't noticed what he was doing, she was way too far gone. After secretly shooting enough material he finally relaxed, and drank a beer and brandy, followed by the same again. He hadn't brought any cigarettes but he didn't need any, he could just inhale the air.

At two o'clock the bar began to empty, and Tom and Nina supported each other to the car, arguing about who was sober enough to drive. Being half-drunk was bad enough, but in the darkness of the parking lot they stumbled together on the uneven ground. In the cloudy night, the only light was the glow from the windows of the Crazy House. At least they found their car easily enough, it was the only one there, in the dark corner beneath the tree. Everyone else must have walked from their homes in the nearby towers.

As Tom opened the car door, put the key in the ignition, and laid his camera on the backseat, heading for the passenger side, pleading with Nina to drive, his heart missed a beat and then pounded like a piston. A shadow behind the tree, moving. The rustle of shoes on gravel. Behind him.

A heavy hand pulled him round.

"You're a real dope, you know?" American accent. Texas?

"What do you mean? Who are you?" Tom said, feeling the pounding of his heart with his hand. "Shit, man, you scared the life out of me." Nina looked across the car, seeing the outline of the man who stayed in the shadow. "You don't learn, do you?" the man said. "Coming out here at night, anything could happen, don't do it again."

"What are you talking about? What do you want?"

"Look over there." He nodded to the other side of the parking lot. Three men stood looking at them. Tom hadn't spotted them before. "Friends of yours?" the man said. "I don't think so."

The three men didn't move, didn't talk, just looked.

"Get in the car," the stranger said, "and beat it! Now!" Nina slipped into the driver's seat, and even before Tom had slammed his door she accelerated away.

Only when they crossed the bridge over the Sava and were well away from New Belgrade did Tom's small voice break the silence. "What was that all about? Our guardian angel?"

Nina drove silently on, as Tom wondered aloud, "So who were those three men? Why were they just standing there? Did they come from inside the bar or were they waiting outside? And why, at two in the morning?"

Nina said only, "And that man. The American. Who was he? And what was he doing there?"

In the dark Tom shrugged his shoulders.

Streetlight washed across their faces as they drove through the deserted city center toward the apartment.

"I sobered up pretty quickly," Tom said. "I can tell you that."

"Me too."

They continued in silence until Tom wondered aloud again, "So did he help us? Did we need help?"

Nina shook her head. She had no idea. She kept her eyes on the road, staring through the alcohol, driving slowly, safely. Fortunately the streets were empty.

As they passed the university Tom said, with a furtive glance, "So, Nina, we're close. What do you say, my place or yours?"

"Yours, of course."

"Really?"

"Don't get any ideas. Those men didn't get you tonight, if that's what it was all about. They don't know where you live now. But they may know where I live."

"You sound pretty cool about it."

"Believe me, I'm not. But I'm glad Sasha isn't here. Anyway, it's not your place, it's my friend's. I should make sure you don't steal anything."

"Of course. You should take an inventory."

It was past three in the morning when Tom removed the African rug and fell onto the sofa in the living room. "It's itchy!" He took his shoes off and stretched out, unbuttoning his shirt.

"Why not make yourself at home?" Nina said.

Tom patted the seat next to him. "Join me."

Nina slipped off her shoes, put on soft music and, holding two glasses of wine, joined Tom on the sofa. They toasted each other, and their narrow escape, and drank and fell silent. The only light was a round pool from a table lamp. It was peaceful and their bodies moved closer until Nina lay against Tom and they stared quietly into the cozy dimness. The house was enveloped in slumber and they felt their eyes closing. Nina pulled the African rug over them and they snuggled against each other on the narrow sofa.

In this way they fell asleep and when Tom awoke in the morning, Nina was gone.

He washed his face and brushed his teeth and worked out how to use the shower. As the water coursed over his body he suddenly thought he should hide the tapes. There was no hotel safe here. What if the goons show up again? They must have checked the tapes and realized he'd given them blank ones. He became nervous, finished up quickly, hurried to find a place to hide them. Still in his underpants, he counted: he'd shot eleven tapes so far. Probably used about half of each tape, so that was about five or six hours of material, and it was all good stuff.

He walked slowly from room to room, looking for a hiding place. Living room, two bedrooms, corridor ending in a window alcove, kitchen, bathroom, guest toilet. Nice apartment. He wasn't looking for Fort Knox, just somewhere out of the way. On top of the cupboard? Too obvious. In the kitchen? Inside a big pot? Not bad. He pulled open a deep drawer but it turned out it was just a facade, covering three regular drawers. He opened the top one and pulled back in surprise.

Inside was a brown leather holster. An empty box of ammunition. There were papers and check stubs and a black leather wallet. Instinctively he looked over his shoulder to check he was alone. The wallet held a stack of visiting cards, a credit card, bills, and an outdated ID card: 31/12/2005. It must be the friend: clean-shaven, thick dark hair, handsome. Penetrating cold eyes looking straight at the lens. But what froze him, what caused his heart to palpitate, was not the icy gaze of Nina's friend but the symbol on his card.

It was gold, gray, and blue, a sword piercing a circle and a cross. It was the badge of the BIA, the Security Information Agency of Serbia.

Tom watched his hand tremble. He slid the ID back inside the wallet and slowly closed the drawer. Holy cow. BIA? Nina's friend? Nina? Had he missed something? Did they always know what he was doing and where he was because Nina was telling them? Could that be? Why would she? Were they pressuring her? Through Sasha? But why? What's the big deal? Everyone does stories on Mladić, what had he done to upset them? And Nina. Would she lie to him? No way.

But—could she?

Why?

No.

He didn't know what to think. If the friend is in the BIA, is he one of them? One of whom? Why did Nina bring him here? She seems very familiar with the place.

Tom's mind began to spin. Nina could not betray him. Could she? And what's to betray? That word again: betrayal. He felt the anger coming. He opened cupboards, slammed them, went into the living room, pulled at drawers, scanned the bookshelves. Damn. What kind of a Serb is he, he must have a drink somewhere. He searched the apartment. There must be a stash. Had he found the only teetotal Serb in the entire Balkans? A spy, no less.

He went to the fridge, to the freezer, Aha! He pulled out the bottle of vodka, looked for a glass, dispensed with it and swigged from the bottle.

What's going on?

Tom remembered the cassettes. He backed out of the kitchen, looking for another hiding place, urgently now. The bench in the alcove opened for storage. He laid the bag of tapes inside, covered it with small cushions, and closed the lid. That's good enough. For now.

I won't tell Nina where they are, he thought.

Just in case.

No, can't be. Can't be. But, then . . . he tried to remember, what had she looked like when she said she couldn't carry on? Terrified. Yes, definitely. So scared that he hadn't wanted to try to persuade her. He'd let her walk out of the door because he saw that it was too much for her. But then she came back. What happened to change her mind? And so quickly.

Why did she really come back?

He went back to the fridge and poured half a glass of vodka, threw back most of it, refilled the glass. That word rattled around his head: betrayal. He'd betrayed Nick, led him into danger and hadn't saved him; yes, he'd betrayed him. Nick had trusted him and he had killed him, as good as. His tinnitus was screaming now, cutting through his head, fueled by drink. Screaming—just like Nina. Oh, Nina.

He looked at the glass and held it upside down, held it to the light to make sure. There wasn't much left in the bottle, he had better not kill the lot, not polite.

He remembered his hip flask and drained it. Now it was his own humiliation he couldn't escape. His strength had betrayed him. He'd shat himself. All the way back in the car, with Nick dead in the backseat, he'd smelt his own dirtiness, sat on it. And Nina, bleeding and silent, staring, in shock.

Was that the drive from hell?

His mind was spinning, he lay down but it got worse, as the tinnitus screamed, he sat up and leaned forward and hung his heavy head between his legs, tried to stand, and staggered and fell back with all his weight into the chair.

They'd all betrayed him. Those bastards at the network, nobody helped, there was a service and after a couple of months a memorial for Nick. He hadn't gone, Nina had dropped out of sight, those were long dark nights, he didn't remember any days, the curtains had been drawn for months. It was his own fault though, he admitted that later, he never answered the phone or the door, didn't allow anyone close, just drank and smoked and, when he scored, did some coke.

And when he finally went back, what was it they said? Oh, yes: burned out. Goddamn right, burned out. Yvonne Drasser, executive vice president piece of crap, up yours too.

He lashed out at the sofa.

"What's the sofa done to you?" Nina said brightly. He hadn't heard her come in. "I've brought some bourekas. Cheese, mushroom, spinach. I'll just heat them up a bit. Good morning, sleep well?"

Tom stood up, as best he could. "You bitch."

She stopped at the kitchen door. "What?"

"You bitch, you heard me."

"What are you talking about? Because I left early? You were snoring, I didn't want to wake you. And don't call me that. Heat up your own damn bourekas!"

"Who are you? What do you want from me? Whose side are you on?" He moved toward her but with half a liter of alcohol swishing around an empty morning stomach, he swayed and staggered back onto the sofa.

"You're drunk. Are you drunk? Do you know what time it is, it isn't even ten o'clock."

"Come here, babe, I'll punch your lights out."

"Stop it."

"Sorry, not babe, I meant to say bitch."

"What is it, Tom? Are you all right?" As she approached him, holding the bag of bourekas out like a shield, he lashed out with his leg and caught her a glancing blow to the shin.

"Ow, that hurt, are you mad?" She threw the bag of bourekas at him, catching him in the face, flakes of filo settling on his chest like snow. He put one pastry in his mouth. "Mmmh, mushroom, can you heat it up?" He settled back with the bag, waited for the sofa to settle down, resumed chewing, and offered the rest to Nina. "Just a bit, I like them warm but not too much."

"Yes, you must be crazy. You think I'm going to make you breakfast after what you just said? And you kicked me. What the hell's wrong with you?"

Tom was lying back with his legs spread, breathing heavily, his face ashen. His chest began to rise and fall, and his brow glistened with perspiration. He began to moan and heave and sit up.

"Oh, no," Nina shouted, "not on Aleks's rug!" She lunged forward and grabbed the bag of bourekas and held it open at Tom's mouth just as his body jerked and with a loud bark he hurled into the bag, vomiting up liquid and dark lumps of mushroom. He fell back, spent, wiping his brow.

Nina shook her head mournfully. "That was a kilo of bourekas."

"That's better," Tom said, his voice barely escaping his windpipe. "Who is Aleks?"

Holding the sodden bag away from her in case it came apart,

Nina rushed to the kitchen. She wrapped the stinking bourekas in plastic and put them in the bin. She returned with a wet dish-cloth. "Here, hold this to your head."

"Ugh," he whispered. "Disgusting. Somebody vomited on my chest." Nina helped him out of his shirt and ran water over it in the bathroom.

After a few minutes, Tom stood, and when the room almost stopped moving he picked his way to the bathroom where he threw up into the bowl. Nina found him on the floor, slumped against the toilet, half asleep, in his underpants.

She flushed the toilet, held a towel under the cold-water tap, and cleaned his mouth and chest, wrung it out and held it against his forehead. His breaths were long and heavy, his eyes squeezed shut, but his hand closed on hers and held it.

In this way they sat silently on the bathroom floor, each lost in their thoughts and sighing. It's easier for me, Nina was think-ing, I have Sasha, a life. He hasn't got anyone, he's kept himself so apart, alone, he's torturing himself. He doesn't need to, he must stop. She shifted and, still holding Tom's hand, she hugged his bare chest from behind and rested her head against his, feeling his hair, wet and soft.

"Tom?"

"Yes?"

"Are you all right?"

"Yes."

"Are you cold?"

"Yes. Hold me tighter."

She did. And bit his ear.

"Ouch!"

She stood up and came back with a dressing gown.

He tied it around himself and they laughed together. "What was all that about?" Nina asked.

"Why, do I need a reason?"

"Yes, why were you so upset?"

"Because I ran out of drink. What sort of a Serb is this Aleks guy if he only has half a bottle of vodka in the freezer? Of course I got upset."

"No, Tom, really? What happened?"

He led her by the hand into the kitchen, opened the drawer, and took the BIA card from the wallet. "I found this. Who is he?"

"What do you mean? He's my friend. I told you. Why are you going through his things?"

"You didn't say he's in the BIA."

"Because he isn't. Or, sometimes he is. He's something in military security, I don't know what exactly, they're all mixed up anyway. He probably works with the BIA sometimes. He probably has lots of ID cards, to get into buildings. Half the men here are something to do with security. That's the messed-up country we are. But that isn't the point. I love him, we grew up almost like brother and sister, he often helps me, he's one of my best sources."

"How close are you?"

"Very close."

"Very?"

"Yes."

"You seem to know his apartment very well."

"It's a lovely apartment."

"You know where everything is?"

"Yes, I do."

Tom paused, not wanting to go there.

"Isn't it bad for him then, if I stay here?"

Nina held a kettle under the tap and put it on to boil. "Tea or coffee? Coffee, I think, espresso. Double. You need it."

"Thanks."

"Anyway, he's coming back this afternoon. Earlier than I thought. You can ask him yourself."

Waiting for the water to boil, and while Tom bent down to take a banana from the bottom drawer of the fridge, Nina drew back her leg, balanced herself with one hand on a chair, took aim, and kicked him hard in the backside. He fell against the fridge door, knocking his head against the hard edge. "Ouch!" He whirled round. "Hey!"

"That's for your kick. Now we're even." The kettle began to whistle and Tom laughed as she turned to pour the water. "No espresso left," she said. "Instant."

"Fine."

"What's next then?" she said, as they sat with their drinks in the alcove, looking out at raindrops beating the window, and the trees dripping and bending in the wind. The sky was dark and heavy. "What strange weather," she said. "It was sunny half an hour ago when I came in."

Tom closed his eyes and held them shut. "I need time to feel better. My head hurts. Look, let's stay away from New Belgrade for the time being. We need to set up some interviews. Not the usual suspects, the spokesmen, prosecutor's office, analysts. Is there any way to talk to people really involved in the hunt for Mladić? Police, intelligence, you know?"

"Tom?"

"Yes?"

"Why is this so important to you? Really? You know, with all these people threatening you. And me? And please look at me."

He opened his eyes. "Why? Are you frightened?"

"Yes, of course."

"Then why are you doing it?"

She thought, To be with you? but said, "I asked first."

"Okay then. Look, first of all it's not 'all these people.' It's the same people all the time. Second, this isn't a war, it's peacetime, I don't have to be afraid of anyone, I'm just doing my job."

Nina interrupted. "And me?"

"You too . . . Look, it's a fair question, and the truth is, I can't say."

"Why you care so much?"

"Yes." Tom pursed his lips as his eyes wandered and he considered the matter. Why did he? Just because it's a good story? He dismissed that right away. That applies when it's a two-minute story you shoot in a day. Not for an hour doc that can take months and can get you into serious trouble. Maybe already has. For justice? Because Mladić is evil and needs to be caught? Gimme a break, I'm no Lone Ranger. So why, then? To impress Nina?

"Truth—I don't know. It's important, it counts . . ."

"Many things are important," Nina cut in, "many things count, but you're not doing them, you're doing this. Why this, what's so important to you about this story?"

"You don't let go, do you? Honestly, I don't know."

"Have you ever been attacked before, on a story?"

"What are you, a lawyer?" Tom had to think about that. The list was long: Somalia, Rwanda, Kosovo, Gaza, Haiti, Bosnia, Lebanon, Iraq, Iran, it went on and on. All the best places, at the worst times. He shrugged. "No, things have happened, but actually attacked, apart from Sarajevo, no, never."

"Yet here you've been attacked twice in a week. Doesn't that tell you something?"

"Yes, it damn well does, that we're on the right track, and

fucked if I'm giving up just because a few goons don't like what we're doing."

"A few? The BIA warning?"

"Look, are you on or off? Are you going to help, yes or no?"

Nina sniffed. She had already made up her mind, and unlike Tom she knew exactly why she wanted to go ahead.

"Let's ask Aleks when he gets here, about who to talk to," was her answer. "He always has good ideas, he knows what's going on. But don't worry, he isn't one of them, he's on our side. It's complicated. Yes, the BIA must be helping Mladić, everyone knows that, but it isn't policy, I don't think. It's like rogue elements inside the BIA. The trouble is they may go right to the top. Aleks's friends are all pro-Western, they're young, they want to join the European Union, move away from Russia, but they have to be careful, very careful. It's always been a matter of perspective. Is Russia on the edge of Europe or is Europe on the edge of Russia? Either way, Serbia is pulled in both directions, trapped in the middle. And the services are still riddled with xenophobes and communist relics. Aleks can tell you more of the inside stuff, I only know what he tells me."

"I look forward to meeting him. I think. In the meantime, I better get dressed." Tom pushed himself to his feet, closing his dressing gown a little late. Nina put the cups away and stood at the entrance to Tom's bedroom, watching him pull on his shirt.

"Too much beer," she said with a smile. He sucked in his stomach, slowly so she wouldn't notice.

"You can relax. Let it out. It's a sign of a life well lived."

He patted his tummy. "Not where I come from. It's a sign of approaching obesity, senility, and probably bankruptcy."

"Bankruptcy?"

"Whatever. Not good."

"That shows how messed up America is. You can't even enjoy life without feeling guilty."

"You don't have a stomach."

"I'm a lot younger than you. A lot."

"Thanks. Shall we have lunch? You're making me hungry. And by the way. Sorry."

"Sorry for what?"

"For all the things I was thinking. And am thinking."

The two top buttons of her blouse were undone.

"What are they?"

"Never mind." The best thing about this documentary, he thought, is Nina.

With the rain pelting down, they stayed inside. Nina made phone calls to arrange interviews, Tom logged tapes, and they ate spaghetti and canned vegetables. "I was planning on bourekas," Nina said, and laughed, that blousy infectious Balkan guffaw, coarsened by alcohol and cigarettes, softened by sensual promise.

Tom loved it; it made him chuckle.

But Aleks was not amused when he heard it all, from beginning to end. At first he had listened calmly, seated at the table, drinking coffee. But the deeper they got into their tale, the more agitated he became, and when they described the three men and the American in the parking lot at night, he began pacing. He was about Nina's age, mid-thirties, fit and strong, lean and somehow menacing. An operative, Tom thought, not a desk man. Good to have on your side. If he really is. Who is he, anyway? Her friend? Lover? He tried to read their body language. But when Aleks finally spoke, it wasn't what Tom wanted to hear.

"You can't stay here, you know that? Another night or two if it helps, but no more. If I were you I'd do what they say, leave, it's just a film, there are plenty more you can do. Why get hurt?" He began to speak in Serbian to Nina, but switched back to English. "Nina, I'm sorry to say this, but you shouldn't be involved in this. Nobody cares what journalists do. But if they start caring, then it's because you know too much, you've rattled them. Any idea how?"

"Rattled them." Good colloquial English, Tom thought. Where did he learn it? "No, none at all," Tom said.

"It's obvious to me," Aleks said. "You said you waited at the cemetery, you followed them, good. They saw you, not so good. They followed you, or someone did. And where you went too far, you went into a building, right?"

"Yes, just the lobby."

"Did you film there?"

"The outside, a bit, yes, and in the lobby. Just the graffiti, the mood, why?"

"Obviously it's the building Mladić was in. Otherwise why would they care? Everything you've done, hundreds of other journalists have done, and nothing happened to anyone. You've done two things differently, the cemetery and the building, so that must be what upset them. Can you show me the building on the tape, you remember where it is?"

"Yes."

"Anyway, he isn't there anymore, they don't take chances. That's why they want you out of here, you've blown one of their safe houses already, they probably don't have many. They don't have the money they once had."

"How do you know?"

"I know. And if they're warning you, you should go. Or if you

stay, definitely drop this story. You don't know who you're dealing with."

"Everyone says that. So who am I dealing with?"

Aleks gave names and described the people as if he knew them,
and some of them, he did. When he gave a list and said Mladić
was protected by a combination of politicians, secret service,
criminal gangs, former militiamen, all the flotsam of the war, not
so much the army anymore, Tom interrupted him.

"Wait, wait a moment, this is so interesting, can I get this on
camera? I don't have to show your face." He stood up, as if it was
clear Aleks would agree. Instead Aleks waved him back to his seat.

"There's a better chance I'll walk on water. Do you think I'm
crazy? Haven't you been listening to what I'm saying? This is no
game, these are all people who kill."

"But I can darken your face with low exposure, I'll only light
the background, I'll disguise your voice, it will be impossible to
recognize you."

"You change the voice in the studio later?"

"Yes, yes."

"And if they confiscate your tapes first, then what? They'll recognize me then, right?"

"I'll film from behind, I—" Nina laid a hand on his arm,
pressed, as if to say, Drop it.

"No chance," Aleks said, noticing Nina's hand on Tom's arm.
"Let me go on. Write it down if you like, that's the best I can
do. They're all in bed together, all for their own reasons. A very
dangerous combination. Now the president, Boris Tadic, he means
it when he says he wants to catch Mladić. He does. You know
what it costs Serbia not to be in the European Union because they
won't let us in till we turn him over? A billion euros a year. That's

what Mladić is costing us. I don't have to tell you that this is a poor country. We're the ones in prison and he's the free man. We are hostage to him. Tadic is a brave man. You know what happened to Zoran Djindic, in 2003?"

Tom nodded. "Of course."

He was prime minister and had called for the arrest of Serbian war criminals, especially Ratko Mladić. Within weeks he was assassinated, one shot from three hundred meters, while he was moving, straight in the heart. Police believed it was a Mafia hit after he also called on the police to move against the crime families. But the assassin was believed to have been a special forces sniper. Nobody else could have made the shot. Tom intended to use pictures of the funeral in the film.

"Wasn't it a mafia hit?" Tom said.

"But don't you see," Aleks said, throwing out his hands, "they're all the same people. Mafia, special forces, some politicians, the church even, secret service, not all but some, the wartime militias, they are all in this together. That's why it's so dangerous. You don't know who is listening, looking. The BIA wouldn't get its hands dirty. They'll get someone else to do it, focus attention on someone else, like the mafia. They are very, very clever. Think of an octopus. All those tentacles are protecting Mladić. But the head, the body, unseen—it's inside the BIA, some secret unit there."

They talked all afternoon. By the time Tom had asked for the third time to film the interview, he was almost begging, but Aleks was unmoved. "For you, it's a film. For me, it's my life. Nina too. You can leave. We can't."

Aleks took his computer, showed pictures of massacres, of the militia leaders, family video of Mladić dancing at a wedding, walking in the woods, with his wife, and before her suicide, with his daughter, all the while linking it in time and significance. It was the best briefing so far. Aleks must be right inside; he knows everything.

But Tom couldn't help wondering, Why is he telling me all this? Just because of Nina? I don't know him, he doesn't know me. Shouldn't he be more careful?

"That's why I have to be so careful," Aleks was saying. "Nobody knows how many different security services there are inside the BIA. Who reports to whom, about what, which orders are real, which are for the record—half the time we're tracking down people who are paid by our own bosses. It is very dangerous, and corrupt. Some of us want to change things. So I repeat, don't get Nina caught up in this."

As dusk fell and they got up to stretch their legs, Tom put away his notebook. "Thank you, that was fascinating," he said. "You gave me a lot to work on."

But again he was thinking: Intelligence people never say a word more than they have to. He doesn't know me from Adam, I could be anybody. If I reported this conversation to his bosses, he'd be finished. They'd say, Only the spokesman can talk to the press. He knows that. So what's his game?

Nice guy though. But . . . him and Nina?

In the kitchen, as they all watched the kettle, waiting for it to boil, one last question occurred to Tom. "So there's still the big mystery. The guy who appeared out of nowhere in the parking lot? Who was he?"

"You said he was American? Texas?"

"Texas, maybe. American? Yes."

"So ask the Americans."

At lunch the next day Tom examined the leek and potato pie. He punctured the pastry with his fork, enjoying the escaping steam.

"There's something pleasing about that, right?" he said to Sam Morissey. "The way you can see the pastry almost relax, like it's sighing. And look at the crust, baked to perfection." He held a forkful, waiting for it to cool, and took a drink of beer. "Pils. Love it."

"You seem mighty pleased with yourself," Morissey said.

"I wouldn't go that far. But yes, it's all beginning to fall into place."

"Nina, you mean."

Tom laughed. "No, not Nina. I wish. What about you? You got someone? I heard you were living with an English girl. Sandra? Is that right?"

"Yeah, Sandra . . . Didn't work out though. Three years we were together. I don't blame her really, she walked out, I'm never in one place long enough. I gotta give up this shit."

"What shit?"

"Don't go there. You know what I mean. I was in D.C. once for eighteen months and then again for seven months, that's it in fifteen years. I got a great place there, in Georgetown, gated community, all that crap, full of African masks, Arab carpets, Meissen porcelain . . ."

"What porcelain?"

"Fragments, anyway. Maid dropped most of it. A fridge full of champagne and one egg. You should stay there one day if you like, eat the egg. Really. May as well. Someone should."

Tom laughed. "Maybe I'll take you up on that one day."

"So what about Nina? She's a sweetheart. You should get in there. She got anyone?"

"I don't really know. Maybe. There is some guy but I don't really know what's going on there."

"What's his name?"

"Dunno."

"Serb?"

"Could be. Don't know."

"This is delicious. I'm gonna have another one." Morissey called the waiter over and ordered a cheese pie and two more beers. "So what have you been up to then," Sam said. "You said you were getting somewhere."

Tom told him about his escapade in New Belgrade, at the Crazy House, and then got to what he wanted to know. His account of the nighttime parking lot was a lot more humorous in the telling— all heads turned to them several times as they laughed—and he ended with a question: "So who would have saved us? Assuming he did? There were three of them, just eyeballing us. If the guy hadn't been there, who knows what would have happened. He was American."

"You're lucky," Sam said, picking the pastry crumbs off the plate. "You think he was someone just passing by?"

"Oh, right. In the dark, at half past two in the morning. Rambo out walking the dog."

"Who do you think he was? And why do you want to know?"

"To thank him, of course. Give him a reward. Seriously, what the hell's going on?"

"Why do you think I would know?"

"Because it's your job."

"Okay, how much is the reward?"

"Lunch."

"Good deal. Okay, you're paying. That would have been my guy out walking his dog."

"Really?"

"Yeah. Of course. What do you think? Look, I've told you before but you are just too dumb to get the message. So pay attention. You are rocking the boat. Rowing in deep waters. Up shit creek without a paddle. How many ways can I say this? You have upset the wrong people. So I'm having you followed. Keep you out of trouble. There's probably someone photographing us right now. The last thing the ambassador wants is a dead American reporter just when we're trying to show how democratic Serbia is becoming."

"So it's okay any other time?"

Morissey smiled and raised an eyebrow.

Tom sat back and let out a long breath. He considered Morissey with his gaze. This is getting out of hand. The bad guys are upset with me, the almost-as-bad guys are following me—what have I got myself into? As the waiter cleared the dishes, Tom said, "Do you want a fruit salad?"

Morissey nodded.

Tom's mind was racing. He had great material, Nina was as keen as him, he knew he would end up with a great doc. What could go wrong? He'd be done in a week or two and out of here. But what about Nina? What's going on between her and Aleks? A shoulder to cry on? More than that? He felt himself growing uncomfortable as he understood how much he hoped that she was not hiding something from him, something about Aleks and her, just as he and she were rediscovering each other. He thought of her watching him dress. Gotta lose some gut. He smiled at the thought of her.

"You haven't got much to smile about, you know," Morissey said. "So what are you going to do?"

"I'm going to Knin tomorrow."

Morissey changed before his eyes. His body tensed like a hunting dog's. "Why Knin?"

"I'm not sure, but we're setting up some interviews there. It's something I was told. Maybe it rings a bell with you? Somebody told me that the truth about Mladić lies between Knin and Srebren-ica. Knin is in Croatia, right, about seven hundred kilometers, a day or two's drive?"

"What's that got to do with finding Mladić?"

"That's what nobody seems to get. I'm not interested in find-ing Mladić. That'll never happen. What I'm interested in is why nobody else has found him. The government, the police. You guys, for that matter. There's a big cover-up going on and I want to find out what it is. I mean, why, after all these years, is it still so im-portant for some people to protect the guy? It isn't loyalty, that's for sure. In the Balkans loyalty won't get you a warm beer. They'd sell their grandmother for half a glass." *Thanks for the phrase, Aleks.* "This is a morally bankrupt region on several levels. Ev-eryone has sold each other out five times over, so it's hard to be-lieve that all these different groups are hiding Mladić just for old times' sake. There must be something very special about him, some very good reason to still hide him."

Morissey sighed and shook his head. "Tom, you are one stub-born son of a bitch. Why? If someone has such a good reason to hide Mladić, what's your reason to want to know why?"

Good question. Sam must have been talking to Nina. Tom leaned back in his chair and considered his answer. When it came, it came slowly, thoughtfully. Tom didn't often talk from the heart. Who with? "Sam, how long have we known each other?"

"Twenty years?"

"About that. We've had our ups and downs, both of us, right?"

Morissey snorted. "You got that right."

"Well, in all honesty, I've had a ten-year down. Longer. And it's too long. You know what happened to me, right, everyone does; I'm a poster boy for depression, post-traumatic stress, all the rest."

"You sure look like shit. I'm joking. Sorry. Sure, Tom. We've all been there."

"Not like this, trust me. Anyway, there's a couple things going right for me right now. Nina, I don't know what will happen there, but we have a connection, something so real . . . Nothing has happened between us, but I feel it, I hope she feels the same. I don't know yet. And the film. I really care about this. It is a shame on our world that Mladić has not been brought to justice. But I guess what really drives me there, if I'm honest, is it's personal. For me, and for Nina too, and it's pushing us together. We both feel the same. You know what I mean, better than anyone, when we got back to Sarajevo. I'll never forget that, Sam, how you helped us. And you took care of Nick's body. It's a special bond we have, Sam, you and me, and Nina is part of it. So this film, it's a way of putting things right. It's a way of getting Nina and me out of the hole. It's about time, too. It didn't start like that but I feel that when this film is done, I'll be all right again, and so will she. And maybe we'll get together, like we should have before, before Nick and all that. You know what I mean?"

"You mean, you need this film?"

"Yes. Yes, I guess so."

"To heal?"

"Exactly, yes."

"To release the inner you."

"Well, I wouldn't—"

"Give me a fucking break. Where do you get this New Age crap from? I told you, you're not going to get healed, you're gonna get Vlad the Impaler up your ass with a rod and a hammer."

They were physical opposites, the large man slumped behind the desk and Sam Morissey, slim and erect. What they shared was a life in the shadows and, occasionally, when their national interests merged, information.

Darko Panic, whose name appeared comical on paper but who Morissey had learned was a man not to cross, invited him to sit. "Thank you for seeing me so quickly," Morissey said, accepting a cigarette and lighting up. After some brief agency gossip, he outlined Tom's plan to visit Knin, and what he hoped to find there. "It's an interesting phrase," Panic repeated, drumming his fingers on the desk. "'The truth about Mladić lies between Knin and Srebrenica.'"

"Yes, it is; this reporter is barking up the right fucking tree."

"You say he is a friend of yours. Does this complicate matters?"

"No."

"I was there, you know that? In '95. July to August."

"Yes, I know."

"I was with General Mile Mrksic in the north of the Krajina. We fought bravely but we were overwhelmed."

"I know you were. I was in Sarajevo, attached to the UN."

"I know you were."

They both laughed, the inference clear; they knew a good deal about each other. It was their job.

Panic leaned back in his chair, puffing on his cigarette. Here we go, Morissey thought. Storytime.

"It was the biggest land battle in Europe since World War Two, you know that?"

Tom nodded. *I'll give him three minutes.*

Knin, once home to twelve thousand Serbs, had been the capital of the Serb enclave in Croatia—a hundred and twenty thousand Serbs surrounded by four million Croats. The Croatian army, fighting for independence from Serbia, attacked the Serb enclave with two hundred thousand men, outnumbering the Serb

fighters five to one. They needed a swift victory before Serb reinforcements arrived but failed to overcome the brave Serbs until
suddenly, inexplicably, the Serbs fled.

It was never fully understood why they yielded.

It appeared their hero, though, was Darko Panic, who by now
was executing daring pincer movements with pens, pads, and the
telephone serving as the capital, Knin. Morissey nodded, applauding his exploits, until he felt a yawn coming and finally interrupted.

"So, anyway, this reporter, Tom Layne."

"We have to stop him."

"Yes."

"You have warned him?"

"Of course. He's stubborn as a goat."

"Leave him to me."

"No, that isn't what I meant. Or rather, it is, but be careful. The
ambassador doesn't want an international incident here. And listen, he's traveling with a girl. Do not touch her, understand?
Leave her out of it."

"A pretty girl?" Panic stubbed out his cigarette. "Leave them
to me."

Tom and Nina set off at dawn. Taking turns at the wheel, they
crossed into Bosnia, stopping for lunch, for old times' sake, on
Modrac Lake in Tuzla, which had been the headquarters of US
forces in Bosnia. Seeing the soldiers all bulked up in their flak
jackets and helmets and boots, local kids had called the American presence "the invasion of the Ninja Turtles."

They continued along the valley floor and through the forests
to Banja Luka, becoming progressively more silent the deeper
they drove into the past.

Banja Luka, which trips prettily off the tongue, was a byword for Serb atrocities, thanks to the nearby Manjača concentration camp, where rape became a weapon of war. Sixty thousand Bosniaks and Croats were forced from Banja Luka or fled for their lives—so-called ethnic cleansing. The ten years of intense fighting that dismembered Yugoslavia largely passed the city by, yet when they drove past the house where they had spent a memorable month with Nick in the early nineties, reporting on a massacre here, mass rapes there, shooting and shelling everywhere, they passed with only a glance.

Houses along the way still stood in ruins. The romantic journey Tom had envisioned through green valleys, frolicking naked in cool springs, became a dour drive. He wanted to ask Nina about Aleks but was afraid of the answer. Surely if they were an item she'd have said so?

When they finally reached Knin late at night, hungry and wrung out, to find the Ivan Hotel had only one room left, a double, and the restaurant kitchen was closed, they had no strength to look elsewhere. All they could do was beg the receptionist for cold cuts and beer and fall on the bed without unpacking.

They took turns in the bathroom and when Tom came out in pajamas, showered and ready for sleep, Nina was already tucked up in bed.

Her eyes were half closed, a mischievous smile played on her lips, her hair flowed around her. The blanket clung to her as if she had smoothed it down, molding to her body. His eyes sparkled and a smile began to spread.

"Well, well, what have we here?" he said. "Am I invited? And what is the dress code?"

Nina slowly and lasciviously lowered the blanket, inch by inch, her eyes locked on Tom's, her hair flowing, his blood rising, only to reveal her blue pajama top, buttoned to the neck like a little girl's. She laughed and wriggled to make room, just as there was a sharp knock on the door.

"Room service?" he said.

"Hope so, I'm starving."

Another rap, too hard and fast to be polite. Tom lifted the little metal cover and peered through the spy hole. A man in a white jacket.

He adjusted his trousers, opened the door, and the receptionist entered carrying a tray of sausages, cheeses, and bread, with two bottles of beer. "Don't touch the plate," the man said, placing it on the desk, "it's very hot. Don't know why. The food is cold."

They sat up in bed and ate and drank like a married couple. "You're making crumbs," Nina said, brushing them onto the floor.

"Careful," Tom said, "you'll knock my beer over."

"Then don't leave it on the bed, put it on the table," Nina said, leaning over Tom and placing his bottle on the nightstand. "Who stands a bottle on the bed? It's bound to fall over. Then the sheet will be all wet."

"God, you're such a nag." Tom took it back. "This is how to stop a beer from spilling." He drained it and sighed, lying back, his hands folded on his stomach. He opened his mouth as Nina looked at him. She said, "Please tell me you're not going to burp."

Tom laughed. "Actually, I was going to ask you something."

"What?"

Aleks? "Shall we make love?"

"I beg your pardon?"

"Shall we make love? We've had dinner in bed, there's nothing on television, we may as well make love."

"I've got a headache."

"Really?"

"No."

"Don't you want to?"

"Watch television?"

"No. Make love."

"Yes."

"Yes what?"

"I want to make love."

"Really?"

"What time is it?"

Taken unawares, Tom looked at his watch and yawned. "It's twelve forty. We've been on the road all day." Another loud yawn.

His yawn made Nina yawn, after which she said, "You're too tired. If you were younger it would be all right, but it's your sleepy time."

Tom lay flat and curled up. "No, you're quite wrong," he murmured. His eyes closed and Nina could just make out the slurred words, "Let's make love, before you change your mind," and his voice became a drone and Tom was fast asleep.

Nina watched as the smile faded ever so slowly, leaving his lips parted and his eyelids relaxed and his cheeks too, and his breathing was slow and even. He would have sweet dreams tonight, she thought. Her own eyes closed, even as she remained sitting against the backboard, and there they were, in her mind's eye, holding hands so long ago, as she had watched him in his bed in Sarajevo. I've seen Tom come out of sleep and now I've seen him go to sleep, she thought, but I've never slept with him.

She edged down the bed, fluffed up her pillow, turned off the light, and snuggled against his back. She took his hand and recoiled. It was a fist, hard as rock.

She turned onto her back, her eyes open, disturbed by his

hand's roughness, so at odds with the loose surrender of his sleep. Was he already having a bad dream? His clenched hand told the true story. His body was at rest but even in sleep his tense, alert brain was sending a signal to his extremity, to his weapon, to his fist, and it made her sad. Did she too sleep on the edge of fear? Is that why her bed was always such a mess in the morning, half the covering on the floor, pillow at her feet? Did he cry out in his sleep? She knew she did, her lovers told her; she sometimes even changed her top in the middle of the night, she perspired so much, even in winter. They say time helps. Really?

Lying here now with Tom, holding his fist, she felt her breathing quicken as it all came back, yet again. One of them had tried to be gentle, which was even more disgusting, and she heard herself shouting, sobbing, and then panting, as she surrendered, unsouled.

Nina wiped the sweat from her brow and realized she was gripping Tom's hand as tightly as his was clenched.

She felt her way to the bathroom and splashed her face with cold water and dried herself. Leaning over the sink, she caught herself in the mirror, by the streetlight's bluish tint through the window. Awful. Those lines around the eyes, the crevice between them, her unruly hair with their gray roots. She shook her head slowly at her reflection, and looked through the door at the outline of Tom sleeping, and she wondered: Had they really come all this way just for a few minutes of video?

Yes.

No.

It was for more than that.

For what then?

Back in bed, after climbing in carefully, not to awaken him, she took Tom's hand again and stroked it gently, for a long time, until she felt his grip begin to soften and the fingers uncurl and heard the pattern of his breathing change too and in this way, breathing together, she fell asleep at last.

But it was not to be a quiet sleep, for again the mountain closed in, rain poured into the valley, waters rose, suffocating her like a hand gripping her mouth, she could only fight to breathe through her nose. Nina woke with a start. She sensed an absence, and just as she remembered where she was and felt with her hand and found herself alone in the bed she heard the toilet flush and the bathroom door opened and she followed Tom's light footsteps to their bed.

As he pulled the cover over himself and settled down she murmured, "I'm awake." Tom didn't answer but pulled her to him and hugged her from behind, warm and strong.

"Thank you," she whispered.

Tom smiled to himself, and answered, "Me too."

She wriggled backwards, pressing herself into him, and pulled his hand to her chest and kissed it. She sighed.

"It's strange, isn't it?" he said.

"No."

He kissed her neck and she shivered.

"Tom?"

"Yes?"

"Do you think about it sometimes?"

"It?"

"You know."

He sighed. "Put it this way. Sometimes I don't think about . . . it."

As they lay quietly in the dark, Nina felt her eyes heat and a tear form and it traveled slowly down her cheek, followed by another, until her tears tickled Tom's hand and he held her while she cried. Finally she said, "I used to cry a lot. It made me sick, I would cry and then be sick. Can I tell you something?"

"Yes."

"I haven't told anyone this before."

"If not me, who?"

She fell silent and Tom waited, listening to her breathing, and gently kissed her neck again.

"You can tell me," he said. *Maybe I can tell you too.*

"I went through a bad period," she said, finally, "don't think badly of me."

"I won't. What happened to you?" he said. "Tell me."

She sighed. "At first, after you left, and I went home, my friends were good, they tried to help, but I pushed them away. I couldn't tell them what happened, and so I couldn't bear to hear them ask. And then, I went a bit crazy, I suppose. Looking back on that time, it's as if anything ordinary wasn't enough for me. Everything I did I went too far. I drank too much, smoked too much, lots of hash. And sex. Lots of sex. With men I hardly knew. I didn't want to see anyone twice. But it was like I was punishing myself. Tom. Is it all right if I tell you this?"

"Yes."

"I have to tell someone, I have to say it." She began to cry, but shuddered and stopped. "Goran, my husband, I wanted him to beat me. While we made love. He wouldn't. I hit him instead, I provoked him, until he held me down, held my arms to stop me hitting him, and he made love to me while I was pressed down, and the harder he held me, the better it was. It was sick. I hated myself."

Tom had gone cold, and as Nina went on and on, describing the acts in more detail than he cared for, he wished she would stop.

But who am I to judge? he thought. She was as angry and lost as I was. I should have dealt with it through rough sex too; at least it would have been more fun.

"And you?" he heard her say. "What about you, Tom, tell me what happened to you. What really happened."

"It's my turn, is it?"

"Yes. I told you, now you tell me."

"You've never told anyone that before?"

"No."

"And is there more?"

"Oh, yes." She tried to laugh. "But another time. Tom, tell me about you."

She turned around and pushed Tom until he turned too and now Nina held Tom from behind, her arm around his waist, and he held her hand in his. "Go on, tell me something."

"What? What do you want to hear?"

"What do you want to tell me?"

"Nothing. What's to say? You know I lost my job and all that. Went off the rails a bit. It took me a long time to admit anything was wrong, that I needed help. You know, people don't really want to hear about your problems. 'How are you?' God forbid you should tell them."

Nina squeezed his hand. "Tell me about your girlfriends. Is there anyone special?"

"What, today?"

"Yes."

"Yes, there is, actually."

"Really?" He felt her body tense, her hand tighten. "Tell me about her."

"Actually, you may know her."

"Really?" That got her attention. "Who? That producer? Amber?"

Tom smiled. "No, taller. More beautiful."

"Who?" Nina tried to remember who else had come with Tom to the Balkans.

"Sort of chubby, a little bit. Sweet face. A bit messed up, but then who isn't? Curly hair. Clever. Funny. Sexy as hell."

After a tense pause: "You want to know who she is?"

"No." *Yes.*

"You."

"Me?"

"Yes. You. You're my special girl. There's no one else."

Nina didn't respond, but her body spoke for her. She seemed to melt into him and her fingers uncurled from his and her hand lay across his stomach, familiar, careless. Now was the time to ask about Aleks, he thought, but as she sighed deeply and he felt her warm breath on his neck, and it became even and long and after another long sigh and more gentle breathing he understood that Nina had fallen asleep. He felt her warmth embrace him and before long he joined her.

A few hours later, after sheepish glances over coffee and eggs, after filming general scenes in town and up at the Knin fortress, from where ruled at different times the Croats, Hungarians, Venetians, Turks, Austrians, French, and Serbs, after getting lost and after several telephone explanations from Dusan Grubor, they found the old man's home at midday. His stone cottage on the outskirts of town reminded Nina of her mother's home. Its garden was thick with wild bushes and sweet-smelling almond trees; the entrance door to the house was made of thick wooden planks. A doleful dog barely budged as they walked up the pebbled path. Tom had to step over him.

But when Grubor opened the door, Tom could have taken his

head in his hands and kissed his crown. If anyone wanted a Serb from central casting, and Tom did, here he was. Grubor's nicotine-stained gray mustache flew out like wings, his ears and eyebrows did the same from a florid, wind-beaten face, and his thick white hair was topped by the national hat, the woolen Sajkaca, which sat on his head like a vee-shaped boat, in battleship gray. Braces over a white linen shirt held up his shapeless black trousers. In ethnically cleansed Knin, where Croats had kicked out the native Serbs a decade earlier, he may as well have worn a sign around his neck with the words *I am the last proud Serb and I will not be moved.*

The corridor's uneven ceiling was low and whitewashed, with cracked wooden beams, and a wall was lined with woolen coats on hooks.

Grubor invited them in with an expansive gesture and made a lecher's show of remembering Nina. Tom slid by carrying a backpack with his camera gear.

While Grubor limped off—*an old war wound*—to the kitchen to make coffee, Tom moved the sofa so that light from the window would fall on the corner where he would seat Grubor, and he pulled up a chair for himself. He set up a small sun gun on a stand behind the sofa to light the peeling wall, with its ragged display of framed family photos, and set up the camera on the tripod by his chair. As always, he would shoot the interview himself, while asking the questions. Nina would translate.

"That didn't take long; we're ready whenever you are, Mr. Grubor," she said as he entered with a tray of coffee and biscuits, and a bottle of brandy. Just as they toasted each other, and as he began to say that he was expecting his wife at any moment, the door opened and in she came, an elderly lady with a white bonnet covering her hair, followed by two big young men.

"My sons," he said proudly. "Here for mother's home cooking. They surprised us, they're staying just a few days. They live in Belgrade." Their bulk filled the small room and blocked the natural window light but they quickly excused themselves to eat in the kitchen.

Grubor loved to talk about the good old days, yet didn't have much opportunity with his Croat neighbors. When the Serbs controlled Knin he had worked in the mayor's office in community relations, which had mostly meant persuading the Croats to leave town. It wasn't difficult. Serb militiamen posted pamphlets naming certain Croat families as traitors and within days the families had fled. New pamphlets went up each week, all over town.

This happened throughout Krajina, where Serbs had lived alongside Croats for hundreds of years until Yugoslavia broke up in 1991. Seizing the moment, Serbs grabbed about a third of Croatia, dreaming of linking with their brothers and sisters in Serbia and Bosnia to carve out at last their mythical "Greater Serbia."

Yet when the Croatian army struck back four years later, in the summer of '95, Knin collapsed within thirty-six hours and the self-proclaimed Republic of Serbian Krajina collapsed with it.

Why?

Why did the undefeated and ferociously proud Serb fighters just melt away?

That was Tom's question for Dusan Grubor.

For when they did, a hundred and fifty thousand Serb refugees fled too, driving cars, tractors, pushing carts with their possessions, running for their lives, their dream of an expanded Serb homeland in tatters.

Tom hoped this colorful old Serb would have some answers: Why did Knin fold so quickly? Where were the Serb reinforcements? And above all, what did that have to do with the continuing freedom of Ratko Mladić?

Later, the part of the interview that Tom marked for use seemed to raise more questions than it answered. But as he listened to it back in Belgrade, he could only shake his head in wonder at the perfect, if shocking, way the interview had come to a sudden close.

Grubor, whose weathered peasant face called out for the viewer to believe every word, was jabbing with his finger. "Where was the army? So? Where was the Yugoslav army? Milosevic was behind every move we made, we got orders at the mayor's office from his liaison officers, everything we did was coordinated with Belgrade. They helped us plan our defenses of the city. Get ammunition. Stock up on food. And then when the Croats attacked, in fact even before, his officers ran and we were on our own. Where were the reinforcements? Ha, all talk, they sold us out." He puffed angrily on his carved pipe as the ash glowed and clouds of sweet apple smoke enveloped them all.

"So, why didn't they?" Tom had prompted.

"We were betrayed, that's why. I know for a fact that the plan was to keep fighting until the Yugoslav army came to help, a day or two at most, and also General Mladić, but nobody came. They betrayed us. Why? I don't know. So much for Greater Serbia."

Whenever Grubor paused, Tom looked at Nina for a translation.

As she leaned forward and spoke into the microphone, she accepted another small cup of coffee from one of the Grubor sons. In his massive hand the cup looked like a dollhouse miniature.

When she finished translating, Tom asked another question. The camera was focused tightly on the wonderfully expressive face of old Dusan Grubor and he heard his own voice off camera, leading up to his key question.

"So the Yugoslav army didn't come to help. But it wasn't really their war, was it? It was the war of the local Serbs. So what about General Mladić. Ratko Mladić was the local Serb army leader. Were you expecting help from him?"

"Of course!" Grubor almost shouted. His face began to twitch, his mustache, his eyebrows, his ears. "Don't you understand? It was the big betrayal. He was afraid. Some hero! Where was he when we needed him? He was the traitor, do you know what it looked like here? There were bodies everywhere, people running . . ."

"But why? Why wouldn't he come to the rescue? He wanted a Serb land here, no?" Tom asked, pushing for more information, hoping for the money bite.

"Look, everyone here knows, there must have been a deal. A deal that the Serbs made, Milosevic, Mladić, I don't know, someone, maybe both, with the Croats. They sold us out, Martić and Babić were pawns."

"The local Serb leaders," Tom interrupted, explaining for future viewers. "One was a dentist, the other a policeman. Both indicted for war crimes."

"Outrageous! Martić was extradited to The Hague, Babić committed suicide. I knew them both well, a tragedy. It was no coincidence that neither Milosevic nor Mladić came to help. They sold us down the river. Who to? Why? I don't know. You find out. They're traitors, all of them. Traitors."

And then Tom heard, on the tape, his phone ring. He had fumbled to turn it off, recognizing the US number of the network news desk in New York. It was their third call. He'd already ignored them twice in two days. What do they want? He hadn't heard from them in months.

Just as he had apologized for forgetting to turn off the phone, there was a loud knock on the door, followed by shouting.

It was instinct now. He slid the catch on the tripod and took the camera in his hand, still rolling from the interview.

Grubor looked in surprise and alarm at the door, which flew open.

Three men in jeans and leather jackets—It's a friggin' uniform, Tom thought as he watched the tape later—pushed into the room, shouting at the old man. Nina jumped up in alarm. Tom stood too, pressing his back against the wall, pulling wide on the lens. Grubor remained in his seat, shocked. There was more shouting as Grubor pulled himself to his feet, trembling, outraged at the intrusion into his home. One of the men stepped toward him and pushed him and his bad leg buckled. He grabbed the arm of his chair and fell back into it.

Then Tom was surprised. The other two men ignored Grubor and came straight for him. On the tape there was a sudden movement and shake and from a wide shot showing the drama in the living room, dark shapes loomed forward and blocked the lens. It was the bodies of the two men, one of whom grabbed Tom by the jacket and spun him around and raised a fist.

"Hey, get off," Tom shouted, and pulled away, breaking the man's grip. The camera recorded a whirl of motion and flashes of face, legs, floor, furniture, and then it was all a spinning blur as the camera fell and settled on its side, showing furniture and legs horizontal to the ground.

Just as the man moved in again, with Nina and Grubor shouting, the kitchen door burst open and Grubor's two huge sons took it all in with a glance. One ducked back into the kitchen while the other lunged at the man holding Tom and threw him into the chair, which clattered against the wall. The man stumbled but quickly recovered, his hand went into his jacket and came out with a knife, a long hunting knife, which he held at arm's length while he stood, panting. He shouted something and gestured to the son to get out of the way.

Then the second son was in the room, followed by his mother's wide eyes peering around his massive frame. He had a hunting rifle at his waist and pointed it at the legs of the man with the knife. He shouted at him and the meaning was clear. Tom had the camera in his hand again, and as he watched the tape later, he thought of a good line for the wide shot of the confrontation: "A hunting rifle against a hunting knife, no contest."

More shouting in Serbian, or Croatian, Tom didn't know which. The men looked at Tom and Nina with hatred, and at old Grubor, tense in his chair, and said something, and they were gone.

There was a moment of stunned silence as they all looked at the open door, then at each other, before everyone started talking and shouting at the same time. Mrs. Grubor ran to her husband, who brushed her away and struggled to his feet.

The two sons were now at the door, shouting after the men, while Tom filmed them from behind, their animated frames filling the doorway.

He glanced at Nina and suppressed a grin. "Got it all," he said, and couldn't help himself. He laughed out loud and shouted, "This is great stuff."

By three o'clock they had drained two bottles of homemade brandy.

The Grubors were puzzled. The men had barged in shouting at Dusan to stop spreading lies, but there was nothing new about that. The neighbors didn't like Dusan Grubor, partly because he was a Serb but mostly because he was an ignorant conspiracy theorist who insulted the Croats by arguing that they had done a deal with the Serbs; no Croat would do that, they had won the war fair and square, they had reinstated exclusive Croat control of their own land for the first time since 1080 through brains, brawn, and bravery, not skullduggery.

But the strange thing about the attack was that the three men were not neighbors and they weren't shouting about glorious King Dmitar Zvonimir, whose thousand-year-old image hung at the entrance to town. They were strangers. Grubor had been their excuse, but Tom was clearly their target, and if it wasn't for the spontaneous visit by the two sons, who had decided to surprise their parents, it could have all ended very badly indeed.

Instead it ended with two empty bottles of brandy and Nina pleading with old Grubor not to open another one. He insisted, almond slivovitz, he'd made it with the nuts from the garden, unique to the house, can't buy it anywhere, and only when Igor, the younger son, said he'd take the bottle for the road did his father give up and ask his wife for coffee.

Grubor was in fine fettle, after all the excitement. "He'd have shot him too," he insisted, laughing at Igor, who had fetched the gun. "Right, Igor?"

"Of course not," he said. "You think I want to get into trouble? I'd have smashed him on the head with it." They laughed uproariously, as they had for an hour already. "Do you know why we named him Igor?" Grubor said.

"Not again." Igor smiled.

"After Frankenstein's lab assistant. When he was born we thought he had a hunchback, but he didn't. Nice name though." Grubor laughed so hard his lower teeth popped out until he pushed them back in with his tongue.

They decided that the elder son would stay with his parents, in case the men came back, and Igor would drive with Tom and Nina back to Belgrade. He was going the next day anyway; this way he had a lift.

His bulk filled the whole backseat of the small rental car, and they felt safer with him. "If they do anything again, I'll hit them with the almond slivovitz," Igor told his father as they parted in front of the house. "Even worse for them, they can drink it."

They set off at four in the afternoon to drive through the night when the roads were clear. Nina and Igor soon fell asleep but Tom was deep in thought.

Those three guys. Only the BIA would have sent them. They must be following me, or tapping my phone or something. Not so unusual in Eastern Europe. There was that time in Prague he got lost at Hlavní Nádraží station and couldn't find the platform for the train to Prešov. He smiled at the memory. A complete stranger came up and said: "Platform eleven."

Still, these guys attacked me. They bungled it. They won't bungle it again.

He looked in the mirror at Igor, who now was staring out of the window, and at Nina sleeping. I should stop being so selfish. Nina should not be involved. For that matter, nor should I. But . . . but . . .

The BIA want me off the story. Why?

They're hiding Mladić? Okay, but so what? Everybody already believes that, so what is so special about this doc that they want to stop me badly enough to threaten and hurt me? I'm on to something. But what?

What am I missing?

As trees flashed by and the headlights lit up the road that wound through sleeping villages, dark since nine P.M., he went through everything he had learned, and always returned to the same conclusion: Grubor must be right. There must have been a deal. And probably still is.

And it all came down to Mladić, commander of the Bosnian Serb army. If he didn't come to the rescue of the Knin Serbs, was that because he didn't want to, or because someone told him not to?

That's the story. Who? Why? It must be something big. Secret. Enough for the BIA to want Mladić out of circulation. Alive but quiet.

And what about this: Why did the Serb forces pull out of Knin so suddenly? Why did they resist the Croats well, and then suddenly pull the plug? The deal must have included them.

If I can find out why, that could lead me to what it's really all about: why nobody wants to find Europe's biggest killer since World War II.

The BIA shows I'm on the right road. But they know why and I don't.

What am I missing?

Gotta find out soon, very soon, before I get hurt.

What about Nina?

He took his eyes off the road to glance at her again. Still fast asleep, her head sunk into a pillow against the door. His eyes darted back to the road and back again to Nina. Yes, she's dribbling. A smudge of drool at the corner of her mouth glinted when moonlight pierced the trees and lit up, for an instant, the interior of the car.

He smiled as he drove.

A few kisses, some hugs, that's all there's been. A night in bed talking. A kiss twelve years ago.

And I never got over her.

Nobody gets me like she does. Last night with her was the best sleep in years, even if we only slept three or four hours. And she'd said the same.

He sighed as he drove. Settle down? With Nina?

It's time.

Don't lose her again, you bloody idiot.

At four in the morning they crossed the dark Sava river, houseboat lights sparkling like stars, and drove through the deserted Belgrade streets to Aleks's apartment.

It was two days before Tom saw Nina again; she had gone to see Sasha at her mother's place outside town. He had been busy shooting pretty pictures of the castle, the river, the pedestrian center in Belgrade, and doing a couple of interviews in poor English. They hadn't given him much, but the second one, a government official reborn as a Serb Orthodox priest, had given him a lead: a former colonel in military intelligence who ran a private think tank. "He always surprises you with his ideas," the priest had said. "And he knows a lot. Fluent English too."

Killing time until he had to leave to meet the colonel, Tom was drinking coffee and reading Ivo Andrić's *The Bridge on the Drina* and wishing he could write like that when his cell phone rang. The caller ID showed the news desk in New York. Again. He sighed and put the book down. May as well take it, couldn't keep hiding.

"Mr. Layne?"

Someone new. "Yes."

"Just a moment, please, I have Amber Brooks for you." There was a clicking sound and beeps as the call was transferred. *Just a moment please, I have Amber Brooks for you.* Gimme a break. Now the assistants have assistants.

Actually, he knew Amber was nobody's assistant, never had been. She was a tough cookie and he liked her, always had. Great field producer, and he'd heard that ever since she left London for New York she had moved steadily up the ranks. At least one person there knew what she was doing. What could she want to talk about? A story idea? He put his feet up and sipped his coffee.

"Tom, you there? At last. You're hard to get hold of, we've been calling you for days, why didn't you call back?"

"Why should I? Didn't you get the memo? I don't work for you guys anymore."

"That's what I wanted to talk to you about. Did you hear the news?"

"Guess not. What?"

"There's been a bit of a shake-up around here."

"That's news? Who have they fired now? You?"

"Not exactly. Guess what? Boone is out."

"You're kidding me! How did he ever last so long?"

"Guess who's taking over?"

"How should I know? I've been long gone. Someone from outside?"

"Me."

"You? Really? They gave you the job? Executive vice president, whatever?"

"Yes."

"Wow. Well, truthfully, that's the first good move they've made in a long time. You'll be great, I mean it. Well done, Amber. All those executive meetings though, you'll have to mind your language."

"Fuck off!"

They laughed; old mates from the field. Amber had been one of the few who persisted when Tom had gone off the rails, she had kept trying to break through his armor, phoning, even dropping by unannounced. But it didn't do any good, and eventually Tom had moved apartments and dropped out of sight altogether. Until about four years ago when he had started offering freelance reports and documentaries, mostly to PBS and Discovery, but sometimes to the network. His very first doc, which he shot himself, on the surprisingly low percentage of humanitarian aid that actually reached the people that needed it, that wasn't swallowed up by so-called administrative expenses and first-class travel for NGO executives, had won him his third IRE award for investigative reporting, his first as a freelancer.

He was back, but the rap was that he was hard to deal with. That was strictly for the executives though; anybody who worked with him in the field loved him.

"So listen," Amber went on. "Fancy title and all, but in addition to overall news coverage, I'm in charge of hiring and firing now."

"Well, you can't fire me, they already did."

"No. But I can fucking hire you."

Pause.

Extended pause.

"Oh no. I don't think so," Tom said.

"Listen, this is the long and the short of it. You're still the best foreign correspondent around, and we want you back. Okay?"

"You're just blowing smoke up my ass."

"Second best, then. After Jim Maceda at NBC."

"Now I know you're shittin' me."

"Did you see his Afghan series? His stuff from Russia? That's what we should be doing. Look, think about it, will you? Chief foreign correspondent. You get the title back. A serious raise from last time. Think it over, will you?"

"How long have you had the job?"

"Three days."

"And you called me three days ago?"

"Tom, you were the first call I made."

It may have been because his mind was still on Amber's offer that Tom almost missed the colonel's bombshell. They were seated at Vuk Vlachs's desk, in his crowded corner office in the Serb Institute for Military and Security Research, in the hills of Topčider, near the cemetery, when Colonel Vlachs answered a question about the fall of Knin by saying the army of Ratko Mladić was too busy in Srebrenica. But just then Tom had had a sudden insight into Amber's offer: if she decided so quickly to bring him back on board, and she had mentioned a good raise, and he really was her first call, then she must be desperate and he could parlay that into real money, which God knows he needed. Freelance documentaries barely kept him in cigarettes, and that was after he cut back to a pack a day. But did he honestly want a real job again?

He was about to follow up with a planned question on how come the Croats had managed to field two hundred thousand troops, five times the number of Serb defenders in Krajina, when he realized what he had just heard. He zoomed in for a tighter shot of the colonel's face. His graying hair was short and swept back, his eyes were set deep in a tanned, lined face. His pipe had gone out in his hand.

"Srebrenica? Too busy in Srebrenica, you said?"

"It seems so. It is very strange. Just when Croatian troops were moving into Krajina in the summer of '95, Mladić takes three Serb army brigades out and concentrates them in Srebrenica almost three hundred miles away. Next thing, Croatian troops take Knin and kick out the Serbs, unhindered. And what is Mladić up to? He's kicking out the Muslims from the east, also unhindered. Moreover, for some reason that nobody understands, the Muslim military leaders left Srebrenica weeks before the Serb attack, even though everyone knew the Serbs would attack Srebrenica at any moment."

Tom adjusted the exposure to compensate for a sudden drop in natural light. A cloud must have drifted across the sun.

"Think of it," the colonel went on. "The Serbs are kicked out of the west, where they were a minority. And in the east, the Moslems are kicked out, where they were a minority too. In both cases, two minorities leave, putting up no real resistance, after their armies all but abandon them. It's too neat. Ask yourself: Why did the winners have it so easy?"

"I don't know. So why did they?"

"Because there must have been some kind of agreement, a deal."

"To do what?"

"My guess? Educated guess: they agreed to ethnically cleanse the east and west, without a fight. Each side gets its territory clean of the worrisome local minority."

The light went on. "And it all went wrong," Tom put in, "when Mladić suddenly massacred nine thousand Muslims who hadn't left yet. Who had nobody to protect them, because the leaders left days before. Mladić was supposed to let them leave too? Instead, he killed them."

"Exactly."

"But who made the deal?"

"That's the big question. Because nobody admits to it."

"And the reason they don't admit to it," Tom said slowly,

underlining what he knew would be the key moment in the interview, emphasizing it for the audience, "is that whoever made the deal is responsible, even if indirectly, for the Srebrenica massacre? Europe's worst mass killing since World War Two."

"That's what I think. And ethnic cleansing. But I can't prove it."

"And who could?" Tom zoomed into an even tighter close-up.

"Only the man who did it. And nobody can find him."

"And who would that be?"

"General Ratko Mladić."

Behind the camera Tom smiled. *Jackpot. Music. End of part two. Cue commercials.*

In her apartment later that evening, Nina had one big objection to what Tom had learned. "It's too complicated. Nobody can follow this, especially a television audience; they won't have enough time to absorb it. Look, the Croats defeat the Serbs in Krajina, the Serbs massacre the Muslims in Bosnia, but what have the Croats got to do with the Muslims, and the Serbs with everybody else? Who's making a deal with whom? And why? And who cares? It's history. It's too much, you've lost me, and I live here!"

Tom laughed and poured another brandy. "True. But you know what, I do. I care, because of Nick. And us. And everyone I ever met here when we worked the story for five years or more. And more reasons too. And don't forget, if the BIA is so desperate to stop us, there must be a good reason. But let's leave it for a bit." He looked around the room. "Nice apartment." It was the first time she had invited him in. "Where did you get all your stuff?"

A sheepish smile played on Nina's lips. "Sort of a combination. The Turkish rugs are all from Goran, he gave them to me when we split." Several were spread randomly on the parquet floor, another draped the sofa, and a kilim with desert browns and dull orange, like rust, covered the table. "Or rather," she said with a shrug, "I took them. Most of the furniture too. We're still friends. He's a good dad for Sasha." She paused, and she said again, her voice trailing off, "I was the problem, not him . . ."

As Tom chewed that over, she said, "Are you hungry? Would you like some eggs?"

"A little. Maybe . . . uh . . ."

"Fried?"

Tom followed Nina into the kitchen where she cooked some eggs and prepared a salad while Tom burned the toast. They heated a bowl of vegetable soup Nina had brought home from her mother—"Organic, picked by Sasha in her garden."

They talked about how cheeky Sasha was becoming and her mother's interfering; and the new mortgage rate, which Nina was trying to reduce; and Tom told her of Amber's offer, which excited Nina. She said a steady job with a top network was her dream, better than arranging the same old interviews and stories for the foreign media, who all thought they were so smart and original: "'I've got a great idea.' Yawn, yawn. 'A documentary on Ratko Mladić.' Boring!" Tom chuckled. She went on, imitating his accent. "Lissen to mah noo geeniuhs approach: Waa nobody caan faand him, it's scandalous!" Now Tom had to grip the counter, he was laughing so hard.

When they had eaten, Nina took a cigarette from Tom and fell onto the sofa next to him.

"What about the briki?" he said, striking a match.

"The what?"

"The briki."

Nina followed Tom's eyes to the top of the packed bookshelves and the line of coffee pots with long thin handles. "Oh, don't say briki, that'll get you in trouble with the Turks. Briki is the Greek word. We say dezva. They're nice though, right? It's hard to find real copper and brass ones these days, they're all aluminum or stainless steel. Would you like some good Turkish coffee?"

"Oh, no thanks, it would keep me awake all night."

"That's the idea."

Tom laughed and took Nina's hand. "Why, what do you mean?"

She stood and unpinned her hair to let it fall loosely onto her shoulders, running her fingers through it. "I'll get some drinks instead." As Nina went back into the kitchen, Tom took off his shoes and stretched out on the sofa, his feet up on the leather ottoman. *I could get used to this.* Minutes later Nina returned with a bottle of wine and two glasses. "Make yourself at home," she said, "why don't you."

"Maybe I will. And why don't you slip into something comfortable?"

"Clark Gable? Humphrey Bogart?"

"Possibly someone stole the line from me."

"You know, I think maybe I will." She had returned from a meeting at her bank and was wearing a black linen trouser suit and an embroidered white on white blouse that Tom, as she poured the wine, was thankful was opened to the second button. Flimsy lacy black bras, best guide to character.

He watched Nina as she kicked off her heels and walked into her bedroom, and moments later he heard the sprinkling of the shower. He smiled to himself. Should he walk in, surprise her? Or would it even be a surprise? Probably not. The surprise would be if he didn't.

Such sweet tension, he thought. Without realizing, he had pulled himself up and sat erect on the sofa as if about to meet his girlfriend's father. He observed himself: his breathing had quickened, like an anxious boy.

He wondered, What will she wear? Anything? Balkan girls: so delightfully retro, romance is romance, candles, perfume, slinky see-through, scanty clothes, they're not afraid to be sexy, to enjoy their bodies and display their womanhood. Cigarettes, chocolates, and cognac. Painted nails and false eyelashes. He shifted in anticipation. He looked at himself: the usual, jeans and a sweater, his jacket thrown over an armchair. Have to smarten up my act. Especially if I take Amber up on her offer. Which I won't. Or will I? If I can do longer pieces for the magazine show, and be the go-to guy for the top stories . . . but then, that's what I was, he thought. What could I do that is new? Documentaries? There are so few slots and—

The door opened and he looked up with a smile, trying not to seem smug.

Nina entered looking as if she was about to wash the floor. Baggy, faded track pants, a shapeless sweater, and her hair pinned up like a bush in the wind.

He laughed out loud.

"What?"

"Nothing. I was just thinking, that's all."

"About what?"

"The wine. It's good wine."

"It's a local wine, from my mother's area, it wins prizes."

She sat by him on the sofa, where they drank in silence, increasingly aware of each other, until like a boy in the back row of the cinema, Tom moved his hand ever so slightly toward Nina, who did not respond like a shy young date. She put down her glass, took his hand, and kissed it.

Tom was moved, he had a sense of time compressed. He held Nina's hair from her face and brought his lips to hers.

"Hmmmmm," she said at last.

"Me too."

They gazed at each other, their fingers intertwined, as the moment lengthened.

"Shall we?" Nina said, looking up into his eyes.

"Sure, why not," he said.

"Oh, I can think of a few reasons," she said.

"No, no, I was joking," and he led her toward the bedroom door. They kissed until, hand in hand, they walked inside, Nina first, and he closed the door.

It was a small room, lit by a single cluster of candles on the bedside table, which touched Tom. She must have taken care to light them after her shower. A fluffy white duvet was pulled back in welcome, on a big bed, and they needed all the space it offered. First, for Tom to sit as Nina stood before him, so close their knees touched, and she pulled her sweater over her head, releasing her hair, which tumbled about her bare shoulders. She turned to offer the clasp to Tom, who unsnapped her bra and dropped it on the bed. As she remained with her back to him, Tom held her and pulled her toward him and, wonderingly, drew his lips across the small of her back, and with his hands traced the curves of her body, which was so soft and silken as he placed his hands on her stomach, and as he pulled her tighter to him she shivered. With the tenderest of kisses where her buttocks melted into the small of her back, Tom slipped his hands into the sides of her pants and gently pulled them over her hips and along her thighs and her calves until, with a flick of her foot, Nina stepped out of them. It was the same with her knickers, a flick and they were gone.

And when she turned to face him, he wiped the tears from her eyes, and she those from his.

There was no journey of discovery, no cautious prodding of boundaries or tentative marking of the trail, just a long embrace and the longest exploring kiss, until a decade of longing took hold of them, and even that big bed was not enough to hold them. Tension built and gripped them like a coil and finally released them and they fell apart, panting and laughing their heads off.

Finally Tom managed to gasp, "Oh my God, that was amazing."

Nina was spread-eagled across the bed. "It was all right, I suppose," she said between gulps of air, her heart thumping. "What just happened? I think I'm having a heart attack."

Tom felt her heaving chest. "Are you all right? Seriously. It's banging away like . . . I don't know what . . . like . . ."

"Us?"

He laughed. "Yes, us." He kissed her breasts and fell back with a shout. "Wow!"

The next time they paused to catch their breath Nina was hanging over the side on her stomach, and Tom was pulling her back onto the bed. They lay on their backs, panting. All that had not happened in the past decade seemed to happen all at once in this small room, until they knew, absolutely and with finality, what the years ahead would hold for them.

"I'm glad you didn't drink any coffee," Nina said at last. "Imagine then." She took his head between her hands and they kissed and embraced but when he rolled onto his back again and she rolled onto him, despite his frustrated groans and his fullest attention to the task at hand, his flesh failed. "You're not sixteen," Nina said, stroking his thigh, "don't be greedy."

"I am, I am sixteen. At least, you make me feel I am."

"Well, I'm not. Don't hurry. Let's talk."

As they held each other, the years peeled back and back, to that time when she had woken him in his underpants in the Holiday Inn.

"I wonder what happened to that little boy, with the harelip," Tom said, lighting her cigarette with his. The red dots glowed and faded, glowed and faded. "What was his name?"

"Petar."

"Right. And his mother?"

"Ema."

"Yes. I hope they had better luck than we did."

"Yes, well, our luck has turned now. At last. Tom?"

"Yes?"

"When did you first know you loved me?"

"I love you, do I?"

"Yes."

"I don't know. I wanted to sleep with you from the first moment we met, when we were looking for a fixer and we had a drink at the bar, after you left CNN. In Zagreb. That big hotel by the railway station. Is that love?"

"No. Seriously. When?"

"Why? When did you know you loved me?"

"Seriously?"

"Yes."

She stared into the dark, until at last she tried to answer. "Is it possible," she asked, "to fall in love with a phantom? We didn't speak for more than ten years but in that time I fell in love with you. Is that possible? With the memory? I invented you, and then I fell in love with my invention, because it helped me, I suppose. When I went for walks I imagined we were holding hands. We talked, and you were the only one who understood me. Like

Sasha, he had an imaginary friend for years. I don't know what I would have done without you, your memory, I was lost for so long. I knew you would call me one day. When you were ready. Do you know what I mean?"

If anyone did, Tom did.

He finally answered. "Me? I knew I loved you when I lost you."

As he talked, Nina wept, in the dark, the candles long since exhausted, like them. Tom held her tight and whispered in her ear. It was easier that way, reliving it aloud for the first time.

"When I heard you scream, and I called out to you, as I called your name, at that moment I knew I loved you. But just as I knew I loved you, I knew I couldn't help you, and I died in that moment. I couldn't help you. I couldn't even help myself, when I thought I was going to die. And the last thing I ever was going to say was your name, and so I knew that I was going to die happy, in some strange way, with your name on my lips. Happy that I knew I loved you. So strange. I dreamed of that for years, of you, that feeling of finding you, having you, losing you, all wrapped up in an instant, in the moment of my death. But I didn't die. Same thing in my dreams; I never died, in my dreams I lived on, for us. I think I knew we would come together again, one day, when the time was right. Right for both of us."

All this Tom whispered into Nina's ear, tickling her with his breath, and he cradled her as she cried.

Tom kissed her eyes and tasted her salty hot tears, and kissed her lips and continued, strangely calm, as if the words were an act of deliverance, a sacrifice at the altar. Somewhere inside he knew, this is what he needed, and Nina needed it too, he just knew it, this is what he had missed for so long, the release, the freedom, of permitting himself, safely, to say the truth.

"I love you, Nina, I love you, and I've never loved anyone like this, never, nobody, Nina, just you." Her shoulders were shuddering, she was sobbing. "When I knew I was going to die, I knew I had to live." Her head was buried into his chest, feeling his heart thudding against her damp cheek.

At last, as they held each other in silence, feeling each other breathe, in the same instant they both said the same words: "So why didn't you—"

They laughed. "Go on," Tom said.

"No you, you say it."

"All right. So, why didn't you phone me or e-mail me? That's what you were going to say, right?"

"Yes, I was," she said. "Why didn't you?"

"I don't know. I couldn't face it."

"It was the same with me. Whenever I wanted to call you, which was almost every day, it brought it all back. It was too painful. And I thought you must be trying to forget it all. And so I got on with my life too. Got married. Lovers. Fights. It was all a lie. I was empty. Lost."

"Me too. Totally."

"And now, it's over. Those times. They're over."

"Yes." Tom kissed Nina on her forehead, slick with perspiration, which glinted as the first rays of daylight cast an early gray into the bedroom. "It's over," he said. He looked at the shifting shadows of the curtains on the wall, and thought, And if we say it often enough, it may even be true. He turned on his side, and snuggled into Nina's back, stroking her hair. "Let's get some sleep."

His first thought when he woke, and felt the warmth of her body against his, the gentle undulations of her breaths, was of thanks. But as his thoughts began to tumble one upon the other, and cleared, he knew that they were becoming too close. He had wanted to protect her; instead she was being drawn back in. The safest thing would be to finish filming as soon as possible, to get a few more shots and leave. He stroked her hair and held some locks between his fingers, enjoying the silkiness and the closeness. But then what? He would leave Belgrade and Nina would stay? They'd be apart again? Could she come with him to New York? Would she? With Sasha? To his little one-bedroom?

As he slipped out of bed for an early breakfast with Sam Morissey, at a cheap café on Knez Mihailova Street, Tom thought, My life is going to change, I almost feel like a prayer of thanks, if I were a praying man.

But don't rush: first things first.

And first, what a night! He had left Nina dead to the world. She can't be together with Aleks, he thought, not after last night, that was real passion, not a bit on the side.

Second, he would not be separated from Nina again. Never, ever. He'd need a bigger apartment though than his dump in the East Village. Maybe he'd call Amber, after all. As the taxi deposited him near the café and he entered, he thought, It's true: there really is a spring in my step.

Third, he needed to speed things up, be done with the doc.

"You're looking chipper," Morissey said, "coffee?"

"Oh yes."

"Things looking up?"

"In every sense, yes, actually."

"You found Mladić?"

"You're getting boring, Sam."

"Excuse me. So why so bright?" He looked at his watch. "Eight thirty."

"It was your idea to meet so early." They chatted over sand-wiches until Tom got to the point. "I told you I was going to Knin, right?"

"Yes. And I said it was a bad idea."

"Well, sorry, you were wrong. I'm making progress. But listen, you know people, is there any way you can help me on this? I need a shortcut, finish the doc and leave."

Tom laid out what he knew so far, and the more animated he grew, the thinner Morissey's lips became. Tom didn't notice the firm set of Sam's brow, or the fixedness of his gaze, or the impa-tient drumming of his fingers.

The only part of the fracas in the old Serb's house that Tom left out was that he had filmed it. "So the goons left and you never saw them again?" Sam said.

"Yes."

"How many times have you been attacked now? Three, four? And they've never laid a glove on you? One thing you can say about these guys, they're fucking incompetent."

Tom laughed. "That's my luck."

"Well, I wouldn't count on luck, my friend."

"I know. That's why I want to finish the shooting as quickly as possible and get the hell out of Dodge. So. Can you help me?"

"With what?"

"I told you. If there was a deal, who made it?"

"And if there wasn't?"

"Of course there was. Look, when the Croats attacked Knin, Mladić—"

"Okay, okay, I get it." Morissey stopped Tom with a wave. "You've got conspiracy theory up your ass. Look, how about if I get you a sit-down with someone in the BIA who should know. Probably on background though, I doubt he'll want to be filmed.

But someone who knows all their dirty little secrets. Wheels within wheels and all that stuff you journalists like to make up."

"You mean I'm just spinning wheels?"

"Wheel, yes."

"You think?" They knocked coffee cups.

"Here's to you getting out of town in one piece," Sam said. "Now, seriously, let's get down to the real stuff. How's nifty Nina?"

"Mind your own business."

"That serious, is it?"

"Leave her out of it."

"Oh, it is that serious."

The table in the apartment's dining alcove held plates of spicy pork-and-garlic sausage, smooth white cheeses with walnuts, chunks of flat bread, and a large bowl of sopsky salad, which Nina knew would remind Tom of Slovenia, where they had eaten it every day: vegetables sprinkled with white cheese. Nina opened a bottle of Prokupac and offered the taste to Aleks.

He swirled it in his mouth, as if he was chewing it. "Perfect," he pronounced, and with a flourish, Nina filled the three glasses. "To us," she said as they clinked.

"To us," the men repeated, and Aleks said with a broad smile, "Does that include me?"

"Oh, yes," Nina said. "It always will."

"But not in the same way." He drained his glass in one swallow and refilled it. Tom sensed a tinge of sadness.

"So." Aleks raised his eyebrows. "Straight to business then. You wanted to tell me what happened in Knin?"

The more he listened, the more poker-faced he became. He laid down his knife and fork and moved his mouth only to drink. His eyes bored into Tom, and when Tom had finished, telling him that he had been rather nervous as he drove home at night, on the lonely roads, scared that bad guys might stop them, Aleks did not respond.

Instead he made a little sandwich with the bread, sausage, and cheese, and chewed thoughtfully. Tom and Nina exchanged glances. "Another bottle?" Aleks said, and without waiting for an answer went into the kitchen and came back with a bottle and the opener. As he worked the cork, he said, "You know, Tom, before, I thought you should drop this whole idea. But now, listening to you, I think two things."

He paused as he wrestled the cork out with a pop and filled the three glasses. "It's very good, isn't it? Monks have been making it since the Middle Ages." After a sip, and an appreciative sigh, he went on. "It's interesting, what you've been saying. Very. I can see why Nina says you are a good journalist. And I've changed my mind—what I think now is that you should not drop this film. You are getting somewhere. Where, I don't know. But obviously, powerful people are afraid of you. You should carry on. If you are not afraid. Anyone would be. It is no shame. But it would be a pity to stop now."

Tom nodded thoughtfully. He hadn't wanted advice. He wanted a lead. "But do you have any idea who would know who encouraged ethnic cleansing? That led to the massacre? Who would say so on camera?"

"Forget about anyone talking on camera. But off camera, maybe you can find out more. Continue doing what you are doing, you seem to be moving in the right direction, but there is another thing I wanted to say." He looked at Nina, their eyes met, and he made a slight gesture with his head toward the kitchen.

"Cherry pie," she said as she gathered the plates and carried them into the kitchen. "With cream."

As she left the room Aleks leaned forward and almost whispered, "You must, I repeat must, stop involving Nina. The closer you get to the truth, the more dangerous it will become. They want to stop you and, believe me, they won't mess it up again. Are you prepared for that?"

Tom glanced around, glad that Aleks had waited for Nina to leave. As cupboard doors opened and closed and pots clanged in the kitchen, he said, also whispering, half to himself, half to Aleks, "Of course I don't want us to get hurt."

"But you will carry on?"

"Yes."

"All right then."

First came the sweet aroma, and then Nina with a cherry pie covered in cream and berries, and three mugs of black coffee.

"Oh, wow," Tom said, "this is perfect." They ate quietly, finishing the wine while the coffee cooled.

As Nina served them each another slice, she said, "I heard you whispering, you know. I couldn't hear what you said but I can guess. And Aleks, there's something you don't know. I don't think you understand why this film is so important to Tom. And to me, too. You may think you know it all, but you don't."

She drank her wine and began to talk, with determination, as if challenging herself to continue. They needed Aleks's support, so he had to understand them. The time had come to tell him all the things she never had.

How Nick was killed.

That she was raped.

That the two men who did it were the two men they followed from the cemetery and who came into the café, and then into the hotel room. Mladić's men.

That she could never tell him before, or anyone, even her mother.

Until Tom came. And now . . . well, you know. They were both damaged, and this was helping them. Nothing else had.

Aleks stared at her as she talked, and his chest rose and fell heavily, but he didn't respond for a long time and as dusk fell and the room darkened, Nina drew the curtains and switched on two table lamps. Tom had also listened in silence and now he too waited. He had nothing to add. What must Aleks be thinking? Of the Nina he once knew, of the Nina he knew now, maybe her story explained things to him; maybe she had changed. They had grown up together, they were close, closer than siblings.

How close?

Too close? Maybe they were once, but now it's over?

He waited.

Finally Aleks stood and said, "Why are you telling me now?"

"So that you understand Tom. Why he's so determined. And me. It's more than just a documentary. And also . . ." Her voice trailed off as she looked at Tom.

He finished her sentence. "And also because we don't want any more secrets. From each other . . ."

Nina said, taking Aleks's hand, ". . . and from anyone we love."

Tom looked at their clasped hands.

That night, asleep in Nina's apartment, he had a dream that jolted him awake. A new one. He was in a dark forest, looking for stolen tree trunks. He came across piles of them, buried in mounds of rotting foliage, their ends jutting out. He felt triumphant: I found them. They were long and there were piles of many more, lying on top of each other, all concealed, and he was curious and they seemed to point into the forest and he followed them deeper into the woods when a man with no substance, like a shadow, emerged from the darkness, looking at him. Tom stopped and the man came closer. Then more men emerged from the forest and walked toward him. Tom realized he had made a terrible mistake. When he had found the stolen trees he should have left and gone for help, not followed them into the forest. Now the men were closing in and it was too late and he tried to turn but he couldn't move his feet and there were too many men around him. He had a sinking feeling that all was lost, that it was too late, that he had made too big a mistake, that it was his fault, and the men came closer, and closer, and were bigger and bigger, and Tom was smaller and smaller and he was being blotted out. He opened his eyes, his mouth was open, he was palpitating, he was sweating, and Nina breathed gently beside him.

Tom never remembered a dream, especially if it upset him, but waiting in a small antechamber in BIA headquarters to talk to Morissey's contact, reading in *Time* magazine about the sudden death of Slobodan Milosevic in a prison cell in The Hague three weeks earlier, he was left with a sense of his own vulnerability, and the dream returned in full, or at least he felt it did. Shadowy men closing in on him, until he woke with a start. Again, he felt his heart beating a shade too fast.

As he sat back with closed eyes, wondering whether the speculation was true that the former Yugoslav leader, Mladić's protector, had been poisoned, it occurred to him: If people poisoned Milosevic, were they the same people who wanted to keep Mladić quiet?

And he thought, If they can get to Milosevic, who had been in jail for four years, what was the problem knocking him, Tom, off any time they wanted? Nobody believed Milosevic when he complained that he was being poisoned, until they found him dead on his bed. Now here he was, ignoring warnings to lay off the Mladić story. Dumbass! Why not forget the doc and call Amber and go back to the network? That's what Morissey had said when he told him of the interview this morning. Much better money. Take Nina and Sasha to New York. He could see the BIA guy, Morissey had said, but better to forget the whole deal. And the talk was background only. Deep background. Not that there was a difference. It was either on the record or it wasn't. Who came up with this jargon?

At that moment the door opened and a young man in a gray suit asked if he would like tea or coffee? And please follow me, the deputy head of security is ready.

Tom got to his feet and picked up his shoulder bag. "You won't need that, please leave it with the secretary," the man said. Tom shrugged. He had already been body-searched.

The man smiled. "Your telephone too. Just routine precautions. Your things will be safe here, they will be behind the desk."

Sure they will. They had already emptied the bag and checked what was inside. Now they'd have time to download his phone contacts. Except he'd left the phone in the apartment. He'd learned that a long time ago—never leave your phone at the entrance to a government building. You may as well give them a printout of all your contacts and PIN numbers. All he entered the room with was his notebook and pen.

"Welcome to my humble abode!" The official stood with a smile and came round his desk to shake his hand, and guided him by the elbow to the chairs around a low coffee table.

Tom disliked him instantly. Humble abode, my ass. His slicked-back hair, his smarmy voice, his handshake like a vise: *What's he trying to prove?* He had the body to back it up, though.

As the deputy security chief unbuttoned his jacket to sit down, he revealed a barrel chest, muscled and defined, even through his shirt, and biceps that filled his sleeves.

He got straight to the point, in fluent English. "So, Mr. Layne, I understand you do not believe that we are serious in our hunt for Ratko Mladić? Is that correct? I have been asked to, as you say, set the record straight."

Tom was a bit taken aback at his directness. "Well, I wouldn't put it as strongly as that but yes, I do have a few questions."

"I'm afraid I do not have much time, so please allow me to tell you what we are doing, and if you have any further questions I will try to answer them, as time allows."

"Fine. Is it all right if I take notes?"

"Yes, but of course, do not quote me or the BIA, this is strictly not for publication."

"I understand. Thank you for taking the time."

When Tom recounted the briefing to Nina later, while he was typing up his notes, he shook his head in wonder. "Who are these people? In every capital they're the same. They think they're so smart, and we're so dumb. He said they're going to form an 'Action Team.' In quotes. My ass. I asked him why it took so long to put together a team—ten years. They're 'this close' to catching Mladić. They don't want anyone like a bull in a china shop 'tipping him off.' I asked if he was thinking of anyone in particular. He even trotted out that old trope of ten thousand police looking for Mladić every day, and posters everywhere. Like hell. I've seen precisely one, and that was in airport arrivals. That's really going to help. I actually laughed when he said that."

"I wouldn't laugh at those people, they're evil," Nina said, "they have no limits."

"Aleks too?"

"They're not all the same."

"He didn't say anything I don't know. The usual stuff about why aren't we worried about the Croat and Muslim war criminals, why just the Serbs? They turned over Milosevic and got nothing, no EU membership, NATO, nothing. And now all they got was his corpse. I told him the first thing I filmed when I arrived was his burial. He did tell me one thing I didn't know. You know what music they played at Milosevic's funeral? 'Midnight in Moscow' for the old communist! That'll be a good line in the script. I don't know why he bothered to see me. Or why Sam thought it would help. And by the way, he looked weird. I would have had to film from the right side, almost profile."

"Why?"

"He's got a huge mole on his left temple."

The deputy head of security was more circumspect, and yet as direct, in his first phone call after Tom left.

"So how did the meeting go?" Sam asked.

"What meeting?"

"That bad, eh?"

That night Aleks took Nina out for a drink, without Tom, and his message was just as brief: Go home to your mother and Sasha, stay in the village until this blows over.

Tears filled her eyes. She took his hand, caressed it, and implored him to help Tom. "Please! He needs this and so do I, we both need it." She fell back on the clichés which more and more seemed true. They were gaining closure. They were escaping from the past. They were finally doing something, and what's more it was bringing them together, back to where they should have been a long time ago. "You know what I have been through now, you know me maybe better than anyone else. Oh, Aleks. You helped me when I needed it, but it can never be the same as Tom. You know that, don't you, Aleks?" She brought his hand to her lips and kissed it. "And soon, in just a few more days, he will leave anyway."

"And what about you? The two of you?"

Nina, already leaning forward to hold his hand, slumped further, her shoulders sunk toward the table, until she looked up with half a smile. "Only good things," she said. "I don't know what, but only good things."

"One thing, Nina."

"Yes?"

"Please excuse my question. But we are such special friends. Why didn't you tell me you were raped?"

Nina's eyes hardened as she dropped his hand, searched for an answer. "What for? Aren't all women raped?"

"That's why?"

"No." Her chest heaved as she forced herself to answer, avoiding his gaze. "I was too ashamed, Aleks. Too dirtied. I couldn't tell anyone. Now, with Tom here, it's different somehow, he knew what happened, was part of it, he suffered too. At night we talk for hours, you know. I had never talked about it. Not even once. To anyone. Hardly to myself. I tried to ignore it, I put up a barrier, between myself and the horror inside me. And with Tom, well, it all came out, and now, I feel so much better that I told you too, so much better." She went for, and managed, a smile.

Aleks also succeeded.

"Don't worry about Tom," he said finally. "I know what I'm doing."

But did he? What Aleks could not tell Nina was that the uncertainty about the cause of Milosevic's death had rattled the back office. His own small BIA unit had become involved two weeks earlier, reporting directly to the chief of staff of the prime minister, and through him, secretly, to the office of the war crimes prosecutor. And his information about Tom's progress, and the attempts to scare him off, formed a new piece of the larger puzzle. After speaking to Tom the first time, he had himself presented a plan of action and it had been approved within a day. A true "Action Team," not one for the media. Nobody else inside the BIA knew of their new mission. Another wheel added to the wheels within wheels.

His men were following Tom. 24/7. Waiting for him to be approached again.

Whoever made a move against Tom would be followed, and as the net widened, it would lead them closer to Mladić. But Nina had to stay away from Tom. When civilians were involved, things always went wrong. Their job was not to intervene, but to watch and follow.

Tom Layne was bait.

But they didn't come for Tom.

They came for Nina.

It was Morissey's idea. He had warned the BIA deputy chief of security to lay off Tom Layne. He may not look it, with his laid-back, run-down style, but he was too famous in America, even if his last coup was ten years ago. He wasn't Bill Blow from the *Belgrade Bugle*. If anything happened to him, star reporter, blast from the past, it would cause a diplomatic shit storm.

So, what to do?

Hit the bastard where it hurts most. His squeeze, Nina. She's an unknown half-Muslim. Disappear her.

. . .

What a cliché, straight from the movies, Tom thought, although usually it's the husband who doesn't show for dinner. He had taken the Turkish rug off the table in Nina's apartment, found a white cotton tablecloth with embroidered red roses around the edges, laid it with the best plates and cutlery he could find, bought some spring flowers for a centerpiece, opened a bottle of red wine, lit two candles that stood in egg cups in lieu of candleholders, had all the ingredients chopped and ready, all set to cook his piéce de resistance, artichoke pasta in a cream of mushrooms and onion, and Nina was late. Very late.

He sat on the sofa, sipping wine, and getting annoyed. He opened the fridge and stared forlornly. That'll surprise her most of all, he thought, his own sopsky salad. Cucumbers, tomatoes, red pepper, chopped up, oil and vinegar, little bits of feta cheese scattered on top . . . it looked so tasty he put some on a plate and ate it, sitting on the sofa and checking his watch.

He didn't want to phone her, it was to be a surprise. At first he'd enjoyed missing her, it made him happy that he did. It was a sweet feeling, of loss mixed with anticipation, of a warm place waiting to be filled, a juvenile feeling, he thought, that he had not felt for anyone since . . . ? He smiled. Since he had missed Nina herself, when he had left her that time in Sarajevo. In London he couldn't wait to get back to her. And then. Well, we all know what happened. Where the hell is she?

He should have called her during the day, just to check. Maybe he'd phone her now, after all, he didn't have to say dinner was waiting. He hadn't seen her since the day before, after he'd gone out to shoot some pictures and she had gone off to see Aleks for dinner, and then had decided to spend the night at his place.

She had laughed when he had asked a week earlier what was

going on with her and Aleks. I used to fancy him, she had answered, when we were fourteen. But we were second cousins, it was forbidden, there was enough interbreeding in the mountains, that's all she needed. No thanks.

Did she protest too much?

Last night she had called to say she had had a few drinks and didn't want to drive and would sleep over in Aleks's spare room. He hadn't worried, at first. But unable to fall asleep, he had put himself in her shoes. What excuse would I come up with? Too drunk to drive? Sure, the perfect excuse. But surely she wouldn't lie to him? Would she? Sleep with him and Aleks at the same time? No. Would she?

But now, worrying on the sofa, he thought, if she really did sleep with Aleks, she'd have called him in the morning, to reassure him, even if she was lying through her teeth. That's what he'd have done. But she hadn't called all day. He had spent the day logging the best parts of the interviews from the day before, and filming a heartbreaking interview with a survivor of the Srebrenica massacre, who was now a human rights activist in Belgrade, and only now he realized she hadn't phoned him even once, which she normally did several times a day.

He went back to the fridge to look at the ice cream he had bought for dessert, which they would eat with the little chocolate bonbons that he knew she liked.

He had been thinking. When the film was finished, Nina should come with him to New York, but what about Sasha? He hadn't even met him yet. Would Nina want to uproot him? They had not had that conversation yet. It was all lovey-dovey. But what next?

He had already made the first move and he was anxious to tell Nina about it. She'd approve.

He took his computer and opened the document he had saved as "Amber," and glanced through his notes of their conversation. He had called her with an idea.

"How about, if I come back, you promote my return by running this documentary on Mladić? You buy it, for you at a special high price, and you call it 'first in a series' of documentaries by daa-de-daaa, new chief foreign correspondent et cetera, main point being this doc is going to make news and you can break it on the network, and at the same time promote your coup at hiring back one Thomas Layne, at an obscene salary, of course. How about it?"

Amber had been thrilled at him coming back, even though he hadn't promised yet. She had a whole plan of action to get the news division back to number one, and he was a key part of it, but as for the documentary, she had said, "I don't know. That's up to Specials, they're in charge of docs, we do so few—"

He had interrupted. "Who is in charge of Specials?"

"Will Klein."

"And above him? Who does he report to?"

"Uh, that would be me."

"Exactly. So make it happen."

"Okay, no guarantees, but it's a good idea. If the doc is any good. Is it?"

"Oh yeah. I've got amazing stuff, lots of your intrepid correspondent, breaking new information about why Mladić hasn't been caught, and a conspiracy theory that seems to be holding up. I just need a few more days to nail it down and I'm done. The shit's going to hit the fan when we show the doc."

Amber's voice went soft, a shade quieter. "And how is Nina?"

Amber had also lost touch with Nina, as well as with Tom, and it had always hurt her, how they had both pushed her away.

"She's beautiful, and wonderful," Tom had said, and no more. "This film is really helping her, I think."

That was five hours ago.

Where is she?

At ten o'clock, and after staring at the door a hundred times to see if it was opening, and having finished the sopsky salad, he called her cell phone, blowing the surprise.

No answer. That's strange. Ten minutes later he tried again. Same thing.

He called Aleks, who was in a bar, judging by the noise. "Wait a minute," Aleks said, "I can't hear, I'll go outside."

After bangs and scraping sounds and the background noise of music and voices and cars, Aleks was back. "What's that about Nina?" he said.

"Do you know where she is, is she with you? I've been waiting at the apartment all evening and no sign of her."

"Well, she's not here, did you call her?"

"Of course. No answer."

"That's strange. She always has the phone with her. In case Sasha calls."

"I know. But I called her several times, starting an hour ago, and no answer."

"Let me try. I'll call you back," Aleks said.

Aleks walked to an awning a few houses from the bar, where there was less street noise, and dialed Nina's number. He let it ring till a recorded announcement said the caller was unavailable, and then he tried it again.

He held the phone at his side. Where did she say she was going? She didn't. He cast his mind back. He hadn't seen her that morning. She had received an early phone call and he had heard her leaving the apartment soon after. And she hadn't been home? All day? Where did she go? He felt the tension in his stomach. And a chill. He immediately made the connection. Tom—them—Nina. Straight from the playbook. First, threats. Second, minor violence. Third, the pressure point—wife, child, and if they didn't exist, girlfriend.

Or maybe she's at a movie or something?

Survival 101—there's no such thing as a coincidence.

He called Nina's mother, even though it was late. When she finally answered the phone, short of breath and muttering about waking up poor Sasha, she said no, she hadn't talked to Nina today. Is she all right? Not sick? She normally calls at least twice a day.

Aleks assured her that everything was fine. He called Tom back. "Nothing?" he said.

"No, I'm still waiting in the apartment."

Aleks already knew that. He was getting hourly updates.

"Call me again in half an hour, I'm on my way."

When Tom called back at eleven o'clock to say there was still no sign of her, Aleks was just parking the car outside.

"Are you hungry?" Tom said. "Artichoke pasta?"

"Sure."

At midnight, as they finished the pasta, Aleks's phone rang. His office had been checking. "Okay, thanks," he said into the phone. He laid it slowly onto the table and looked up at Tom. "No news is good news. She isn't in any hospital. She isn't in the morgue. No car crashes involving her car. Police are looking for it."

He got up and went through the drawers until he found Nina's photo collection. He took a recent picture, and five minutes later gave it to a man who had knocked on the door. "The police will have this in ten minutes," he said. "They'll scan it to their vehicles, and their stations. Ten thousand police will have it by the morning."

Right, Tom thought, next to Mladić's picture. He held his hand before him. Steady as a rock. He poured a brandy and held one out for Aleks. He watched Aleks pacing, and suddenly stop, his face going tight.

He made another call and spoke in rapid Serbian, faster than usual, but Tom made out the word "Amerikanac."

"What was that?" Tom said. He was marveling at Aleks's efficiency and calm, even as he felt more and more useless. If your girlfriend goes missing, he thought, it's good to have a spook in the family.

"I've taken some of my men from an assignment they had. Moved them to Nina's mother's home. Just in case. Because of Sasha. Until we know what's happening I'm going to assume the worst. If someone has taken Nina, they may take Sasha too. Don't ask me why. Maybe I'll move him from there."

He made another call. "That's taken care of. Sasha and Nina's mother will be taken to a safe house, they'll be out of their village within the hour."

If someone has taken Nina? Only now was the penny beginning to drop. Until now Tom had been anxious and annoyed, half blaming Nina. But—taken Nina? Who? Why? Because of him? And then her mother and child? A wave of nausea made him giddy and he had to grip the table and lower himself into a chair. He had blamed himself when Nick was killed and Nina was raped. For years he cursed himself—he had taken them there, it was all his idea. And now, it was happening again. It was all his idea, he had persuaded Nina to help him, almost insisted she remain when she had said it was too dangerous. And now look! He slumped forward, holding his head in his hands. He was useless, helpless. Thank God for Aleks.

As Aleks paced and Tom grew more and more nervous, and guilt and fear for Nina threatened to overwhelm him, and he poured himself his fifth brandy and lit yet another cigarette, Aleks's phone rang again. More rapid Serbian from Aleks, this time in a pleading, urgent voice. Tom froze, staring at Aleks, who explained when he ended the call.

"Nina's mother. She didn't believe my men, so they put her on to me. It's okay now, they've left the house. They're safe."

"But safe from what?"

Aleks shrugged. "Maybe I'm just overreacting. Maybe she went to see a couple of movies. Maybe she met an old friend and went for a few drinks too many."

"But she would have answered the phone?" Tom said.

"Of course she would," Aleks said, dialing her phone again and getting the same recorded message.

"Well, she isn't here with me. Why are you calling me? Maybe she's with a lover, ferchrisssake, what time is it?" Sam Morissey said when Tom woke him at four in the morning.

By now Tom was a wreck, lying on the sofa, his pants unzipped, staring at his phone. He'd almost finished the brandy when Aleks pulled the bottle from him. It wasn't hard—his grip was weak and his head was spinning from alcohol, nicotine, and fatigue. He had agreed with Aleks: this was no coincidence. Aleks, who understood these people, said she must have been kidnapped to put pressure on Tom, who they couldn't touch because he was a famous American journalist.

There was a knock at the door. A man came into the apartment and gave Aleks a headphone splitter so that if anyone phoned Tom, Aleks could listen in without using the speaker.

By now Tom had finally gotten the message: the doc is over. It isn't worth getting Nina hurt.

If she wasn't already. Bile rose at the thought that somebody might be harming her, and all because of him. He didn't know what to do, he squirmed in his seat, stood and sat, drank and smoked, listened and waited for his phone to ring. If only he hadn't been so stubborn. Just another stupid film that nobody even wanted. Who cared about Ratko Mladić? All he cared about was Nina. Oh, please, please bring her back.

"Aleks?" Aleks was half asleep in the easy chair.

"What?"

As the alcohol wore off, and as he recovered a bit after dozing for an hour, his mind must have cleared somewhat, because Tom had a good question. "If it is Mladić's men who have done this, why would they care if I'm an American journalist? They could not care less if I'm well known or not. They're murderers and thugs. So if someone does care enough to take Nina instead of me, maybe it isn't Mladić's men?"

Aleks yawned and stretched and looked at his watch. "Good morning, Einstein. It is Mladić's men. But guided by someone in the BIA. Anyway, whoever it is, they'll call soon."

"How come you're so calm?" Tom stood and zipped up his trousers and stretched, with a yawn that was almost a yell.

Aleks went into the kitchen and came back a few minutes later with two cups of black coffee. "Because I know what's going on. They're playing my game. They'll let you sweat all night and call at dawn. You take the call, so they know it's you, and then give me the phone. I'll do the talking."

"What do you mean?"

"You know the film you are making is over, right? That will be the condition."

"Of course." Tom couldn't care less about finishing the documentary. Anyway, he had enough material already to do a good one, how good did it have to be?

The first light of dawn revealed a clear sky and a deserted street. Tom opened the window to let in fresh air. After a night of smoking and alcohol and dozing, the living room smelled like a stale nightclub. "You said they're playing your game. Who is they, and what's the game?" Tom asked.

"This whole thing is a BIA operation from the beginning, it's obvious. I don't know who in the BIA, but their fingerprints are all over it. Your luck is that they would never do anything against you directly so they're using all these cheap thugs who keep messing up. Or maybe they're supposed to mess up. I wouldn't be surprised if that's what the BIA wants. A gentle scare. Or you'd be in the hospital a long time ago after an unfortunate car accident."

He looked at his watch. It was six o'clock. He made a long phone call, and then explained to Tom. "All BIA units will get an update. My cousin Nina Ibrahimovic has disappeared. That will let whoever did this inside the BIA know that this is personal. They took the wrong person."

A moment later, at six twenty, before the BIA could have done anything, Tom's phone rang. Aleks took a last swig of coffee, inserted the earplug, and nodded at Tom to accept the call. They heard breathing, fast and heavy. "Tom? Tom?"

He nodded to Aleks, a tear formed in his eye. "Nina? Are you all right? We've been so worried—"

He heard a yelp and a voice interrupted in English with a thick Serb accent. "Thomas Layne, if you want to see—"

Tom didn't hear the threat. Aleks grabbed the phone and began to talk into it, without listening to a word from the other side. He spoke for a minute, as Tom looked on, his heart racing. Aleks spoke slowly and deliberately, making sure the other person understood every word, and not only the words, but the message too. When he stopped talking he did not wait for a response. He simply hung up the phone. He looked at Tom with an expression of smugness and . . . what? Doubt? Tom hoped not.

"What did you say? What did they say?"

"If I'm wrong, they'll call right back. If I'm right, we'll get a call from Nina to pick her up somewhere. Or she'll take a taxi and just come here. We'll know very soon."

"I can't believe how calm you are."

"I told you. They're playing my game."

"But what did you say to them?"

"I told them Nina is my close family, I gave them my name, my number and rank in the BIA, a couple of my operations they will be familiar with, and I said that if anything happens to Nina, anything at all, I will start with their children, work my way through their wives, end up with their mothers, and only then cut off their balls. I said they should immediately check with their BIA handlers whether they really want to destroy themselves, all for a, excuse me, stupid American reporter."

"Oh, I see."

"Words to that effect."

"Well, as long as it works."

"And I told them to free her immediately."

"Good."

"I also said that you have stopped making the film."

"All right."

"I mean it. If you carry on they will simply leave Nina out of it and go after you again. Only for good. Step four, so to speak."

Tom shrugged. "All I care about right now is Nina. But tell me something. Who is behind all this? What have I done, or what have I found out, that is serious enough to start all this?" He followed Aleks to the kitchen, where they made fresh coffee.

"I don't know. I'm not too sure I care. I also want to find the war criminal Mladić who is holding the people hostage with his very existence. The reasons some may have for hiding him are not really my business."

But that's the real story, Tom thought. That's where I come in. Or did. Finding Mladić is a local story. Why people are hiding him could be a much bigger story. "Between Knin and Srebrenica." What am I missing? What?

The phone rang. Tom looked at Aleks in alarm, his heart racing from normal to off the chart in a second. They were calling back. So was Aleks wrong after all? Aleks indicated, Pick it up, and he put a plug in his ear.

"Hello?" Tom said.

"So, a fine mess you've got yourself into. I told you to drop it. Has she turned up yet?"

"Good morning, Sam, how are you?"

"Better than you. At least I went back to sleep. How about you, sleep well?"

"Fine, thanks."

"Like hell. So what's up? Did you hear from anyone? Is Nina all right? What's going on?"

Aleks had been writing feverishly on a pad: *Sam Morissey? US embassy?*

Tom nodded: *Yes.*

Aleks made a throat-slitting gesture. Cut the call. Tom nod-

216

ded. "Gotta go, Sam. Thanks for calling. I'll call you as soon as I know something for sure."

"You do that. I hope Nina's all right. Call me later."

"Thanks, Sam. I will. Bye now." He tapped the End Call key. "What?"

"You're close with Sam Morissey?"

"Yes, we've known each other for many years. You know him? He's a good friend."

Aleks cocked an eyebrow.

"What?" Tom said.

"He's a good friend the same way I'm a good friend. By which I mean, don't trust him an inch."

"You mean I shouldn't trust you an inch?"

"That's different. I'm family, with Nina anyway. Morissey is close to the top people at the BIA. He's a liaison man. CIA, BIA, same same."

"I know that. But he's only ever been good to me. He helped Nina too, way back when."

"Well, just remember. He'll do his job. If helping you is part of his job, fine. If it isn't, he'll drop you like a live hand grenade. I know. I'm the same."

"Unless it's family."

"Right. Unless it's family. And you're not family."

Aleks was right again. An hour and a half later, as the eggs were frying, Tom's phone rang. Nina was crying. "Where are they, where are they?" she kept saying.

"Who?" Tom said. "Nina, are you all right, where are you?"

"I'm at the cottage. Sasha. Majka—Mama. There's no one here. Where are they? Are they all right?"

Aleks took the phone and explained. He told her to stay there, he would send a car and driver, but Nina insisted she could drive herself, she was all right and she had her own car. She wanted to see Sasha, now, immediately, where is he? Her voice was breaking, high-pitched, almost hysterical. She hadn't slept all night, they had threatened her, scared her, she wouldn't say how.

Aleks tried to reason with her. "Nina, you'll frighten Sasha," he said. "You need a rest. He's all right, he has no idea anything was wrong. Let your mother take him home again and when you're rested, tomorrow, the next day, then go and see him. If you see him now, you'll scare him, he won't understand why you're so upset." Aleks went on and on; he wouldn't stop until Nina agreed. "I'm right," he said. "The main thing now is not to upset Sasha, it's hard enough for him anyway. He should keep his routine. It's all over now. Just come home and in a day or two, when you want, send for Sasha again."

And so, an hour later, they heard the metallic click in the door and before they could open it for her, Nina was leaning in the doorway, the sagging dark bags beneath her bloodshot eyes speaking for her. As Tom and Aleks watched, she stepped by them, as if in a daze, took her coat off, hung it up in the closet, walked into the kitchen, and lit the gas beneath the kettle. From the cupboard she extracted three cups and saucers, put a teaspoon of sugar into each cup, carefully arranged spoons on the saucers, leaned with one arm on the marble counter, and began to cry.

From the living room Tom and Aleks heard her weeping and went to her and held her. She turned round and hugged them both, and they each felt her heartbeat and the dampness of her tears, as the whistle of the kettle became shriller and shriller.

And after Aleks left, they went to bed, where Tom held Nina tight until she fell asleep in his arms. For long minutes Tom held her, his mind blank but for a sense of thanks. Finally, unable to sleep, he inched himself clear, brushing her hair from his face, wriggling his arm from beneath her chest, until he edged his leg clear from hers and ever so smoothly raised himself from the bed and tiptoed out, leaving Nina sighing and turning and quietly sleeping. The door slipped from his hand and slammed shut. "Shit!" He froze at the door, waiting for her call, but all he heard was her even breaths. He dressed and on the way back from the bathroom, entered Sasha's room.

It had touched him when Nina had gone straight to Sasha. Of course she would. But he hadn't anticipated it; he had assumed she would come straight home. But for any mother, home was where her child was. Not the new lover.

He sat on Sasha's little bed, with its white sheets printed with blue clouds and its soft eiderdown, and as he gazed at the barn-yard scenes on the yellow wallpaper—cows chewing the cud, fluffy white sheep, ducks waddling in a row—Tom felt wrapped in the warmth of the room. The bedside lamp was round with black and white checks, a soccer ball lamp. Nice. I wouldn't mind one of those, he thought. In the corner was an untidy pile of Lego pieces. I should buy him a present, he thought. Chocolate. He remembered, from way, way back, a friend of his mother's had brought him chocolate. His mother had said, Chocolate isn't good for him. Her friend, bless her, had answered, I don't care what's good for him. I want him to love me. He chuckled, and his throat caught.

His eyes fell on a storybook, in Serbian. He picked it up, leafed through it. Pictures of a wolf and a little girl in red. Must be Little Red Riding Hood. As he turned the pages, his mind seduced into calm, fragments of images imposed themselves, the pictures on the page became images from his film.

So it was over. No big scoop.

Pity, he thought. I'd like to nail Ratko Mladić. At least find out the real story. Because it wasn't only about Nick and him and Nina. What about all the others, those who were massacred? Especially in Srebrenica. What got him into trouble today must have something to do with the massacre, something to do with Mladić being there and Mladić not being where he was needed, in Knin, in Krajina. Srebrenica. Knin. The missing link. If there was a deal, who made it, and with whom? And why? And why is it still so important to keep it quiet today?

He hadn't been in Srebrenica, he'd been almost everywhere else though. Mass graves were all the same, and he'd seen plenty. In fields on the outskirts of villages, at the edge of the woods, you saw pits recently dug, or mounds of shoveled earth, with broken shin bones sticking out of boots; earth-covered bodies decomposed into each other; skulls with hair, finger bones with rings, fragments of rags stiff with earth.

He stood up suddenly. He didn't want to sully this sweet bedroom with such thoughts. He went into the living room, threw himself onto the sofa, took a pillow, and stretched out.

Srebrenica. It didn't help that he had only seen the carnage on television through a haze of whiskey and drugs, lost in loneliness and insomnia. At first he hadn't cared. Not my problem anymore, he'd thought. He knew the network wouldn't renew his contract, which was up three months later. By then he was on borrowed time, he hadn't worked in a month and had no intention to. His salary landed every four weeks in his bank account, and he spoke to the news desk with about the same frequency.

He lay with his head resting on his hands, looking at the ceiling; even now, eleven years later, he had a pang of regret. At first the press couldn't find the survivors. He knew what he'd have done if he'd been there. He'd have gone to Tuzla, where the Mus-

lim army was based and where the Srebrenica Muslims were trying to go. But it was forty miles away, forty miles of rough trails
through Serb-controlled forested mountains, and although thousands set off on the journey, walking by night, sleeping by day,
strung out for miles, few arrived. Serbs mowed them down in the
fields and hunted them in the woods, and all along the way, mass
graves marked their progress, or rather, the end of the road for
hundreds at a time. They had called it the Trail of Life and Death.
He thought, I'd have started in Tuzla, and backtracked, met them
along the way, walked with them. What a tragedy. What a story.

Instead, he lost his job.

And Mladić, his onetime chess partner, who had basically done
him in, had promised the Muslims who weren't smart enough to
flee that he'd look after them. He had patted boys on the head and
commiserated with the men, and then killed them all.

Still, one thing he'd have to do in his film, if he ever made the
damn thing, was to give some context. Everything the Serbs did
to the Croats and the Muslims, the Muslims and the Croats
had done to the Serbs, and worse. In World War II the Croats
killed close to half a million Serbs. The Muslims had been killing
Serbs for centuries. For the Serb militiamen, this was payback
time. In Srebrenica Mladić had boasted, to a television camera,
surrounded by his exultant comrades, "Finally the time has come
to take revenge on the Turks."

"Genocide" is a word used by the judges, Tom thought, when
it's too late. Where were they before the word, when they could
have prevented the massacres? Looking away. Holier-than-thou
bastards.

Tom emptied a glass of wine and looked at his watch. One
thirty in the afternoon. Nina's been asleep for three hours. And
for most of that time he'd been torturing himself, replaying in his

head the war, and his own professional demise. Had he dozed off too? He'd hardly slept all night.

He yawned as he poured another glass. If you don't stop genocide, are you an accomplice? Of course you are. Mind you, he wasn't any better. What had he been doing? Getting smashed in a dark room, feeling sorry for himself. And what was he doing now? Giving up on the doc, just when he was getting somewhere.

The worse he felt, the more he thought of Nick, which is what always happened when he felt like shit.

And Nick's family; what a disaster when he had gone there to tell them about Nick's last moments. Them all sitting around the room against the walls, parents, cousins, everyone, and him facing them. He saw it in their eyes, unable to meet his, their brief handshakes, the long silences. Nobody had come out and said it but it was obvious what they were thinking: How come you're alive, if he's dead? What, you ran away? You led him there and then you didn't help?

The wine bottle was empty, so he filled the glass with brandy. Plum brandy, good mellow stuff. He sighed, emptied his lungs with a loud exhalation, and wiped the sweat from his brow.

Ratko Mladić. Wanted for genocide and crimes against humanity. Whose men killed Nick. And raped Nina. Mladić. The One Who Is Getting Away. Again.

Before she fell asleep, Nina had told him, at first through tears and then, after he kissed her and stroked her, more calmly, what had just happened. One threatened to rape her. He didn't even know he already had. The other one had stopped him. He'd given her water, stopped the big one from harming her. But he was weird.

When they had let her go, and took her back to her car, he had waited till they were alone, and had asked for her phone number.

Her phone number? Can you believe that? And in a tone of wonder, she had drifted off to sleep.

Tom stood at the bedroom door and listened to the comfort of Nina's even breathing. He crossed the threshold, gently closed the door, and moved to the bed, in the dark, and as he undressed found himself thanking God that she was home and whole and in doing so understood that this was the beginning of something new and wonderful for them both. All he had to do was give up on the film, or at least, make do with the material he already had, which wasn't half bad at all. He could always try to find out the truth from sources outside Serbia, military institutes and the like in Europe and America. He smiled to himself as he pulled up the cover and snuggled against Nina's warm body. He just had to get them all out of Belgrade and safely back to New York.

I'm going to begin a new life, he thought, and it's going to be quiet and peaceful and all the things I've ever wanted, and even as he banished a distant small voice that whispered "Who the hell are you kidding"—he fell into a deep sleep.

And he woke the way he had long wanted. The heaviness began to lift and in the farthest reaches he became aware, in the dimmest way, of a change in his breathing, and in the breathing around him, of Nina's breath. It was sweet against his skin, like a warm breeze on a cool spring day, stirring his chest, where her head rested and he breathed in the musk of her hair and his breath caught and his heart raced as he understood that Nina's lips and tongue were teasing his chest and her hand was hovering and twittering above his belly. Like a butterfly glancing him with its dainty wings, her hand drew circles barely touching him until, rested, strengthened, contentment and excitement filled him and he rose to meet her. It was as if each knew the rest of their lives was starting here and now.

The next afternoon the trouble started. Nina wanted to go to her mother's to collect Sasha, but wasn't sure about Tom. She couldn't just bring Sasha home and announce that this strange man was staying in her room. She needed time. They should meet first.

"You mean I should move out? That's all right, I can get a hotel."

"But I don't want you to go."

"So I'll stay then."

"But what about Sasha?"

"So I'll go?"

"I don't know!"

Tom took her by the hand and led her to the window alcove, where the sun cast a warming glow on the little table and easy chair. "Here," he said, and pulled her onto his lap. She rested her head on his shoulder and he played with her hair, lifting her mane to his cheek and caressing her loose tresses. "So soft," he whispered, brushing her ear with his lips.

She whispered back, "What will we do? I thought of you for so long and I'm so happy to be with you. But . . . now what?"

"I can't live without you," Tom said. "I don't want to. Would you come back with me to New York? I'll take the network job, we'll get a bigger apartment, it'll be perfect. It'll be easy." He turned her toward him and kissed her on the lips and they held their kiss, a gentle, loving promise, until she separated and he asked again, "Will you come with me?"

Nina turned on his lap and snuggled into him, and he embraced her. Her eyes were open.

"Are you thinking of Sasha?" Tom asked.

"Of course. His grandmother. School. His friends. The language. Many things. Tom, look, maybe it's a little too early to talk of this, we need time . . ."

"I don't. I know exactly what I want, I don't need any time at all . . ."

"Yes, but it's so much easier for you. It's just you, you can do what you like, go home, have a job, we'll live with you. It would be beautiful. My dream. But I can't just leave, just like that. It takes time. My apartment; what would Sasha feel? My mother, who would help her? She's almost eighty, and alone . . ."

"She can come too."

Nina laughed. "You're sweet."

"Not really. I didn't mean it." He laughed, trying to recover when he felt her body stiffen. "Just joking. Of course she can come. We'll get an even bigger apartment, there must be a Serb club she can join."

"Don't be silly. It isn't funny. Anyway, she's Muslim. I couldn't leave her here all alone, we're all she has. Tom, I love you, but let's not rush things."

"I love you too. I suppose I could stay here, as long as it takes, until you're ready."

"But what about your film?"

That's true, Tom thought, what about it? Just throw it away? Wait till we're in New York and then finish it? There's no great hurry, unless they find Mladić, and there isn't much chance of that.

And then all at once in a startling crescendo, his phone trilled like a bird, Nina's phone beat a drum solo, and there was a knock on the door.

Nina walked toward the door while she answered her phone

and admitted Aleks, proffering a bouquet of flowers, into the apartment. Seeing they were both on the phone, he went straight into the kitchen to find a vase.

Nina, by the fireplace, went pale.

Tom, sitting in the alcove, was listening to Amber's offer. She had gotten straight down to business. Whatever his last final salary was eleven years ago, they would increase it by 50 percent and he would get the full benefits package, 401k, health insurance, the lot. Maybe she could arrange a signing bonus. He heard her out, and said he'd get an agent to deal with it. But when she said he should start at the beginning of the next month, a fortnight away, he had interrupted. "What's the hurry? I want to finish the doc. And what did Specials say, do they want it?"

"They want to hear more about it. I said you'd call them direct. But the idea of using it to reintroduce you to our viewers, that we all love. It's a great idea. But the thinking is, nobody cares about this guy Mladić. Why didn't you go after Osama bin Laden? The doc needs to be a total winner otherwise it'll weaken the brand."

"What brand?"

"You, of course."

"I'm a brand?"

"You will be by the time we're finished. Times have changed, Tom. No one's just a correspondent anymore. You're a brand. Or you're nobody."

"Spare me the claptrap. Who should I call there? Klein? And by the way. Fifty percent increase over eleven years? I'll need a lot more than that. Just saying. My agent will deal with it."

"About who to call about the doc, I'll let you know. About the money, the more you get, the bigger my payoff, right?"

"Of course. Goes without saying. All that black market diesel in Sarajevo. I hear you bought an apartment with that."

"No, just a car, Tom, just a Mercedes. But Tom?"

"Yes?"

"We don't joke about that stuff anymore. Okay?"

"We?"

"You know what I mean."

"Sure. You mentioned it first. I was just kidding."

They swapped some gossip and Tom hung up, smiling. He looked over to Nina and saw Aleks was holding her hand, each staring into the face of the other.

"What is it?" Tom said, walking to them.

"You know I said that weirdo asked for my phone number?" Nina said, looking past his shoulder.

"What, you really gave it to him?"

"Yes. That was him. He just called."

Tom's jaw dropped. "Don't tell me he wants a date."

"He does want to meet. Not with me though."

Tom looked at Aleks, and back to Nina.

"Huh?"

"He wants to meet with you."

"Me? I think I should play hard to get. Always best on a first date."

"Why do you make a joke about everything?"

"Nina, it's a defense mechanism."

"I see."

"That's pretty amazing, isn't it?" Tom said. "What did he say, 'This is the nice kidnapper'?"

"Don't be silly. He just said, 'Do you know who I am,' and I said yes. I recognized his voice right away." She paused, a distance crept into her eyes, as if remembering something.

"And," Tom prompted.

"So I said, 'What do you want?' And he told me, just like that.

He said he wants to meet you, somewhere safe, away from everyone, just the two of you. And that you have nothing to fear."

"That's it. Nothing else?"

"No. I said I was with you. He said he would call me again in an hour and you should say when and where. Anywhere that makes you comfortable."

"Does he speak English?"

"I suppose so. He said just the two of you."

Aleks was pacing, his mouth tight. "Let's sit down. Think about this."

Nina added, "And he also said no camera."

Screw that, Tom thought. A public place. He can't pat me down. I'll have the hidden camera in the shoulder bag.

"First, let's go through what we know about him, all right?" Aleks said. He was thinking, This is the break.

As they talked and plotted, adrenaline flooded Tom's body. He was up for this, he was back in the game. What a documentary he was making. Whatever this guy wants, it must be big. He turned back to Aleks, who was summing up what Nina had told him.

"So he's physically shorter than his mate, he was always kinder, even though he's just as violent, and it sounds as if he has a mind of his own. He's been part of Mladić's circle for a long time. He must be ex-military, not just a relative or low-level something, he was in that village right in the beginning, in a war zone. Nina, was he kinder then too?"

She snorted. "He raped me. I wasn't thinking, Oh, he's kinder than the other one. They were both disgusting pigs. I don't remember anything about it and I don't want to."

"In the hotel room, he hung back," Tom remembered. "It was the bigger one that did the talking."

"It sounds to me as if he's smart," Aleks said. "He wouldn't be part of the inner circle if he was a dope, and he lets the other guy get out in front, do the rough stuff. But he's always there. And now he wants to meet." He rubbed his chin, looking for the catch.

"So what do you think he wants?" Tom said. "And where should I meet him?"

"Could it be a trap?" Nina said.

"No," Aleks and Tom said at the same time, each for his own reason, each unsure about the truth. Tom said, "He wants to talk, but what about?"

"Go and find out," Aleks said. What he didn't say was that he would have Tom followed, and then they'd follow the other man, call him "K." Was K breaking away from his circle, or loosening his ties? Had he had enough of whatever they were doing? A possible snitch? K has a message for Tom. What could K know that Tom cares about? Only Mladić. Or something to do with him. I'll call the team, he thought, set K up. We'll record the meeting with Tom, follow K, pick him up, turn him. He sounds like he's ripe. Set the meeting up for tomorrow. By the next day, we'll have a guy close to Mladić. We'll have to get Tom out of the way immediately, though. K will think Tom ratted him out. Not good for Tom. All this flashed through Aleks's mind in the time it took Tom to say, "Do you think he wants to talk about Mladić?"

"Go and find out," Aleks said again.

"All I can say," Nina said, "is it's lucky I didn't bring Sasha back. I knew it wasn't over."

"Where should I meet him, do you think?" Tom said. "And when?"

"Tomorrow," Aleks said quickly. "Let him sweat a bit." He'd need time to get the job okayed, to organize the team, set a place and get it wired. At least they were back in place following Tom. They could just swap targets. But he needed the green light, and technical help. A day should do it.

Nina's phone rang again. Her voice shook as she spoke, and she hung up after twenty seconds. "He wants to meet right now, within the hour, or it's off. He says it's now or never. He'll call back in ten minutes."

"Tell him never. You meet tomorrow," Aleks said. "He's bluffing. He's the one who wants to talk."

"Why?" Tom said. "I'm ready. The sooner the better." He was thinking: Why delay? What's in it for Aleks? This guy is too shifty. Tom still didn't know whether to trust him. So far, in everything to do with Nina, Aleks had been an ace. But when it came to him, to Tom? Why would Aleks care? He trusted Aleks to look after Nina, but not in any other way. He went straight to his pile of camera gear and took the shoulder bag with the hidden camera, checked the batteries and the tape. "I'm ready to roll, let's do it. But where? Nina, where do you think?"

The man in the long raincoat and rain hat sat silently next to Tom on the bench by the Sava river for five minutes before Tom understood he was the man he had come to meet. Above them the brick ramparts of the Belgrade fortress loomed dark and heavy against the gray sky that threatened to unload at any moment, and a chill wind blew in from the water. It occurred to Tom, if Nina tried, she couldn't have recommended a worse place to meet. The wind would kill the camera sound, and what excuse can he have for holding the bag on his lap like a granny. It was on the bench, facing the water. He looked at the man sharing the bench, willing him to get up and leave. Surely it was too cold here. If he didn't leave he'd have to find another bench for the meeting. But as Tom glanced at him, the man spoke.

"Thank you for coming to see me," he said, in heavily accented but good English. Tom pulled away from him, startled. He didn't look anything like he did before. He had a mustache and glasses and his cheeks seemed fuller, rounder. The very fact he wasn't wearing jeans and a leather jacket was a disguise in itself. Tom didn't dare take the bag and turn the camera on yet. The man was not to be underestimated. He must have been sizing him up.

Tom nodded. He couldn't bring himself to say to the rapist, "It's a pleasure," but there was a catch in the man's voice, a lilt in the few words he had said, that suggested he was troubled, sincere. He wasn't ingratiating, or wheedling. Does he want help? Without thinking, Tom responded as he would in any ordinary encounter with an acquaintance.

"I'm sorry I chose this place to meet. It was sunny an hour ago when you called. Weather sure changes fast around here."

"Thank you for coming so quickly. Yes, I think we will get very wet soon. If you don't mind, we can go to a café near here, it is small and quiet. I understand if you don't want to go, if you don't trust me. But I am also concerned. I must not be seen with you."

"I should have disguised myself too, I didn't think of it."

"Not necessary." The man smiled. "What do you say? Café or pneumonia?"

"Well, if you put it like that," Tom said, standing up. He could film much better in a quiet, dry place. As they walked, he said, "What is this about?" but regretted it straightaway. He wanted it all on camera. "Don't tell me," he said. "Let's talk over a coffee." They quickened their steps as the first raindrops, light and sparse, quickly became heavy and torrential. Tom crouched as he walked, protecting his bag, and hugged the walls, benefiting from shop awnings and protruding roofs, until they entered the first café they came to.

"It isn't the one I meant, but this will do," the man said, taking off his dripping coat. He hung it on a wall hook by the table. Tom removed his own jacket and for a moment they contemplated drops of rainwater pooling on the floor. The man said, "You can call me David."

"Is that your real name?"

"No, but I've always liked it. It will do for now, for us."

"David" ordered two coffees and two cheesecakes. As he spoke to the waiter, and while Tom surreptitiously turned the hidden camera on and pointed the bag at David, Tom marveled at the sudden turn of events. He'd been about to give up. Instead, here he was with a mild-mannered mystery man across the table who had raped and kidnapped Nina, threatened him, presumably was protecting the man at the top of Europe's "most wanted" list, had been present at Nick's murder, and liked extra cream with his cheesecake.

"You have a sweet tooth," Tom said. He could just as easily have said, You are a bastard rapist and murderer.

"My curse. Every roll of my stomach is a year's worth of cream and chocolate."

"And beer."

"I don't drink."

"Then you're the first Balkan I ever met who doesn't drink. You smoke?"

"Yes."

"That's good then. Here, have one." Tom knocked a cigarette from his pack of Marlboros and offered it, and they both lit up.

"So," Tom said, hidden camera recording on a wide shot. The

sound should be perfect, he thought. They had taken a corner table and were alone but for two women several tables away. It was quiet, secure, out of the way. "Here we are, smoking and drinking coffee," Tom said, speaking just as much to a future American audience eight thousand miles away as to the strange man opposite, "and you want to tell me something. What is it?" He couldn't help smiling as he spoke. He could just see it. End with the question as a tease. *End of part three. Cut to commercials.*

Dramatic final chapter coming up.

Tom didn't know how right he was.

The man glanced around, leaned forward, and spoke in a whisper so low that Tom could barely make out what he was saying. Worse, he thought, the microphone wouldn't pick up a thing. "I can't hear," he said. "Sorry, there's nobody listening, can you speak just a little louder?"

David fixed Tom's eyes with a look of steel. "Can you hear me now?" he whispered.

Tom shook his head. "Not clearly."

"You want me to speak louder?"

"Yes." Tom looked at the two women. They were deep in conversation. The waiter was sitting at a table across the room reading a newspaper. "Nobody is listening."

"If you can't hear me, try harder. Can I trust you?" Tom could barely make out what he was saying. "I must know if I can trust you."

With his elbow Tom surreptitiously nudged the bag closer to David to pick up his sound. He looked up to see David smile in triumph, sit back with a grin. He pointed at the bag with his finger, then wagged his finger in Tom's face as to a naughty schoolboy. He whispered, "You are a journalist and I know that the temptation must be great. But turn off the recorder. Now. Or I walk out and you will regret it forever."

For an instant, a vestige of hope, Tom began to protest his innocence, but David's grin just grew bigger while his eyes became colder. Tom sighed. "Okay," he said. "You win." He put his hand into the bag and turned the camera off. *Pity.*

"No more hidden microphones?" David said, looking at Tom's jacket. Tom shook his head. "I'm afraid not," he said, "I'm not that smart."

"So next time you will know better," David said. "Always have a backup."

Tom shrugged. "Never too old to learn. So, what do you want to tell me?" *Dammit.* He felt deflated; he knew he was about to miss the turning point of the documentary. Now he'd have to re-create the moment somehow. With actors? A long standup? Return to the café later and say, 'At this table he told me . . .' Let's hear what he has to say, it may not amount to much. If he couldn't get it on camera, he almost hoped it didn't.

David stirred three sugars into his coffee and ate a forkful of cheesecake, piling cream on top. He licked his lips. "Good," he said. "You like yours? You've hardly touched it."

"It's fine, thank you."

"It's like this. You know who I am and what I have done."

"Of course."

"And what I am doing."

"Not really. Protecting—"

David silenced him with a hand on his arm. "No need to say the name. Now listen, I have a proposal for you. Do you want to make some money? A lot of money? And get a scoop at the same time?"

"A scoop?" An overused word, for books and movies. "What do you mean?"

"I mean a scoop. Listen," and here David pulled Tom toward him by the arm and whispered, and this time it wasn't just to see if Tom was recording him. "I know where he is. Right now. He won't be there for long. Don't ask me why, but I want to turn him in. I need money, there's five million euros on his head, and I want it."

Tom's heart was slamming against his ribs. He fought to control his breathing. *Holy shit! Appear calm.* "So turn him in. What do you want from me?"

David was gripping his arm. "I don't trust anyone there, the BIA, the chief prosecutor's office, half of them are protecting him. If I told anyone there, I wouldn't live long enough to walk out the door."

"So you want me to do it?"

"Yes."

"Why not a local journalist? Why bring me into it, an American?"

"Don't you understand? Everyone is in this. If not the journalist, then his boss, or the lawyer they'd consult, or the person they go to with the information, or someone in his office. It will all get back to the source within moments. I'd be a traitor, you know what that means here, I'd be dead meat in minutes. You, they won't touch. I know how they think. You came across the information, you passed it on, you're already history, your role is over, no need to do anything to you. It wouldn't be about revenge or punishment or warnings to others. You found out, you passed it on. Mind you, why take a chance, I'd advise you to leave immediately anyway. You just give the information to the chief prosecutor's office and the Dutch at the same time, they will have to act, and you get on a plane. But only talk to the chief prosecutor himself, Vladimir Vukcevic, directly, with no one else in the room, even though it's probably bugged. Whisper in his ear. Go for a walk. Something. He'll tell you who to talk to with the Dutch. They'll bring in The Hague. They'll have to act."

"But then I would get the reward."

"Exactly. And the scoop. You would use that word for this?"

"Oh, yes."

"Good. Then you give me four million, and keep one for yourself. All you have to do is tell Vukcevic in a way that nobody hears you. And the Dutch. And maybe he'll tell them instead of you. This all has to happen quickly, while my friend is still where he is. Although we'll still be okay, if he moves; I'll know about it and where he moves to. And don't tell this to anyone, you hear, not a soul, not till it's all over. Only one man. Vukcevic."

A million bucks. A genuine scoop. Tom tried to take it all in. Could he get access to Vukcevic? Of course, no problem, he'd already asked to interview him. He'd call his office right away. They had said they'd get back to him shortly, it could even happen today or tomorrow. Certainly next week. "Listen, I know you won't let me interview you, I understand, but how about if we just go over some of what you said and I'll record the sound on the camera, but no picture, sound only? I can change your voice digitally, nobody will know who it is."

"Don't be an idiot. How many people could it be?"

"I could say that—"

"Impossible. No. So? Will you do it?"

"Of course. You bet." *There must be a way to get some of this on tape.* "So tell me then, where is he?" *An apartment in New Belgrade?*

"Not so fast. First speak to Vukcevic and the Dutch, tell them you will have the information in twenty-four hours after you speak to them. In the meantime they should start things moving."

"But why would they trust me?"

"Because they're desperate. But they will want something from you, some kind of proof. Just say this to Vukcevic. He'll know what it means. Only somebody deep inside would know this. Tell him, and use these words, tell him, 'There is a mole in the BIA. A black mole.'"

"A what?"

"A black mole. Use the English word. He'll know."

Tom nodded. He had nothing to lose and everything to gain. This guy really is THE guy. Is he really just in it for the money? What else could it be? Remember, he may not look it, with his false mustache and glasses, but this is a true badass. That stony look when he said turn off the recorder. If looks could kill . . . He had almost forgotten who he was talking to. The man who raped Nina. Yet there was no way to associate this man licking the last bits of cream off his finger with the killer and rapist that he really was. Aleks had said he must be smart. He must be brave too, taking this risk to shop his boss. Or a fool.

"One thing though," Tom said. "If I do this—and I will, I will— why trust me? How do you know I won't just keep all the money? Run off to America with it."

"That's the easy part," David said. "May I?" Without waiting for an answer he took a big scoop of Tom's almost untouched cheesecake. "Pity to waste it." He savored the cake, licked his lips. "If you don't give me the money, I'll find you and kill you. Very slowly. I do hope you believe me."

Tom pushed the plate of cheesecake away.

Aleks had moved fast. The moment Tom had left for his meeting he'd worked the phone, and by the time Tom returned, barely able to contain his excitement, Nina was standing at the apartment door with their packed bags, hers and Tom's. Whatever the meeting was about, Aleks had said, they should change their location. You don't deal with these people and expect a quiet life. Just in case, he had found them another place to stay for a few days. Before Tom could even tell them what had happened, Aleks was driving them both across town to an empty apartment. All protective, he said. Why make it easy for the other side, if there is another side. Maybe there isn't. But just in case. Keep moving.

Tom wasn't sure how much to tell Aleks. Could he trust him? Who was he really? The only certainty was that Aleks was a bit too smooth. But he'd realized, on his way from meeting David, he had no choice. He trusted Nina and she trusted Aleks. And anyway, he was getting in way over his head, and by now it was all or nothing.

In the car, when Tom told them what David had offered, Nina had gasped, as if she had been expecting a hot shower and the water came out cold. Aleks had been so shocked he had guided the car to the side of the road and parked. "He's going to rat on Mladić? He must be suicidal."

"He seems to have it all thought out," Tom said. "Should I trust him?"

"Why not? What's the risk?" Aleks said. "He gives you some information, you pass it on, they do with it what they want. If they find Mladić, you're a hero and rich, and if they don't, you did your duty. No, he's the one who needs to trust you. If you talk too much, he's dead." Aleks drummed the wheel with his fingers. "Why you? Why did he pick you? How does he know you won't give him away." It wasn't a question. He was thinking aloud.

Tom answered anyway. "He says if I cheat him, he'll kill me. Slowly."

"Oh, I'm sure of that. Well, anyway, I suppose it doesn't matter why he chose you. You need to call Vukcevic."

"I already did. I have an appointment next week."

"Next week?" Nina said.

"I can take care of that," Aleks said.

The chief prosecutor's office had none of the aura of the BIA headquarters, no guarded gate or manicured lawns and tended woods or multiple buildings to get lost in. Vladimir Vukcevic's operation was housed in a shabby building on a nondescript busy road in central Belgrade. On the other hand, there was no linoleum swept clean of blood, it occurred to Tom. These are the good guys, in theory.

A woman behind a grille in the entrance continued her phone chat until Tom almost pushed his face through to get her attention. She glanced at his ID and waved him into the lobby where he walked around an unmanned metal detector and stood lost at the elevator shaft. Everything about the place, Tom thought, suggested "Irrelevant." A woman balancing a large pile of documents and box files asked if she could help, and directed him to the fourth floor, turn left at the end.

As soon as he gave his name to the young man he found behind a desk, the official phoned his boss and led Tom into the adjoining room.

Impressive, Aleks, Tom thought at the door. He got me the meeting in two hours flat.

Vladimir Vukcevic, with a trimmed gray beard and gray hair swept up and back from a high dome, and the red cheeks of a jovial uncle, beamed as if he'd just heard a good joke. He was a state prosecutor until 2003 when the National Assembly elected him Serbia's chief war crimes prosecutor. But apart from some minor successes, he had little to laugh about. All the main targets of the International Criminal Tribunal for the former Yugoslavia remained at large. A big new poster lay on his desk showing a flow chart of Serbs wanted for genocide and crimes against humanity. On top was Ratko Mladić.

The two men shook hands and as they made small talk Tom arranged his camera on a tripod. He'd film it all on a static wide shot because he knew he would have to leave the camera and approach Vukcevic. This was going to be unorthodox in every way.

When the microphones were in place and the camera was rolling, Tom said, "Sir, I have come for a reason that is rather strange for me, to say the least. I wanted to interview you anyway, as you know, but something came up that you need to know as soon as possible. Thank you very much for seeing me at such short notice."

Vukcevic acknowledged Tom's preamble with a nod of the head and a dismissive gesture with his hand, as if to say, Don't bother, and said, "I understand. I also understand that you have a close friend within the Security Information Agency and he recommended that I meet with you immediately. That's why you are here, but can we please be brief, I have a short window, I must leave the building in fifteen minutes."

"Well, I'm not sure where to start," Tom said. *There's this guy, he raped my girlfriend, killed my best friend, likes cream with his cheesecake, and anyway, he says that . . .*

"Just get to the point."

"Yes, well, this is going to seem a bit strange, but I have been given a message for you, I can't say from whom, but I have been instructed to whisper it into your ear."

"My what?"

"Your ear, sir."

Despite the import of his message, Tom couldn't help but chuckle to himself. This is all on camera, great stuff for the doc. *"My what?"* He could hear the editor laugh out loud when he saw the tape.

"Whisper into my ear?"

"Yes."

"Why, do you think my room is bugged?"

"I don't know. Do you?"

Vukcevic laughed. "I wouldn't be surprised. All right then, come over here and whisper into my ear. You won't be the first."

Tom left the camera, went behind the desk, leaned over Vukcevic, and began to murmur into his ear, covering his mouth with his hand. The prosecutor listened intently, his eyes fixed and distant, until his body jolted straight. Tom barely avoided getting his nose smashed. He resumed his whispering, his hand cupped over his mouth and Vukcevic's ear.

When Tom said, "There is a mole in the BIA. A black mole," Vukcevic instinctively rubbed his left temple.

Tom pulled back, and then remembered there was more. He cupped the prosecutor's ear again and whispered, "He said I should tell the Dutch too. Who should I speak to there?"

Vukcevic nodded to indicate he had understood, pointed to himself, indicating he would take care of the Dutch, and waved Tom back to the other side of the table.

His red face had not turned white but he seemed paler, a firmness had set into his jaw, his breathing was heavier. He looked down at the table and slowly turned the Wanted poster toward himself, and stared at the photos of General Ratko Mladić. There were two. One showed him staring at the camera: square faced, piercing blue eyes, lips thin and parted, salt-and-pepper hair brushed back and flat. A military shirt. The other was a profile, leaning forward in a civilian suit, elbow on the table. In both he looked hard, aggressive, mean.

Tom was holding the camera and panned from the poster up to the chief prosecutor. He too was now looking hard and determined as he made a note on his writing pad. Could this be it? They had had thousands of tips. Mladić was driving a taxi in Vienna. Farming in Russia. Living in Montenegro. But this had the ring of truth. Nobody outside understood the true significance of the man known as, but never, never ever called, to his face, the Black Mole. He ran the dirty tricks department of the BIA and it was best to stay far away from him. This American journalist could not possibly know anything about him.

When Tom turned the camera off, he silently pointed at the photos of Mladić and moved his finger to the word and number alongside. The highlighted word was in Cyrillic but the number was English: five million euros. Tom looked at Vukcevic with the obvious question in his eyes. Vukcevic nodded.

If we get him, it's yours.

Tom packed his gear and shook hands, and even before he had left the room, Vukcevic was speaking fast into the telephone.

In his brief time inside, thirty minutes at most, night had fallen. As he waited for a taxi, his backpack of gear hanging from his shoulder, he cursed the weather yet again. Sunny and light when he went in, dark and raining when he came out. He pulled up his jacket hood and peered through the rain at the hazy headlights flashing by, searching for a lit taxi sign showing it was free. Just as the rain began to pelt down and bounce off the sidewalk and he thought he might end up sleeping here, a taxi stopped right in front of him. A woman got out holding a newspaper over her hair and as she rushed up the stairs, he ran down, threw his bag in first, and sat down heavily.

It was only then that he remembered he didn't know where he lived. Moreover, the driver didn't speak a word of English. Tom pointed at his telephone.

Nina picked up at the second ring. "How did it go?"

"Where do we live?"

"What?"

"The address. I'm in a cab, it's pouring here. You speak to the driver, tell him where to go."

When he arrived at the apartment, a top-floor flat in a quiet leafy road, Nina was waiting with Aleks and two of his colleagues. "This is Thomas Layne," Aleks said, and the two men shook his hand. The introductions were not mutual.

Both men wore leather jackets and jeans. At least they're our leather jackets and jeans, Tom thought, as he put on dry clothes and unpacked his camera gear.

"I don't want to be rude," he said to Aleks when he got him alone in the kitchen, "and I'm sure you know what you're doing, which is more than you can say about me, but wasn't the idea not to tell anyone about this?"

"They are good men. They'll follow you if David calls tonight. Keep you out of trouble."

"Is that necessary?"

"Yes. And remember the address this time."

Nina came in and kissed Tom and took Aleks's hand. "What's that about trouble? It's getting late, are you hungry?"

The three of them put together a light meal of sandwiches, salad, and beer, and took it into the living room where all five ate around the coffee table, waiting for David to call Tom. But the call didn't come and at midnight the two men left, followed shortly afterward by Aleks.

As soon as they were alone, and they moved toward each other, Tom's phone rang. They looked at it but as Tom went to answer, Nina stopped him with her hand on his arm. "No, don't answer it."

"Why, it's him, it must be at this time."

"No, don't answer. He may want you to meet him somewhere now. Don't go. Not alone. Not at night. Aleks said so, he knows what he is doing. Let it ring. He'll call again in the morning."

"But it may be urgent. I don't want to miss this." Tom picked up the phone, still ringing, but Nina grabbed it from his hand. "No! Maybe they can trace the call to where you are."

"Why would they? And who?" The phone stopped.

"You heard what Aleks said, you can't trust anyone. Vukcevic has told someone and that person told someone. He also told the Dutch. That person told someone too. Tom, please, wait, do what Aleks says."

The phone rang again, its falsetto ringtone a bird's mating call. It made Tom smile, but not this time. Nina put her thumb against the battery pack and pushed until it snapped out and the phone went silent. "There," she said with a smile.

Tom looked forlorn. "Now, now," she said, "I'll put it back on in the morning." She took his hand. "Come to bed," she said, leading him to their new bedroom. "I'll make it worth your while."

"I'm too wound up," he said. "How can you think of nookie now?"

Nina pulled him by the belt.

"All right, all right. I'll come to bed with you if you come to America with me, as soon as this is all over." At the doorway he pulled her into his arms and kissed her and turned her around and held her from the back, cupping her breasts and kissing her neck. "Okay? Deal?"

"Oh, I like that." Nina squirmed as Tom slowly nibbled his way to her earlobe and caressed her ear with his tongue. "Oh, stop, it tickles. No. No, don't stop."

She turned and they kissed again and Tom edged her backwards until she came against the bed and he kept pushing until her feet left the floor. "Stop it, I'm falling," she cried and pulled him on top of her.

"So will you come to America with me?" he said, as she opened his belt buckle and he unbuttoned her blouse and slid it off, one arm and then the other.

"Why, now you're making conditions? Unconditional love, that's what I want."

She helped him out of his trousers and looked at his underpants.

"I mean it," Tom said. "Will—"

"Ssssshh," she whispered, putting her finger to his lips, and then between them. "Ssssshh."

It wasn't long after they fell asleep that Sam Morissey pulled off his coat and threw it over the chair in the corner of the official's room. "Don't worry, I wasn't asleep," Sam said. "I was up dealing with the security of the Western world—the ambassador's daughter didn't come home for two days, not for the first time, and I had to read the riot act to a horny literature student from Beatrice, Nebraska. Literature, ferchrissake. No wonder he's got nothing better to do than screw the ambassador's kid. So—what's so urgent?"

As soon as he sat in the chair two more men entered. That was unusual. It was normally just the two of them. He looked at his watch. Four thirty in the morning. That was unusual enough too. What's up? The deputy head of security nodded at one of them, who began talking in English as if they were continuing a conversation.

"When the senior officers were told who the target is, two of them, separately, no names in front of our friend, called our people. We've confirmed it. They haven't told their units who it is yet, just that it's a high-value target and they should stay on full operational alert. They're all in place, ready for the order."

The second man spoke. "We're just waiting for them to be given the time and place."

"So we have to be quick. Why not just move him?" their boss said.

"Because we don't know the source of the leak. It could be anyone around him."

"Replace them all."

"We can replace ours. But they're not all our people. What if the leak is from one of his? And if the SWAT teams raid the place and it's empty, they'll know he was tipped off. Again. Not good. Times are changing. Too many people are looking at us, especially the Dutch, and the Court of Justice people in The Hague. It's getting complicated."

"You know who we're talking about?" the deputy security chief said, fingering his temple.

Morissey shook his head. "How could I? Who?"

"Mladić."

"What?" His antennae quivered.

"Mladić. Vukcevic has someone, someone who says he knows where he is. He hasn't got the address yet but he's so confident he'll get it, and soon, he's persuaded the police and special forces to stand by. They're on top alert."

"So move him."

The first of the two men interrupted. "I just said why we can't."

"But you have to," Morissey put in. "Okay, it won't look good, but it's better than him being caught. That's out. Do it, move him."

"No," the boss said. "Internal politics. But there is another way." All three were now looking at Morissey.

"Okay, so what is it? What's it all got to do with me?"

The three men exchanged glances. "A lot," the boss said. "The source. He's one of yours."

"One of mine? What do you mean? From the embassy?"

"No, an American. The journalist. He interviewed Vukcevic and spent half the time whispering in his ear. We couldn't pick up a word."

At the word "journalist" Morissey's heart sank. *Don't tell me. That guy is a trouble magnet. He's like a bulldozer on automatic. What the fuck!* "Tom Layne."

"Yes."

"I'll wring his fucking neck."

"That won't do much good. He's just the middleman. Someone is using him. And if you wring his neck, that someone will just use someone else."

"How do you know it was Layne?"

"Because he was still in the room when Vukcevic made the call."

Shit. "So first move Mladić! Then find out who the leak is."

"But now the chief prosecutor and The Hague Tribunal and the Dutch mission here all know that Mladić is about to get picked up—"

"So what? So it all falls apart. A bum steer. It happens all the time. Listen, let me make myself clear. We do not want Ratko Mladić arrested. That will kick up a shit storm of biblical proportions. If you don't—"

"I know, I know," the deputy security chief said, "and let me say one thing to you, my friend. We are all in this together. So no threats please. But let me say, and this is not news to you, that if anything did come out it would not change much for us; little is expected of us anyway. Unfair, but that is the way it is. Your country, however, will have no excuse. You will be revealed—"

"We better not. For your sake."

"Oh, for my sake? A threat? A personal threat?"

"No, of course not, that's not what I meant. Listen, let's not get sidetracked here. We have the same interests, we're on the same page, and we have the same problem. What are we going to do?"

Showtime! Kneeling on the floor in the living room, his camera gear arranged in rows, Tom went through every piece, polishing the lenses, replacing all the batteries, putting fresh tapes into the main camera and the hidden camera, checking the microphones. He smiled to himself as he worked. It's all coming together. Nina had all but promised to come to New York with him, they're going to get Mladić, the bastard, he'll finish the doc with a great climax, he'll get his job back with the network at a much bigger salary, it's all looking good. And he could get a million euros thrown in, if it works out. He even began to whistle, his tuneless "Star Spangled Banner" . . . *Oh, say can you see, by the dawn's early light.* He looked outside. Half past eight and morning light barely making it through black clouds. What awful weather. He checked his lights, made sure he had spare bulbs, and double-checked the sun gun that fitted on top of the camera. Ready to rock and roll! He had filmed himself passing on the message and then . . . *O'er the land of the free and the home of the brave . . .*

Nina laughed and hugged him from behind. Tom had risen early and brought her breakfast in bed: a boiled egg, toast, and coffee. They had smoked their first cigarette together, passing it from hand to hand, leaning back into the pillows propped against the wall. And they had fantasized about the apartment they would have in New York City. Maybe I'll buy one, Tom had said, it's about time. At my age. He'd gone through all his savings by hardly working for so many years, but he could be looking at a million-euro windfall. That's a million dollars plus. Anyway, if he took the network job he could get a big mortgage. Two bedrooms by the park, or maybe down in the Village. East Village is cheaper, up and coming, maybe three bedrooms down there. Big kitchen for you to cook in. "For you, you mean," Nina had said. With a nice view. A good school for Sasha. She could find work, maybe as a translator at first, she could write for the Serb press, be their USA correspondent.

Bed talk. Fantasy time. "Let's take it a step at a time," Tom had said, "as long as we get there in the end." Then the phone rang and they both froze, and Tom took the call, his heart beating. But it wasn't "David," it was Aleks, asking if David had called yet.

"No," Tom said.

"Because something is up at work. They're keeping it tight but they're excited about something. Maybe it's related. Call me if you hear something. But remember, be vague, no names."

"Got it." They hung up.

Only minutes later, as Tom finished arranging the camera gear in the backpack, and had stuffed extra batteries in the side pocket, his phone rang again. This time, fully psyched and raring to go, he grabbed the phone. But again it wasn't David.

"Hey, Sam," Tom said. "What's up?"

"You owe me one, pal. I know the only way to get rid of you is to give you what you want, so listen, you're going to get a phone call in a moment, from the BIA. They're going to offer you a scoop.

Take it. They won't tell you what it is, but I'm calling to tell you it's what you most want. Okay? Something's going down and you're going to get the exclusive. All right? I set it up for you so you owe me. It may be an overnight, I don't know, but it's for real so bring your purple toothbrush."

"A scoop?" He hated the pretentiousness of the word, even if he was sitting on a big one. Tom was thinking intently as he listened. Nothing from Sam comes with no strings attached, there was always an angle. On the other hand, he'd always looked out for Tom, going back a couple of decades. "Why me?" Tom said, playing for time. Could it be based on his David tip? It's got around already from Vukcevic and the BIA doesn't know that he himself is already involved? Is it connected? Or something else? A coincidence? He remembered what Aleks had said: no such thing.

"Give me a hint, Sam, I need to know what I'm getting myself into. What's it all about?"

"Can't say, buddy, sworn to secrecy. But it's big. Huge. Like I said, it's what you want." There's only one thing I want, Tom thought, and he knows what it is—Mladić. So maybe it's my tip, and he doesn't even know that. "Well okay, great, thanks for letting me know. I'll expect their call then."

"Yeah, be ready, any minute. I just wanted to give you the heads up. And get some credit, dinner's on you next time, buddy, you got that? And good luck, Tom. You're a good man."

"Wish I could say the same about you." They hung up simultaneously.

I'm a good man? What does he mean by that? Why say it? Sounds like an obituary.

Well either way, it's good stuff for the doc . . . *Oh, say can you see, by the dawn's early light . . .* He was whistling again, sitting side by side with Nina opposite the marble fireplace, looking at the phone on the coffee table. Her head lay on his shoulder, as they waited for the phone call that could lead to the arrest of Europe's greatest villain, the man who had shattered their lives, the pieces of which they were only now beginning to put back together. Tom sighed, thinking of Nick. By now he had trouble summoning him up—the weight of his presence had always been measured only by his own guilt, which with Nina's help was becoming lighter, freeing him. Part of him had always known it wasn't really his fault, but it was a small part. The bigger part was guilt, or if you like, self-flagellation. Assuming responsibility must have served some other purpose, but God knows what. Someone at DART had said the real way to commemorate a dead person is to live your own life fully. Why had he taken the burden upon himself so heavily as to almost throw his own life away? Nina had asked him that several times. When he had told her that her rape was always on his conscience, she had become almost angry. "You made yourself a victim because we were victims. You made it easy on yourself by taking upon yourself our pain. Well, let me tell you, I don't need you to share in what happened to me. It had nothing to do with you. It's mine, mine alone."

She wanted to free him, he could see that, to make him take control of his own life again, to no longer fester in an ancient wound. He was certainly drinking a lot less. And by helping him, she was helping herself. She may be much younger, he thought, but in wisdom each Balkan female year equals two or three of an American male. He put his arm around her shoulder and kissed her forehead. I love you, he thought, and then he said it.

"I love you too, Tom."

But suspense diluted the message. Their minds were elsewhere. The waiting became torturous. The more the minutes dragged by, the more Tom wished he'd taken the call last night. He should have insisted. They sat, Tom and Nina, looking at the phone, willing it to ring.

When the phone rang, they watched it trill several times before Tom blew out air, as if psyching himself up before a race, and took the call.

It was a name too complicated to recall, speaking on behalf of the same deputy head of security he had already visited, off the record. He is offering the reporter the opportunity to witness a special forces operation taking place in the context of Serbia's responsibility vis-à-vis the international criminal tribunal for the former Yugoslavia. Complete secrecy must be maintained; you will surrender your cell phone for the duration of the operation. You are permitted to film the events as they unfold. You must sign a commitment to abide by all instructions pertaining to the security of the operation and its implementation as well as a liability waiver. You will be accompanied by an official state photographer and you will be the only member of the press invited. If you agree, present yourself immediately to the BIA headquarters main entrance at Kraljice Ane Street. Prepare yourself for a possible overnight.

Tom had been scribbling furiously, taking notes. "What is your name again?" he asked, but the line had already gone dead. He looked at the phone and then at Nina. She had pushed her head next to Tom to listen.

"How do you know it is real?" she asked before Tom could speak. "It may just be a way of making you come to them and then they can lock you up."

"Why would they lock me up? I haven't done anything. But

could it be? They're going to get Mladić and I'll be the only journalist there? Is that possible?"

"Frankly, no."

"So what is it then?"

Nina phoned Aleks. "He'll be here in five minutes," she said,
"he's just buying fresh bourekas. Potato, mushroom, and cheese.
He knows the way to my heart. Straight through my stomach. I'll
put on the coffee."

"I'll get ready. Actually, I am ready." Tom put his toothbrush
and toothpaste into a small plastic bag and stuffed it into his backpack's side pocket along with his notebook and pen. "Is this too
good to be true?" he muttered. The best he had hoped for was to
find the link between Mladić, Srebrenica, and Knin, which ad-
mittedly was a bit of inside baseball. But to be there when they
capture Mladić? Oh man! He felt the excitement building. And
an exclusive facility? It'll be a piece of cake. I won't even have to
think, they'll take me by the hand. This is going to knock Amber
off her feet. What a way to start a new job.

"Nina," Tom said, joining her in the kitchen as she stared at
the kettle on the gas. "Seriously, we could have a terrific apartment in New York. And if I get Mladić's arrest, it'll be a great news
story. I'll get on the show with that as soon as it happens, and keep
back most of the action stuff for the doc. It'll put me in a great
place to negotiate with the network. So, you'll come? Tell me, put
me out of my misery."

Nina poured water into two of the mugs as she weighed her
response, which came in a slow, wondering voice. "You know, it's
all a bit of a game for you, isn't it?"

"What do you mean?"

"Well, for you it's just a story. Great pictures, great scoop, you'll get your great job back, great salary, it's all great, great, great for you, isn't it? And greatest of all, beautiful younger woman comes home to live with you in your great new apartment in great New York."

Whoa. Where did that come from? What do you say to that?

"It was the same in Bosnia. Not only you, but all the foreign press. A great story. While for me, and my friends, it was our life. Our life and our country were collapsing around us, and for you it was all just one great story after another. You know, every time some photographer said, 'Dude, great picture,' it was like a knife in my gut. You won promotions, won prizes, earned more money, while we ... while ... we picked up the pieces. Buried our friends. Rebuilt our homes. I wanted to be a lawyer. But that got lost with all our other dreams." She put down her coffee and took his hand. "I'm not criticizing you, Tom, really I'm not. That's just the way it was. If there was a war in America it would be the same. Foreigners would come and report and commiserate and go home to their families and forget about you. At best they'd have a reunion twenty years later to celebrate the good old days. It's your job. It's what you do. But when you're all so happy—Oh, wow, I'm gonna film Mladić getting arrested—well, you know, for me, it sounds kind of juvenile. For me, it's different. It isn't just a story. It's my life, my country, it's all just one big continuing tragedy, and all you care about is getting a better contract and making a better film."

"Okay, that's decided. I won't go."

"Don't be silly. Of course you will."

"So what's your problem, then?"

"I don't have a problem. Maybe you do."

"What do you mean by that?"

Saved by the bell. Nina went to open the door to find a jovial Aleks holding out a paper bag with bourekas. "Look," he said.

"Fresh, tasty, hot." He kissed her. "And the bourekas aren't bad either."

"You're in a good mood this morning."

"Did David call yet?"

"No," she said.

"Well, he better. Otherwise we've got nothing."

Again Tom all but bit his lip. Why didn't he take that call?

Nina continued, "The BIA did."

That slowed Aleks down. "The BIA?"

"Yes. They've offered Tom an exclusive. They didn't say what."

Aleks phoned his office. They didn't know anything about it. "Who called you?"

"The office of the guy Sam set me up to see," Tom said. "Deputy head of security."

"Which one? There are several."

"I don't know. They're not very generous with names."

Aleks snorted. "That's true. Here, I've got three of each."

Tom took a mushroom boureka and munched quietly, and sipped his coffee. "He said I should come immediately."

"Hurry up and wait. We learned from the army. Whatever it is, you should take a book; nothing happens on time. And it may not even be in Belgrade."

"What if it's a trap?" Nina put in. "To get Tom there and then arrest him."

"Only one way to find out. But don't worry about that, it isn't a trap. And if it is something not good, and who knows, I'll be nearby. Don't worry about that, Tom."

"The worst thing you can say to someone invited to the secret service of any country," Tom said, "is 'Don't worry.'"

"But what about David? What if he calls?" Nina said. "Or what if he doesn't call? Presumably this whole operation is based on that call."

"You're right," Tom said. "This is getting complicated. Presumably this whole BIA facility is about a source telling them where Mladić is, and they don't know that source is me. If they take my phone, David can't get hold of me and the source, who is me, doesn't tell them where Mladić is after all. And I come home with nothing. That should make you happy, Nina. Why the hell didn't I take that call last night!"

"He called last night?" Aleks said.

"Someone did. Late."

"And you didn't answer?"

Tom looked at Nina. "It's a long story," she said.

Aleks sighed and shook his head. "Okay, let's move on. Tom, how about you don't take your phone, Nina, you keep it, and take the call from 'David.' He'll trust you. You give me the information and I pass it on to Vukcevic. Or you do, Nina. One of us."

"If David tells us, if he isn't scared off," Nina said. "What if he wants to see Tom in person again, he won't tell me over the phone."

"So you go see him. Tell him Tom is sick. Or tell him the truth can't hurt."

"That way we could have it both ways," Tom said. He didn't want to lose out on the tip-off. But he couldn't lose the BIA opportunity either. It might be related, it might not be. "Anyway, it's been nearly twenty-four hours, he hasn't called, and the BIA has. I should go with what I've got, a bird in the bush and all that."

When the taxi dropped Tom off at the sweeping driveway to the BIA headquarters, an impatient young man in a gray suit was already waiting for him inside the guardroom by the metal barrier. A uniformed guard emptied his backpack and laboriously checked each item, switching everything on and off, opening and resealing each tape cassette, even inserting a long needle inside the toothpaste to make sure there was no solid object inside. After Tom had passed through a metal detector, the escort, apologizing for all the bother, issued him with a numbered identity tag, which he pinned to his jacket lapel, and led him through the entrance lobby into a maze of corridors and stairways and across a courtyard into another building.

Waiting for another elevator, Tom tried to make light of his sinking feeling. "In my experience, the higher you go in a building the safer you are," he said with an attempt at a smile. "The lower you go . . . well, you know what I mean." Except in South Africa, he added, where in apartheid days the cops threw so many people out of the top-floor windows locals called police headquarters "The Flying School." The man in the suit acknowledged his attempt at humor with a smile a shade too grim for comfort.

In the elevator he pressed −3. As Tom contemplated the keyboard's red light illuminating each further descent his stomach began to tighten. Had he made the mother of all mistakes?

They turned left and again took off through empty corridors, arriving finally at a waiting area with sofas and chairs and a coffee machine.

"Please wait here, someone will come for you soon," the man said, and left.

Tom made a cup of coffee, praying that David had called and that Vukcevic had got the message and that this whole BIA thing was related. After fifteen minutes he began to wish he had taken Aleks's advice and brought a book. There was a pile of magazines: *House and Home,* Serb style. Dark wood, hunting trophies, each bathroom with a slim naked woman washing her hair. The almost-naked men were all dark and handsome with socks stuffed into their briefs. A travel magazine specialized, judging by the pictures, in bus tours to Stalingrad circa 1960.

Come on, ferchrissake. Tom consulted his watch for the tenth time. Ten to twelve, he'd been here almost an hour, without seeing a soul.

Could Nina have been right? Did they bring me here just to keep me out of the way? What do they want from me? But it started with Sam, he told me not worry, I'd get a scoop. Could they be using him too? No, he's been around too long, he's nobody's fool. Not like me.

The longer he waited in isolation, the more convinced Tom became that he had been played for a sucker. He didn't get nervous. He wasn't worried they'd do anything to him. What could they do? And one day, it would all be a great story to tell in the bar. That consolation had got him through most of his professional life.

Still. Come on! Where are they? He stood up, stretched his legs, walked to the door. It was the only way in or out. Was it locked? Just as he turned the handle, the door opened, almost knocking him backwards. It was the young guy in the gray suit again. "Sorry to have kept you," he said. "Please follow me."

He didn't say where and Tom didn't ask. Tom shouldered his backpack and went with him in silence back to the elevator shaft. As the door opened, Tom said, "Up or down?"

"Down."

Tom snorted. "Thought so."

More walking in echoing corridors that ended at a thick iron door with two long levers for bolts. Morissey, Tom was thinking, it isn't dinner I'm gonna give you for this, but a knee in the balls. The man pushed the door open onto what looked like a cavernous underground parking lot. The ceiling was low and crisscrossed with pipes and thick cables and supported by pillars. He heard the echo of footsteps and loud voices bouncing off concrete walls and as they rounded a corner his heart leapt.

There were about fifty men in groups of around ten, all dressed in black with black balaclavas around their necks, ready to be drawn up over their faces. No insignia. Each seemed more square-jawed and muscular than the other. At least half had shaven heads. Hanging from their wide leather belts were handcuffs, truncheons, pistols, bulky pouches, and on the ground before each of them was a backpack and a bottle of water. Farther away in the shadow he made out a man addressing a group, all dressed the same way, but these were all holding long automatic rifles. Behind them was a line of black SUVs and a collection of nondescript cars, of the kind nobody would look at twice.

A young man approached in jeans and an olive green fishing vest stuffed with camera equipment. As Tom's escort made a brief introduction and left, the man said, "I've been waiting for you; I was afraid they'd leave before you got here." They shook hands.

"Unavoidably detained. Sorry, what's your name again?"

"Bojan Bogdanovic. Call me Bobo. I grew up in New Jersey. You're Tom."

"Yes." He looks just like the police, Tom thought, probably a cop too. "So what's the story here?"

"We'll get a proper briefing at some point. I'm the in-house photographer here and I also escort the press sometimes. So I'm your escort now. Stay close to me all the time, okay?"

"Sure. Do you know what's happening? And who are these guys?"

"Police special forces. Operating with the BIA today. They never say what's happening till the very last moment. But it's some kind of arrest operation, and judging by the number of people here, probably several arrests. One of the officers will brief us soon."

"Can I film here?"

"No way, don't take your camera out till we have left HQ."

"Any idea when we're going?"

"No."

"Where?"

"No."

They sat on folding picnic chairs by one of the SUVs, which Tom now saw had blacked-out windows. Some of the police commandos were stretched out, sleeping, while others smoked and laughed, and one group of the sharpshooters played cards. When an officer strolled by, Bobo called out and got a terse response. "They're waiting for the green light," he said, "it should have come by now. He said he hopes it isn't a false alarm."

Tom's stomach clenched. He stood, threw out his arms, and yawned. His eyes closed in self-reproach. He blew it. He should have waited for David's call. It was obvious. Vukcevic had put everyone on alert, waiting for Tom to call with the info, but Tom couldn't get the info because he was stuck in the basement.

But surely Aleks would know how to pass on the information from David. If David gave the info to Nina.

If David ever called. And apparently he hadn't. Too many ifs. But what else could I have done? He thought, Bye-bye million euros. Bye-bye scoop. What a letdown. And all because Nina wouldn't let me answer the phone.

Someone was handing out coffee and sandwiches. Bobo made sure Tom got one but otherwise kept to himself. Tom munched with no appetite, thick slices of ham and thicker slices of cheese, with some kind of mayo spread. So much for all his experience.

So much for a great end to the doc. Why oh why didn't he wait for David to call. Asshole!

He walked in circles, embarrassed by the nerdy squeak of his sneakers on the tarmac.

He should find a toilet, he needed to pee. But just as he opened his mouth to ask Bobo where to go, there was a whistle, and a dozen men ran to their chief, who was unfolding a large map. Each took out a smaller map and followed the instructions of their leader, making notes on their own maps.

The other men fell into groups of eight, standing by their backpacks.

"Looks like it's a go," Bobo said. Tom's heart was pounding. They got the call? They're going to pick up Mladić? Oh man, oh, God, this is great. He stood with his backpack in his arms, ready to jump into whichever car he was assigned.

A minute later a door opened and a group of men in civilian dress walked straight to the commandos. One of the youngest took the lead and began to talk, in a quiet, calm voice, even before he had reached the men. The hard-faced police listened without a change of expression. All in a day's work. Tom strained to try to identify the name Mladić, but could not. The man speaking handed things over to an older man who seemed to be giving a pep speech rather than handing out information. When he finished, he went up to each man, shook his hand, and turned and left.

The unit leaders gave final instructions, their men shouted some kind of Serb marine-like hoo-ha, and ran to their vehicles.

"So?" Tom said to Bobo.

"So?" Bobo said with a tense smile. "Let's go."

"Is there a toilet around here?"

"No time. Later."

. . .

Bobo explained as their car squealed through the tight turns of the underground parking lot. "There're going to be some arrests," Bobo said. "They still haven't said who, but they never do until the very last moment. Complete need-to-know basis. Everyone carries phones, so they're afraid somebody could tip somebody else off. Know what I mean?"

Tom nodded but couldn't help himself. "Mladić? Could it be Mladić?"

Bobo laughed out loud. "Ratko Mladić? Sure, it could be. It could be the queen of England too, but I doubt it. Mind you, it would be good if it was. Mladić, I mean. Or Karadjic. Time to clean house."

They sat in silence as their driver clung to the tail of the SUV convoy. Next to him was a severe, preoccupied man with a thin neck and thinning hair who hadn't spoken a word, not even of greeting. Both were in plain clothes. The police commandos in their black jumpsuits were in the black-windowed SUVs. It seemed to Tom that whereas they had left in one long convoy, groups of vehicles were peeling off, and after twenty minutes they were down to two SUVs and two cars.

He was calculating all the way and knew they'd need more than eight commandos and two cameramen to pick up the feared Ratko Mladić. Moreover, they weren't heading over the river toward New Belgrade but out of town. They had left the clusters of apartment buildings well behind and now the rows were thinning and soon it was all fields and meadows until finally they came to a stop at a clearing off a narrow road bordered by tall hedges. A good place not to be seen. Tom prepared his camera but Bobo stopped him with a hand on his arm.

The thin-necked man, speaking on the phone, got out of the

car, gesturing for the commandos to gather around him. Bobo translated, in a whisper. "There're a number of arrests going on right now. They'll do one here, hand him over to the local police station, and then they'll join a bigger operation."

Tom listened grimly. Hope yet. Maybe Mladić is next. "So who is the guy?" At that moment the briefer handed out color photos of the target. Heavyset face and broad shoulders. Short, light brown hair. Brown eyes, thick eyebrows, thin lips. About forty years old. "Mladić's driver," Bobo said, with an appreciative nod, "one of them. Maybe you're right, they're closing in on the guy. Maybe today's the day."

"Can I film yet?" His bladder was painful, he needed to piss, but he was missing great pictures, he needed this scene to set up the arrest. "Not yet," Bobo said. "They don't want anyone identified." Just as Tom began to walk off to find a corner to pee in, he heard Bobo call, "Okay, here you go, you can film now." The men were pulling up their balaclavas to cover their faces. Only their mouths and eyes were visible through slits. The crew of joking men became a fearsome bunch. Tom began filming as each clicked the magazine into his semiautomatic, pulled back the slide and loaded the chamber, and the two men with automatic rifles slammed in their longer magazines. They pulled on flak jackets. So did Tom and Bobo. Locked and loaded, the special forces climbed back into their vehicles, led by their little Honda, with Mystery Man in front again talking on the phone. On the outskirts of the next village an unmarked police car pulled out ahead of them and they followed it through a few streets and turns until they came to a halt outside a small house in a row. Two workmen fixing a culvert looked up, nodded, and walked away. It was one thirty in the afternoon.

Even before Tom had got out of the car the SUVs had emptied

and four armed hooded men in black walked quickly through the gate and along the side of the house to the back, while two of the men stopped at the front door and two more covered them from the gate.

The thin man walked past them all and knocked on the door. A woman in an apron appeared and disappeared as if pulled back by a rope as the masked men and the briefer pushed past her. Tom was at the briefer's shoulder, filming every moment, hearing each sound on the small bud headphone pressed into his ear. Ten seconds after she had opened the front door they had their man. He was sitting in the lounge reading a newspaper and didn't have time to understand what was going on before his hands were cuffed and he was on the floor with his nose in the carpet.

Tom had it all on tape, the door flying open, the masked men in black assaulting the man in the chair, flurries of arms and heads and shouting and yells of protest and the newspaper torn from the man's hands and torn by boots stamping over it.

The man's wife was shouting, clawing at the arms of the plain-clothes briefer who was explaining to her, telling her to calm down, and then to shut up. You didn't need to speak the language to get the message. Tom focused on her furious, terrified face and then pulled out wide to her husband on the ground, arms behind his back, a commando kneeling over him and now pulling him to his feet, holding him upright, her husband red-faced and panting so hard he could barely breathe, he had to bend and suck in air, trying to say something. In the small room everyone was shoved by someone else and Tom struggled to keep his shot steady.

When things calmed down and he finished a shot Tom said, "What's he saying?" Bobo was snapping away next to him.

"Says he's just a driver, he didn't know who he was driving, every day someone else, he got orders and he did what he was told."

"Was he driving Mladić?"

"Yes, he said so, but he says he just drives whoever he's told to drive."

A kind of calm descended upon the room. The husband stood upright, his hands handcuffed behind his back, two masked commandos holding him by the arms, his wife quietly crying, the briefer talking on the phone.

Tom said to Bobo, "Please, for me, ask him when he last saw Mladić."

Bobo translated as Tom panned from the man's handcuffs, around his body, and ended on the man's face as Bobo finished the question. Nicely framed, Tom waited for Mladić's driver to answer. But the man only looked with contempt at Tom, his snarling lips and glaring eyes expressing more than any answer he could have given, if he had wanted to give one, which he didn't.

They were in and out of the house with their quarry within three minutes, giving neighbors no time to gather and protest. A local policeman remained with the wife to make sure she didn't phone anybody, warn anyone else who might be on the list. Tom had hardly stopped rolling; it was his first piece of real action, except for when he had been the target himself. And as they raced out of the village, a smile spread across his face.

"Good stuff?" Bobo said.

"Oh, yes. Where to now? Another one?"

"Yes, but they won't say who."

Tom's smile was wiped off by a burning sensation in his gut. "I've really got to piss."

"Can't stop now. Why didn't you go in the house?"

"Oh right, there was really time."

· · ·

An hour later, after local police took custody of the handcuffed driver, with instructions to take him to BIA headquarters in Belgrade, and after Tom was finally able to empty his bladder, they drove fast to join two more units on the outskirts of town. Six SUVs, six civvy cars. Tom was over the moon. He'd had a piss, he'd shot ten minutes of great material, about two minutes of the arrest of the driver as well as some good rolling shots through the window and also of the back of the driver's head while driving, passing traffic seen in the side mirror, the usual, moody stuff that he'd need to help tell the story.

He couldn't help congratulating himself. If David called, had spoken to Nina, and Aleks had passed on the message—in his name, of course—he'd be a million euros to the good. Not that it was about the money, of course, it really wasn't, but still, a million euros goes a long way when you can barely afford a bottle of scotch. Not that he wanted one. Off that stuff, for good. That's a promise.

If he really gets the Mladić scoop. Oh, man.

Their extended convoy broke into two and now even Bobo was getting excited. Team leader in front was on the phone all the time and Bobo gave Tom the odd hint from what he overheard. "It's something big. A lot of people involved. Coordination. More than one target. Several together. Apartment block."

"Could there really be a shoot-out?" Tom said. With a crunching sound he pulled the Velcro fastening of his flak jacket tighter across his chest.

"Who knows? Mladić always said he would never be caught alive. But if you ask me, that's all talk. He's been on the run, what, ten years? More? And now he's supposed to be sick?"

As the car navigated Belgrade's heavy afternoon traffic, Tom

wondered why it wasn't going down at night. Isn't that the way
it's done? Dawn raids, when the target is groggy with sleep, too
dazed to respond, quick getaways through deserted streets with
no gawking neighbors getting in the way. Fast and clean. Or is
that just the movies? Now the streets are crowded, it's afternoon,
they'll be wide awake. Better for filming though. He cradled his
camera on his lap, ready to roll.

Who will it be? Mladić? Oh, he hoped so!

He wished Nick could be here. He hadn't thought about him
much lately. Nina had been right, he'd become morbid, reliving
painful details as if it was his solemn duty to remember every
crushing moment. At first it had been a tortured blur, an anguished affliction with no center, an awful memory whose details
were brushed out. Then over the years he'd wake up sweating, or
he'd be struck in mid-sentence, as another fragment of memory
shot to the surface, another piece of the puzzle fell into place.
The muzzle flash. The mournful mooing of a cow in the distance.
Nick's shadow disappearing as he fell. He too had felt his legs
giving beneath him, as if he was collapsing in sympathy; it had
taken him years before he suddenly recalled that sensation and
remembered he had supported himself against the car's hood.
And it was at least five years before he had realized that it wasn't
his own mock execution that tortured him but his guilt that
Nick did die. And because of him. He had decided to do the
story. He had decided to take that road. He should have been
driving; he would have driven through the roadblock, Nick was
too inexperienced. It was all his fault.

"Are you all right?"

"I was just thinking, that's all. Sorry, what did you say?"

"You're sweating. Is the flak jacket too tight? He said that when
we arrive it will be different this time. One man will take him,

when he comes out of the store, the grocery store. We can't film because it is too dangerous. There will be too many people around. We'll just draw attention."

The leader in front spoke some more, looking at their reflection in the driver's mirror, which he had twisted to see them. He had a soft, calm, commanding voice that fought his scrawny, chicken-neck appearance. He'd make a great interrogator, Tom thought. You wouldn't see it coming.

Bobo went on, "He says from there we'll go straight to headquarters and you can film them there."

"Them?"

"I don't know who. He didn't say."

"Can you ask him if I can film through the window, from inside the car, nobody will see me, from a distance, I'll be on the end of the lens. Is that all right?" Otherwise why be here, he thought.

Bobo translated, and the man hesitated, then nodded. "He says yes, but don't raise the camera till he says, okay? And don't film his face."

"Sure, tell him thanks."

When they reached the edge of the forest of tall apartment buildings that constituted New Belgrade, instead of entering the maze of streets and pathways, they pulled into a gas station while the other two SUVs and their civvy escort vehicles drove on.

They backed into parallel positions, by the entrance to the bathroom in the back, noses out, ready to leave in a hurry.

"Are we hiding?" Tom said.

"Looks like it," Bobo said, and leaned forward to the skinny leader, who as always had his phone to his ear. When he ended his call Bobo spoke to him in a low voice and the man answered before taking another call. Bobo sat back in his seat. "We're just waiting for the green light. We're going to get him coming out of a grocery store but he hasn't gone in yet."

"Who?"

"He didn't say. And I didn't ask."

"Why not get him going in?"

"Because on the way out he'll have his hands full. It will slow him down a bit."

It was late afternoon when Mystery Man took a call and they suddenly pulled out from the garage, sped up to the stop light, and just made it through on yellow. A minute later they jerked to a halt at a sleepy little shopping center. Old men dozed alone on concrete benches, a couple of children sat on a seesaw watched by mothers in athletic pants and a woman emerged from the grocery store carrying a brown paper bag.

One SUV parked behind them, another continued past and came to a halt thirty meters away at the other end of the square where a path led to the nearest apartment building. Tom thought, Why so conspicuous? Two big black SUVs. They should carry a sign, Don't look at me, I'm undercover.

After all their waiting, Tom almost missed the moment. He was pointing the camera at the SUV's passenger door, rolling and waiting for the hooded men in black to emerge. He didn't notice the single large man in civilian clothes get out of the other side and saunter round the SUV to the grocery store, where he waited at the entrance.

Then their mystery man got out and said nonchalantly, "It'll be over in a moment," and Bobo focused his camera on the doorway. He told Tom, "You're looking the wrong way." Just as Tom said, "What do you mean?" a man came out of the store carrying two laden bags. Tom swung his camera round. Mystery Man spoke to him, and the man looked around. His eyes rested on the first SUV, and the second. The second man in civilian clothes took him by the arm. Tom zoomed in.

Holy cow. Tom saw him on close-up at the end of his lens. David. The two men walked him to the first SUV and took his shopping as he climbed into the vehicle. His face looked blank, as if he had expected this. They must have told him there was no point fighting and a quick look at the black SUVs parked so close must have persuaded him. That's why they made them stand out so much, to show the futility of resistance. As the man with the chicken neck closed the SUV door he was left holding David's bags. Walking back to the car he looked inside, took out a carton of cigarettes, and gave both otherwise full bags to an old man in a cardigan on a bench. He looked after him in surprise and rummaged inside, exploring his bounty.

Tom was calculating: So they picked up David. What does that mean? Did he ever make the call, did he give away Mladić's hideout and now he's been picked up too? They're arresting Mladić and everyone around him? What's going on?

"Who was that man?" Tom asked.

It was minutes before they could get an answer from the leader. He was talking animatedly into his phone, at one point raising his voice and laughing, and when he ended the call and Bobo asked him a question, it took him half a minute to respond. "A bodyguard," Bobo said at last. "We're going back to BIA headquarters. So what do you say, did you get a good story?"

"It's been a good day," Tom said, but his mind was already far away. Is that all? Should he be disappointed? Or did another unit pick up Mladić?

He heard a fluttering sound, the fine rustle of paper displacing air, and smiled at a gathering pile of green, or whatever color euros are: a million, stacked at his feet. And if David spends the rest of his life in jail, who knows, maybe five million?

"What's funny?" Bobo said.

"Nothing. Just thinking." No, he couldn't do that, he had a deal. Don't get greedy. A million euros. Holy cow!

A million euros. A great doc. Nina waiting for him. Are things looking up, or what? Tom closed his eyes as they drove, more slowly now, back to headquarters. A glow of satisfaction washed over him, and as he lay back against the seat, half asleep, a smug grin spread over his face.

There were five men that night in the BIA's holding pen, a small internal courtyard with one metal door and wire netting above. On all sides were walls with windows that looked down on the yard, and high above was the roof. Tom leaned out of one window to film the men below who were slouching and talking. They had probably been allowed out of their cells just so that he could film them. Armed guards stood in each corner of the yard. It was brightly lit by floodlights that threw shadows of the men onto the walls. As he filmed, one of the men noticed and pointed. The prisoners looked up.

Later he cursed himself for not ducking back in. Instead, Tom looked away from the viewfinder straight into the eyes of David, and his flesh went cold. Even from two stories high, Tom could see the bodyguard's eyes narrow and darken and his fury seemed to shoot up like arrows. Too late, he pulled himself into the room, and again cursed himself. What do I have to act guilty about? He leaned out again and continued to film, as David stared up at him.

Was that a threatening look? Did it matter now, anyway? Tom felt a surge of relief as he recognized another of the prisoners: it was the other bodyguard, the one who had pulled the camera from his hands in the hotel room and tried to smash it. By now Tom knew what was going on. He was witnessing history. The BIA was rounding up Mladić and his entire support network, arresting them all in a nationwide sweep, and he, Tom Layne, had the scoop. Yes, at last he'd use the word. A genuine scoop. Nobody he had spoken to knew where Mladić was, but apparently he wasn't in Belgrade or he'd be here now. He must have been hiding outside after all and would be brought here soon, or the next day at the latest. He asked about filming Mladić exclusively, but even if the rest of the media had it, he already had enough exclusive material to make his documentary an award winner. This is what the world had been expecting for eleven years. And he was alone with it!

Was it all because of David? Had he called and given Mladić away? And then got caught in his own net? If so, Tom was already a million euros richer. If not? So what? He'd never been after the money, he had wanted a good doc and maybe to take care of Rat-face Mladić. And he'd done it.

At last Tom pulled back from the window into the room and made way for Bobo, who leaned out with his telephoto to take stills of the prisoners below.

Tom had all the pictures he needed. The hunt, the arrests, the prisoners. Mladić must be caught somewhere else. Now he couldn't wait to get home, back to Nina, and to compare notes with Aleks. He'd know where Mladić was being held, what would happen next, maybe the killer's swift extradition to the International Court of Justice in The Hague. The longer the government held him in a Belgrade jail, the more likely it was that his supporters, Serb nationalists, the militias, would take to the streets to free their hero. That's what everyone feared when

Mladić was finally arrested: revolution in his support. Would it start as soon as the news broke? Tom smiled: Layne's back! In the right place at the right time.

With the operation now over, an official allowed Tom to use his office phone. He didn't want to call Nina in case someone was listening, and he'd see her soon anyway, so he phoned Amber in New York. He had to tell someone about his scoop, even if it couldn't be reported until there was an official BIA statement, and he wanted to build up Amber's excitement, to increase the price for his doc, get her on his side so she could sell it to Specials. He looked at his watch. Eight o'clock in the evening in Belgrade, two in the afternoon in New York.

"Sounds wonderful, Tom, congratulations," Amber said, after hearing him out. "But will you get Mladić on tape?"

"I don't know yet, I hope so. But if not here, then we'll get him in The Hague. The perp walk. You should get someone from London to go over and wait for him."

"We can get that from Reuters or AP, or Dutch TV."

"No, I need our own coverage for the doc, it'll be better."

"Okay, I'll send someone over. What about trouble on the streets in Belgrade?"

"I'll cover that for the doc. If it gets big, send in some more people for news."

"I'll send in a crew now, just in case. And Tom?"

"Yes?"

"Well done. Really. It's great to have you back on board."

"Hey, not so fast. Speak to my agent!"

Amber laughed. "Agent? And you lose ten percent? That'll be the day." She hung up, leaving Tom looking at the phone, heaving a huge sigh of satisfaction. What a day.

. . .

There was only one place to celebrate and that was in bed, but to say Nina's mind was elsewhere was to put it mildly. As soon as he entered the apartment and told her about the arrests she had only one question: "Are you sure it was the other bodyguard too? Both of them were arrested?"

"Yes, definitely. I saw them both in the yard."

She could feel herself palpitating as she fought to control her emotions. *The pigs will pay.* At last she said, "I wonder if I should testify against them. For rape."

Tom took her hand. "It's possible. Let's see what Aleks says."

"Tell me again, though, when David looked up at you . . ."

"Oh, I forgot!" Tom shouted. "So what happened? Did he call me? David. Did he call?"

A million-plus bucks rode on her answer. She looked at him, her face blank. *Was she teasing him?*

"Did he?" he shouted. "Tell me, now, don't play games."

"Is that really all you care about? The money? When the man who did those terrible things has finally been caught, and his horrible henchmen too?"

"No, it isn't all I care about. But I do care about it some, oh yes. Tell me, did he call, yes or no?"

Nina stood, shaking her head. "It is all you care about, the money. My country's worst criminals have been caught, and the people who raped me, they will be punished, that is what is important."

Tom felt like grabbing her and shaking her. "Of course you're right. But why are you torturing me? Please tell me. Did . . . David . . . call?"

"Yes."

"Really?"

"Yes. I met him. For a moment on a street corner."

Tom felt himself go faint, he felt the hairs on his nape rise, he had to sit down. "And he said where Mladić was? What did he say? What did you say? You told Aleks? Oh, my, God. A million euros. Oh, my, God."

"And it isn't about the money?"

Tom didn't answer. He was looking over her shoulder, and caught himself in the mirror: his mouth was open and his face was crinkled in the biggest grin he had ever seen. He looked like a circus clown with a painted smile, but it was real.

Nina said, "I think you should give the money to a charity for his victims."

"I will. You. I'll buy a flat in New York and we can live in it. We're victims too, you know." He let her go and sat on the sofa, scratching his chin. "Really, Nina, you know what this means? It means we can start our life together with our own place, no mortgage . . ." His mind was off and running and everything was falling into place. He was thinking Lower East Side two-bedroom apartment, the best school for Sasha, him back at the network, maybe even having their own baby . . . He smiled at Nina. She'll be happy there, we all will . . .

And so to bed. It turned out Nina wasn't too serious about giving the money away, and in the slithery playfulness of the shower she continued to tease him in other ways, until in bed she moved beyond teasing and, at last, they fell asleep in each other's arms and slept like children until the morning.

The radio news and then the TV news came and went with no mention of the wave of arrests. "It's probably still going on, that's why," Tom said, stirring the coffee and pouring a cup for Nina. "Picking everyone up." He phoned Bobo to see if he knew what was happening but gave up after seven rings. "He's probably out with them; he shoots everything they do."

"We can go back to my flat now," Nina said, taking Tom's hand as they sat on the sofa. "Bring Sasha home. It's all over. You know, I feel as if it's easier to breathe. Knowing those two men will be punished at last. For what they did to me.

"There is something strange though," she continued, as they sat quietly, waiting for Aleks to come with his daily morning delivery of warm bourekas. "Everybody assumed that the BIA always knew where Mladić was, even that they were hiding him. So if they arrested him because David told me where he was, and I told Aleks, and he told Vukcevic, does that mean that it really was news to the BIA? That they weren't hiding him after all? Or was it one part of the BIA acting against another?"

"Or does it mean," Tom said, "that they were finally forced to act against him exactly because it was Vukcevic who told them? They could hardly ignore exact information given by the chief prosecutor. Especially if the Dutch knew too and were probably telling the Americans and everyone. They had to do something."

"We forced their hand?"

"I guess so. David did. Amazing, isn't it. What about the reward, will they publicize it?"

The jangle of the bell interrupted them and Tom opened the door for Aleks, who hugged him with one arm while holding the bag of bourekas in the other. "The ace journalist," he said, laughing. "You made me a hero with David's information. Now you're going to break the biggest story in the Balkans since the war. And guess what, by way of saying thank you, you can interview me on camera. Back of the head though."

"Really? Why?" Tom said, taking the bourekas. "Anyway, who says I want to? I've got such a great story, who needs you?" But he had already thrown the bourekas to Nina and was opening his camera bag. "Just kidding. Let's do it before you change your mind."

Aleks laughed again. "Slow down, coffee first."

As they ate and drank, Tom arranged the gear. He set a chair for Aleks in front of the window and opposite that placed a chair for himself, next to the camera on the tripod. He placed a microphone on each chair that they would clip on when the interview began. He wouldn't use lights. Within five minutes he was ready, and led Aleks to his chair and clipped the mic on his shirt. He exposed for the light outside, making Aleks's face so dark he was unrecognizable. "Okay, ready?" Tom said.

"What, I'm looking at the camera?" Aleks said.

"Don't worry, you're so underexposed you'll come out black."

"No way," Aleks said, turning the chair round and sitting with his back to Tom. "It's this way or no way. Anyway, what does it matter, if I'm just a black outline?"

Tom sighed. "All right then, as you like."

"And you'll change my voice? Digitally?

Tom gave a louder theatrical sigh. "If you insist."

But he stopped sighing when he heard what Aleks had to say. He was transfixed. He didn't even ask a question, just let him talk. It was the missing link. He had his story. If it was true.

Did it matter? As long as he had someone legit saying it. He'd have to get a reaction from Washington though. Maybe a studio interview after showing the doc?

"Don't ask me how I know this," Aleks began, speaking to the window, his voice sounding distant and hollow because he was speaking in the wrong direction. But Tom wasn't worried; he knew the lapel microphone would pick up perfect sound. "And I can't swear it is true, but it explains a lot. I have been talking to some of my people who should know. The phrase you used once, that someone told you that the truth about Ratko Mladić lay between Knin and Srebrenica? Well, now I think I know what he meant. I stress, *I think*. And it is dynamite. Especially for your country. Listen. In 1995, ethnic cleansing took place in Croatia and Bosnia, as everywhere for years, but this was different. I'll tell you why. Everyone knew that there would be even more bloody fighting, and in the end the Serb minority living in Croatia, in Knin and Krajina, would lose and after great loss of life would be chased out. And the same in Bosnia. Everyone knew that the Muslims around Srebrenica would lose to the Serbs and after great loss of life they too would be chased out. So someone got clever and arranged that both communities, instead of fighting to the end with many useless dead, would get up and leave quietly, or at least, leave after a short war with minimal loss of life. So that someone arranged for both armies to pull out at almost the same time, leaving behind civilians with little protection, who would then have to leave voluntarily. Clever, but too clever by half, as it turned out. Why did someone want that?"

And who? Tom thought, his heart pounding. At last he had someone saying on camera what he had heard. But where did Mladić fit in? He was about to ask when Aleks continued.

"Why did someone want that? To make it easier afterward to arrange a peace agreement among the Croats, Serbs, and Muslims, that's why. Someone organized ethnic cleansing, or as they may have seen it, the wise transfer of populations, in the hope that it would reduce loss of life and make peace easier afterward. But who was that someone? Because of course, it went horribly wrong, as all plans do in the Balkans. Because Ratko Mladić, who under

the secret agreement was supposed to arrange for the Muslim civilians to leave quietly, massacred them instead. So who was the
genius who put the lives of thousands of Muslims in the hands
of a psychotic murderer?" He paused.

Tom quickly asked, "Who then?" He didn't want Aleks to slow
down. This was an amazing interview. It was the heart of the story.
If it was true.

"The great manipulator, the Great Satan, the United States of
America, of course. Who else? From the best of motives, to the
worst of results. Washington sanctioned ethnic cleansing that led
unwittingly to the worst massacre in Europe since the Second
World War. And after Mladić was quickly indicted by The Hague,
twice, for genocide and crimes against humanity, he had the
Americans over a barrel. Their innocent and well-meaning dip-
lomats had delivered the Muslim sheep to the slaughter; they had
as good as put the gun to their heads. So the Americans had no
choice but to go along with Mladić's deal: my safety for my silence.
And if something happens to me, as you say so colorfully, the shit
will hit the fan. Everyone will know that indirectly America
caused the Srebrenica massacre. That's why Mladić was able to
hide so easily. Because nobody wanted to find him."

"Until today?"

"Precisely. Until today."

So now the shit hits the fan? Tom asked some more questions
and Aleks answered them knowledgeably and plausibly, but Tom
was barely listening. If that was true about the Americans and the
massacre—and he'd go back to the colonel from the research institute to see if he could find some proof—his doc would blow
America's Balkan policy wide open. More foreign meddling, more
playing God, more trying to fix the world, and messing it all up.
He was making not only a great documentary but an important

one. He glanced over to Nina with a triumphant grin but she was sitting on the sofa staring into the distance. Her mind seemed elsewhere. Her eyes were puffy: from too much sleep, or lack of it; she seemed preoccupied.

Later, when Aleks had left, he asked her what she had been thinking about. "I looked over and you seemed a thousand miles away."

"Twenty-five or so, actually."

"What do you mean?"

"I was thinking of Sasha. At my mother's. They've all been arrested, the danger is over. I want to collect him. Now. I miss him."

"Of course. But Aleks just told us the biggest news since I don't know what. Do you realize how big that is? It's huge. I have to get someone else to say it too, though. Of course Washington will deny everything. But it'll give the doc legs. Wow, what a story."

"You see, I told you. It's just a story to you."

"It's more than a story, if it's true, and I aim to find out. And anyway, with Mladić arrested, he may say something about it." He thought a moment, and added, "If he has a chance. They'll find a way to shut him up."

He went to the phone to try to make an appointment to meet Vukcevic again. He needed to get his reaction to Aleks's story, and there was another small matter: five million euros.

But as he picked up the phone, it rang, startling him.

It was Aleks at BIA headquarters, and as Tom listened silently, his heart quickened, his lips tightened, he glanced nervously toward Nina. Within minutes there would be an official announcement. Listen to the news at the top of the hour. In three minutes. A wave of arrests across Serbia. Must go. And Aleks hung up.

"I hope you like Sasha," Nina said.

"What?" Tom said. "Sasha? Of course I will. That was Aleks, he sounded stressed. Let's listen to the radio, he said they'll announce the arrests." He was thinking, I should go to the main square with the camera, wait for any protests at the news about Mladić. This is what they were always afraid of: Serbian nationalists demanding his release, attacking the police, demonstrating at government buildings, street fighting and nationwide protests. And he'd be in the thick of it. Right place, right time. He wondered if Amber's network team was in place yet, and who they were. They could have a celebration drink together, he thought.

They sat around the radio, Tom nervously drumming his fingers, Nina chewing her lip. It was the lead story on B92, Nina's favorite station, renowned for being independent and accurate. And as Nina listened, her brow creased, pen in hand out of habit, Tom strained to understand the pronunciation, the harsh, masculine tones. As the announcer launched into a long list of people arrested, Nina ignored the names but translated their positions with Mladić: driver; bodyguard; another bodyguard; cousin; landlord; uncle, and the longer the list, the lower Tom's stomach sank. What about Mladić? Wouldn't they mention him first? Is this some cultural thing, where they leave the best till last? He remembered what the first guy arrested had said: "I'm just the driver, I just get told what to do." So who told him? Where was the boss in this list, the senior figure? These were all bit players: drivers, guards, cousins.

Even before the news item was over, Tom felt like puking. Don't say it had all been for nothing. What was going on? As the list of names ended and the announcer began to speak to another person, and Nina looked over at Tom, numbly shaking her head, Tom blurted out, "Where the hell is Mladić then? Unless they arrested him but just didn't say so yet. What do you think?"

In response she grabbed her phone and called her cousin, who answered on the second ring. Aleks sounded nervous, distraught, there was shouting in the background. *"A sta je sa Mladićem?"* she asked. "What about Mladić?"

As she listened, her mouth widening, she shook her head at Tom and when she hung up, she slumped onto the sofa, and said, finally, "He got away. They went to the address David gave us, and he was gone. An empty apartment. No sign of him. They did forensics, found his fingerprints everywhere. But Mladić? Gone."

Ten furious minutes later, as they groaned and cursed and threw cushions, it began to sink in.

It fitted. Mladić, the chess player. When the king was in danger, he kept moving, sheltered behind the main pieces, and sacrificed the pawns. And the BIA fell for it. Or rather, the BIA probably arranged it. Instead of stalking the pawns until they led to their leader, they knocked them all off in one go, warning the king, giving him time to escape, to hide in another dark corner. They'll get the headlines, arresting Mladić's support network, but they won't get Mladić.

Oh, how unfortunate! Once again the clever bastard slipped out of our grasp. But don't worry. We're on the case. We have an Action Team. Ten thousand policemen looking for him. We'll get him in the end. Just not this time. Meanwhile, stop pressuring us, Europe, America, International Court. See—we're doing our best.

Like hell! As Nina switched off the radio Tom cursed and threw a cushion to the floor. She joined him with a string of Serbian curses. "It was all a show," she shouted. "Theater. And we fell for it. We helped them. Oh, so naïve! You must not use those pictures you shot, Tom, you will only help them by showing all the arrests, them picking up the little people. Tom, you must destroy the pictures, make sure they are never seen, it's just propaganda for those evil manipulators, those bloodsuckers, those murdering rapists!"

Like hell, Tom thought, what about my doc? It happened, I filmed what happened, that's the news. Why it happened? That's not my concern.

"Let's not get into that right now," he said. And as an afterthought, he all but wailed, "So much for a mortgage-free apartment."

"And it's not about the money?"

"Of course not, I'm joking. I didn't even know about it until a couple of days ago. I'm just saying, we could have used it."

He was thinking: No million euros. No Mladić. No happy ending for the doc.

"Damn!"

"Seriously, Tom," Nina said, stepping toward him. "You will only help them by using those pictures. They show the BIA arresting a few nonentities, but outside it will look like a massive security operation that tried to catch the big fish who wriggled away. Your pictures will give them legitimacy. That's why they invited you to film it. If it was Serb cameramen the world could say it was a setup, a con. But you, you give them credibility—the famous American who got the scoop. You see it, don't you, Tom, you must not use those pictures."

"Don't be silly, you give me too much credit. How do you know there weren't other cameramen with the other arrest teams? They were working all over the country. You think I was the only witness?"

"They said so."

"Oh, suddenly you believe them."

"Even so, none of them would be believed like you."

"Look, that's the guts of my film, the best stuff, I have to use it."

"So don't make the documentary then."

"Oh, sure. So why did I come here then?"

Nina's face went hard. "I have no idea."

Morissey wasn't much better. When Tom almost shouted at him for setting him up, Morissey went cold and spoke slowly, measuring his words. "Listen, you dope, you have no idea what I have done to help you," Sam said, ice in his tone. "You could have been in the hospital by now, with your face plastered over and your arms and legs too. Suspended from pulleys. Drinking through a straw and pissing through another one. On a good day. But my job is not to help you. My job is to do what is best for my country. And yours. America, in case you forgot. Maybe I can tell you a bit more, not on the phone. We'll meet for a drink. You're a good guy, Tom, we're friends. But you can be a fucking idiot too. Don't you get it? Nobody cares about Mladić anyway."

Tom said, "Anyone with morals does."

"That counts you out then. All you want is to sell your documentary."

"But what about Mladić?"

"Forget it. He's gone. And look at the plus side. You've got someone much better. Nina is a gift, Tom, a fucking gift; she's way too good for you."

Tom had to smile. "You're right about that, at least," Tom said. Sam could hear his tone soften. "I'm blessed. I just need a couple more interviews here, then it's back to New York, both of us."

"A new life."

"Yes. A new life." He savored the words and said them again. "A new life. Sounds good, eh?"

"Sure does. I'm jealous."

"But just one thing, Sam. When Mladić didn't help the Serbs in Krajina and moved his army to Srebrenica, didn't Washington realize that he—"

Dial tone.

The next day the slate sky threatened but held off its deluge, darkening further as dusk fell, holding the gray suburbs in its damp grip. The waters of the Bolećica barely rippled as the narrowing road took them along its banks and out of Belgrade. "It's from two words," Nina was saying, as if by rote, "*bol* means 'pain' and *leči* means 'to cure,' so literally we call this river, 'the water that heals the pain.'"

"I could use a drink of that today," Tom said, as most people did when they heard the name.

"I don't think so," Nina replied, "it's mostly sewage."

In the summer the fields were a sea of blue, heralding the plum harvest, but now the orchards were like an army stretching its bare arms to the sky. "There are forty million plum trees in Serbia, six for every one person," Nina was reciting, gazing out of the car window, "and most of them seem to be around here. This is fruit-growing country. Plums, cherries, peaches, apples, apricots, you name it."

Tom, taking a bend slowly in the rental car, glanced at her as she went on: "We'll be there in a few minutes. It's Zaklopača, a nice little village, lots of refugees from Bosnia and Croatia, Serbs, who settled here after they had to run away during the wars. They changed the nature of the community. But I hope you like it, my mother does, and Sasha loves it. I love it here too. We all do."

For most of the thirty-minute drive Nina had either been silent or had been talking in an increasingly stilted manner. She had been all bustle and excited energy when they had packed and returned to her apartment, but the closer they got to her mother's village, the more she seemed to be prattling. Prattling: that's the word, Tom thought. She seems nervous. Or maybe just excited at seeing Sasha again and taking him home. She had said, "I hope you like Sasha." "Of course I will," Tom had replied, "why shouldn't I?"

He was looking forward to meeting Sasha. He'd have a son, all packaged and delivered, seven years old. They'd find a school for him in New York. Back on a network salary he'd have no trouble paying school fees. They'd have to get him private English lessons right away, but kids pick up languages quickly, from friends, TV, from his dad. Tom chuckled to himself.

"What's funny?" Nina said.

"I was just thinking about Sasha, teaching him English. And I suddenly thought of myself as his dad." He chuckled again: "Daddy! About bloody time!" He took one hand from the wheel and slapped Nina's thigh.

"Don't do that, it hurts," Nina said. She gave him directions until they pulled up in front of a low house that stood in its own stand of trees on the outskirts of the village. "Cherry and plum," Nina said. "It smells so beautiful in the autumn. My mother makes jam and brandy. The best." She remained sitting, her hand on the door handle.

"So let's go," Tom said. He had parked in the small driveway and opened his door, but Nina hadn't moved. "Nina? Are you all right?"

Nina stepped out of the car and closed the door, and smoothed her skirt. "Isn't it beautiful air here," she said, "so much clearer and cleaner than in Belgrade."

They heard a door slam and a child shout. A woman's voice, high-pitched and angry, the child crying. Nina hurried up the path with Tom following: "He's probably hungry. Misses his mom."

So much for the storybook reunion. Little boy swinging on the garden gate waiting for Mommy, leaping into her arms with a big hug, the TV moment. Nothing is ever what you imagine, he thought, life just doesn't work out that way. How many times had he expected a happy ending, a joyous reunion, the Hollywood scene, and then life had got in the way? He'd filmed a birth once in a refugee camp and instead of the joy of motherhood, the girl had rejected her baby, made the nurse take it away. She couldn't bear to bring another poor child into such a miserable world. Or the two Jewish brothers who had each believed the other killed in the Holocaust and, reunited after sixty years, had been too embarrassed to hug. They just stood there like two schlemiels, staring at each other, ruining the climax of the story he had worked on for two months.

Life doesn't always play ball, he thought, that's what makes it life. There's no script.

He followed Nina into the house in time to see her harried mother breathe a huge sigh of relief and hug Nina. Nina moved past her, calling out, "*Sasa, Sasa, to sam ja, Mama.*"

Tom smiled and stretched out his hand in greeting. "I'm Tom Layne," he said to Nina's mother, who looked surprisingly young, even with her bedraggled hair and haunted eyes. He felt like adding "your future son-in-law," but she could be his sister, so he didn't. He couldn't make out her name, she was rushed and nervous, wringing her hands and watching Nina's back as she entered the living room and shut the door. The mother turned and went into the kitchen. From the living room there was the sound of something smashing: a plate, a cup?

Through the door he heard the muted sound of Nina's sweet,

low voice, comforting, reassuring, almost pleading, and then the boy's voice, groaning, calling, whining; and a jumping sound, feet hitting the floor, again and again. Nina, soothing, saying his name, over and over, "Sasa, Sasa, Sasa," as Sasha made the same groaning sound. Tom listened from the hall, unsure what to do. What's going on?

He waited at the front door, smelling the damp grass and the sweet cherry buds, hearing the shouting, Nina's calming voice, and the boy's anguished wail.

Then, all quiet but for the patter of falling rain.

About two minutes later the door squeaked open, and Nina appeared, carrying Sasha, in shorts and shirt. His thin legs were wrapped around her stomach, his arms around her neck, his head lay on her shoulder. With a serene Madonna smile Nina mouthed, He's tired.

In his mother's arms, Sasha was already sleeping, clinging to her like a little monkey. She took him to the car in the rain and Tom helped lay him across the backseat, and Nina's mother put a pillow under his head and a blanket over him. Sasha's breathing was quick and loud, as if he still had a way to go to calm down, but he was fast asleep and that, clearly, was a relief to the two women.

Back inside, Nina's mother took Tom's hand again, speaking in Serbian. Tom smiled and half bowed and looked at Nina. "She says she is sorry for the poor welcome and she has made some tea. And she is offering you some of her homemade slivovitz. Plum brandy."

Thank you, Tom gestured with a nod and a smile.

He looked around the little living room, liking its low wooden rafters and whitewashed walls, and shelves of figurines and little bottles. There was a large cross above the mantelpiece, and two deep, worn leather chairs at the fireplace. They sipped the tea, smiling at each other. But not for long. Conversation between mother and daughter became animated. Nina's mother, whose name he finally understood to be Andjela, appeared to be lecturing Nina, who nodded, downcast, pensive. She answered briefly, in a cajoling manner, but her mother overrode her, emphatically, as if laying down the law to her daughter.

In a lull in the conversation Tom took Nina's hand. "What is it, Nina, is there a problem?"

"Not for me. For her."

"What is it?"

Nina sighed, shifting uncomfortably. She shrugged her shoulders. "I'll tell you later, not now."

But when Andjela left the room and the silence between them became loaded, Nina said, slowly, as if bored, "My mother says she can't look after Sasha anymore. Not for so long. A day or two, yes. A week or two, no. It's too hard."

Tom waited for more but Nina fell silent. She drained her tea, took Tom's cup, and left the room.

More animated conversation through the door. Tom waited uncomfortably. Poor little kid, Sasha, he thought. He was just tired, so what? After a few minutes he stood, thinking he would join them in the kitchen. Or go to the bathroom. It was getting embarrassing, all this drama and him just hanging around.

Rather than skulk he opened the door and walked into the kitchen with a smile. Andjela was standing, talking rapidly. Nina was sitting, looking dejectedly at the floor. Tom came behind her and massaged her shoulder. Her neck muscles felt like rope and he gently dug with his thumbs and rolled his knuckles along her nape, thinking, If her mother is an example, she'll age well.

He couldn't understand much as they continued talking, but

a few words sounded familiar. He could make out: *Specialista. Klinika.* He felt Nina stiffen, she was shaking her head, her lips tight, as if saying No, no, no.

Tom knew better than to ask. Instead he said, "Shall I collect Sasha's things? Put them in the car?"

"Upstairs, it's all packed, in a suitcase and some carrier bags," Nina said. "Let's leave. Now."

At the door he shook Andjela's hand, and she pulled him to her for a hug and kissed him on each cheek, and said something with a smile, keeping his hand, looking at Nina and back to him. "She says you're handsome," Nina said. "She says if I don't want you, she'll have you."

Tom laughed. "Tell her I agree."

They hesitated at the door, and ran through the rain to the car. Tom drove slowly back the way they had come, sheets of rain lit by sweeping headlights. They were silent, listening to Sasha mumbling in his sleep in the back. There was a sticky, sliding sound on the plastic of the seat, as Sasha's legs moved like a dog running in his dreams.

A tight smile played on Tom's lips. What a couple of days, he was thinking: You gotta laugh. Mladić, the One That Got Away. With all his filming and interviews and research, what had he really added to the sum total of knowledge of the man and his time? Not much. That he was protected by the BIA? Surprise, surprise. That the Americans were involved? Big deal. He couldn't prove a thing. He had one guy on camera, with no name or face, speculating. Better than nothing, but not enough.

He'd have his job back though, that was something. And he had a good documentary. The pawns getting rounded up, him getting pushed and shoved around would help. Bit of drama. Not a great doc. But good. No real ending, no grand finale, that's the trouble. No Mladić. Still, he hadn't expected to find him in the first place; the doc was supposed to be about the failure to find him, so in that sense, this was perfect.

Pity about the reward!

Sasha. What's with him? He glanced at Nina. She was asleep. Or pretending. It was obvious the moment they closed the car door that she didn't feel like talking.

It was also obvious something was up with the boy. He'd picked up the word "*Klinika*" and he knew what that must mean. When there were no cars behind, Tom slowed down and looked over his shoulder. Sasha was on his back now, his head hanging over the edge of the seat, his hands and legs at rest beneath the blanket that somehow still covered him. His long black hair had settled over his cheek. In his brief look, Tom took in long eyelashes, sharp features surprising on a little boy. He didn't have the pudgy roundness of a child.

Keeping his eyes on the road, feeling his head droop, Tom drifted into his Trove of Consolation, that place to which he often retreated, his memory bank, which took him from Sasha to all the other children he'd met along the way.

He thought of Petar, as he often did, the harelip kid in Sarajevo; whatever happened to him? And that little boy, what was his name? In Gaza. The one who was paralyzed from the waist down after he'd thrown stones at Israeli soldiers and earned himself a bullet in the neck. Yusuf, that was it. His benefits checks from the Palestinian Authority bounced. I wonder how he is, Tom thought. Is he still in that little bed in that dark room playing with the pulley contraption his father made to exercise the one arm that he could move? No, he must be grown up. Still alone in that sad bed? I should go back and check on him one day.

He thought of the thousands of matchstick children with distended bellies and clumps of iron-wool hair starving to death in the camps of Somalia, Ethiopia, Sudan, and the weeping man in Wad Kowlie whose hand he held after he buried his fourth daughter. Of the albino children in Uganda who people kidnapped and killed to mix their bones into magic potions, and the white-haired girl who told him robbers had stolen her sister's right leg because it was the most valuable part of the body. They got two thousand dollars for a leg.

From outside, a steady whine of tires on tar, and wind. Cars flashed by, their yellow lights hazy in the rain. One on high beams blinded him and he had to shield his eyes and slow down; the car behind honked loud and long as the annoyed driver pulled out sharply to overtake.

He yawned, his extended groan loud in the silent car where mother and child breathed evenly in their sleep.

That girl in Cambodia? She was so sweet, with her wide eyes and long limbs. In school she was learning to handle a gun in case the Khmer Rouge attacked her village, and at night she studied by candlelight to be like her father, who had been killed because he was a teacher. She wanted to be a teacher too, even if they killed her for it. Her mother made very sweet tea.

In Banda Aceh after the tsunami when the teacher read out the roll call of first graders. He called out fourteen names before a child answered. Twenty-four of the forty-two in the class were taken by the ocean.

And that girl he'd overheard in the Tel Aviv hospital, crying to her parents with any child's cri de coeur, "Why me?"

That's what he should do—forget Mladić, do a doc on all the children he had met over the years, all the suffering kids. What happened to them? He'd love to know.

And now, there's Sasha. What happened to him? What is Nina's secret?

As Sasha and Nina slept in the car, dark but for the flashing lights from oncoming cars, Tom felt a tear welling in his eye, which he brushed away with the back of his hand.

It was after they arrived home and Sasha woke and had a tantrum and he watched Nina's patient, calming response, restraining Sasha as he stood before her and jumped on the spot, and clamped his hands to his ears as if to shut her out, as if all the noise and light and excitement was too much for him; and as she firmly brought his hands down to his sides, all the while looking in his eyes and talking in a quiet, soothing voice, and she finally managed to distract him long enough with a Lego toy until he sat down and focused on it and began quietly moving it from side to side, smiling like an angel; it was while watching all that, that Tom fell in love with Nina, if he hadn't already.

He wanted to hug Nina, to hug Sasha, to take them into his arms and make everything all right for them. From the chair, his eyes followed their every movement, entering their lives, a visitor who didn't want to leave. As if he had heard his thoughts, felt his gaze, Sasha turned his eyes to him at last and their eyes held. The boy's were dark and sunken. It must be lack of sleep.

It was after eleven o'clock and Nina wanted Sasha to go to bed, but now she stood back and watched.

Tom didn't move as Sasha came toward him. Nina said something to Sasha and Tom heard his name, Tom Layne. She was telling Sasha who the strange man was. Now Sasha approached him boldly, and stopped in front of him. He was taller than Tom had expected, and thinner. Locks of thick black hair had fallen over his forehead and Tom reached out and pushed them back with a smile, stroking his head while at it, and said, "Hello, Sasha."

The boy answered and as Tom looked quizzically at Nina she translated. "He says, 'What time is dinner?'"

Tom smiled again and took Sasha's hand. It was tiny in his, like holding a chicken's foot. "I don't know," he said. "I think it's time to go to bed."

The boy said it again. "What time is dinner?" And again. And again. "What time is dinner?"

At last Nina came to him and took him by the hand. He pulled away and resisted, kicking. She couldn't pull him from Tom's side, so Tom took his other hand and together they walked him to his room and undressed him and took him to brush his teeth. Sasha gurgled and spat and brushed and spat some more and gurgled again and they took him to bed as he said in a fading voice, "What time is dinner?" He was asleep before his head hit the pillow and they tucked him in and kissed him and left the room, pausing to gaze at him from the door, which they left open so that they could hear him if he woke, so that a chink of light fell into the room and he would not be alone in the dark.

Tom and Nina went hand in hand to the kitchen and stood looking at the kettle on the gas. Nina sighed and turned to Tom as she stretched to take cups and saucers from the cupboard above the sink. "I'm going to sleep well tonight," she said, as if it was her greatest wish.

"Me too," Tom said.

Tom took the cups from Nina's hands and pulled her to him. She snuggled against him, burrowing her head into his chest as he held her tight. "We've seen a lot together, haven't we?" she said.

He answered with a kiss, stroking her hair, which was as soft as Sasha's, and the moment extended, comforting and intimate. When the kettle began to whistle he gently shrugged her away to turn it off. If life offered new beginnings, this was the moment, but he couldn't put his hope into words, and what he said was, "So why didn't you tell me about Sasha? About his problem?"

Later he thought: If only I hadn't used that word.

Nina froze. "What problem?"

"You know. Sasha."

"What about him?" Nina didn't move, a tea bag dangling from her fingers. "He hasn't got a problem. Have you?"

"Come on, you know what I mean, I just—"

"No, I don't know what you mean. Sasha has a very mild form of autism. So does half the world. Is that the *problem* you mean, is that a problem for you?"

"No, no, of course not, he's adorable, I just mean, why didn't you tell me? I would have thought—"

"Well, don't think." She poured the boiling water onto tea bags in two mugs and took them into the living room where she sank into the sofa, still holding the mugs. Tom took one and sat next to her.

"It's almost midnight," she said.

"Yes. And I've been thinking."

"Not again."

"About us. About what's next."

Nina sighed. "So have I."

"You have?"

"Of course."

"So, what's next?"

"I don't know."

"I do."

"What?"

"New York, of course. I want you to come with me. Both of you."

"I was in New York once. Twice. I hated it."

He sipped some tea and placed the mug on the coffee table, and took Nina's mug and put it next to his. He took Nina's hand and looked into her eyes, and then away, as if he was plucking up courage.

"You're not going to ask me to marry you, are you?" She leaned her face into his, noses almost touching. "You've gone all serious. You aren't, are you?"

When Tom hesitated, she smiled. "You are, you are going to ask me to marry you. Go on then, ask me. Or, rather, please don't." She leaned back into the cushions, and folded one leg over the other, knocking over a cup. Tea flowed across the table and onto the floor.

"Oh," she said, but with a hand on her leg Tom stopped her from rising.

"Don't worry about it. Listen," Tom said, searching for words. "Marriage wasn't exactly what I had in mind, right now; first things first. But now that you mention it, if I asked, what would you say?"

"I'd say Cool Tom Layne is flustered."

He burst out laughing. "You'd be right. But seriously, listen, what I was going to ask is—"

"Will I marry you?"

"No. Well, maybe, but listen for once, please. What I wanted to say is, will you come to New York with me? And Sasha too. I love you so much. We've been through a lot, and we weren't to-gether when we needed each other. We've wasted so much time. Now I feel like we're starting all over. And I don't want to leave you again, I want to be with you. And Sasha too."

Nina held Tom's hands, her face inches from his again, and kissed his nose, then stood and came back from the kitchen with a cloth to mop up the spilled tea. Tom watched her. "Will you?"

She sighed and said, "Let me just wring this out."

"Are you playing for time?"

"Yes, I think so. Can we talk in bed?"

But in bed, Nina pulled Tom to her and brought his head to her chest and nibbled at his neck and ear and soon he kissed and nibbled at her and Tom felt Nina tremble beneath his touch, and he felt fire beneath his skin. Their bodies glistened together. Later Tom fell asleep with a fulfilled smile, satisfied by her body's answer. As for Nina, gazing at his peaceful face, she was left with more of a question. Had their passionate joining set the seal on their future? Or was it more in the way of a farewell?

A presence infiltrated Tom's sleep until he emerged groggily to feel a bony little body next to his. Sasha's penetrating eyes were wide, staring at him. "G' morning," Tom managed, moving onto his side, pulling the blanket over his bare chest. Sasha smiled. "It's time for breakfast," he said brightly in Serbian, "it's time for breakfast," and repeated it half a dozen times. "It's time for breakfast, it's time for . . ."

Tom was saved by the shrill clanging of the phone and after a brief conversation Nina's call, "Tom, pick up the extension, it's for you," and there was Amber.

"Hey, Tom, you sound terrible, what time is it?"

"I don't have a clue. Too early."

"Well, six hours' difference. It must be twenty past seven where you are. In the morning."

"Okay. Whassup?"

"Long and short. Slight change. New idea. Based in London

instead of New York? Chief foreign correspondent. All the benefits. You'd be better off than in New York. Here you'd have your
salary and then you're on your own; in London you get the same
salary plus all the perks. The usual—accommodation, cost of living, the rest."

That brought Tom to his elbow.

"Education for the kids?"

"You? That'll be the day. But sure, the whole package. The
thinking is that we may anchor a new show partly out of London
and you could do that too. And if it happens, more money of
course. It's a great opportunity, Tom. Think it over, let me know
as soon as possible."

"Yes."

"What do you mean? Yes, what? Yes, you'll think it over."

"I just did. London, here I come."

"Fantastic. Can you be there Monday? I gotta run, that's great
news, Tom, Monday, okay? The desk will call you to coordinate,
there's an early assignment. I gotta run though, bye for now."

"What's the rush . . . It isn't a Royals story, is it?"

"They'll tell you about it, bye now."

"Wait . . . No." The phone went dead. Tom looked at it and felt
the smile spreading. It is a Royals story. Still, this is going to work
out. Nina didn't like New York anyway. But London . . .

Nina came in with a cup of coffee and sat on the bed, handing
it to Tom. "Good call? You look happy."

He sipped the coffee and put it down. "Come here," he said,
"let me kiss you." He pulled her down but she resisted.

"Not now, Sasha . . ."

Tom said with a smile, "I have good news and better news.
Which first?"

"The good news."

"The good news is you don't have to live in New York. The better news is, we're going to London."

"What, with my problem child?"

"Don't be silly. I used the wrong word, that's all, I'm sorry. I love Sasha, and you. We'll all live together, it will be perfect."

She didn't answer, just took his hand in both of hers and lay next to him on the bed, and brought his hand to her lips. They lay in this way and minutes passed until Nina said, "Tom, I think I loved you in Sarajevo, I always did, our love has been bornished in fire."

"You mean burnished in fire? Burnished?"

"Yes; poetic, yes?"

"And has stood the test of time?"

"Not poetic. But, yes." Her chest rose and she heaved a sigh so great that her body seemed to lift and fall. "But what about Sasha? I have to think of Sasha. Here I have my mother to help me. He has a good school and friends who do not think of him as having a problem—"

"I—"

"Wait, let me talk. Please. I know you didn't mean anything bad, but it hurt me, it hurt me very much, I can't think of Sasha as having a problem, and I don't want to go somewhere where people think he has one. He's a bit different, that's all. And he doesn't speak a word of English and I don't know if he can learn. Other children may make fun of him. I couldn't bear it."

"But I'll be there, I'll be with you . . ."

"No, you won't, you know you won't, Tom, you'll be away from home like you always were, you're a foreign correspondent, so you'll always be traveling. We'll be alone in London. I won't be able to work . . ."

"Your mother can come."

"Oh, yes. She doesn't speak a word of English either. Tom, think about it. Really." She put her arm around him and held him to her and kissed his cheek and slipped her hand beneath the cover and between his legs and said, "Think, think, Tom; not with this, but with this," and she touched his head with hers.

"Anyway," she said, "I've been thinking, for both of us. Someone has to," and she withdrew her hand.

It felt to Tom like an abandonment, an emptying of warmth, as he waited for her to continue. They were lying side by side, Tom under the cover, Nina on top, separated by an inch of material, but in her pause Tom felt the distance grow. "So you've been thinking," he said at last, pulling himself up in the bed. "What about?"

Nina continued to gaze at the ceiling, and sighed, as if gathering herself, when from the kitchen came the crash of breaking glass and a high-pitched exclamation and in Serbian, *"Izvini, Mama."* Sorry, Mama.

Nina smiled and raised her eyebrows. Tom didn't respond.

As Nina called out in Serbian, "I'm coming, don't move, you'll cut your feet," he thought, She's right, of course. What could he offer her in London? Or New York? He'd be traveling most of the time. And she couldn't even come on trips with him, she wouldn't leave Sasha alone for long, never would be able to. The only people you can really rely on are family and he didn't have any and her mother, Andjela, was here. She'd be crazy to leave. And he'd be selfish to ask her to.

He was lying against the backrest, bare-chested, his hands folded on his stomach and wondering, Can you be filled with emptiness? Or is that an oxymoron?

He could hear the sweeping of a brush and the scraping of glass shards and Nina's voice probably telling Sasha to move out of the way. He heard Sasha's footsteps fade away as the child wandered off, looking for more trouble.

What had she been about to say? Maybe he was wrong.

As he heard the click of Nina igniting the gas to make coffee, he thought, There must be a way to persuade her. Think, Tom, think. Don't blow it.

And he did think, all day, accompanying Nina to school where they dropped off Sasha, waiting for her in the café opposite the bank where she was again trying to persuade the manager to reduce her mortgage by even a fraction, at the grocery store afterward, idly fingering produce, until an assistant brusquely asked him to stop bruising the tomatoes. Nina took them from his hands and put them in her basket.

He was thinking about the sadness he was feeling, and the more intimate the day became with Nina, the sadder he felt.

Bringing Sasha home from school, silently preparing their evening meal together, allowing Sasha to teach him how to say hello in Serbian before preparing him for bed, and Nina bustling from task to task, Tom felt it all beginning to slip away, like the wisp of a beautiful cloud.

Ema! That was it. The harelip kid's mother. He felt a sense of relief as he turned over in the dark. In his sleep he'd been searching his Trove of Consolation for her name and had woken with a crushing sense of frustration that he had forgotten it.

Ema Cordas, it all came back now. Not only had she been separated from Petar for two years, but her husband Aleksandar had been away somewhere—wounded. Had she seen her boy again? Did he have the operation on his harelip? Did they all survive the war?

Now that was a mother with a problem. But Tom knew better than to say that to Nina.

Repressing a rush of resentment against her, he shuffled closer to Nina and laid his arm along her bare thigh and tried to go back to sleep.

But whenever he thought of the harelip kid, he saw Nick, who in Tom's mind seemed younger and younger until he was no more than a child himself, whose life had been thrown away. And that thought unsettled him so that now he lay wide awake, on his back, his mind clearing, as he thought of Amber's job offer in London. A good job, to be sure, but to do more of the same? Why? And was he still up to it, even if he wanted to? He had been able to report on every disaster, tragedy, and war for twenty years and more, because instinctively he had erected a wall between the drama outside and his emotions within.

Even though tears sometimes came to his eyes when mothers wept for their children or fathers broke down, he turned away and concealed them from the crew, and soon moved on, to the next victim, the next deadline, the next story. He had never allowed himself to feel sad. No time. Another party, another girl, another assignment, another city, another tragedy had taken care of that. Until Nick's murder blew it all away.

Then the wall had crumbled, the demons burst through—all the tears sealed inside him from so many other people's tragedies had burst the dam and drowned him.

Tom's lips curled in a bitter smile. Demons burst through, indeed! I'm enjoying this, he thought. Feeling sorry for myself.

Somebody had to. For years he'd felt so alone, so disconnected from everyone around him that he thought he'd never have a normal life again: get married, have children, get his career back. Working freelance had paid the bills but not much more. It had all stressed him out so much that during the day the thud of a dropped book would make him duck, or at night a sudden memory often shocked him awake, sweating, and he would feel his heart pounding and sometimes he even had to vomit. He became furious for no reason, threatened people, though he had never actually hit someone.

They had a fancy name for what he'd gone through: posttraumatic stress disorder. But for years he thought he knew better; it wasn't that complicated.

He had lost it, that was all. Burned out. Toast. All he needed was another drink.

Until, not so long ago, thanks to his friends at the DART Center, the trauma workers who helped journalists like him, he'd finally understood: Don't diminish yourself. These are real emotions you're feeling. And if they hurt, well, good. About time.

Sad is good.

And now, another realization, another piece of the puzzle.

He wasn't sad about the past. He was sad about the future.

A future lost, if he lost Nina again.

His hand rested on Nina's warm skin, and he exerted gentle pressure but there was no response. Her breathing was even and quiet.

Another thought: Grief is love, for if you love, you grieve its loss even before you have lost it. Love is fear, and Tom was afraid. Afraid as he had never felt before, even when he thought he would die, even when Nick was killed, even when he heard Nina scream when she was raped.

For this was a different fear. It was sweet, it was longing, it was fear of something he wanted, not that he didn't want.

He wanted Nina. So warm, so loving, so knowing, so beautiful. And that made him afraid.

Face it, Tom, you're fifty-two, you love her, and it's all very simple: you're shit scared of losing her.

Really, he thought, why didn't I call her for all those years? Truly, a lost decade. He'd been so angry at everyone, especially anyone connected to his work, he'd wanted to escape, and especially not to think about Nick and all that. But you can't escape from what is embedded inside: the flash of Nick's mischievous smile, the gunshot's boom, Nick's fading eyes, his own failing legs, and shitting himself. Mostly he'd been angry with himself. For getting Nick killed, Nina raped. And he'd got away without a scratch. Why?

Lying on his back, his head cradled in his hands, Tom stared up into the dark, feeling lonely, yet bathed by a sense of comfort. He hadn't got up for a drink, he hadn't had a nightmare, he wasn't furious at anyone, his heart was calm, he was merely filled with a kind of sweet uncertainty, a longing for love, something really simple: to sleep forever by Nina's side.

He turned and pulled himself against her and cupped her warm breast with his hand and felt her untroubled breathing. She never did say what she had been thinking and all day he had been afraid to ask. If it was something good, she would have said it. You only put things off if they're difficult. What could she have to say that was so hard?

Don't be a dope, you know what that is. Nina's not coming to London.

Oh yes she is, he thought as he hugged her, and melted into her, and drifted away, even if I have to kidnap her, Morissey can help, and with that kind thought, and a full heart, Tom finally fell asleep, with the words of a song playing in his mind: I've been lonely, too long.

. . .

The tickling of air, a gentle puff that teased his cheeks, coaxed him from sleep. His heavy eyes opened with a smile, expecting to kiss Nina's lips above him, and in her stead he saw in the dim light from the corridor the outline of a blurred boyish face inches from his, with round lips blowing into his eyes.

What time is it? It must be the middle of the night.

Sasha, kneeling, loomed even closer and pursed his lips and blew again. Sasha's own eyes were narrowed as he applied himself to his task. He drew his head back to survey Tom's reaction, until, leaning down again, his head extended from his neck like a tortoise's, filling Tom's vision with his indistinct features, he continued to breathe gently into Tom's eyes until Tom pulled back into his pillow, and suddenly blew hard into Sasha's face.

Sasha pulled back and stuck out his tongue. So did Tom. Sasha wiggled his tongue around and Tom did the same. Tom made a popping sound with his lips and Sasha did too: puh, puh, puh. They spoke in puffs and as they did so, Tom put one hand on Sasha's head and stroked his hair.

Lying on her side, Nina watched through the shimmer of half-opened eyes, trying to breathe calmly, not to let them know she was awake, absorbed by the beauty of this moment. When was the last time Sasha had looked someone in the eyes? Or been so taken by a stranger? Or shown such trust? Tom was so good with him. Why did she always feel like crying when Tom held Sasha?

Sasha was crouching, supporting himself on his knees and his hands, which were on either side of Tom's head, and as they puh-puhed each other, and blew into each other's faces, and wiggled their tongues, Sasha's arms slowly bent at the elbow until he lay quietly across Tom's chest, and rose and fell with his breathing.

Gently, not to disturb the sleeping boy, Tom inched his other arm from beneath the blankets and put it around Sasha's thin back. He pulled Sasha gently toward him until his mop of soft hair nestled in the crook of Tom's throat.

Nina watched Tom hug Sasha and kiss his forehead, and leave his lips there. Nobody but family had ever held Sasha like this. Tom's eyes were closed and so were Sasha's, his long black eyelashes fluttering in his sleep. Knowing that Sasha was at peace, Nina felt the heat of a tear in the corner of her eye and a sob rose in her throat.

Tom heard, or maybe felt, her involuntary shift, he opened his eyes and glanced across Sasha's head, and his eyes met Nina's, inches away, and they held, and they both smiled—serene and wistful—and their heavy eyes slowly closed together, and sleep took all three to a shared and peaceful place.